D0037028

ALSO BY ALLAN TOPOL

Dark Ambition

Spy Dance

CONSPIRACY

Allan Topol

AN ONYX BOOK

ONYX
Published by New American Library, a division of
Penguin Group (USA) Inc., 375 Hudson Street,
New York, New York 10014, U.S.A.
Penguin Books Ltd, 80 Strand,
London WC2R 0RL, England
Penguin Books Australia Ltd, 250 Camberwell Road,
Camberwell, Victoria 3124, Australia
Penguin Books Canada Ltd, 10 Alcorn Avenue,
Toronto, Ontario, Canada M4V 3B2
Penguin Books (N.Z.) Ltd, Cnr Rosedale and Airborne Roads,
Albany, Auckland 1310, New Zealand

Penguin Books Ltd, Registered Offices:
80 Strand, London WC2R 0RL, England

First published by Onyx, an imprint of New American Library,
a division of Penguin Group (USA) Inc.

First Printing, January 2004
10 9 8 7 6 5 4 3 2 1

For my wife, Barbara, who, with her love of piano, helps me with the major chords as well as the grace notes

Prologue

The normally cool and unflappable Yahiro Sato was furious. Someone had found out about his trip to Buenos Aires.

"Repeat what you just told me," he said tensely to Tera-sawa.

The bodyguard was in the ornate lobby of the Alvear Palace Hotel, in a corner behind a white marble pillar, speaking on a cell phone rather than the house phone to minimize the chances of an eavesdropper.

"I was down here keeping my eyes open, as you directed, when a man walked into the hotel. I don't know his name, but I've seen him before in Tokyo. He's one of Prime Minister Nakamura's lackeys."

"You're sure of that?"

"Absolutely."

"Okay. Then what?"

"I moved off to the side behind a post so he couldn't see me, but I heard him when he went up to the reception desk."

Sato gripped the phone tightly. "And?"

"He told the reception clerk that he was with your party. He wanted a room close by the presidential suite."

How could he have known that's where I was? Sato asked himself. There had to be a leak among the clerical people in his office. When he got back to Tokyo he'd fire the lot of them. Radical surgery for a serious cancer.

"So he was put in room eight-twenty," Terasawa continued, "two doors away from you. He's already gone upstairs. What do you want me to do?"

There was only one possible conclusion, Sato decided. Nakamura had sent the worm to spy on him, to see whom he was meeting. He glanced at the gold Rolex on his wrist. It was already seven-fifteen in the evening. He had asked the American to fly down from Washington and come to the presidential suite at eleven. When he arrived, Nakamura's worm couldn't be permitted to see him under any circumstances.

Sato held the phone close to his mouth. "Distract the man," he whispered. "Any way you want. And make sure he stays distracted until we leave town at noon tomorrow."

Terasawa closed up his cell phone and put it in his pocket. He would enjoy dealing with the spy. As he ran his hand over the long scar on his left check, a souvenir from a knife battle during his youthful days with the Yakuza, a plan was already taking shape in his mind.

Up on the eighth floor, Hayaski waited until the bellman had been gone for ten minutes before he peeked out of the door into the wide blue-carpeted hallway to make certain it was deserted. Then, in his stocking feet, he tiptoed into the corridor and planted three tiny round silver metallic objects, each the size of a watch battery, under the edge of the carpet, along the wall, spaced at equal intervals between the elevator and the presidential suite at the end of the hall. All three were motion sensors that would trigger an alarm in Hayaski's briefcase and let him know when someone was walking in the corridor. He could then go over to the door of his room, look out, and see who was entering Sato's suite. In the event he missed them going in, he would remain at his open door until they emerged. Then he would take their picture with a tiny handheld camera that resembled a pen. If Sato left the suite, the sensor would go off and Hayaski would follow him. It was a perfect plan. Nothing could go wrong.

Knowing that the alarm would alert him, he could relax in the suite, maybe doze off a little, because he was still jet-lagged from the long flight. Hayaski ordered dinner from room service. Yet when it arrived, the Argentine beef he had heard so much about was tasteless and stringy when compared to Kobe. The Argentine beer was watery. He had never been to the country before, but he was beginning to see why it was second-rate. As he ate, Hayaski became irritated. He had been sent a long way on a stupid assignment. What difference did it make with whom Sato met? The man had no chance of being elected prime minister. He was a joke out there on the right-wing fringe.

Once the waiter had cleared the dishes, Hayaski picked up the thin booklet on the television set, which described the pay movies that were available. All were in English or Spanish, so he couldn't understand much of any of them, but that didn't bother him. The erotica offering was *Hot, Wet, and Wild*. He'd get what he wanted from that movie even if he didn't know what they were saying.

Before he turned on the television set, the alarm in the briefcase rang. Hayaski turned it off. Still dressed in pants and a white shirt, he hurried to the door and opened it. An elderly man and a woman were staggering down the hall, speaking English loudly and slurring their words. They had obviously had too much to drink at dinner. He watched them go into a room across the hall. Then he closed the door and returned to the television set.

Fifteen minutes into *Hot, Wet, and Wild,* three naked women were in a hot tub fondling each other. Hayaski was propped up in bed against a pillow. He'd slid out of his pants and tossed them onto a chair. His erection was sticking out of the opening in his white cotton boxer shorts.

The alarm rang again. He turned it off and ran over to the door. As he peeked out, he saw a gorgeous woman with long black hair walking from the elevator in the direction of the presidential suite. She was tall, almost six feet, wearing stiletto heels and a black leather jacket that ended halfway up her thighs. He couldn't tell what she had on underneath because the coat covered up the rest. Yet he could clearly see her curves. Maybe Argentina wasn't such a bad place after all.

As she came closer he shut his door, deciding to rely on the peephole until she was past so he didn't seem to be eavesdropping, particularly if she was headed for Sato's suite, as he expected. *You lucky bastard,* he thought with envy.

To his astonishment, she stopped in front of his door and knocked softly. Worried about being seen by someone so close to Sato's room and compromising his mission, he kept his door shut and looked out through the peephole.

"Yes, please," he said, in English.

"They sent me from the agency," she said.

He didn't know what the hell she was talking about.

She responded to his silence by untying the belt of her black leather jacket and letting it hang open. Underneath she was wearing a flimsy see-through bra that held only about half of her voluptuous round breasts, and a sheer G-string that covered a fraction of her thick black pubic hair.

Hayaski gaped. Stunned by what he saw, he was frozen to the spot.

When he didn't open the door, she closed up her jacket. "They must have made a mistake," she said. She turned and started to walk back to the elevator.

Hayaski couldn't stand it anymore. She must have gotten the room numbers mixed up, he decided. If he acted quickly, Sato's loss would be his gain. He opened the door and grabbed her by the arm, pulling her into his room. "No mistake," he said.

Once the door was closed, she held out her hand. This time he knew what she meant. That was a universal gesture. He walked over to his pants, reached into his pocket, and peeled off several hundreds from the roll of dollars he had for the trip. That seemed to satisfy her, because she put the money in her jacket pocket.

He began groping her, but she pulled away. She gave him a little feel through his cotton pants and said, "Later. First I'll dance for you."

She pointed to the bed. When he was sitting there, she turned off the television set and turned on the radio. She tried a number of different stations until she found what she was looking for: a tango. She hung her jacket over a chair and kicked off her shoes. Then she began dancing near the door, writhing to the music in a sensuous, undulating motion, swaying and twisting with the rhythm. Hayaski's mouth fell wide open, his cock hard and swollen. He had never seen anything like it in his life. The women who stripped and danced at the Roppongi bars that he liked to frequent were rank amateurs compared with this one.

Hayaski's staring was interrupted by the sound of the alarm in his briefcase. He cursed loudly. With all of his heart he wanted to ignore it, but his sense of duty was too strong. He reached across the bed and turned off the alarm.

Before he had a chance to go to the door and look out, the woman wheeled around and grabbed the doorknob. Twisting it, she unlocked the door.

"Hey, what . . ." Hayaski cried out, but he knew exactly what was happening. He charged toward the door, keeping his body low and close to the ground. Leading with his right shoulder, he knocked her out of his way. He slammed into the door, hoping to blast it shut, which would kick the lock on and give him time to call hotel security. But he was too late. The door was being opened by a force that was greater than his own.

With a sudden kick the door flew open, flattening Hayaski against the wall, then knocking him to a sitting position on the floor. Through a daze he watched a Japanese man wearing a suit and tie and white gloves, with a long, ugly scar on one cheek and a gold tooth in the front of his mouth, close the door. He handed the woman some money. In a few seconds she put on her shoes and her black jacket and left.

The man with the scar picked Hayaski up high in the air as if he were a baby and tossed him onto the bed on his back. Then he climbed up and straddled Hayaski, pressing his knees against Hayaski's arms. He removed a piece of piano wire from his jacket pocket. Hayaski's mind told him to fight back, to resist, but his assailant was too powerful.

Hayaski watched in helpless terror as his assailant looped the piano wire around his neck and pulled it tight. His eyes bulged as the pressure made him cry out in pain. At last his body gave one final shudder.

Terasawa let go of the wire and climbed off the bed. He reached into Hayaski's pants and took out all his money,

American and Japanese. After tossing Hayaski's wallet on the floor, he removed a condom from his own pocket and placed that on the table next to the bed.

The cops would have no doubt that Hayaski had been robbed and killed by a prostitute he had invited into his room. They wouldn't make any effort to investigate. When so many Argentines were the victims of crime, why bother to investigate the murder of a Japanese tourist who was stupid enough to invite a stranger to his room to get his rocks off?

As Terasawa was preparing to leave the room, he looked around for the Do Not Disturb sign, which had fallen to the floor in the melee. He picked it up and placed it on the outside of the door as he left.

He was confident that no one would enter the room before noon tomorrow. By then he and Sato would be gone.

When he was back down in the lobby, he called Sato on his cell phone. "Mission accomplished."

At ten-forty-five, the dining room table in the three-bedroom suite was fully set. The waiters had departed, leaving behind platters of smoked salmon, caviar, smoked whitefish, cold meats and cheeses, bowls of exotic fruit, a basket of bread, a bottle of wine, and a large pot of coffee.

Sato poured himself a cup of coffee and walked with it past the baby grand piano in the living room toward the high floor-to-ceiling windows that provided a view of the broad Avenue Alvear below. The nighttime traffic was heavy, stop-and-go, on the wide streets and boulevards of the Recolete, which sliced through what was considered the most fashionable area in all of South America. The city had always reminded Sato of Milan.

The end of winter in Argentina and the beginning of

spring matched Sato's mood. All things were possible. The conclusion of the long-running Japanese economic nightmare. The end of the even longer Japanese military weakness, relative to its historical enemy: China. All that was needed was proper leadership in Tokyo, and a meaningful program to emerge from the depths of weakness and subservience. Sato was ready to supply both of those.

Looking out of the window, he tried to get a good view of the entrance to the hotel. He had no doubt that the American would come. The man's desire for revenge had to be overwhelming.

Promptly at eleven o'clock he heard a firm knock on the door. He put the cup down and straightened his silk Hermes tie as well as the jacket of the double-breasted navy blue Brioni suit.

"I'm Yahiro Sato," he said as he closed the door behind the American.

Sato waited to see if the American shook his hand or bowed. He did neither.

"I know who you are." The reply was terse. "I read the newspapers."

Sato pointed to the dining room table. "Perhaps we can talk while we eat." He started to move that way.

The American remained fixed in place. "I didn't come here to eat," he said in a gruff tone that Sato had heard often from powerful Americans over the years. "I've come a long way. Tell me why you wanted to see me." The tone was impatient. "Why you sent me the note that said 'November twenty-first, 1949.'"

Sato sighed. He preferred to pursue a discussion like this in a slower, more orderly manner, but he had no choice. "I want your help in removing the one obstacle blocking my objective of evicting the American military from Japan and rearming my country in order that we can challenge China for control of Asia."

His words produced a skeptical expression on his visitor's face. "What are you telling me?"

"If Senator Boyd is elected president, then I won't be able to implement my program. I can't let that occur."

"What do you care? Why not implement your program regardless of what the American president says?"

"Unfortunately, it's not that easy. If your president opposes my program, the Diet will never approve the necessary constitutional change or back me on the withdrawal of American troops. Both President Webster and Crane would support me. You know I'm right on that. I've made every effort to win Boyd over, but—"

"You'll never win him over. He'll placate the Chinese in the hope that they'll curb their growing bellicosity, and we'll all live in peace and harmony." He snarled. "Ridiculous claptrap."

Sato walked over to the dining room table to pick up a red folder.

In stony silence, the American watched Sato place the folder on a glass coffee table.

"Inside," Sato said, "you'll find the information you need. You'll know what to do with it."

"What makes you think I'll help you?"

The question hung in the air. The American looked at Sato for an answer, but Sato turned away, walked back into the dining room, and poured himself a cup of coffee. The man was left alone with his remembrances.

Everything about that day in early October of 1949 was firmly embedded in his mind as if it had happened yesterday. He had been seven at the time, living in Shanghai in a courtyard house with his mother and his father, a missionary from the United States. They had just finished breakfast, and he was putting his books in his bag for school when five Chinese soldiers burst into the apartment, guns in their hands. The red stars on their caps caught his eye.

From then on their lives were ripped apart. The nightmare began as his father was hauled off to a Chinese jail and charged by Mao's government with being a spy for Chiang Kai-shek. Six weeks later, on November 21, the nightmare reached a crescendo. Nor did it end. For the boy it continued on and on.

Sato watched the American roll up his hands into fists. The man's eyes were on fire.

"My father was framed for political reasons to strike a blow at the American government and the Christian religion."

"So now I'm offering you a chance for revenge against Mao's successors."

The American sat down, opened up the folder, and leafed through the contents.

"You'll find in there," Sato said, "an envelope with a fax and telephone number in Tokyo, should you wish to reach me. Ask for Nara, and relay the information to the woman who answers to that name. Use the code name R.L., letters I selected at random, for this and any other communications. In Japan I have a special electronic device that will scramble the numbers on any call you make to me. No one will be able to connect us from those calls."

Sato was aware that he hadn't received any response from the American. Still, he pressed on, sounding confident that his visitor would do what he was asking. "I also want your help in writing speeches that I give in Japan and in the United States that will make me sound reasonable. Not like the way Alex Glass has been describing me in the *New York*

Times, as some type of fascist. Together we can change the political face of Asia."

Sato decided to stop. There were deep creases in the American's forehead. Remembering was painful. After a full two minutes the man stood up. Sato held his breath.

"You can count on me," he said. "I've waited a long time for a chance like this."

Sato saw the thirst for revenge—always the strongest of motives. Sato knew that he could depend on the man. R.L. was sufficiently well placed and powerful in America to get the results Sato wanted.

Chapter 1

Waiting for a jury to come in, C. J. Cady thought, *is the trial lawyer's living hell.* He took a bite of the turkey sandwich on his desk and washed it down with diet Coke. This made two nights in a row he'd had dinner in his assistant U.S. attorney's office in the courthouse in Washington. Hopefully this was the last one.

A jury could be out two hours or two weeks. There was no way to tell when they would reach a verdict. This jury had already taken two days. In the meantime Cady hadn't been able to do any other work. The high adrenaline levels from the demanding days of the trial had left him drained emotionally. He kept wondering whether the long jury deliberation favored him or the defense, while at the same time he kept replaying in his mind over and over again portions of the testimony. Monday-morning quarterbacking, rehashing whether he had been foolish to ask that final question of a witness, or too timid to ask the one on the tip of his tongue.

Cady stood up, surveyed the room, and grimaced. He liked an orderly office, only a few piles of paper on his desk, each one precisely where he knew it was. But after two weeks of trial, the office was a total mess. Boxes of exhibits were piled on the tattered brown leather sofa and the dirty beige carpet, standard government-issue. Volumes of transcripts were stacked in several piles on his desk, each of them filled with scraps of yellow paper to mark an important portion of testimony. One wall contained framed conviction orders from six of his favorite cases, arrayed neatly like trophies that line an athlete's wall. In a corner was his tennis racket, which hadn't been used in weeks.

He crossed the small office to the dirty window on the far side. With all of the money GSA spent to maintain the U.S. Courthouse in Washington, a showplace for the country's criminal justice system, it always amazed Cady that they couldn't figure out how to wash the windows.

Outside, it was dark already. Cady removed the gold pocket watch with the letters H.C., his grandfather's initials, engraved on the back, and glanced at it, as if surprised that the daylight had departed. It was almost seven-thirty. But what difference did the time make? There was nobody waiting by a phone for a call from him explaining when he would be home. Somewhere in the not-so-distant past, Janet had taken up with the tennis pro at the country club, and a bitter divorce had followed. Fortunately they didn't have children.

On the other hand, he had no difficulty remembering when Pam, the latest of the significant others who had shared his spacious Cleveland Park home in upper northwest Washington, had moved out. It was June 28, his forty-second birthday, when a leg of lamb, the main course of what was to have been a romantic candlelight dinner Pam had made, burned to charred remains. He had refused to suspend a deposition in an important case. Pam called him an unfeeling WASP, a workaholic, a cold fish, and an emotional cripple as she packed to leave. Maybe she was right, but he worked hard because he wanted to. He could easily have spent his life living off the trust fund that his grandfather,

Hugh Cady, had created when he had sold out his air-conditioning company, but Cady wanted to do something worthwhile with his life, and that was what he was doing in this trial.

From his vantage point on the third floor, he watched a damp and chilly rain pounding the streets below. A scattering of solitary men in tan raincoats and dark suits, under black umbrellas, hurried past on foot. Lawyers who had worked late, he guessed. A homeless man, bearded and scraggly, one of the legions who inhabited the streets of Washington at night, was seeking shelter in a doorway of an office building. Across the street, beneath the overhang of the Canton Duck restaurant, a hooker was watching the passing traffic, with her yellow raincoat open to reveal a bright red dress cut halfway up her thighs.

The ringing of the telephone jarred Cady. He was tempted to cross the room and grab it, but he decided to let Margaret, his secretary, answer. Seconds later the message came through the intercom: "Judge Hogan's secretary called. The judge wants you in her courtroom in thirty minutes."

"Did she say whether they've got a verdict? Or is Hogan sending them back to the hotel for the night?"

"I tried to find out, but she wouldn't say."

"Call Anita and Ed, and tell them to meet me in the courtroom."

Afraid if they were out much longer, he would end up with a hung jury, Cady wanted a verdict. Now, tonight. Jim Doerr, his boss, the U.S. attorney for the District of Columbia, had already warned him that if there was a hung jury, that would be the end of it. Doerr refused put the witnesses through another round of intimidation by Boris Kuznov's

Russian gangster friends who ran a prostitution and extortion ring in Washington.

On his way out of the office Cady stopped at Margaret's desk. "You want to go upstairs with me? You've invested lots of your time in the Kuznov case."

"You know how superstitious I am," the heavyset African-American replied. "I'll wait right here."

"You still pushing the theory that I win if you remain here, and I lose if you go to the courtroom?"

"There was only one time I went with you, and that was the only case you lost."

"That's nonsense."

"It may be, but I'm staying right here."

Cady laughed. "Okay, okay, but if we win, Anita and Ed want to have a party. Will you join us?"

She raised her hand. "I'll pass tonight. After you get back from the courtroom, if there's nothing left to do, I think I'll take off. Nancy called to say Mary Beth's not feeling well. I figured I'd stop by their place on the way home."

Cady glanced at the picture on Margaret's desk. Her granddaughter, Mary Beth, was a cute little kid with pigtails, who was missing a couple of teeth in front. "What's wrong with her?"

"Sounds like the usual. Cold and flu. It's getting to be that time of year."

"You want to leave now? That's okay with me."

"Nope. I'll wait right here for the verdict. I want to be the first to hear it."

"If there is a verdict."

Margaret watched him go through the door. Then she returned to typing.

After a couple of minutes the telephone rang.

"Mr. Cady's office," she said, expecting it to be a reporter calling about the Kuznov case.

"Is this Margaret Taylor?" a man's unfamiliar voice asked. Instinctively she felt something was wrong. "Yes, this is Margaret," she replied in a weak voice.

"I'm calling from the Washington Hospital Center. Your daughter, Nancy, asked me to call. It's Mary Beth. They had to rush her in here."

"Oh, God. What's wrong?"

"We've got her in intensive care. You'd better come now. And come to the emergency-room entrance."

"I'll be right over."

She slammed the phone down and raced to the closet for her coat. Heading toward the door, she remembered Cady. She hastily scrawled a note on a yellow pad: *An emergency with Mary Beth. I had to leave. Good luck . . . M.*

In an instant she locked the door. Soon she was moving as fast as her legs would carry her down the marble corridor of the courthouse.

A solitary figure stepped out of a telephone booth on the third floor. Wearing a long tan raincoat with the collar pulled up high behind his head, he waited until Margaret turned the corner to the elevator. Then he walked down the dimly lit hallway, clutching a brown legal-sized envelope tightly in one hand and the key to Cady's office in the other. His walk was certain and self-confident. He wasn't prone to indecision or second thoughts.

At the door to Cady's office, he stopped and glanced both ways along the corridor. It was deserted. He slipped the key into the lock. A perfect fit.

Less than a minute was all he needed in the office. Then he was gone, disappearing into the shadows of the building, and after that into the mist and rain that enveloped Constitution Avenue outside the courthouse.

In the high-ceilinged, wood-paneled courtroom Cady sat alone at the government counsel's table, waiting for Judge Hogan to take the bench. Anita and Ed were in the first row of the gallery, where all of his subordinates sat during a trial. Cady believed it was critical to give the jury the idea that he was one government lawyer in an old wrinkled suit arrayed against a battery of high-priced uptown lawyers in their fancy Italian suits. And that was how it was now. Bart Fulton was surrounded by two of his partners. At the end of the table Boris Kuznov was trying to force a smile onto his evil, craggy face.

Cady guessed that the call had reached them at a posh uptown restaurant like the Prime Rib or Galileo. He didn't care. He had been a partner in one of those powerful firms, with offices in half a dozen American cities and four more in Europe and Asia, before catching Janet in his bed with the club tennis pro. That had forced him to reexamine his life and find something worthwhile to do with the rest of it.

Behind Anita and Ed, the gallery was filling up with reporters. It was amazing how quickly they descended on a story, like vultures going after a fresh carcass. In the last row Kuznov's wife, Masha, sat, trying to distance herself from the proceedings, Cady thought. During the trial his sharpest confrontation had come with her. She had screamed that he was a paid executioner, trying to destroy their lives. She knew very well that if the jury found Kuznov guilty, Cady would insist on his extradition. He'd bet that Masha would never go back to mother Russia with charming Boris.

Cady leaned back in his chair, waiting patiently. The

sound of the bailiff's shrill voice—"Oyeh . . . oyeh, this court is now in session"—brought Cady to his feet.

In appearance, Judge Hogan was a gentle-looking woman with soft gray hair and sparkling blue eyes behind silver-framed glasses. She had a grandmotherly look that belied her reputation as the stiffest sentencer in the district court. The judge nodded to Cady and Fulton.

"We have a verdict, gentlemen. Bailiff, will you get the jury?"

A tingle of excitement spread through the gallery. Cady felt the same surge, waiting for the verdict to be announced.

The foreman, a retired employee of the postal service, was a tall, thin man with a full head of gray hair. At the judge's instruction he rose slowly, with dignity, clutching the verdict form tightly in his hand.

"Do you have a verdict, Mr. Foreman?" Judge Hogan asked.

"We do, Your Honor," was the nervous reply.

The clerk walked across the room, took the piece of paper, and showed it to the judge. She glanced at it, displaying no emotion, and returned it to the foreman. "Would you announce your verdict?"

Cady held his breath.

Silence gripped the courtroom as the foreman fingered the paper for an instant.

"On count one, we find the defendant guilty. On count two, we find the defendant guilty. On count three, we find the defendant guilty."

Cady released his breath in a whoosh. As a tide of elation spread through his body, he glanced over at Kuznov. The defendant was impassive, presenting a stony face to the world. In the back Masha moved toward the door and slipped out of the courtroom.

Minutes later, when the judge concluded the hearing, the press surged to the front of the room. One group surrounded Cady, and the other Fulton and Kuznov. Press coverage had been massive, but Cady had followed his usual rule of never talking to reporters. A lawyer could only lose that way. The most he could do was enjoy an ego trip, and Cady had no need for that.

He stuck with his rule now, though he could hear Fulton's angry voice: "It was a miscarriage of justice, and of course we will appeal." Clutching his briefcase, Cady pushed through the circle of reporters, mumbling, "No comment, no comment."

"Ah, c'mon, C.J.," a reporter pleaded, "you've got to say something this time."

"No comment."

Outside in the corridor, television cameras were turning furiously. Cady pushed past them as well, heading for the privacy of an inside staircase with Anita and Ed behind him. When they reached the third-floor landing, Cady finally relaxed. He threw an arm around each of their shoulders.

"We did it," he said. "We won. I can't thank you two enough."

"You're the one who did it," Carl protested.

Anita said, "I've got a bottle of champagne in my office. Give it a couple more minutes to chill."

"I'll be there," Cady replied. "Don't start the party without me. I wouldn't miss this for the world."

They separated, and Cady headed down the long corridor. He was surprised to find the door to his outer office locked. Reaching into his pocket for his key, he let himself in. Then he saw Margaret's note. Oh, God, that was awful.

He was so sorry. Maybe it wouldn't be that serious, after all. He'd call her later tonight to see how Mary Beth was.

Continuing into his own office, Cady flung the brown leather briefcase toward the sofa, where it landed with a thud on piles of papers. "Yes," he shouted as he moved toward his desk chair. "We nailed that damned Kuznov."

Suddenly something in the center of his desk, on top of the mess of papers, caught his eye. It was a brown legal-size mailing envelope, blank on the top except for his name, which was neatly typed on a white label. Cady was certain that it hadn't been there when he left for the courtroom. He sat down and ripped open the envelope. Inside he found a bundle of documents held together by a butterfly clip. On top was a piece of plain white bond typed with a note:

> *Dear Mr. Cady:*
> *It has come to our attention that Senator Charles Boyd was first elected to Congress ten years ago after a campaign financed by a large illegal political contribution. Senator Boyd violated the law then. He continued to violate it with votes that he cast, bought by this money, for many years. He should be prosecuted now, and these facts should become publicly known before the presidential election. Documents supporting the statements set forth above are enclosed.*

There was no signature. No other marks on the paper to identify the author.

Cady leafed through the attached documents. A deed of sale, an SEC decision, and a criminal court conviction caught his eye. Margaret must have still been here when the envelope had been dropped off. She could tell him who had brought it. With long, fast strides, he walked back into the outer office and checked the Rolodex on Margaret's desk for her daughter's telephone number. Nancy answered on the first ring. "It's C. J. Cady down at the U.S. attorney's office."

"Oh, yes, Mr. Cady."

"Listen, I'm sorry to bother you, because I know Mary Beth's sick, but—"

"Oh, that's nothing. She's just got a cold and a runny nose. You know how kids are."

"But I thought . . ."

"What is this? First my mother and now you."

"What did you say?"

"Mother just called from the Washington Hospital Center. Somebody had called her at the office to say that Mary Beth was in intensive care. What kind of nasty person plays a prank like that? Mother was frantic with worry. She's on her way here. Do you want me to have her call you?"

Now Cady understood how the envelope had ended up on his desk. "No," he said slowly, "I don't think so."

He returned to his office and closed the door. Seated in his black leather chair, he began reading the documents that supported the charge against Boyd. Then he suddenly stopped. He dug into his cluttered desk drawer, looking for the little white booklet with Jim Doerr's home telephone number. Before he could find it, the phone rang.

"The champagne's chilled," Anita said. "It's party time."

"Listen," Cady said, "a personal emergency has come up. You and Ed had better go ahead without me."

"Oh, I'm so sorry. Anything I can help you with?"

"Afraid not. But thanks. I'll work it out."

He dumped the contents of the drawer on the desk in order to find the office telephone directory.

A teenage girl answered the phone in Doerr's Georgetown house. He heard her shout, "Daddy, it's for you." She
sounded irritated that her father would be tying up the line
during prime evening phone time.

"Hello?"

"It's C.J. Sorry to bother you."

"Nonsense. I should be calling you. I heard about *our*
victory in the Kuznov case on a news bulletin on TV. Congratulations. But I do appreciate your calling to make sure I
knew about it."

"Unfortunately, that's not why I'm calling."

"What's up, then?"

"I think we'd better do this in person. May I come out to
your house?"

"Can't it wait until morning?"

"Afraid not."

Cady knew that Jim Doerr had little enthusiasm for his
job. Until four years ago he had been a successful practi-
tioner with a large Washington law firm, specializing in
white-collar crimes. He had jumped on the Webster band-
wagon early, organizing the preparation of policy papers
evaluating the country's criminal justice system. He was
hoping for the A.G.'s job, but that went down the tubes
when the president's old crony, Hugh McDermott, got the
nod. Doerr had accepted the U.S. attorney job as a stepping-
stone to a judicial appointment, which thus far had failed to
materialize.

"You're not going to like my conclusion," Doerr said
after listening to Cady, "but I think it's right under the circumstances."

"What's that?"

"I'm a political appointee, and the president who appointed me is in the midst of a reelection campaign. I can't possibly get into this."

"Should I take it to Attorney General McDermott, then?"

"That would be worse. Hugh is the president's closest adviser. He's his campaign manager."

"But he's also attorney general of the United States."

Doerr looked annoyed. "Of course I know that. All I'm saying is that at this point you can't take it to him."

"So what do I do?"

Doerr shrugged his shoulders. "You're on the civil service side. You should investigate this as you would any anonymous tip involving a public official. It's your case. Run with it. Follow normal procedures. Keep me posted in the same way you did in the Kuznov case."

Cady looked down at his hands. This case was potentially explosive, and here his boss was saying he didn't want to touch it. "Suppose I tell you I won't do it?"

Doerr glared at Cady. "Then I'll have to tell you to look for another job. You're the best I've got. I'd hate to lose you, but I wouldn't have any choice."

"Thank you for your vote of confidence," Cady replied, not trying to conceal his sarcasm.

It was raining as Cady walked down the steps of Doerr's house to R Street. He was clutching his briefcase with the Boyd documents so tightly that he suddenly realized his hand, damp with perspiration, was aching. He felt very much alone, angry at Doerr, but not surprised. He had learned long ago that in Washington it was SOP for political appointees to let civil servants take the fall while they pursued their own agendas. Yet even by those standards, what Doerr had done was despicable. For chrissakes, Boyd was running for president.

Cady was too absorbed in his thoughts to notice the man

in the long tan raincoat, lurking around the corner, mostly concealed by a parked SUV. The man was watching Cady carefully.

The grim expression on the prosecutor's face told the man everything he wanted to know. When he had left the package for Cady, he had been confident that Doerr wouldn't lift a finger to get involved. Now he knew he had been right.

Cady was on his own—precisely what the man wanted. He had snared a powerful hunter. Next, he would begin placing food in the hunter's path, leading him to a defenseless prey.

Chapter 2

Maria Ferrari was her real name, but since the age of twelve she had insisted that everyone call her Taylor. At the funeral of her mother, a victim of leukemia, she had told family and friends, in the grimy shadow of a steel mill in Donora, Pennsylvania, that she wanted to be called by her mother's maiden name, and she wouldn't respond to any other.

Now, twenty-six years later, she was seated at the kitchen table in Charles Boyd's Georgetown house with the senator and Bob Kendrick, who shared the responsibilities with her for running Boyd's presidential campaign. As morning sunlight filtered in through filmy white curtains, she was drinking coffee while studying the results of the most recent presidential polls.

A smile lit up her face, and she pushed her jet-black hair to the side. "We're in the lead," she cried. "We're finally out in front."

Kendrick reached for the papers in her hand. "Three percentage points isn't much," he said somberly. "Barely outside the margin of error. With a month to go we have to stay in a full-court press."

She slapped him on the back. "C'mon, Bob, a month ago nobody gave us a chance. What this proves is that the senator's message is getting through."

Kendrick laughed. "You mean the New Age crap you packaged for him."

"Oh, don't be such a cynic. The American people believe in the senator. They know that he wants to change the system of 'politics for politicians' and do something for the people." As both men knew, her emotion and conviction had played a large part in Boyd's surge. "They understand that he wants to build on the diversity of their country and turn it into a common purpose—a better life for all Americans."

"It's okay with me," Kendrick said. "The main thing is for him to sound good. I've done enough of these presidential contests to know that's what it's about—not substance. You're writing the speeches. Just make him sound like he cares. Like he feels the people's pain."

"But he does. That's the point," Taylor insisted.

She turned toward the senator, who was amused that they had been discussing him as if he weren't there. Dressed in a lightly starched blue shirt good for television cameras, he had a broad smile on his face. *Now he even looks like a winner,* Taylor thought.

Since the end of the convention, the senator had faced an uphill battle, as challengers often did against an incumbent, trailing President Webster in double digits. He had never worried but kept pressing forward. The pace had been mind-numbing, his sleep minimal, but he had managed to keep his sense of humor.

The image he projected was an honest reflection of what he was, Taylor believed: a sincere and intelligent man who could be trusted. That was why she had joined his campaign, and when it came down to the bitter end, that was why he would be elected president. In the confines of polling booths the American people would agree with Taylor that the senator was someone who cared about them and their problems of raising children, getting adequate medical care, funding their retirement, and paying for heat and gasoline.

"Look here," Boyd said. "You're both telling me the same thing. I'll keep pushing the New Age theme as hard as I can. Now, let's talk about energy. Taylor, when do you want me to give the speech you wrote on that topic?"

Kendrick interjected. "If you give that speech, it'll hurt our fund-raising with corporate America and people who drive gas-guzzling SUVs."

"I don't care," Taylor said. "The burning of fossil fuels by Americans at such a prodigious rate is destroying our environment and producing global warming." She thought with sadness about the destruction of the permafrost she had witnessed two summers ago when she had been hiking and mountain climbing in Alaska. "A radical reduction has to be a top priority for this country."

"Most Americans aren't as smart as you are," Kendrick fired back.

"Then we have to educate them," Taylor replied with determination.

The senator raised his hand. "Listen, Bob, the reason I'm running is because I want to lead this country in the right direction. It's a good speech. When and where do you guys want me to give it?"

Taylor glanced at the schedule on her laptop. "Thursday evening in Chicago. There's a dinner sponsored by the Midwest Business Council. It's ideal because the Chicago metro area has gotten a huge percentage of its power from nuclear energy for decades without an accident."

"Good. I'll do it."

Taylor's ebullient mood drained away as she saw the senator's wife, Sally, coming toward the kitchen. *Jesus, that woman is always trouble. What does she want now?*

Sally trundled across the floor dressed in tight-fitting black stretch slacks and a red Stanford sweatshirt. She was a pathetic figure, Taylor thought. Reasonably pretty when she had been young, she had spent her days since then in an unsuccessful effort to fight off the ravages of time. She looked every bit of her fifty-seven years. Already a large-framed woman, she was bulging with flab.

"I have to talk to you, Charles," she announced. "Alone."

He glanced at Taylor and Kendrick. "Give me five minutes, would you, guys?"

Taylor grabbed her laptop and retreated with Kendrick to the living room.

"You were with them both yesterday in Pennsylvania," she said to Kendrick. "Do you have any idea what Sally's up to now?"

"Her highness wants him to go over to St. Michaels this weekend when we do prep for the debate. She says there are fewer distractions."

Taylor grimaced. "What's her real agenda?"

Kendrick lowered his voice to a whisper. "What I've been able to deduce is that she's invited some hot new Italian painter to spend the weekend as a houseguest. She wants him to exhibit his work at her gallery. She figures that she can land this budding Michelangelo if he's exposed to the man who might be the next president of the United States."

Taylor looked worried. "We can't let him do it. The final debate is next Monday night. That's five days from now. It's critical that he spend the weekend here in Washington preparing. We'll never get him to focus over there."

"I couldn't agree more. But it's not going to happen."

Taylor rested her head on her hand and stared through the window, feeling glum. Outside, a light mist was falling, coating the first leaves of autumn on the ground. An expression popped into her mind: Snatching defeat from the jaws of victory.

Over her shoulder she heard the senator calling them back to the kitchen. He looked harried. Under Sally's watchful gaze, he announced, "The day after that Chicago speech, I want to go to St. Michaels for the weekend."

Pretending that Kendrick hadn't tipped her off, Taylor acted stunned and upset. "You can't do that. Friday morning you're supposed to be in Charleston, South Carolina. Friday afternoon there's a fund-raiser back here for Washington lawyers. Then Saturday and Sunday we have to closet ourselves in your house in Georgetown and get ready for the debate Monday night."

"We don't need two full days to get ready."

"This debate will probably decide the election. We've worked too hard and come too far to let it slip away." She was pleading with the senator with her eyes.

"I have to agree with Taylor," Kendrick chimed in. "She's right."

"She's always right about everything," Sally said, looking at Taylor and Kendrick and shaking her head. "I can't believe you two. I really can't. How can you be fighting against Charles's going to the country for the weekend?"

"We're trying to run a campaign," Taylor said.

"Oh, you certainly are. The two of you want Charles in the White House because that way you get the big jobs in government. You don't care how tired he is," she snapped.

"That's enough," Boyd said.

But Sally wasn't finished. "Jesus, Charles, when you wanted to come to Washington, I sold my business. Now I've got my gallery so that it's almost as good as one of the top New York places. All I'm asking from you is one weekend in the country. One lousy weekend. Is that so much? If you're around, I'll be able to land Emilio Cipriani for his new showing."

"For God's sake," said Boyd, who had been sick of her for years, "I can't get into all of this now. Bob and I have to fly up to New York. I've got people waiting."

"I don't care who's waiting. For the past year I was willing to take all of your stuff and theirs as well, and to be on call for your presidential campaign because at least you made an effort to be half decent to me. I figured if you won, it would be exciting for us in the White House. But ever since the convention, you don't even know I exist. I've had it. I've had enough with a capital E!"

Sally stormed out of the room, leaving Taylor horrified. They needed her to make campaign appearances with the senator. They'd be dead without her. Moving quickly, Taylor cut her off in the living room before she could go upstairs.

Sally's jaw was set. Her blue eyes had a glint of steel. "You don't get it. You really don't. So I'll make myself clear with a capital C. Either Charles comes to the country this weekend, or I'm leaving him. It's as simple as that. Now you decide."

Taylor hesitated for a second. Looking at Sally, she knew this was no bluff. "He'll go to St. Michaels."

Back in the kitchen, without signaling Kendrick, Taylor said wearily, "I'll change the schedule. We'll be able to do the debate prep in St. Michaels."

Boyd nodded in approval. "Crane can go to Charleston for me."

"He doesn't play well in the South," Taylor said matter-of-factly.

"Then why'd *you* want him on the ticket as vice president?"

She was taken aback by his testy tone. "Because you had no other way to get the nomination."

"He'll have to do the best he can. And you can talk to the Washington lawyers Friday afternoon. They're your clan anyway." He looked at Kendrick. "Get our stuff together. We've got a plane to catch."

Once Boyd was upstairs, Kendrick shared a commiserating look with Taylor. "You'd better tell me where you're going to be for the next couple of days in case I have to reach you and can't get through on your cell phone."

"I'll be at campaign headquarters today, and tomorrow at my office at Blank, Porter, and Harrison."

Kendrick scowled. "Why are you still spending time at the law firm? From here on out the campaign should be a full-time job for you."

"C'mon, Bob. My deal with the senator has been fifty-fifty all along, and you know there's been no problem. Every speech and every position paper's been ready on time."

"That may not be good enough anymore. We're down to the short strokes now."

She could understand his frustration. It was a feeling she shared. She would have liked nothing better than to be working full-time for the campaign, but she was already in trouble at the law firm for spending so little time on firm business. Kathy, her secretary, had reported hearing partners grumble in the corridors: "Why are we paying her half her salary?" The nineties were over. Lawyers in large firms were expendable these days, and Taylor couldn't afford to sever her relationship with the firm.

"What are you worried about?" she asked.

"Shit happens at the end of every campaign. Things come flying out of left field at a thousand miles an hour. You've got to move fast or they'll knock your candidate out of the ballpark."

The furnace room at campaign headquarters was going full blast when Taylor arrived. It looked like a makeshift temporary office. Battered metal desks and chairs, hastily rented, had been tossed almost at random in the large center bull pen and a series of small offices along the outside walls of the building. The constant *click, click* of word processors and the humming of laser printers filled the air. Members of the brain trust, all of whom Taylor had handpicked, mostly in their twenties, hurried around with papers in their hands, composed memoranda and speeches in front of computer screens, or assembled in twos and threes to argue about an idea and how to formulate it. As Taylor made her way to her corner office, she greeted the staffers. Someone had mounted on her wall a blowup of the results of the day's *Post*/ABC poll that showed the senator leading Webster by three percentage points.

Taylor worked at her desk through the noon hour, eating a yogurt while making notations in the margins of the briefing books for next Monday's debate. She had just turned a page when the sound of the intercom jarred her. "Saul Cooper from the *L.A. Times* on line one."

Taylor picked up immediately. "Coop, if it's tennis, I'm sorry I can't play this evening. I'm buried here."

"I wish it were tennis."

She detected a grim edge in the normally jovial Cooper's voice. "What's up?"

"We better talk in person. For certain conversations, I hate using the phone. You never know."

"I'm tight on time today. Can we do it tomorrow morning?"

"This can't wait."

Cooper was not prone to exaggeration. He had something urgent to tell her. "Where and when?" she asked.

"How about a park bench in the center of Franklin Square? I can get there in fifteen minutes."

"It's raining, Coop."

"It was raining this morning. It stopped. Don't you ever look out your window?"

"I've been busy."

"Fifteen minutes?"

"I'll be there, Coop."

She marked her place and grabbed her coat, taking an umbrella just in case. But Coop was right: The storm had passed.

She arrived first, sat down, and watched him approach from K Street, cutting diagonally across the park with long strides. Cooper, a widower at forty-seven, was tall and wiry with graying black hair that was thinning in front. He was carrying a white paper bag and wearing a dark blue raincoat that was so beaten up, she'd bet it was the only one he had ever owned.

Sitting down on the bench, he opened the bag. Inside was a pint of Ben & Jerry's ice cream, which he pulled out along with two plastic spoons. "Cherry Garcia, your favorite."

She smiled. "You know how I love ice cream, Coop. This is a treat. It's also the nicest thing anybody's done for me all week."

For several minutes they ate in silence. Taylor tuned out the campaign and watched the pigeons sturdily pacing among the golden leaves. Finally she said, "I guess you didn't drag me down here to eat ice cream."

"Unfortunately not."

"Okay, give."

"I want to tell you something as a friend."

His solemn tone set off alarm bells. "You've got my attention."

"About half an hour ago I got a call from Ed Dawson, one of our reporters who works out of the San Francisco office."

"And?" She was holding her breath.

"Ed told me that there's some serious digging going on up in Napa about Senator Boyd's past. Rumors are starting to surface that there's some skeleton in Boyd's closet that could hurt him and change the election."

Cooper's words shook Taylor to the core. A scandal at this late stage would wreak havoc on the campaign. It took her a few seconds to recover her composure. "Who's doing the digging?"

"I asked Dawson. He said that he doesn't know."

"Then how'd he find out about it?"

"First he got an anonymous tip. Then he made some calls to check on what he'd been told. He's just begun his own checking."

Taylor cried out, "C'mon, Coop. An *anonymous* tip?"

"Hey, don't shoot the messenger. At this point we don't know much. I wanted you to have everything I did ASAP."

"Skeletons in the closet," she said in an angry, bitter voice. "That type of character assassination finds its way into every presidential campaign sooner or later. You know that, Coop. You've been in this town a long time. President Webster and his distinguished attorney general and campaign manager, Hugh McDermott, must be behind it. McDermott's a sleaze, and they're getting desperate. So they'll plant stuff like this. You guys in the press always take the bait."

The veteran newspaperman shook his head. "For your

sake I hope you're right, but it's a little more complicated than that."

Wide-eyed, Taylor stared at him, waiting for the other shoe to drop.

"Dawson also heard in this anonymous call that the U.S. attorney's office in Washington will be launching an investigation of the senator."

His words rocked Taylor back on the bench. Even the existence of an investigation like that would destroy the senator's chances of winning. She tried to keep up a brave front. "Well, they won't find anything. He's a good man. That's why I'm working with him."

She bit down on her lip. "It's all so damn frustrating." She squeezed her fingers together, breaking the plastic spoon in two. The ice cream that had tasted so good a few minutes ago was curdling in her stomach. "We've run our campaign on the high road, concentrating on the issues, presenting a program for change and improvement for the American people. Now that we're winning, this is how Webster and McDermott respond."

"Did you really expect anything else?"

"I suppose not, but still I won't get into the gutter with them and start slinging mud."

"I'm not telling you how to run your campaign. So far you're doing better than I ever imagined."

She hesitated for a second. Then she gulped hard and asked, "Will your paper publish tomorrow what you told me about the rumors in Napa?"

Cooper waved off the idea. "We don't have enough for a story. Not yet, anyway. I don't think it would be responsible journalism to publish what we have now. Fortunately, as the head of the Washington bureau, I get a veto on a story like this."

She breathed a sigh of relief.

"I'll let you know if I hear anything else."

"Thanks, Coop. You're a real friend. Anytime, day or night, get to me."

Chapter 3

Closeted alone in his office, Cady read every document in the brown envelope four times. If they were all accurate, there would be a powerful case against Senator Boyd.

In any other situation, he'd set off with zeal on the investigation, but he was still bothered by the way in which the materials had arrived in his office and Doerr's immediately backing off. He needed a sanity check before he fell into a trap. He'd consult with his longtime mentor before taking the next step.

He checked his watch before calling. By this hour of the afternoon, he expected the Chief to be working at home.

Betty answered the phone.

"I hope I'm not disturbing you," he said.

"C. J. Cady! We haven't seen you in ages, since our party in June. You should be ashamed of yourself, neglecting your old friends like that."

Her words made Cady feel guilty. In the past he had visited Betty and her husband, Chief Justice Gerhard Hall, every couple of months. Since the summer, he had been swamped. Now he was calling when he needed something.

"Well, you're forgiven anyhow," she said. "I know how busy all of you boys are. Let me find Gary for you."

While waiting for Hall to come to the phone, Cady

thought about his wonderful relationship with the chief justice over the last sixteen years. It began when Hall had hired Cady to be one of his four law clerks, working in the chambers of the chief justice in the Supreme Court building. Cady was one year out of Yale law school at the time and clerking on the D.C. circuit. The year he spent working for "the Chief," as Hall was affectionately called by his clerks, was the most enjoyable and stimulating of Cady's life. Since then he had maintained a close relationship with the jurist.

The Chief came on. "Cady, what a pleasure to hear from you. How have you been?"

"Pretty well, sir. I have to apologize for disturbing you at home, but I'd very much like to see you today, if I may."

"You sound so serious."

"I'm afraid I am."

"Come on over as soon as you can."

The Chief lived in a rambling old house on Garfield Street in Cleveland Park. He had occupied the same house ever since he arrived from Cincinnati more than twenty years earlier to take his position on the Supreme Court. He and Betty were childless, but his law clerks provided a constant source of young visitors.

Betty answered the door, dressed in a pale green woolen dress. She took him to the Chief's second-floor study and then departed. Seeing the Chief hunched over a brief on his desk, Cady was struck by the pallor of his face.

"Ah, Cady," the older man said, looking up from the brief. He pulled a thick pair of reading glasses from his face and dropped them on the desk. Then he rose and greeted Cady with a handshake. "You must feel good about the verdict in the Kuznov case."

"I do. Were you surprised?"

"Pleasantly. It only takes one juror to hold out with a reasonable doubt, and from the press coverage, your key witness . . ."

"Olga."

"Yeah, Olga seemed shaky, to say the least. Well, anyhow, you did the country a service. Maybe INS will deport some of Kuznov's buddies with him. We don't need them here."

Cady felt some of his tension ease away. "I can't tell you how happy I am to hear you say that. Your opinion means a great deal to me. Already I'm glad I came."

"But that's not why you're here."

"Unfortunately not."

"Okay, fire away."

Feeling the Chief's penetrating gaze on him, Cady took a moment to gather his thoughts. "When I got back to my office last evening after the verdict, there was a package on my desk. A brown envelope with my name on it. Nothing else."

"Who delivered it?"

"That's part of the problem. I don't know. But whoever it was, they tricked my secretary into believing there was a medical emergency with her granddaughter." He paused and ran his hands through his hair. "What a scum. Once she was gone, they left the package. I was in the courtroom at the time. Margaret always locks the door when she leaves, so they must have had a key to get in."

"What was in the envelope?"

Cady wasn't sure he wanted to go on. "I know it's not right for us to be having this discussion. I don't want to cause you any problems."

The Chief smiled. "I'm past the point that you could cause me any problems."

It was an odd comment, Cady thought, but he let it drop.

The Chief repeated, "What was in the envelope?"

"Bottom line, an anonymous tip that Senator Boyd violated the law relating to campaign contributions when he first ran for Congress. With supporting materials."

The Chief let out a long, low whistle. He began tapping his fingers lightly on the desk. "What's your instinct tell you? Is the tip serious, or is this just a fabrication to blow smoke and affect the election next month?"

"My gut tells me the charges could be real."

"Did you talk to Jim Doerr about it?"

Cady nodded. "Recognizing his responsibility as U.S. attorney, he ducked and told me it was my problem to deal with."

The Chief raised his eyebrows. "Jim didn't want to get into it at all?"

"You've got it."

Hall resumed the tapping of his fingers on the desk. "Who has a key to your office?"

Cady dismissed that lead. "They're everywhere around the building."

"Okay, let's look at this another way. Why would somebody do this now?"

"Because they want Boyd out of the campaign."

"In that case, why not simply leak it to the press?"

Cady pondered the question. "They think it'll be more effective if I confirm the facts."

"Suppose you don't act. Just trash the envelope?"

"They still have the option of going to the press."

"You think McDermott's responsible, or someone else who's working on Webster's campaign?"

Cady nodded. "That's the first thought that crossed my mind. What about you? What do you think?"

"I'm not sure. My gut tells me it's more complex than just an election dirty trick."

"So what should I do?"

The Chief thought about Cady's quandary for a minute. Finally he said, "I think that you should do whatever you would do if this letter concerned another high-ranking official who wasn't a presidential candidate. Make sure you keep careful notes and records of what you're doing and why."

"Should I go to Hugh McDermott?"

"Not now. Keep Doerr informed and let him make that call. By rights, McDermott shouldn't get involved. I'm afraid that our attorney general has the ethical standards of a bootlegger in Prohibition. Besides, since there's a chance he might be responsible, or somebody working under him, you shouldn't go to him until you have to."

"I've got the press to worry about as well."

"Do what you can, but don't worry about the press. They are going to pick it up sooner or later. Nothing's safe from them these days. Not even the conferences among justices on the Court."

Hugh McDermott was distraught. At seven o'clock in the evening, the attorney general was in his office. His gold cuff links with the presidential seal were off, his sleeves rolled up. His vest was unbuttoned to release his protruding gut, his glasses on his forehead and his Church's shoes on his desk. He kept examining every presidential poll he could get his hands on. All of the results pointed to the same conclusion: Webster had lost the lead.

But how the hell had that happened?

When the telephone rang, McDermott waited for one of the secretaries to answer. Then he remembered they had both gone home. He picked up his regular black phone, but the ringing continued.

In a rush, McDermott grabbed for the red one, of which he was fond of telling people, "Only the president has the number. Not even my wife."

That was only partially true. One other person had the number as well. Since Webster was occupied in a state dinner this evening with the president of somewhere or other, it had to be her.

"I'm sorry to bother you at the office," Gina said in her sensuous, melodious voice.

McDermott was alarmed. He had told her never to call on this phone unless it was an emergency. "It's not a bother when you call, honey."

"I know you're so busy." She sounded apologetic. "Something happened this morning. I didn't want to call, but it's been bothering me all day, you know, and so I hope you won't be angry."

McDermott took a deep breath. "I could never be angry at you." She was obviously frightened, and he wanted to reassure her. "You can tell me what happened."

"Well, I went shopping in Sarasota this morning. I was out walking, pushing little Jimmy in his stroller, on the road that runs along the water toward Longboat Key. You know?"

"Yeah." He was anxious for her to get to the point. "And what happened?"

"A car pulled over and this guy jumped out on the passenger side with a camera. He took a couple of pictures of me and the baby. Then he got back in and drove away."

McDermott could feel moisture forming under his arms and soaking his shirt. Jesus, not this. Not now. He tried to sound calm. "Did you happen to get a license plate number?"

"No, but it was a large black car, like a Cadillac or a Lexus. Like that."

Which certainly narrows the field, McDermott thought.

"It scared me half to death," she said. "So why were they doing that, Hugh?"

He knew damn well why they were doing it. Someone would show him those pictures when they tried to blackmail him. "You wouldn't like the world to know you had a second family, would you?" they would say. *Oh, shit.* Why did this have to happen? Why now?

Still, his immediate objective was to settle Gina down. "Well, after all, you are a former Miss Florida, honey. My guess is that you looked so good that some tourist stopped to take your picture. He figured it was cheaper than buying a magazine with good-looking, sexy women."

She purred. "Do you really think so?"

"I'm sure of it. What were you wearing?"

"My little white shorts and that pink halter top you bought for me when you were down here last weekend. You know."

"You mean the one in which those gorgeous boobs of yours are practically jumping out?"

She giggled.

He could feel himself getting hard just talking to her this way. "See what I mean?"

"Yeah, I guess you're right. I never like to press you, but when can you come back again?"

McDermott looked at his calendar. "The president has a Florida campaign stop in about ten days. I'll break away at least for an overnight. How's that, honey?"

"I'll be there waiting for you."

"Are you okay on money?"

"Oh, yeah, thanks. I got your check yesterday."

"Good. I'll talk to you in a couple of days."

Hanging up the phone, McDermott suddenly had a great desire to urinate. He raced into the private bathroom off his office. When he was finished, he clutched his penis in his hand. *Dammit,* he thought, *this is what got me into all of this trouble. This little piece of flesh between my legs that loses thirty years and stands at attention every time I get remotely close to Gina. I should have found a way to keep it under control.* He sighed. *Well, it's too late for that now.*

Back at his desk he stared at the black phone, waiting for it to ring.

From a corner booth in the Szechuan, in Washington's Chinatown, Cady watched Paul Moore climb the tattered red-carpeted stairs to the restaurant's second-floor dining room. Moore was a short, chunky African-American whose body seemed too large for his head. Cady smiled, thinking about the defense attorneys who had been lulled into a false feeling of security by Paul's physique, only to have him lower the boom on their clients with his razor-sharp mind.

Cady stood up to greet him. "Thanks a lot for agreeing to meet me on such short notice."

"You hit me on the right night. Linda's down in Raleigh playing nurse to her mother. Your offer to buy me a Chinese dinner beat the frozen meat loaf I was planning to zap in the microwave."

A waiter was standing nearby with two menus.

Moore said, "Order for us, C.J. When we did that insider-trading case together last year, the one thing I learned was to let you order the meals."

Cady laughed. "I'm particularly good at Chinese dishes. It's that year I spent in San Francisco. I tried as many of them as I could."

When the waiter departed, Moore gave Cady a wry look. "There are no free meals in life. I bet I'm going to have to earn my dinner by coughing up info about something or other."

"Give that man a Kewpie doll."

"What's on your mind?"

"Abdul Azziz. Remember him?"

"Ugh. How could I forget? A complete scoundrel. He'd be a serious candidate for the worst white-collar felon in all of California. At first I wondered if he was malevolent or just stupid. Later I realized that his stupidity was all an act. He was very clever and venal."

"I saw the judge's sentencing order. I was surprised to see that you appeared in court yourself."

"About six years ago, if I remember right."

Cady nodded.

"It was one of the first cases that came across my desk as director of enforcement at the SEC. Abdul Azziz had state department and White House clout. I decided I'd better handle it myself, rather than one of my staff attorneys."

Dim sum and two bottles of Chinese beer arrived. Cady poured some in a glass, took a long sip, and picked up his chopsticks. "What'd you finally get Azziz for?"

"Failure to disclose facts related to liabilities when he issued stock in a Texas oil-drilling company."

"That sounds like a garden-variety Securities Act violation."

"It was. What made it special was the elaborate mechanism of intermediate companies he set up to siphon off cash from the stock issue and put it in his pocket."

"You got eleven-point-two million in a criminal penalty and a suspended sentence. That sounds like a pretty good hit."

Moore was concentrating on getting a dumpling to stay between his chopsticks. "Hardly. Azziz is loaded with gulf oil money. He's hooked into the sultan of Oman somehow." Finally he speared it and popped it into his mouth. "I actually fought against the sentence. I wanted him to do time or be deported because he wasn't a citizen."

"The judge wouldn't buy it?"

"Unfortunately, it didn't get that far. Azziz used a friend at the state department to put in a word at the White House."

"Well, isn't that nice?" Cady felt anger rising in his body. "Didn't that send you into orbit?"

Moore shrugged his shoulders. "After seven years at the SEC, I'm used to shit like that. If it bothered me, I'd have quit long ago. It's part of the system."

"Who was Azziz using for a lawyer?"

"Joe Hughes at Hughes and Baker in L.A."

"Was he good?"

"Very." Moore gave him a curious look. "But why the sudden interest in Azziz? What did he do now?"

"It's nothing recent. It's another old story that's just come to light."

"Another securities scheme?"

"Election fraud this time."

"Nothing about Azziz would surprise me. What did he do?"

Cady hesitated just an instant while he moved around some watercress with his chopsticks.

Moore was smart enough to pick it up. "If you feel uncomfortable talking about it, then please don't."

Cady laughed. "God, I'm getting paranoid about this investigation. For a second I thought I shouldn't tell you. That's crazy."

"Don't worry about it. It's a prosecutor's knee-jerk reaction. When the stakes get large enough, we all become obsessed with secrecy."

The waiter deposited firecracker shrimp and mu shu beef. Cady placed some on each of their plates. Moore was looking at him and waiting.

Finally Cady whispered, "I'm investigating a charge that Senator Boyd violated the election laws when he ran for Congress the first time . . . ten years ago."

Moore droppped his chopsticks and they clattered on the table. "You're doing what?" he asked in stunned disbelief.

"You heard me right."

"Oh, boy. Now I can see why you're concerned about secrecy. Did you volunteer for this beauty, or did Jim assign it to you?"

Cady checked about them before going on. "It arrived on my desk in an envelope from an anonymous source. The materials in the envelope suggest that Boyd was paid fifty million for a winery and vineyard called Mill Valley in Napa near Rutherford. The purchase price was never publicly disclosed. The papers also suggest that the property was worth only ten million max at the time. The other forty million was in effect an illegal political contribution."

"Did the money make that much difference in the election?"

"I did some research today, and I'd say the answer is a clear yes. Boyd narrowly upset Chris Broder, who had held that seat for twenty-four years. Broder had been a ranking member on the House Foreign Relations Committee. The election was decided by only nine hundred and twenty-two votes. Money Boyd spent for television advertising at the end played an important role in his victory." Cady paused to take a bite. "You like the shrimp?"

"Oh, it's great. First you electrify my mind by telling me

about your investigation. Then you zap the rest of my body with the shrimp. Tears are about to start pouring out of my eyes and I can't move my mouth. Aside from that, I love it."

"It is a bit hot."

Moore gulped down the rest of his beer and a full glass of ice water. "Now tell me what Abdul Azziz has to do with this Boyd election business."

"I don't know."

"So you just invited me here to burn out my G.I. tract."

Cady smiled. "The envelope on my desk contained the indictment and the sentencing order in the Azziz Texas securities case you handled. There was no apparent link to the Boyd election fraud charge. I was hoping you could supply that link."

An odd spark lit in Moore's eyes. "What else was in the envelope?"

"A deed to the Mill Valley property. It shows that Boyd sold out to a French company, Maison Antibes, headquartered in Lyon, which still owns Mill Valley. I did some research, and I learned that the president of Maison Antibes at the time of purchase was Henri Chapell. He died two years after the transaction of a heart attack. I couldn't find the names of any other principals of Maison Antibes. That's as far as the information has taken me. Got any ideas?"

Moore nodded. "Just one. It's a shot in the dark."

"What's that?"

"At the time of his conviction in my case, Azziz was an Iraqi citizen living in California. But I also remember that he had lived in France for about five years before he moved to this country."

"You think he could be involved with Maison Antibes or Henri Chapell?"

"The names never appeared in my case, but it's a possibility."

"I need something. I'm at a dead end." Cady took a long sip of beer. He wondered whether he was cleverly solving a difficult puzzle, or simply following a false trail that someone had created for him.

"If you ever meet Azziz, you'll love questioning him. He's such a charming fellow."

"I might have to do that. Any chance you could check the file tomorrow and get me an address for Azziz?"

"I don't have to. Having been there once, I could never forget it. He lives in L.A., up on Sunset, three blocks west of the Beverly Hills Hotel. It's a stone house painted dark green. In the center of the front lawn there's a statue of a nude woman with her pubics painted dark green as well. You can't miss it."

Cady smiled. "I wouldn't think so. You know if he still lives there?"

"I've got no idea. Happily, that was the end of my relationship with Mr. Azziz. But I'll call you in the morning with his phone number from the file. If it doesn't work, the FBI in L.A. should be able to trace him for you." Moore paused to give his old friend a measuring look. "You sure you want to do this?"

Cady nodded weakly. "I feel as if somebody just handed me a live grenade minus the pin."

Chapter 4

Yahiro Sato couldn't have been any happier.

He was sitting in the corner suite on the top floor of the forty-story Sato Industries building, overlooking the Imperial Palace in Tokyo, preparing for a television interview. Much of the day he had spent polishing answers to the questions he would receive, while smoking one cigarette after another and eating sushi from a lacquered tray at his desk.

A month ago, when he had announced that he was a candidate for prime minister in the December 28 election, no one had taken him seriously. *A rich industrialist catering to the militant right-wing fringe* was how one Tokyo daily had described him. Well, now they were singing a different tune. Everyone considered him a contender to unseat Prime Minister Nakamura, and his star was still rising fast. He was even being taken seriously in the United States, thanks to the Alex Glass series in the *New York Times*.

At precisely six o'clock, he heard a knock on the door. That pleased Sato. He liked subordinates to comply with his directives. "Yes?" he said, lifting his head.

The door was opened by Terasawa, accompanied by Toshio Ozawa, an ally and confidante of Sato's for more than twenty years. Dressed in a military uniform, Ozawa was the commandant of the National Self-defense Force, the only quasi-military defense force permitted under the Japanese constitution. If Sato became prime minister and the constitution was amended to permit a full-fledged military, Sato intended to appoint Ozawa as commander-in-chief of the new Japanese military.

Two smartly dressed young women in short black skirts, matching bookends, brought in cups of green tea for the three of them, bowed, and then withdrew quietly, closing the door of Sato's office behind them.

Terasawa took his cup and retreated to a corner of the room. The bodyguard knew his place. Dressed in a dark blue suit, a white shirt, and a tie, he could have passed for a salary man if not for the long scar on his cheek. When he was angry, his face turned to a menacing scowl.

Reaching for the stack of papers on his desk, Sato pulled out several neatly typed pages and handed them to Ozawa. "The spontaneous answers to the spontaneous questions that will be called in by viewers on tonight's television interview."

The normally humorless Ozawa cracked a smile. "Do you talk about China?" he asked.

"Read it. I've ratcheted up the pressure. Let them choke on their own tongues in Beijing."

As Ozawa read the script, he nodded. Only at the end did he wrinkle his forehead. "You deal with the Americans in strong terms."

Sato puffed deeply on his cigarette. "I've made my position clear. All American troops must leave Japanese soil within thirty days of my election on December twenty-eighth, and we will delete Article Nine of the Japanese constitution."

"But you'll need Diet approval for these steps. I'm worried that you won't be able to get it. Too many of the legislators will be intimidated and roll over for Washington. Also, the United States can bring economic pressure. You know that."

"Suppose I were to tell you that the American president will agree with my program and remove all of their troops without even a whimper?"

Ozawa raised his bushy eyebrows. "You know that?"

"Webster has told that to one of my people. He and his top aides are concerned about growing military power in China. They see us as an important offset to Beijing. They also see the Asian conflict as a matter to be solved by Asians. They view American military expenditures in Japan as a drain on their badly stretched defense budget. One that can easily be eliminated."

"And the Democratic candidate?"

"My trip to Buenos Aires last month was a success. I have a plan to deal with Boyd. It's a Japanese politician who's worrying me more right now."

Sato turned toward Terasawa, whose gold tooth in the front of his mouth glistened under the overhead lights in the office. He was the perfect bodyguard, Sato thought, even to the point of speaking English, which was important because Sato traveled so much. The son of a Japanese woman and an American military man who had been stationed in Japan but stayed after his tour of duty to expand a lucrative smuggling operation in and out of PXs on American bases, Terasawa had been christened Paul O'Brien. At the age of twelve he killed his father, a drunken lout who regularly beat his mother, and ran away. He'd lost himself in the underworld of the Yakuza and taken on a name from his mother's family. That was where Sato had found him two years ago. He also liked the fact that Terasawa was smart. When Sato gave him an assignment, Terasawa quickly devised a way to get it done.

"Tomorrow evening," Sato said to Terasawa, "Masaki has scheduled a rally at the Kokuritsu Gekijo Theatre to condemn my visit to the shrine in the afternoon."

Terasawa nodded and leaned forward.

"Masaki and his left-wing communist group have been a thorn in my side since our campaign began. Tomorrow would be a good time to eliminate that thorn once and for all."

Terasawa nodded. "It will be done," he said grimly. Tonight he would meet with some of his friends in the Yakuza. He knew exactly what they would do.

Rather than in a television studio, Sato conducted the interview in his office. For the session he directed aides to install a large flag of Japan, the red sun against a white background, behind his desk where it would be hugely visible.

Sato had provided all of the questions, lobs up to the net, to Mori, a friendly reporter who was conducting the interview. Dressed in a dark suit, pale blue shirt, and a tie, and looking statesmanlike at his desk, Sato was relaxed, easily fielding Mori's questions, plus the call-in questions from viewers.

Following Sato's script, the first viewer asked, "If you are elected prime minister, will you apologize to the Chinese people for atrocities committed during the war, such as the rape of Nanking?"

Sato looked straight into the television camera. "It's time we set the record straight. The number of those so-called atrocities has been grossly exaggerated. To be sure, in any war some soldiers become carried away, but that's much different from a collective sense of guilt, which some of our politicians would impose upon the Japanese people."

"How would you deal with the issue of Taiwan?"

Sato paused, wanting to appear as if he were thinking about the question. "I plan to visit Taiwan next month before the election. In that visit I will urge the residents of the state of Taiwan to select—and I will support—whatever destiny they wish to pursue, whether it be union with the People's Republic of China, a continuation of the status quo, or full independence." Cognizant that his words were tantamount to a declaration of war with China, he had asked Mori to pause before he took the next question to make certain that Sato's words sank in.

The final set of questions from viewers concerned the United States. On this subject Sato tried to portray himself as very provincial, in the style of a traditional Japanese leader. He had to be careful, because the reality of his life was so different. He had started a company that made a novel computer chip widely used in telecommunications, which AT&T had acquired ten years ago. For the negotiations, held in New York, Sato had taken up residence at the St. Regis for a month.

"My program," Sato said, "begins with the repeal of Article Nine of the constitution. That language, written by General MacArthur and imposed on a weak and prostrate Japan, states: 'The Japanese people forever renounce war as a sovereign right of the nation . . .' and that land, sea, and air forces, as well as other war potential, will never be maintained.

"I won't argue about whether Article Nine made sense in the days immediately after World War Two. However, it clearly makes no sense at this time, and it's a humiliation." He stopped and repeated the word *humiliation* for emphasis.

"We've suffered enough for our loss in the war. Our sins didn't remotely approach those of the Germans, who slaughtered more than six million innocent civilians. We, in fact, helped Jews to escape from Europe and safeguarded those Jews under our control in Shanghai. We should now have the right to create and to maintain any military force appropriate for our own defense, just as Germany has that right. Not merely some pasty civil defense force to take action in case of an earthquake or tornado. We don't want the United States to defend us. We want to be able to defend ourselves if our enemies seek to undermine our economy and to destroy the balance of power in Asia. Wars begin when one party is strong and the other is weak.

"Finally, let's not delude ourselves into believing that the American troops are in Japan to defend us. They are here to keep our military in check. That's the reality. Anything else is fiction. It's time that the United States withdrew those troops."

A viewer asked, "How do you believe the American president will react to your proposal to remove all American troops from Japanese soil?"

With black eyes blazing, Sato responded, "I am confident that the American president in office at the end of next January will support my program as honorable for Japan and in the interest of world peace."

Alex Glass was exhilarated as he sat at his desk in the *New York Times*'s bureau office on the twentieth floor of a high-rise in the center of Tokyo, staring at the television set that was blasting out analyses of the Sato interview by Japanese commentators. In the seven years he had been in Tokyo as a reporter for the *Times*, Glass had been looking for the big, big story that he could ride to fame and fortune the way Woodward and Bernstein had at the *Washington Post* with Watergate.

Six years ago he had thought he had it with the global-warming conference in Kyoto, but nobody back home cared very much if increased temperatures eroded their quality of life. For Glass, the only good that came out of the Kyoto conference was the four-week affair he had had with that dish Taylor Ferrari, a member of the American delegation. It had been the first and only time Glass was in love, but not enough to consider giving up his great job in Tokyo and moving back to Washington. Though Taylor had studied Japanese in college, he knew that there was no way she would ever live here. He never even broached the question with her. It wouldn't have worked anyhow. She was seven years older, and he doubted that she was in love with him. *So what?* The sex was great, and she was fun to be with.

That was six years ago. Now he was on the verge of a Pulitzer. The rise of Yahiro Sato and the growth of Japanese militarism was a huge story—the largest involving the United States and Japan since the 1945 surrender. Here was the horse that Glass could ride, and that was precisely what he was doing. A month ago he pleaded for authorization from Steve Terry, the *Times* bureau chief in Tokyo, to do a lengthy three-part series on Sato. Research for that had gotten him squarely in the middle of Sato's organization, and established him as an expert. He was also the messenger sounding alarms for Washington.

Portions of the series were being widely quoted. Alex was now a celebrity. Last week a CNN reporter referred to him as one of the top foreign journalists in Tokyo; "What Glass writes can't be brushed aside," the reporter said. And the series was only the beginning. Now Terry was telling him to provide daily coverage on Sato. Glass was thrilled that he had picked the right horse in this race.

Alex turned off the television set and his computer, grabbed his motorcycle helmet, and rode down in the elevator. He needed to relax for a couple of hours over dinner in one of the clubs in the Roppongi. After that he'd come back and work some more—if he couldn't entice some young beauty into his bed first.

Alex had another reason for feeling good. Besides garnering a Pulitzer, at long last he'd gain the respect of Martin Glass. Then old Dad wouldn't think he was a worthless, lazy dilettante because he had refused to go to work in the family auto-parts business back in Seattle.

Stop kidding yourself, he thought as he put on his helmet while walking toward his Kawasaki. *Old Dad will never be proud of me, no matter what I do, unless and until I join Glass Auto Parts. "The Crystal-clear Supplier."*

When he had spent time with Taylor she had told him, "Stop being such an ass. It's time you gave up the family guilt horseshit."

For Alex that was easier said than done. He had something to prove to his father. He would do it with his in-depth coverage of Yahiro Sato and the rise of Japanese militarism.

Chapter 5

Taylor looked at the computer screen in her office at Blank, Porter, and Harrison and winced. "Ah, damn. Not now."

She reread the e-mail message.

> *I have a new transaction to discuss with you. Can you meet me for breakfast tomorrow at the Four Seasons in Washington at eight A.M.?*
> *Kenzo Fujimura.*

At any other time she would have liked nothing better than to hear from him. Fujimura, a prominent Japanese lawyer whom Taylor had met at the Kyoto global-warming conference, had become a friend and the source of most of her law work, as he funneled American projects to her for his largest Japanese clients in the energy sector, particularly M. H. Heavy Industries, which was buying energy-related companies in the United States. The relationship was mutually beneficial. She knew the energy area from her years as a congressional staffer, and she could draw on the specialized expertise of other lawyers in the 160-person firm—depending upon the project. The trouble was that Fujimura always demanded her own personal involvement. This e-mail was just what she didn't need right now. Not after a sleepless night spent tossing and turning about the information Coop had delivered to her yesterday.

She hit the intercom. "Kathy, reply to Fujimura's e-mail. Tell him I'll be there. I'm going down to Philip Harrison's office."

As she walked along the hardwood corridor lined with rich Oriental carpets, Taylor thought again about Coop's information. She made up her mind that she wouldn't sit around and wait for the senator to go down in flames. If in fact a criminal investigation was under way, she wanted to stop it. The trouble was that she didn't have any decent contacts at a high level in the U.S. attorney's office. *Oh, well.* She'd worry about that later. For now, she'd better try to cajole Harrison to take on Fujimura's new project. If she succeeded, she could limit her role to cameo appearances, and it would not detract from her work on the campaign.

Seeing that Harrison was on the phone, Taylor stopped to chat with Doris, his secretary. Once he spotted her through the open doorway, he waved her in to sit and wait while he finished his call. It was a typical Harrison performance. He was on the speakerphone with investment bankers and lawyers in New York. A step ahead of everyone else, he was spinning out a complex approach for the financial reorganization of an electric utility that the other members of his client's team knew was right if they could only understand it. As he spoke, he paced back and forth from his desk to the bookcases over a strip of worn carpet and fiddled with a plastic object that resembled a cigarette—one of twenty that his wife, Celia, had given the irritable and restless Harrison to avoid having him drive her crazy when he decided two years ago to stop smoking.

As always, the office was devoid of papers. Unlike mere mortals, Harrison, who had degrees in theoretical mathematics and law from Oxford as well as a photographic memory, had no need for the reassurance of having stacks piled up in his office, like most lawyers. Instead he had models of sailboats—his latest in a string of long passions, including chess, astronomy, and Greek tragedies that he read in the original language. Anyone else would simply be sailing boats, but Harrison had to design them as well, intrigued by the scientific concepts that permitted a sailboat to maximize its speed. Articles in the *Washington Post* had covered the boat he would be building to race in one of the top world-class competitions.

Others in the firm viewed Harrison as eccentric and minimized their contact with him. But not Taylor. Not only did he often work with her on projects that Fujimura funneled to her, but he was responsible for her coming as a partner to the firm. After hearing about her work at the Kyoto global-warming conference from some of his energy clients, Harrison had flown to Japan and made Taylor an offer that was too good to turn down and return to her job as Senator Boyd's chief of staff after the Kyoto conference ended. It wasn't the money that did it. He had told her in his usual blunt manner, "I have clients who want to build power plants that don't burn fossil fuels, but can't because of permitting and other environmental issues. If you believe in the cause, come with us and help them get the job done. If you don't, then stop pontificating about it."

The phone conversation ended. He stuck the plastic cigarette in his mouth, sat down behind his desk, put up his feet, and looked at her. There were no greetings. It was the gruff Harrison's way of saying, "What do you want?"

Sitting in front of his desk as usual, Taylor noticed the holes in the soles of his shoes. He was in need of a haircut, but she knew that would be cured soon, because Doris scheduled them for him every four to six weeks in order to ensure that he maintained a good image for his clients.

"I received an e-mail from Fujimura," Taylor said, speaking rapidly, which she always did with the restless Harrison to keep his attention. "He has another transaction for us. Any chance you can take charge?"

"How big and what's the timing?"

"I'll know tomorrow. I'm having breakfast with him."

"For you, anything, my beleaguered friend."

"Do I look or sound that bad?"

"Both."

Without asking, Doris brought in two large mugs filled with black coffee and handed one to each of them. *This man does not need caffeine,* Taylor thought.

Harrison took a gulp of coffee. "How's the campaign going?"

"Don't ask. I've got big troubles."

"You want to talk about it?"

She sighed. "I suppose so."

"That bad?"

"Wait till you hear."

She had no hesitation talking to Harrison. From the time she had hooked up with Senator Boyd for the campaign, she regularly sought the lawyer's advice. He had been an informal mentor since he had lured her to the firm, and he had never betrayed a confidence. Besides, it was Harrison who had persuaded Don Blank, the managing partner, to keep Taylor on with half pay during the campaign.

She reported to Harrison what Cooper had told her in the park yesterday.

In typical Harrison fashion, he cut her off in the middle of a sentence. "You're right. You do have trouble. Big trouble."

"What do you make of it?"

"Can I be brutally honest?"

"Could you be any other way?"

A faint smile appeared on his face. "My guess is that somewhere along the way of an otherwise illustrious career, your marvelous senator may have committed a transgression, either big or small. Probably in California. But at any rate, somebody found out what Boyd did, and they're threatening to disclose it."

"Where does Dawson of the *L.A. Times* fit in?"

"Boyd's transgression probably took place in Napa Valley. They're manipulating Dawson to turn up the pressure on Boyd. It's easy to use the press that way."

"Why do you assume the senator did something wrong?"

"Good point. But it doesn't matter if he's guilty or not. If the mere fact of this investigation is disclosed now, he'll never get elected. Enough people will believe there must be something to it."

"The ultimate dirty trick by McDermott and his stooges, like Pug Thompson." She was raising her voice in anger. "More damaging than stealing documents from the Democratic National Committee headquarters in Watergate, like the—"

"Which backfired on Nixon."

"But not until after he was reelected."

"Let's take it one step at a time. First we have to find out if there really is an investigation. Dawson's source could be passing misinformation."

"Agreed. Any ideas?"

"How well do you know Jim Doerr?"

"Barely. I met him twice at bar dinners and once at a benefit for the Washington Symphony."

"You want me to talk to him for you?"

She was delighted. "I'd love it."

"I know him from the Metropolitan Club. He owes me because I asked clients to make calls for him when he was trying to be A.G."

After Harrison arranged a lunch meeting with Doerr, he turned back to Taylor. "I want to tell you something as a friend."

She tensed up. "I'm not going to like this, am I?"

"Probably not. A couple of members of the management committee came to see me yesterday. They said that your billable hours are way below what they expected under the fifty-percent arrangement."

"What'd you say?"

"I tried to defend you, but law firms aren't kind and gentle places these days. You know that."

Waiting for Harrison to return from lunch, Taylor sat at her desk trying to read the briefs in the Jeffersonville Power case that had been filed with the Mississippi Supreme Court. The case was scheduled for argument in Jackson in December after the election.

But she couldn't concentrate. The news Coop had given her yesterday was disquieting, and the charge was wrong. It had to be wrong. She had known the senator for so many years. He would never have committed a crime.

She well remembered the first time she had met him. It was at a hearing in Napa, California. She was a young lawyer in the governor's energy office, assigned to travel around the state and take testimony from industrial and consumer groups about what should be done to create a fair and reasonable system for energy use and supply. He was the spokesman for the California Wine Growers and Vintners Association, which wanted to ensure that its energy needs were being supplied at a reasonable cost.

Expecting a contentious session with Boyd—which was what she had encountered when other industry representatives appeared and tore into the governor's policy, which they viewed as favoring consumers who had more votes—Taylor was pleasantly surprised. Boyd was polite and mild mannered. He answered all of her questions in a forthright manner, taking a broad view that all interests in the state had to be satisfied, not merely those of his association. He didn't surrender his own position, but without being patronizing he tried to educate her, to persuade her why he was right, always looking squarely at her. In his words, she found principle, not merely self-interest.

She finished the hearing at noon and was loading her briefcase and documents in the trunk of a rental car when she saw Boyd approaching across a dusty parking lot. It was a bright and sunny March day. He was wearing sunglasses and walking with a self-confident stride. For the first time it struck her how handsome he was. She was no longer the state's lawyer.

"Listen, Miss Ferrari," he said in a soft, polite voice.

"You can call me Taylor."

"Okay, Taylor then. I'd like to take you on a little tour around the valley this afternoon and let you know what our business is really about."

He had snowed her with his bright red Lamborghini and lunch at Auberge de Soleil, accompanied by bottles of white and red wine from Mill Valley, followed by a tour of the large château that he lived in on the property. Sally was off in San Francisco for the day, buying for her antiques shop, he explained as they stopped in front of the master bedroom. He draped his arm around her shoulder, leaving no doubt about what he had in mind. She found him more attractive and charismatic than any man she had ever met. He was perfect, but for one fact: He was married. When she pulled away, he didn't press her.

After that day she didn't see him again until he was in his first term in Congress. She was on the staff of the House committee that handled environmental legislation, and he was a committee member. From the start he made an impression on people for his visionary positions. After he was reelected he offered her a job as his chief of staff. She was tired of being pushed around by more senior staff members, so she accepted.

"Great," he said. "You'll be a real asset for a young congressman with higher ambitions."

She smiled. "And what higher ambitions might the young congressman have?"

"There's a small white house at 1600 Pennsylvania Avenue. I'd like to live in it one day."

"My, what a modest fellow."

"My dad used to tell me that if you never shake the tree, you don't get any apples. He also hired the best young winemaker he could find when he began Mill Valley."

"I don't crush grapes."

"But you can help me crush Republican congressmen who are trying to bury me before I get started."

She laughed.

"So you accept the job offer?"

She paused to think. Working for him, she might be able to do something significant and make a difference. "The answer's yes, as long as you stick with your agenda. If the idealism goes, I go."

The idealism never went, but she had become restless, which was why she took Harrison's job offer at the law firm.

Charles had never hit on her again after that day in Napa. Nor had he done anything illegal; she was certain of it. Someone was trying to smear him.

Taylor tried to concentrate on the Mississippi briefs. She was confident that on the merits she should win the appeal, and the injunction halting construction should be lifted. What was making her nervous were the rumors she had been hearing that one of the local officials against the project was a close friend of the chief justice of the state supreme court. She would have to do a good enough job, she reasoned, that they couldn't decide against her even if they wanted to.

Taylor picked up a pen and began outlining her oral argument. When she was almost finished, the telephone rang. It was Doris. "He just got back from lunch."

Less than a minute later Taylor was in Harrison's office. "Well?" she asked nervously.

He pulled the plastic cigarette out of his mouth. "Bottom line," he said sounding sympathetic, "is that there is an investigation under way on Senator Boyd."

She was seething. "That's absurd and unfair."

"Well, that may be, but it's being handled by an assistant U.S. attorney by the name of C. J. Cady. I can't help you there. I don't know Cady."

"I do. We've gone head-to-head twice in environmental criminal cases."

"And?"

"I think I finally have a good break. We got along. I always found him to be professional, decent, and fair. Not a zealot like some of those guys." She had once kidded Cady about being too polite and preppy for the current legal world inhabited by sharks, but she was aware that he could be as tough as he had to be. She also knew that beneath that good-looking face, friendly smile, and wavy brown hair was a sharp legal mind and a determination to get at the truth. Knowing her enemy would be an advantage.

"Doerr wouldn't tell me anything about the substance or status of the investigation."

"Why not?"

"He swore up and down that he has no idea."

"Oh, c'mon."

"Actually, I believe him, but it doesn't matter for our purposes. We still have Cady to deal with."

"We? I'm delighted that you want to join me in the engine room of the *Titanic*."

"That's what friends are for. Anyhow, maybe we can still head this thing off."

"Who do you think's doing this to the senator and why?"

"That's a harder question. The obvious choice is Hugh McDermott and the Republican crowd. Hugh has some lovely fellows working for him, like that psychopath Pug Thompson." Harrison shrugged his shoulders. "On the other hand, you've got Boyd advocating your nuclear-power approach. Those people will do anything, as you and I know." He paused. "And God only knows what other groups you've managed to alienate."

"The answer is plenty of them, including most of the special-interest groups in this town. The antiabortion crowd, the gun lobby, and the radical right, to name only a few. We knew that we'd make lots of enemies by presenting a program to take the government away from special interests and return it to the people. We were prepared to—"

"That's my point. There's no way to determine who's behind it at this time." He stopped to think for a minute. "Have you told Boyd what Cooper reported to you yesterday?"

"Not yet. The senator's in the Midwest. I didn't want to do it by phone."

"My advice is that you get to Boyd ASAP. Repeat to him what Cooper said and make him tell you everything that might be a problem from his Napa days. You're better off knowing what you're dealing with right now before it's public."

"I'm going to be with the senator Saturday in St. Michaels. I'll talk to him then."

"It's a mistake to wait two days. These things move fast when they start rolling."

She considered his advice. "Let me think about it. I want to do it the right way so I don't upset the senator and destroy the momentum he has going in the campaign."

Harrison shrugged. "That's your call. Now I'm going to tell you something you won't like to hear."

Taylor looked at him apprehensively. "What's that?"

"How well did you know Boyd when he was back in Napa?"

"Not well. We met once. He was a witness for the wine producers when I was with the state in an electric power proceeding."

"Did you ever hear of anything that might be a problem?" She shook her head.

"Any business problems before he went into politics?"

"Nothing I've ever heard about, and I traveled with him extensively in Napa during each of his campaigns after I joined his staff."

"You like the senator a lot. Don't you?"

Taylor's face reddened. "We're not having an affair, if that's what you mean."

"Actually, it wasn't. All I'm saying is that if you like the man and you ever find out that what he did was bad, embarrassing, or even criminal, you should encourage him to withdraw from the race, rather than getting dragged through the mud."

"You can't be serious."

"I wish I weren't. Remember Abe Fortas?"

"He wasn't running for president."

"The principle's the same. I'm telling you this as a friend. For a man to lose the presidency is one thing. To get destroyed in the process is another. It's called cutting your losses. You give up the office to save the man."

"But the senator didn't do anything wrong."

"You wanted advice. I'm giving it to you straight."

"You're making me sorry I came in to see you."

"What can I tell you? People play hardball in this town."

He answered his own phone: "Cady here."

"C.J., it's Taylor Ferrari." There was a long pause. "You still there?" she asked.

"A voice from my past," he said in a guarded tone. "I should never have let your client off with a five-hundred-thousand-dollar penalty."

"Of course, you could have gone to trial and lost. Speaking of which, congratulations on your Russian gangster case."

"Thanks. What's up?"

"I'd like to talk to you this afternoon."

Cady was flabbergasted. He knew from the newspapers that she was Senator Boyd's campaign manager. She must have found out about his investigation. The matter had just gone from strange to bizarre.

"Sure. Come at three o'clock," Cady said.

Walking into Cady's office, Taylor remembered once again how striking he was. He was handsome not because of looks but because of the force of his convictions. Adopting a light tone, she pointed to the picture of a rustic mountain cabin in the woods and said, "Now that the Russian case has ended, I figured you'd be out in Mendocino playing tennis and hiking."

"Yeah, well, I've got one or two things to wrap up here," he said. "Once I'm through with them, that's where I'll be. I don't imagine you've spent much time rafting at your place in Aspen either this fall."

His words set off a pang of longing. She'd love to be in a raft on the Colorado right now, with the spray flying off the water, her weary body aching and the sun beating down on her in a gorge between red-rock walls.

"Which reminds me," he added, "last spring when we were wrapping up the Warden case, you and I talked about doing some rafting together in West Virginia."

She smiled. "That was before the election took over my life."

He didn't respond. She had opened the topic. The ball was in her court.

"Listen, C.J.," she said, beginning tentatively. "I appreciate your agreeing to see me. I want to talk to you about your investigation of Senator Boyd."

"What investigation?" he replied, deadpan.

"The one you're conducting."

"Sorry, I can't respond to that. We never talk about ongoing investigations." His voice was polite but professional. "We never even confirm or deny that an investigation is under way. It's Justice Department policy. You know that."

She took a deep breath. "This isn't an ordinary case. The presidential election is at stake. Whoever got this ball rolling did it for political purposes, to knock the senator out of the race and to get Webster reelected."

Cady raised his eyebrows. "What makes you think there's an investigation?"

"I have a source in the media. I can't say more than that."

Cady locked eyes with her. "Listen, you're a sophisticated lawyer. Even if there is an investigation, which I won't confirm, I can't talk about it. That shouldn't surprise you. So I'm wondering why you wanted to see me."

"If you tell me the subject of your investigation, I think I'll be able to satisfy you that there's no factual basis for you to proceed."

Cady sucked in a deep breath and blew it out with a whoosh. He was sympathetic. So far this whole business had the smell of fish that had been dead for three days. A mysterious file in the dead of the night. Leaks to the press. It wasn't fair to stonewall her completely. "All I'll tell you is that it concerns Senator Boyd's first election to Congress. I'm being generous in saying that much."

"Thank you. I appreciate that. Of course, I'd like you to call off your investigation."

He gave her a tight smile. "That's a large order. Personally, I like and respect Senator Boyd and his program, but you know I can't do that."

"*You're* going to decide the presidential election. *You'll* be taking the choice of the next president away from the American people."

He had already considered that point. "If Senator Boyd violated the law, the American people have a right to know that."

"That's precisely my point. He didn't violate the law."

"But unfortunately, I can't take your word for that. Neither would you in my place."

Taylor was feeling waves of frustration. "Listen, C.J.," she said, "I've been in Washington ten years. I know there are plenty of corrupt people in this town. They are in it for the power and the ego trip, but Senator Boyd isn't in either category. You've got to believe me."

How often had he heard that line? "What makes you certain he's different?"

"I've known him for a long time, and we've worked closely together. You don't think I'd put my whole career on the line if I didn't think he'd make the country better?"

Cady didn't dismiss what she said out of hand. Still, how well did anyone know another person?

Taylor pushed on. "The senator gave up a good business to go into politics. He did it so he could help the people of this country. His record in the House and Senate has been outstanding. Even you'd have to admit that."

"This isn't about his voting record."

"What is it about?"

"Whether he committed a crime."

"Doing what?"

"I told you that it concerns the senator's first election to Congress, and that's all I can tell you."

"That makes it hard for me to respond."

"Nobody's asking you to respond right now. You'll get a chance in the normal course."

She was exasperated and her face showed it. "But this isn't a normal case, dammit. A man's running for president. You're about to wreck his life and hand Webster the White House for four more years. All based on some half-assed rumor of something that might have happened ten years ago."

"It's my job to find out if something did happen."

She decided to take a different tack. "C'mon, C.J., you left a large firm to do something good. That's what you told me."

He nodded. "Uh-huh."

"So we both want the same thing: to do what's right for the country."

"Agreed, but at this point it's hard to determine what that is."

"You know there's something sordid in this business. A dirty trick. You're too smart not to know that."

He thought about what she had said. "As always, you're persuasive, but at this point I can't tell what's right."

"But you do know that you're being set up. Doing good doesn't mean being a puppet."

He shot to his feet. "I resent that."

Taylor held up her hand. "All right, all right. I'm sorry I said that." She fell silent, to let them both simmer down, before continuing. "We're willing to cooperate in any way if you'll agree to keep this whole matter confidential. Just give us a chance to respond to any evidence you think you have before you take any action."

He softened his tone as well. "That's a reasonable request. I'll do my best to keep it quiet. I won't go public before you have a chance to respond. You've got my word on that."

Taylor was relieved. She felt as if she had gotten as much as she could. C. J. Cady was fair in his dealings. He wouldn't use the case for his own personal gain.

On the walk back to her office, Taylor decided that Harrison was right. She had to make the call she had been dreading. She had to let the senator know about Cady's investigation. She checked her watch. They were in Chicago this afternoon. In about thirty minutes he'd be back at the hotel for an hour of downtime.

Before picking up the phone, she closed her office door tight.

An aide called the senator to the phone.

"Are you alone?" Taylor asked nervously.

"Yeah. What's up?"

"You'd better be sitting down for this."

"C'mon, Taylor. Stop stalling. What happened?"

She had decided that there was no good way to ease into it. She had to simply throw it out, and they could go from there. "Yesterday Saul Cooper from the *L.A. Times* came to see me. He said that rumors have surfaced that you have skeletons in the closet in Napa, and—"

"What kind of shit is this?" Boyd cried out. "What's Cooper's source?"

"A Bay Area reporter for his paper who's done some digging after an anonymous tip."

"Oh, for chrissake. The Republicans are losing. They're planting garbage like this and using those clowns in the press to spread it. It happens all the time."

She gripped the phone tightly. "It's not that simple. Before you interrupted me, I was about to tell you that Cooper also said there's a U.S. attorney in D.C. who's investigating the charges. I confirmed that myself an hour ago."

Boyd's voice began to tremble. "What di-did you say?"

"A U.S. attorney in Washington by the name of C. J. Cady is investigating the charges. I just came back from a meeting with him."

"What charges?" Boyd said, sounding mystified. "I never did anything wrong."

"The most he would tell me is that it concerns your first election to Congress, and—"

"That's ridiculous. Total horseshit. I beat Broder fair and square. I played it all according to the book. Even sold Mill Valley so I could use my own money to campaign and not be indebted to private interests. This stinks to high heaven. It has McDermott and Pug Thompson written all over it."

Taylor decided to follow Harrison's advice. "Think carefully, Charles. If there are any bad or even questionable facts in Napa, let me know about them. That way I can be ready with our own spin and do some damage control."

"Why don't you believe me?" Boyd said, expressing outrage. "There are no skeletons in Napa."

"Please try it my way. What's the single worst thing you ever did in the valley that you would find most embarrassing if it appeared on the front page of the *L.A. Times*?"

"Nothing!" he shouted. "Whose side are you on?"

She persisted, trying to calm him down. "Please think, Charles. Everybody has something."

"What is this, the third degree?"

"No. I'm trying to help you."

"You sure don't sound like it."

"Well, I am."

He snarled at her. "All right, I'll tell you. I tried to seduce a young female lawyer working in the governor's office about twelve years ago, but she was super virtuous and she wouldn't go to bed with me. How would *you* like to see that on the front page of the *L.A. Times*?"

Taylor turned bright red. *You bastard,* she thought. *You had no right saying that.* Yet she was determined to keep her anger under control. "That's not fair."

When Taylor put down the phone, she was convinced that Boyd was telling the truth, that he hadn't violated the law in his first race for Congress. She was also convinced that Cady's integrity was beyond question. That meant someone or some group was out to wreck the senator's campaign. McDermott, aided by Pug Thompson, was the logical choice, but she couldn't jump to that conclusion from the little she now knew. There were lots of people who wouldn't want to see Boyd in the White House, including the foes of nuclear power and undoubtedly some foreign interests.

She racked her brain, trying to imagine which ones might care enough to try to influence the campaign. In recent speeches the senator was accommodating to China, sympathetic to Israel, supportive of free trade with Europe, and opposed to renewed Japanese militarism under Sato. Were those groups sufficiently offended to try to influence the election? She didn't know, but she was certain of one thing: Regardless of who it was, she couldn't underestimate them.

Chapter 6

Sato was aware that his decision to visit the Yasukuni Shrine in central Tokyo would set off a maelstrom in Japan, Korea, and China, but that didn't deter him. As he got out of his limousine with Ozawa and walked the last hundred yards to the Shinto shrine dedicated to the nation's war dead, the size of the crowd lining both sides of the road surprised him, as did the number of baton-wielding members of the Tokyo police, dressed in riot gear.

The placards were equally divided between those that read, *Sato Yes* or *Self-defense for Japan* and the ones that read, *Sato No,* or *No More War Criminals*—a reference to the fact that among the millions of fallen victims of Japan's wars, the shrine honored fourteen men like Tojo, the prime minister during World War II, who were executed as war criminals.

For the first fifty yards, as Sato walked with Ozawa at his side, the crowd was orderly and silent. Suddenly half a dozen young men burst out of the police cordon close to the shrine and threw themselves down on the road, blocking Sato's path. "Warmonger," they chanted. A score of police ran toward the young men, swinging their batons, determined to clear the path before Sato reached them. When they refused to move, the police forcibly dragged them by their legs off the road.

Sato slowed his pace, letting them clear the path before he reached the point of the protest. Soon after, Ozawa stopped walking, to let Sato continue on alone.

Inside the shrine Sato stood in front of the giant cedar altar and bowed his head.

When he exited the shrine, the television reporter, Mori, was waiting for him with a microphone and a cameraman close by. Ten yards away Alex Glass stood with a reporter's steno pad in his hand and a tape recorder on, wanting to hear what Sato had to say.

"Sato-*san*, will you answer some questions?" Mori asked.

Sato didn't hesitate. He had already approved the questions Mori would ask. "Yes, of course."

"Why did you make this visit today?"

"Many good and honorable men have died for our nation. We have an obligation to remember and honor them."

"But aren't you endorsing what the Japanese government did during the second world war?"

Sato looked into the camera. "We fought the Greater East-Asian War for a noble purpose . . . the liberation of Asia from strangulation by Western colonial powers. Yes, we made mistakes. Like all people we suffered tremendously. However, Asia was liberated. We should never forget that."

"It has been said that you wish to start a new war with China."

"That is totally false. I want the nations of Asia to live in peace and harmony. However, that is possible only if all nations are in a position to defend themselves from any possible aggression. My view is war, no. Self-defense, yes."

"And what position do you think the American president will take in response to your program?"

Alex strained to make sure he caught every word of the answer. "I am confident," Sato said, selecting his words carefully, "that the American president in office at the end of next January will support my program."

Sato's confidence about what the American president would do reverberated in Alex's brain. They were precisely the same words Sato had used two days ago in the television interview. Alex sensed some hidden meaning in those words, but he had to find it.

When he had researched his recent series, Alex had spent several hours in one-on-one sessions with Sato, as well as with several of Sato's close confidants, including Ozawa. He had read enormous amounts of material, everything he could find, by and about Sato. One of the things that surprised Alex was the intense interest that Sato was taking in the American presidential election.

Knowing how Sato operated, Alex was convinced that he was involved in something in the United States that Alex was missing. As he replayed Sato's words in his mind, Alex was certain that he was right—not merely from Sato's words, but from the firm, unequivocal tone of voice. Sato wasn't making an idle boast or wishful prediction.

But how could that be? Alex had studied in detail all of the public statements of Webster and Boyd on the subjects of Japan and Asia. He was persuaded that Webster would support Sato's program. Not only did the president have a neoisolationist view toward foreign policy, but he was concerned about the budget deficit. He saw America's foreign military commitments as a tremendous drain on the country's finances, which had to be reduced.

If Webster were reelected, then Sato would be right. But

Boyd was a different matter. As a member of the Senate Foreign Relations Committee, he had spoken often about his view of America's place in the world. He believed the United States could placate China, notwithstanding that country's growing military might. He would view a rearmed Japan as creating the risk of a war between the two historical enemies, with the likelihood that the United States would be drawn into it on one side or the other. No, Alex was convinced that Senator Boyd would never support Sato's program. With the latest polls showing Webster and Boyd in a dead heat, something in this picture didn't make sense.

As Alex walked back to his motorcycle, he asked himself, *So what's it all mean?*

The answer that came back to him was that Sato was somehow meddling in the American election in a way that would eliminate Boyd's chances of being president. To do that he'd need help, and he'd need it from an American. But whom had he recruited? Alex would give anything to know the answer to that question. And he intended to find out.

That evening the crowd lined up outside of the Kokuritsu Gekijo Theatre, the national theater west of the Imperial Palace near Hanzomon Station, an hour before the doors were to open for the rally. The line extended in a southerly direction almost to the National Diet Building. None of the usual performances in this venue—Kabuki, traditional theater, or a concert—had ever drawn such a crowd.

They were polite and orderly, but their signs and banners told their message: *No War. No Sato.* These were ordinary Japanese people who prized their country's democracy and its relationship with the United States. Many had never attended a political rally in their lives, but Sato's rise in the polls frightened them. The announcement of the rally had stated, *If we don't speak out against Sato, he will prevail.* So they came to raise their voices.

When the doors opened, the crowd filed in until the theater was filled to capacity. People were standing three deep behind the last row and in the side aisles.

Speaking from a platform on stage, the first two speakers, members of the Diet from Prime Minister Nakamura's party, outlined the "Japanese political and economic miracle" since the end of the war. "To be sure," one said, "our economic path has been rough in recent years, but our foundations are strong. We need only stay the course, and our economy will recover." Their message was greeted with enthusiastic applause. Chants of "Sato no . . . war no," filled the theater.

Outside, Alex jumped off his motorcycle and approached the front door. He wasn't late. He had come to hear Masaki, the third speaker, who would be going on shortly.

As Alex approached the front door, he flashed his *New York Times* ID at one of two tough-looking men. "No more admission," the man said. "The theater is full."

"I'm press," Alex said. "*New York Times.*" Figuring that could get him in anywhere, he moved toward the door and grabbed the handle. One of the men roughly pulled him away. He punched Alex in the stomach and sent the reporter tumbling to the ground. He followed that with a swift kick to the balls that left Alex writhing in pain. "The theater is full." The man turned around and left him there.

Inside the theater, Masaki, a brilliant orator, was just beginning his speech, rapidly arousing the crowd to an emotional pitch.

"Sato is nothing but a warmonger and a demagogue," he shouted into the microphone. "It took us decades to recover from the previous round of leaders like Sato, who launched us into the Second World War and nearly destroyed the country."

There was a huge round of applause.

"We cannot permit—"

Masaki felt a wave of heat behind him and stopped in midsentence. From the front of the audience rose cries of "Fire!" Flames were shooting up backstage from the area where scenery flats were stacked.

Once the crowd saw what was happening, they bolted for the doors. Panic ensued. Loud screams filled the theater. Cries of help and anguish erupted as some fell in the pushing and shoving of the frightened mob.

Masaki jumped off the stage to get away from the fire. He too was swept up in the panic, and he tried pushing his way to the closest side door. On the stage, the crackling flames grew higher.

Masaki was in the center of a pushing crowd of people when he suddenly felt a hard blow to his head. "What the . . . ?" he cried out. Then he lost consciousness and fell to the floor.

The crowd tried to move around him. Terasawa had watched while one of his friends in the Yakuza had struck Masaki. Once the speaker was on the ground, Terasawa pushed against the surging mob toward the speaker. Terasawa was wearing specially made shoes for tonight with steel plates in the heels and toes. Once he reached Masaki's unconscious body, he raised one foot and slammed it down on Masaki's head. Then the other foot. He was certain that the first blow had fractured Masaki's skull. The second killed the man.

Chapter 7

"Ah, Miss Ferrari," Carlos, the maître d' at the Four Seasons, said as Taylor descended the large wooden staircase and approached the entrance to the dining room on Friday morning. "Mr. Fujimura has already arrived."

The Washington power breakfast was in full bloom in one of the city's most prestigious restaurants. Thick beige wall coverings and a high ceiling that opened to a more casual garden restaurant above muffled the sounds. The tables were spaced to permit confidential conversation. As Carlos led Taylor to the far side of the restaurant, she nodded to the secretary of the interior and a senator from Maine.

Taylor stopped in front of a Japanese man dressed in an expensive-looking dark business suit, white shirt, and tie. Taylor bowed, and he bowed back.

When they sat down, Fujimura, behind heavy black-framed glasses, studied Taylor. He remembered being struck by her good looks when he met her six years ago during the Kyoto conference on global warming, as well as by her intelligence and her genuine interest in the Japanese way of life. He was impressed that she had not only studied Japanese in college, but had kept up her proficiency with a private tutor since that time. She had grown into an elegant-looking woman, even at eight in the morning, and she had honed her legal skills, which was why he called on her for many of his clients' legal matters in the United States.

"I'm sorry I was late," Taylor said.

"I was early. I appreciate your adjusting your busy schedule to meet me on short notice."

Fujimura nodded to a waiter, who rushed over, took their breakfast order, and quickly departed. "I have a new matter for you," Fujimura said in English that was precise, though a little stiff. "M. H. Heavy Industries wants to buy East Texas Enterprises, a large national gas producer headquartered in Houston. Eight facilities are involved throughout the United States. I would like you to visit each of them within the next thirty days, give me a report on all potential liabilities, and develop a structure for the acquisition."

Taylor felt her stomach churning. She couldn't possibly do what Fujimura wanted in the next thirty days, not with the campaign going down to the wire. She selected her words carefully. "May I suggest a variation of your proposal?"

She allowed a flicker of annoyance in his eyes to pass before she continued. "I'll be in charge of the investigation. I'll make all of the decisions and recommendations, but my partner, Philip Harrison, with whom you've worked before, will organize and handle the visits. He'll develop a proposal for structuring the transaction."

Fujimura's face showed no emotion. "You're my lawyer," he said. "You understand what I want and need. That's why I came to Blank, Porter, and Harrison. There are lots of other lawyers out there." He raised a hand and waved it.

Taylor's knees were trembling under the table, and she sucked in her breath. *That's all I need right now is to lose Fujimura's business. I'll be asked to take early retirement*

*from the law firm. Real early. I've got to find a way to keep
it together for another month.*

Taylor forced a smile and pressed ahead. "As you know,
Philip is very experienced in this type of transaction. He'll
organize his regular team. They're fast and efficient. He'll
report directly to me."

Fujimura deliberately sipped his coffee, considering the
matter.

There was a long silence as Taylor prayed, *Let him go
along with this.*

Finally Fujimura said, "That'll be fine."

By the time they had eaten their continental breakfast, he
had finished telling her about the transaction. "A box with
all of the relevant documents about the acquisition and the
plants involved will be delivered to your office this morning," he said. "For much of the next month you can reach me
at the Hotel Bel Air in Los Angeles, where I have other business, although I expect to be flying back and forth between
Tokyo and Los Angeles a number of times."

"I'll give you periodic reports of our progress during the
month," she said encouragingly.

"Good. Now tell me about the Mississippi case."

Taylor relaxed. Here she was on stronger ground. "The
briefs are in. I'll argue the case December tenth in the state
supreme court."

"What do you think of our chances?"

"On the legal merits, I like our case, but I'll warn you,
Mississippi is provincial."

She didn't have to spell out what she meant. Fujimura
was used to discrimination against Japanese companies in
the American courts.

He began looking around to signal the waiter for the
check, and she could tell that they had completed his

agenda. Yet she had another subject to raise with him. Before doing so, she checked the tables on either side. At one of them four men were engaged in an animated business discussion. At the other was a man who appeared to be in his fifties, with a strikingly beautiful blonde who couldn't be more than twenty-five, Taylor guessed. They were holding hands under the table. Harrison frequently lectured her to be careful what she said in public places, but if she and Fujimura kept their voices down, no one else could hear a thing.

"I read Alex Glass's article in the *New York Times* this morning about Sato's visit to the shrine and Masaki's death at the rally," Taylor said. "Can you help me understand what's happening in Japan?"

He lowered his head and peered at her through those thick glasses. "Your question implies that the two are related, that someone from Sato's crowd was responsible for Masaki's death." He sounded defensive, which didn't surprise her. She was a foreigner asking him about a Japanese internal matter. Though he was sophisticated and spent considerable time in the United States and Europe on business, he still had that clannish allegiance to his island home.

Treading carefully, she said, "According to the article, the police cannot account for the cause of the fire."

Fujimura held out his hands. "It's still early in the investigation. Too early to draw any conclusions."

"Fair enough, but let me ask you this: If Senator Boyd is elected, do you think he will have to deal with Sato as the next Japanese prime minister?"

Deep furrows appeared on Fujimura's forehead. "I don't know," he said softly, trying to mask his concern. "Our economy has been bad for so long that people are becoming desperate. You're a student of history. You know that desperate people sometimes turn to people with radical solutions. A month ago I would have told you that Sato had no chance."

"And now?"

"As you Americans say, it's too close to call."

"We're in big trouble," President Webster said as he tossed the results of the latest *Wall Street Journal* poll on his desk in disgust. "Jesus, I can't believe we blew that big a lead."

Seated at his desk in the Oval Office, the president scanned the three men in front of him: Hugh McDermott, the attorney general and the president's campaign manager; Darren Boudreau, the president's political adviser; and Pug Thompson, in charge of special projects.

In contrast to the scholarly Boudreau, on leave from his job as a political science professor at Georgetown, with a neatly trimmed salt-and-pepper beard, Pug Thompson was a street fighter. That was how he had gotten his nickname, trying to escort a recalcitrant witness out of a congressional hearing room after the chairman ordered the guards to lock the doors. Thompson had decided to punch his way out. Both he and the witness escaped the room, but Thompson suffered a broken nose in the process. It had been poorly set, and it was now the first thing anyone noticed when they looked at him.

"It's the economy," McDermott said. "But there's no need to panic. The average of the six private polls we ran in the last week shows us down by only two percent, with a margin of error of one to three. Virtually a dead heat. Isn't that right, Darren?"

Unconvinced, Webster scowled. "What bothers me is the

trend. We lost ground last week in practically every part of the country. It definitely wasn't a good week for us."

"You've still got the advantage. You're the incumbent," McDermott replied calmly. "Let's stick to our game plan. All you have to do, Bill, is continue to act presidential. Just do your job. I promise you that next week the numbers will be different."

"You're betting I can turn it around in the debate Monday night?"

McDermott nodded. "I know it. I got a report from someone who attended the dinner last night in Chicago where Boyd spoke. The guy's losing it. He wasn't focused. Something's bothering him. When he gets in front of that national audience at the debate, he'll come off like Nixon in the first Kennedy debate. You mark my words."

Thompson shook his head in disbelief. These guys were delusional. "I feel like a minority of one, but I think something more radical is required."

"Like what?" Webster asked.

Thompson was ready. "Sticking to the issues and acting presidential isn't doing the trick. The economy's killing us, and we're losing ground fast. My proposal is that we move away from the issues, and we attack Boyd personally."

Furious, McDermott shot Thompson a dirty look, but he turned away. "How? For what?" McDermott asked, sounding skeptical and annoyed.

"We've got two possibilities," he continued. "One, we've got reason to believe that when Boyd's oldest son, Donny, was a student at the University of California, Santa Barbara, he was arrested on a marijuana possession charge after the cops raided a frat-house party. It was all kept quiet. The kid did public-service work, and the misdemeanor conviction was expunged. But we can find witnesses, pay them to come forward, and resurrect it. It would make Boyd look like a fraud with his big campaign promises about a war on drugs and a new crime bill."

"Great," McDermott said scornfully. "It would also give Boyd's camp every parent in America who's upset about what his child has done, which is almost everyone with kids. Whose side are you on?"

Pug looked at the president and Boudreau for support, but all he found was an expressionless silence.

"Number two," he continued, "we begin carefully and systematically leaking information to the press that Boyd, who holds himself up as a great family man, has been having an affair for the last ten years with his adviser, Taylor Ferrari."

McDermott raised his eyebrows. "Has he?"

Pug looked at Boudreau, who responded, "We don't know for sure. I told Pug that they're very close."

"Meaning you don't know at all."

"They spend so much time together," Pug fired back, "people would believe it."

McDermott felt the perspiration under his arms beginning to wet his shirt. Jesus, he did not want a public morality issue raised under any circumstances.

"That is one shitty idea," he said. "Forget it. If we don't have the facts, it'll boomerang. The press will figure out where the rumors came from."

Pug refused to back off. "We could hire a detective to see if the facts are there."

"NFW. No fucking way. Who's paying you? Boyd? Stuff like that will only lose votes if it comes out."

"Good God," Pug said in a voice dripping with sarcasm. "You're holier than the pope."

Wanting to shift away from an escalating verbal battle,

McDermott turned toward the president. "It's your call, Bill," he said. "Personally, I vote for sticking with the current game plan and tabling these ideas for now, but you're the boss."

The president rolled the issue around in his mind for a moment and wrinkled his nose. "I'm with Hugh on this. No dirty tricks. We'll win this fair and square, or we won't win."

McDermott wasn't surprised. Twenty years ago, when he was a powerful and savvy Chicago lawyer, well connected in state Republican politics, he took a young legislator, a diamond in the rough, from a small town in downstate Illinois out for a drink. Right from the start, McDermott knew that William Webster was a straight shooter, as well as having the charisma and political instincts to be governor.

"Can you stick around for a while, Hugh?" the president asked. "I've got a short call to make. Then the two of us need to talk."

"I'll be happy to. Just let me walk out with Darren and Pug for a minute. I'll be right back."

From the reception area outside the Oval Office, McDermott led Thompson into a small working room across the hall that was empty. The A.G.'s face was flushed with anger as he kicked the door shut. "Don't you try any crap like that again. I told you, run the ideas past me first."

"Okay, okay," Pug replied. "I've got the picture."

"And I'll tell you one other thing: I don't want you or anybody who works for you pulling off any of these schemes or any other stuff like that without approval from me. Is that clear?"

"I wouldn't consider it, boss," Pug said.

McDermott moved in close. He stuck out two fingers and shoved them hard against the middle button of Thompson's white shirt. "I have this campaign under control. I've told you before and I'll tell you again, if you follow orders and do things my way, Webster will get reelected and you'll get a good job in the next administration."

"I'm trying to give us a little insurance."

"We don't need it, asshole. You go off on your own, like the Lone Ranger, and you're out of the campaign on your ass. Also, I'll see to it that you never work in this town again. You can trust me on that."

Pug pulled back. "Okay. I got it. By the way, nice suntan you have, boss. Must have gone south for the weekend, eh?"

McDermott's face grew beet red. He slammed Thompson hard against the wall. "You'd better not be spying on me."

Though Pug could have knocked McDermott down with a single backhand swipe, he refused to fight back. He had done his damage verbally.

After pulling himself together, McDermott went back into the Oval Office. The president was still on the phone. "Tell him that I'll meet with the Russian ambassador at ten in the morning," Webster said. "I can't do it this evening." He replaced the phone in its cradle. "Jesus, Hugh, that was Perry in London. The Brits are anxious for me to meet with the Russian ambassador in Washington, the one whose name I can never pronounce, to get some info about Lernov, the new Russian president. But I doubt if he'll know anything. If he did, he wouldn't tell me anyhow."

"The Lernov thing's got everybody jumpy."

"What do you think I should do about it?"

"Not a damn thing until after the election. Except . . ."

"Except what?"

"Get some TV time one evening next week after the debate to make a speech assuring the American people that you're in control."

"The Democrats will scream that it's political."

"It is, but so what? Fuck 'em. You're the president. You get the advantages of the incumbent."

"Good advice. I'll do it. How about sitting in on my meeting with the Russian ambassador tomorrow?"

"Your distinguished secretary of state doesn't like it when I poach."

"Don't worry about Tom. I'll tell him I want you there. I feel more comfortable with your advice."

McDermott glanced at his gold Franck Muller. He knew that the president had a state dinner tonight. "There was something you wanted to talk to me about after the others left?"

"Oh, yeah," Webster said, remembering where they were before his phone call. "You want a drink?"

"Why not? It's about that time of the day."

Just off the Oval Office was a small pantry. McDermott poured scotch over ice in two glasses, added a splash of water, and handed one to Webster.

"To your new job," Webster said, raising his glass and taking a long sip of the drink.

McDermott was puzzled. "What new job?"

"You're going to get your wish. What do you want most in life?"

"The Supreme Court."

Webster clinked his glass with a smile. "Not just a seat. You'll be chief justice."

"You're kidding."

"Nope. Gerhard Hall invited himself over this morning for breakfast. He didn't want anybody to know why he was here."

"He's resigning?"

"Not yet." His face grew darker. "He was diagnosed with advanced lymphoma. It's unclear how much longer he has."

"When's he going to resign?" McDermott asked anxiously.

"March first unless he just can't function before then."

"That bastard!" McDermott cried out.

"Yeah, I know. He wants Boyd to make the appointment if he wins. Hall was up-front about that. He knows I'd pick you, and he's not one of your biggest admirers."

McDermott sipped his drink, finding it tasted bitter. "It's not just me," he said. "He thinks Boyd would appoint some candy-ass liberal. Somebody who's soft on abortion and thinks it's a good idea to keep the criminals on the streets so they can commit more crimes."

"Well, there's only one way to solve that problem. Isn't there?"

"Damn right. You get a second term."

The president finished his drink.

"You want another?" McDermott asked.

"I'd better not. It's tuxedo time. If it's Thursday, then it's the king of Sweden, and I've got to preside over the usual gathering of penguins and fancy ladies."

"In Washington they're called women."

"I know that. But where I come from, they're still ladies, and there's no press around now. Don't worry; I won't let that one slip."

They both laughed loudly. McDermott rose and started to leave.

"Listen, Hugh, there is one other thing." The president hesitated. "God, I hate asking you this."

"Don't worry. Fire away."

"Let's assume I win, and you get the nomination for chief

justice of the Supreme Court. Do you envision any trouble during the confirmation hearings?"

McDermott was blindsided by the question, but he kept his emotions under control. *Don't show a thing,* he told himself. *You're a good poker player. You know what it's like to keep raising when all you've got is a pair of deuces.*

"What do you mean, trouble?" McDermott asked.

"Well, you know what's happened with some Supreme Court nominees during the congressional hearings. I just don't want to cause any problems for you."

"Oh, those kinds of problems," McDermott replied, forcing a natural-sounding laugh from his mouth. "You don't have to worry about me. Personally, I've got nothing to worry about. And politically—"

The president interrupted. "Politically I don't see a problem. You've been close enough to the middle of the road as attorney general to satisfy a sizable number of Democrats in the Senate."

"Happily, I'm clean as a whistle."

Chapter 8

It all fits together, Cady decided, once again eating a turkey sandwich for lunch at his desk. The evidence against Senator Boyd was clear and convincing. He should convene a grand jury, issue Boyd a subpoena, and see what the senator did.

But he wasn't ready for that. What was bothering him was that the facts in the documents fit together too neatly. Who was it—he tried to remember, maybe Anatole France—who wrote that the best evidence was perjured evidence because it had no loose ends?

Taylor had said to him, "A man's running for president. You're about to wreck his life and hand Webster the White House for four more years."

Maybe she had a point. Doerr was conveniently staying out of the whole business. McDermott had added Pug Thompson to their campaign team, and that guy was capable of anything. McDermott was bad enough by himself.

No, Cady decided. He had to make sure the facts and documents were accurate before he did anything as drastic as convening a grand jury. There was only one way to do that: go to California and check on the facts.

He booked a flight to San Francisco for that evening and began mapping out his strategy for the next two days. By the time he returned to Washington Sunday night, he'd know whether he had a case against Senator Boyd.

Taylor picked up a glass of white wine from the bar and looked around. Two hundred Washington lawyers were milling around in the Mayflower Hotel ballroom, drinks in their hands. Men outnumbered women, but not by much. All had paid a thousand dollars to attend this Friday-afternoon cocktail reception, ostensibly to meet Senator Boyd, but in reality to toss their names into the huge pot from which a number of Washington lawyers would be selected for high-level government appointments should Boyd become president. These men and women, making several hundred thousand dollars a year or more, were salivating at the prospect of taking an 80 percent cut in pay to trade what they now saw as a boring but lucrative job for a great power trip. A few reporters were also working the crowd, accompanied by their camera crews, hoping to gain a useful quote from Boyd. Kendrick had kept the lid on the senator's change of plans for today.

While trying to decide how to break the news that the senator wasn't coming, Taylor felt a sudden tug on her arm. She turned to find Ben Owen, formerly a Washington lawyer, now the Democratic congressman from a suburban Maryland district, who was using this event to troll for dollars for his own reelection campaign.

Ben pulled Taylor into a deserted corner of the room. "Is there something big about to break that'll hurt Boyd?" he asked anxiously.

Dammit, she thought. *Information's starting to leak out about Cady's investigation.* She didn't dare let Ben know how upset she was about that idea. He would take away as much from what he saw on her face as from what she said.

Trying to appear nonchalant, Taylor said, "Nothing I've heard about. Who told you that?"

"One of my aides heard that the U.S. attorney's office here in town is looking into something from one of Boyd's campaigns."

Taylor was furious. That bastard Cady had to be the source of the leak. She sipped her wine, trying to stay calm. "I'll check it out. Sounds to me like Republican wishful thinking."

Some of the nervous strain left his face. "That's what I was hoping, but you never know."

"Our lead keeps growing."

"It's making me nervous. You guys aren't getting complacent, are you?"

Taylor forced a laugh. "Me, complacent? You've got to be kidding."

"You're doing well so far, but there's still a long way to go. I hope you don't blow it."

Taylor was searching for a way to escape. She didn't have to answer to the likes of Ben Owen. Through the corner of her eye she spotted plump Dan Logan, who had organized this affair. He gave her the sign to start.

Striding quickly up to the podium, Taylor tapped on the microphone. She waited until she had everyone's attention. "You may have noticed," she began, "that I'm not Senator Boyd."

"But you're a lot better-looking," a man called from the back of the room.

That prompted a retort from a woman: "Pig." The entire room erupted in laughter.

"Somebody also told me," Taylor continued, "when in doubt tell the truth. The truth is that he was afraid to enter a pool with so many sharks."

More laughter.

"Seriously, the schedule's been a killer. We've got the critical final debate coming up, and the senator needed some prep time up in St. Michaels, away from the crowds. But I'd like to describe for you some of the new and expanded federal programs Senator Boyd contemplates as part of his New Age for America."

"Will they result in more legal business for us?" someone shouted out.

"Doesn't everything?" Taylor responded.

She now had the audience in the palm of her hand, and she kept it that way for the next fifteen minutes with a light but informative talk. When she was finished, the crowd gave her a loud burst of applause. Dan Logan was smiling.

Still furious at Cady for what Ben had said, Taylor cut a beeline for the door and a waiting car outside.

"You son of a bitch," Taylor shouted at Cady on the phone, "you promised me confidentiality. One congressman already knows about your investigation." Her voice was shaking. "How could you do such a thing?"

Cady was taken aback. "You can't be serious."

"I wish I weren't. Ben Owen asked me if I knew about it."

Cady was wondering where the hell the leak came from. He hadn't involved any other lawyers in his office. Even his secretary didn't know about it. The only others he had told were Doerr, Hall, and Moore. Hall and Moore, never. Doerr, conceivably for that judicial appointment. Or whoever left the envelope on his desk Tuesday night. That person could have been the source of the leak.

"You're right to be angry," he said. "But you know me, Taylor. I don't operate that way. My honesty and integrity are critical to my job. I promise you that the leak didn't come from me. I've limited knowledge of the investigation so much that I think the chances of it coming from the government side are almost nil."

He was a straight shooter, she remembered. He wouldn't do something like that. "Then who leaked it?"

"I intend to find out. I'm plenty pissed myself."

Cady meant precisely what he said. If he had been fed phony information to persuade him to file a trumped-up charge, then the point of the leak might be to turn up the heat and get him to move faster. As he thought more about it, he realized the mysterious visitor could have been McDermott, with or without Doerr. He could easily have gotten access to Cady's office to drop off that package. His trip to California was vital.

"Taylor, I'm trying to get to the bottom of this. Just give me a chance, okay? I'm going to be finding out things this weekend."

"The way this snowball is rolling," she said grimly, "by Monday it may be too late."

Chapter 9

Alex Glass was at a dead end. After spending a full day in his office, studying everything he had about Sato for a clue to identify the American working with him, Alex decided to give up. He needed to unwind, and he knew whom to unwind with.

Three weeks ago he had broken up with Yaki for the second time. They were electric in bed together, but she was worried that being involved with a Westerner would kill her chances for advancement at the corporate software firm where she worked. "You have to understand," she had told him. "It's tough enough here being a woman. A serious relationship with a *gaijin* would finish me. So I can't go out with you anymore."

He picked up the phone and dialed her. "Yaki, my love. How about one more evening for old times' sake?"

She hesitated. "You know I can't be seen with you anymore. We talked about all of that."

"Suppose I pick up sushi at that place you love near the Meiji, and I'll park my bike three blocks away. Nobody will ever know. What do you think?" Before she could reply, he added, "I know you're getting wet just thinking about it. Come on."

A softer note entered her voice. "Okay, but just this once."

"Great. I'm on my way."

Tearing through the streets on his Kawasaki in the chilly late-afternoon air, Alex thought about how great his life was in Tokyo. He was someone now—not like he had been in Seattle. His articles were being carefully read. He could call top people in the Japanese government and get an immediate meeting. There had even been a grudging compliment from Dad in Seattle after the series ran in the *Times*.

Yeah, dreary Seattle, the most overrated city in America. But maybe everybody feels that way about their hometown.

The traffic was insane, but it didn't stop Alex. He wove around cars, in and out of lanes. This was why he had decided to get the bike in the first place. It was the only way to get around in Tokyo. Well, there was the subway, but that was too crowded.

He loved this Kawasaki, tuned and cleaned it like it was his baby. He also loved the idea that it made him seem dashing. The motorcycle definitely helped lure Japanese women into his bed. They loved riding with him, clutching his body for dear life while they pressed their breasts against his back. And there had been lots of them. But none better than Yaki.

She was smart and talented, besides being great in bed. A computer hacker par excellence. He had asked her to help him get facts for stories a couple of times. Once she broke into the computer system of Honda Motors to confirm a rumor he had heard that they'd decided to close one of their U.S. plants. Another time Yaki broke into the computer system of JAL and put them on a plane with paid-up seats in first class to Phuket for the weekend.

The red light he'd stopped for changed to green, and he raced away. Then it hit him: If she could do that, she could probably break into the computer systems of all the airlines and check manifests for flights to and from Tokyo. That could be the break he was looking for. If Sato had recruited an American, he probably would not have met him in Japan. Nor would he have gone to the United States. He would have had the meeting in another place, where they were less likely to be spotted together. Probably Europe. It was a long shot, but what the hell. Right now he didn't have anything else to try.

The fax from R.L. in Washington told Sato not to worry. *Everything is proceeding on schedule.*

But Sato was worried, and he intended to give the American some help.

He hit the intercom button on the phone in his office. "Send Terasawa in as soon as he gets here."

"Yes, Mr. Sato," came the demure reply from one of the two bookends in his outer office.

He walked over to the window and looked out. The sun was setting in the western sky over Tokyo. Though Sato was facing east in his corner office, he could see a clear reflection on the window of the adjacent building of the gorgeous red globe, the symbol of Japan's empire, the empire that would be rising again once he was heading the government.

It had been so many years ago, he thought. He had been only seven at the time, but he could still remember his father coming home from the war in Manchuria, a mere shell of the powerful man who had left, beaten down and submissive, ashamed of his infantryman's uniform in the Kwantung army, protesting that neither he nor anyone he knew had committed any atrocities.

Having grown up in a weak Japan and watched the country's once high-flying economy unravel to its current appalling state, Sato was persuaded that the nineteenth-century

Japanese philosophers had it right when they wrote, *Strong army, strong nation; weak army, weak nation.*

At the knock on the door, Sato wheeled around to see Terasawa walking in with bold steps. Terasawa was perfect for what he had in mind.

"I want you to go to the United States," Sato said.

"When do we leave?"

"There is no 'we'. This time you're going alone. You've been there three times before with me. You can speak the language."

"It's not a problem," Terasawa said obediently.

"Good. You'll be following orders from a man in Washington, an American whom you will know as R.L. I'll call and tell him you're coming. He'll decide where to meet you. Don't take any weapons. R.L. will supply what you need."

Terasawa nodded.

"I want you to stay in touch with me. Let me know everything that's happening. I'll tell you when to return."

Looking at the eager face in front of him, Sato was confident he had made the right decision in sending Terasawa. The man knew how to operate without being caught. One way or another, he would stop Senator Boyd from becoming president.

Alex lay in bed in Yaki's apartment, watching the rise and fall of her breasts as she slept with a contented smile. The woman was unbelievable. No one made love like she did, not even Taylor. She was a gymnast. He never dreamed anyone could hold a position like that, on her back on the bed with her buttocks and legs high in the air, while he stood on the floor facing her and sliding in and out of her. Her scent was in the air. Her taste was in his mouth. He had asked her, "Don't you know anything about biology? I'm a man. I can't possibly come again." She had laughed as she went down on him. Jesus, three times in an hour. There was nobody in Seattle who could do that to him.

When he had arrived, he thought they would eat first. He was wrong. She was wearing a short, sheer white night-gown. If he had any doubt about her intentions, she settled it when she took the package of sushi from him and placed it in the refrigerator.

Alex stroked her thick hair, kissed her on the side of the neck, and poked her in the ribs. "Honey, I hate to wake you," he said softly. "But I'm starving."

She purred. "Whatever you want. After what you did to me, I'm your slave."

He waited until they had finished eating to spring his request on her. "I need your great expertise on the computer."

She put down her cup of green tea. "Anything for Alex."

"Remember you once tapped into the computer system of JAL?"

She smiled. "Sure, it's a piece of cake." She liked using American idioms. "You want me to make a reservation for you and show it as a paid ticket, like we did when we went to Phuket?"

"No. I want to know about any trips that Yahiro Sato has taken on JAL or ANA."

He held his breath, hoping that she wasn't troubled by his request. His concern was unwarranted.

"What period of time?" she asked in a matter-of-fact voice.

Alex was trying to recall the exact date of the Democratic convention in Los Angeles. It was around the tenth of August. "Let's say from August first to the present."

Yaki sat down at the computer and began punching keys. With Alex standing behind her and watching in admiration, it took her only eleven minutes to come up with the answer. "On August twenty-eighth he flew from Tokyo to Buenos Aires, Argentina, on ANA. He stayed there one night, the night of the twenty-eighth, and returned to Tokyo."

Alex was elated. The information she had just gotten was consistent with his theory that Sato had flown somewhere— he had thought Europe—to meet with an American and enlist his help in the conspiracy involving Senator Boyd. Buenos Aires was even better. Far less chance of being accidentally recognized. Alex kissed Yaki on the lips. "Thank you so much."

"What else can I do for you?"

Alex leafed through his AmEx airline travel guide. American Airlines and United had the most flights from the United States to Buenos Aires. If he had a list of Americans arriving at the same time in Buenos Aires, it was conceivable that he could pick out the likely choice for the Sato meeting.

"Can you get me passenger manifests on AA and UAL flights into Buenos Aires on the twenty-seventh and twenty-eighth of August?"

She shook her head. "Sorry, I can't get into the U.S. carriers. Since the terrorist attacks on the World Trade Center, they've changed their systems."

He sighed in disappointment. *Think,* he told himself. *There has to be another way to get more information.* What about hotels? Sato always stayed first-class. That meant the Alvear Palace in Buenos Aires or the Hyatt. He had to find out which one. He wrote out a script for Yaki and handed it to her. Then he listened on another phone as she spoke to the hotel reservations clerk at the Alvear in English with a Japanese accent.

"I'm calling from the office of Yahiro Sato in Tokyo. Mr. Sato wants to make a reservation for December tenth."

"What type of accommodation would he like?"

"Please check the computer on his last stay, which I think was August twenty-eighth. We'll take the same thing."

Alex held his breath while the reservation clerk checked. She returned in a bubbly voice, "Mr. Sato had the presidential suite on the night of August twenty-eighth at a rate of one thousand five hundred U.S. dollars."

"Yes. That will be fine," Yaki said. "Use the credit card on file to secure the reservation."

"Thank you. We have everything. The reservation number is two-three-six-nine-one."

"There's one other thing," Yaki said, reading from the script Alex had given her. "In August Mr. Sato also made reservations for someone else. We'd like to make one for that person as well."

"Do you have a name?"

Yaki was ad-libbing now. She sounded flustered. "Mr. Sato's my boss. He gave me the name, and I lost it. Please help me."

The clerk sympathized. "One minute please."

Alex was pacing around the room nervously. *C'mon,* he thought. *Come up with a name.*

"I'm very sorry," the clerk said, "but the other individual must have made his own reservation. It's not part of Sato's record."

Alex wasn't too disappointed. He had learned a lot tonight. His hunch had been confirmed. Sato had recruited a powerful American to work with him, someone who had met him in Buenos Aires on August 28. Once he had that name, Alex would be ready to go into print with his article on the conspiracy being engineered by Sato to make certain Senator Boyd never became president.

But how could he get the name? He didn't know, but it was all he thought about as Yaki led him back to her bed. He was still thinking about it when she was straddling him, moving up and down and moaning with pleasure.

And he was thinking about it when he left her apartment. As he roared through a red light on the now deserted streets of Tokyo, a daring idea was taking hold in his mind. He would arrange a dinner with Toshio Ozawa in the next couple of days. He remembered their last meeting during his research for the series. Over a *kaiseki* dinner, the sake had loosened Ozawa's tongue. He would tell the commandant of the civil defense forces that he was doing an article on Japan's earthquake preparedness. As the evening wore on, Alex would get information about Sato's manipulation of the American election. Chances were, Ozawa would have plenty of information, even the name of the American whom Sato had met with in Buenos Aires.

It was a great idea, but Alex would have to be careful, because the man was dangerous. Alex wasn't deterred. That was the secret of good journalism: You took risks and you ran up every alley. You never knew where you were going to find the story that guaranteed you the Pulitzer. He was almost there. The prospect of all that power was intoxicating.

Chapter 10

Taylor stood alone on a dock jutting into the Chesapeake Bay, watching the senator pilot the *Sally II,* a 125-foot dual-engine Chris-Craft, back in to shore. The conversation she planned to have with him had taken on a special urgency at seven this morning, when Coop had dropped by her Watergate apartment with a bag of bagels and muffins, along with a couple of cappuccinos. "Room service," he had called out, but everything tasted dry once he told her that he had heard from Ed Dawson. Cady had flown to San Francisco and was driving north toward Napa when Dawson lost him. Napa meant he was looking for something specific.

The first one off the boat was Wes Young, a burly Secret Service agent who had played fullback at Penn State. His hazel eyes squinted in the bright noon sun as he scanned the landscape. Another agent followed Young. Then came a tall, handsome man with thick black hair, wild and out of control, who was dressed in old faded jeans and a bulky blue sweater. His face had a ruddy glow from the sun. He was about forty, Taylor guessed. That had to be Emilio Cipriani. Behind the painter came the senator, walking with grim determination and resolve.

Ignoring Taylor, Sally bounded from the house and went

to the edge of the dock, where Boyd was showing Emilio how to tie up the boat.

"How about lunch?" Sally asked. "They delivered the most incredible oysters and crabs this morning."

"Sounds wonderful," Emilio said in English tinged with a heavy Italian accent.

Boyd looked around anxiously until he spotted Taylor, who moved back onto the grass that ran up to the large white house. "You two go ahead and eat," he said to Sally and Emilio. "Taylor and I have to talk. We'll join you up at the house later."

Taylor expected an outburst from Sally. Then she saw her fawning over Emilio and decided that she was happy to be alone with the painter. That way she would hustle him better about her art gallery.

Boyd grabbed two sweatshirts from the deck of the boat, tied one around his shoulders, and tossed the other one to Taylor. "Come on," he said, "let's take a walk."

The property, which the senator was renting for a year from a wealthy friend who spent most of the time in France, was an estate on ten acres of waterfront on the bay. The six-bedroom house and smaller guesthouse were well concealed from the neighbors. Except when Boyd visited, which had been infrequently, the only visitors were a lawn and care-taker crew that came twice a week.

Young and the other agent were following about ten yards behind. "You guys can stay back here," Boyd said to Young. "We're just walking along the water. You'll be able to see us clearly."

For the first minute they walked in silence. Then the sen-ator said, "Any more information on what you told me about the investigation by this guy Cady?"

"I learned that Cady's out in Napa for the weekend. People are beginning to talk."

The senator paused and kicked a stone viciously. It bounced and rolled to the edge of the water.

"On the substance," she added, "about all I know is that Cady's focusing on your first congressional election."

"I didn't do a damn thing wrong. I financed my campaign with the sale of Mill Valley."

"Why don't you tell me all of the facts relating to your sale of Mill Valley ten years ago?"

"That's a good idea." Boyd shoved his hands into his pockets. "Look here, my congressional campaign got off to a good start. Then Broder began cashing in the chips that he had collected from being an incumbent so long. You know how that goes."

He waited for her to nod before continuing. "By August I could see that it was going to come down to money. Broder had been building a war chest for the last two years, and my fund-raising effort was scraping the bottom of the barrel. I needed a pot of new money. The campaign laws placed severe limits on how much I could get from an outside source, but I could pump in as much of my own money as I had. So I started talking to some local bankers to see if I could get a mortgage on Mill Valley. The banks hated the idea because if I won, I'd be in Washington. Without me running the winery, they saw it going down the tubes. And I couldn't blame them. The wine business is always speculative. It would be a risky proposition. So I finally decided to bite the bullet and to sell the land and the business."

"How'd you put it up for sale?"

"The usual way. I gave it to a local agent."

"Who?"

"A man named Harvey Gladstone."

"Is he still around?"

Boyd shrugged. "Never heard from or seen him since."

Taylor made a mental note to call Mark Jackson, a P.I. she regularly used at the law firm, and ask him to locate Gladstone. "Then what happened?"

"Two weeks later Gladstone brought me in a contract for ten million."

She let out an involuntary whistle. "That sounds like an awful lot of money for Mill Valley."

"You have to remember that at that point in time, ten years ago, premium wineries in Napa looked like a growth business. American consumption was up, and we were ready to challenge the French on quality. Since then, of course, the business has gone to hell. I got lucky. I sold at the top of the market."

She nodded. "I guess that's right."

"Also, Gladstone did a bang-up job for me. Somehow he found a foreign buyer with lots of cash."

"Who bought Mill Valley?"

"A French company out of Lyon by the name of Maison Antibes. They're in the wine business in Burgundy. They were anxious to get a foothold in Napa Valley."

"A cash transaction?"

"All cash."

"What about Gladstone's commission?"

"I don't remember exactly. Is that important?"

"At this point, I'm not sure what's important."

"Look here, six percent is the standard commission."

"So you paid him six hundred thousand dollars?"

Boyd nodded. "Yeah, that sounds right."

"Did you make any other payments to Gladstone at the time?"

He looked at her, annoyed. "No. Why would I? He got his commission. That's all."

Taylor thought he had sounded tentative in his answer. In fairness, though, the events had happened years ago. "Who interacted with the French company?"

"Jesus, what difference does it make?" He regarded her with a stern eye. "This sounds like a cross-examination. You're making me feel like a hostile witness."

A chilly wind began blowing off the bay. Boyd untied his sweatshirt and put it on.

"Sorry if I sound aggressive in my questioning, but I'll need to know everything if we're going to have a chance. Cady is one tough adversary."

He smiled. "Don't worry about it. That's what I get for retaining the best lawyer in Washington. What was the question?"

"Who interacted with the French company?"

"Oh, yeah, Gladstone primarily. I spent several hours showing one of their people around the place. That was all I had to do with the negotiations."

"Who was it?"

"I don't understand."

"The person you met with?"

He held his hands out. "I don't remember exactly. He had a French name that sounded like Chapel, something like that."

"Did you have any other dealings with the purchaser?"

"Not until the closing."

"At either of those times, or at any other time, did any of the French people say anything at all to you about politics, Congress, or how you would vote if you were elected?"

"Negative. Never. Not one word."

His story made sense. The French wouldn't meddle in

American politics this way. Who had put Cady on to this bogus case? she wondered.

"Based on what you just told me, Cady doesn't have squat. What we don't know is whether someone fed him forged documents, and if they did, whether he'll be able to figure it out."

The senator blinked at the possibility of forged documents. "What will you do with all of this?"

"I'd like to get one of my partners in the law firm involved. Somebody who deals with white-collar criminal matters full-time, like Ken—"

Boyd cut her off in midsentence. "Nope. No way. It's got to be you alone. I know you. I've got confidence in you, and there's less chance of a leak."

"But—"

"No buts on this."

She sighed in resignation. "Okay. I'll go to see Cady Monday. Try to get him to stop his investigation."

"Do you think Cady will drop it?"

"It's hard to know. Would you be willing to put your statement about the Mill Valley transaction under oath, if I thought that was helpful after I meet with him?"

"Absolutely. I've done nothing wrong. I've got nothing to hide."

The certainty with which he said it reassured her. Still, with everything at stake, she said, "Please go through all of the facts in your mind one more time. Our whole strategy depends on your version of the facts, that you did nothing wrong when you sold Mill Valley. If Cady can come up with evidence to show that there's an error in our story, he'll seize on that and push ahead. I know how prosecutors operate."

"I've had a lot of time to think about what happened. The facts I just told you are absolutely correct."

Taylor believed him. "Okay, I'll deal with Cady on Monday. For the next twenty-four hours we have to forget about Cady and do debate preparation. Otherwise Webster will crush you Monday night, and Cady's investigation will be moot. You'll be out of the race for all practical purposes, which," she added darkly, "is the objective of whoever induced Cady to launch his investigation."

Chapter 11

Clutching a black leather briefcase, Cady opened the glass
door that said, *Napa County Tax Records.* A polite young
woman with short brown hair, wearing a freshly laundered
white blouse and blue skirt, got up from behind her desk and
walked out to the counter to greet Cady. She had the face of
an innocent farm girl. The name tag on her blouse said,
Karen.

He didn't see anyone else in the office. "Pretty quiet, isn't
it?" he said.

"We don't get many visitors on a Saturday. What can I do
for you?"

Cady showed her his DOJ identification, which neither
impressed nor intimidated her. "Like I said, what can I do
for you?"

"About ten years ago . . ." Cady began; then he checked
the papers in his briefcase and gave her the precise date.
"Charles Boyd sold Mill Valley Corporation to a company
by the name of Maison Antibes. I want to know the purchase
price of what was sold and whether it included the business
and the land." He expected her to have some reaction to his
mention of Charles Boyd. Either she didn't relate the Democratic presidential candidate to his inquiry, or she didn't

care, or maybe she didn't even know who was running. He thought it was odd.

"Give me a couple of minutes," she said.

With quiet efficiency she moved back to her desk and a computer. He watched her punching keys. "Do you want a printout?" she asked him.

"Please."

A few minutes later she handed him a single-page document, showing that Maison Antibes had paid Boyd a total of fifty million dollars for the stock of the Mill Valley Corporation, which included the winery and the land. That was consistent with the statement in the materials that had been mysteriously dumped on his desk.

If everything else panned out, Cady decided, he would have a case to take to the grand jury. He began thinking about evidence. It wasn't necessary to have Karen fly to Washington. He could have her authenticate the printout, but original documents would be better.

"Where do you keep the back-up for these records?" Cady asked.

Karen looked puzzled. "This is all we have."

"But when you put the information in the computer, didn't you store the original documents somewhere?"

"Oh, that," she said, nodding. "We only keep back-up for the past five years. For earlier than that, the original documents are discarded. The computer is the only record."

This also sounded odd. "Really?"

"Yeah, that's how we do it out here."

Cady was surprised, but during the year he had spent practicing law in San Francisco, he had learned that anything was possible with the state government in California.

He asked Karen to write on the printout that it was a

record of the state of California, then sign and date the document. He tucked it into his briefcase and left the office.

From Napa, Cady drove north on Route 29, traversing the valley floor with vineyards on both sides, passing the most prestigious producers in the American wine industry: Mondavi, Grgich Hills, and Beaulieu, among others, all properties of enormous financial value. But not fifty million for something the size of Mill Valley, he thought. That winery was a couple of miles to the east along the Silverado Trail.

Continuing north, Cady took a left in Calistoga and drove up the winding road that led over the western ridge of the valley. The view of the lush fields far below was incredible, but Cady tried not to look at it while driving, because the road dropped off sharply. What kept running through Cady's mind was: *I hope to hell Harvey Gladstone never drives this at night when he's had too much to drink.*

Toward the top of the peak sat a wooden rambler that Cady guessed was fifty years old. The outside looked shabby, with faded yellow paint that was peeling in scores of places. In contrast, the front yard was carefully maintained, with clusters of flowers and a vegetable garden on one side.

Cady walked along the cracked cement path that led to the front porch. After he rang the bell and waited for several minutes without an answer, he peeked in the front window, through an opening in the curtains. A woman was talking on the phone. Cady rang the bell again, while watching her through the window.

This time she hung up, walked over to the door, and opened it a crack. She was a gray-haired woman with a leathery, wrinkled face. She had been crying, and was wiping her wet, bloodshot eyes with a tissue.

"I'm looking for Harvey Gladstone," Cady said.

"He's not here," she said, immediately frightened.

"Do you know when he'll be back?"

"He's not in business anymore. You'll have to find somebody else."

She started to close the door, but Cady put his foot in the doorway.

"Are you Mrs. Gladstone?"

She nodded and wiped away more tears.

"My name's C. J. Cady. I'm from the Department of Justice in Washington. I'd like to talk to you." He took his government ID from his pocket and held it up to the crack in the door.

She didn't move to let him inside.

"Please, Mrs. Gladstone. It's important government business."

With great reluctance she opened the door. "But only for a few minutes."

Inside the house, Cady felt as if he were in a time warp. All of the furniture was from the fifties.

She wiped her eyes one more time, blew her nose, and tossed the tissue in a wastebasket. "Look here, Mr. Cady. I don't mean to be rude. This isn't a good time for me. I've got a grandson down in Los Angeles who's real sick."

"I'm awfully sorry."

"Well, there's nothing you can do about that, unless you know where he can get a new heart for a transplant."

She started to sob again. This time she wiped her face with the sleeve of her faded plaid dress. "I'm okay now. You want some cider? It's homemade."

"Yes, thank you."

She fetched him a glass from the kitchen and handed it to him. "I don't know what you want to see Harvey about, but my husband's had two heart attacks. He's not supposed to get upset. Maybe I can help you? That way you won't have to bother him."

Cady looked at her sympathetically. "I appreciate the offer, but I'm afraid that won't work. If you tell me where he is, I promise to talk to him without getting him upset."

"What did he do wrong?"

"Him? Nothing. I want to talk to him about something that somebody else did. I may need him as a witness. So where is he?"

"Fishing."

"When will he be home?"

She shrugged her shoulders. "I don't know. Maybe tomorrow. Maybe next Sunday."

He couldn't tell if she was being deliberately vague or not. "He must have a phone there, or a cell phone. Why don't you give me that number, and I'll call him?"

She shook her head. "He's in the mountains. No phones."

"Then tell me where he's fishing. I'll go find him."

She looked down at the floor. "Sorry, I don't know. When he goes off fishing, he stays in the cabin one of his buddies has up there. Harvey has never told me where, and I don't ask. When a man gets to be his age, he's allowed to enjoy himself, and fishing is what Harvey likes to do. Me, I like gardening and making cider. He doesn't bother me when I do those things. That's how we've had such a good marriage all these years. We give each other space. Are you married, Mr. Cady?"

"Actually, I'm divorced."

"Well, I'm sorry to hear that."

She sounded genuine, and she was obviously upset about her grandchild. Cady, the tough prosecutor, couldn't bring himself to lower the boom on her, though she was giving him the runaround. "It's quite important that I talk to Harvey."

"What do you want to talk to him about?"

Cady would have liked to say it was none of her business, but he didn't want to sound like a tough Easterner. Besides, she might have some information herself. "The sale of Mill Valley about ten years ago. The Charles Boyd property."

"I don't know anything about that," she said.

From the terrified look on her face, Cady realized she was protecting her husband from something more than being upset. He decided to follow the nice-guy routine. "Listen, Harvey hasn't done anything wrong. I'm trying to help him because some other people who aren't as nice want to get him into trouble. But I can't help him unless I can talk to him. Are you following me?"

She nodded.

"Now, I know he's hiding out somewhere. If it's a buddy's cabin in the mountains, then that buddy can drive up and bring Harvey back. I don't care about any of that. But please get Harvey here in this house at nine A.M. on Monday, when an FBI agent will come to question him. Can you do that?"

She desperately wanted to be helpful to this young man. He was decent and kind. But there was no way she could do that.

"I'll do what I can," she replied in a noncommittal way.

"Remember—nine on Monday," Cady said as he walked to the door.

If this approach didn't work, he would have to use FBI agents in the area to find Harvey Gladstone one way or another. Meantime, he had to hustle if he was going to make it to Santa Rosa in time to get the last plane to Los Angeles.

*   *   *

A hundred miles away, north of Mendocino, Harvey Gladstone stood knee-deep in a cold mountain stream in his fishing boots with his line extended in the water. He should have had his eye focused on that line, looking for a nibble, but he couldn't concentrate on fishing. He hadn't come up to this desolate spot in northern California for the fishing, which was so extraordinary that he had already caught six trout today, stashed in a cooler on the bank. No, he had come to escape from *him,* the tough-sounding man who had called from what Gladstone, with caller ID, later learned was a Washington, D.C., pay phone. The man had tried to persuade Gladstone to call a prosecutor by the name of C. J. Cady and explain that the sale price for Mill Valley had been fifty million and that he had received a commission of six hundred thousand, which was six percent of ten million, and another hundred thousand for keeping his mouth shut. On the phone, the man's promise to arrange a new heart for Carl had been enough to convince Gladstone to agree to his request. Instinct told him to wait, though, until Carl received the new heart before making the call to Cady. Well, that was three days ago. The man hadn't arranged a new heart for Carl, but he had repeatedly called with threats.

After the third one, Gladstone decided to take off. He didn't know whose battle this was, but he didn't want to get involved. Besides, the man frightened him. He was convinced that no good would come of it. He had urged his wife, Louise, to leave and fly to Los Angeles, but she couldn't stand the idea of what seemed like a hopeless death vigil for Carl. He didn't think the man would bother her. She didn't know anything about the sale of Mill Valley.

Gladstone's eyes scanned the hills that ran up from both sides of the stream. Nothing was moving in the heavy green foliage. Suddenly he heard twigs snap on the hill to the west.

Startled, he dropped his fishing rod and looked that way. It was only a deer. He grabbed the rod from the water and breathed a large sigh of relief. *You're being stupid,* he told himself. *Nobody could possibly find you here unless Louise told them, which she would never do.*

He planned to stay for a few days, maybe a week or longer, until he was satisfied from the radio he listened to that it was all over, whatever was going on with Senator Boyd. If need be, he'd stay until after the election.

You're safe, he told himself. *Forget about it. Relax and fish.*

High on the hill to the west of the stream, Terasawa crouched in a cluster of berry bushes, ten yards above the point at which the frightened deer had spotted him and burst through the brush. As he watched Gladstone through powerful binoculars, he doubted that the fisherman had any idea he was here. When the deer had moved, Gladstone's face had tensed. Now he was back to fishing.

He was a sneaky bastard, trying to run away like this. All it had taken was a mild threat on the life of the sick grandson for the man's wife to cough up her husband's location. She had said that she couldn't warn him that Terasawa was coming because he didn't have a phone in the cabin and his cell phone didn't work so deep in the mountains. She must have been telling the truth. Otherwise Gladstone would have been long gone.

Wanting to maximize the element of surprise, Terasawa kept low, crouching down among the trees and bushes, treading softly in his waterproof hiking boots, clutching a sharp knife. He was wearing a green camouflage uniform, which he had purchased at a military surplus store, a uniform left over from the Vietnam War, when American soldiers had hidden in the highland jungles, watching a foe the way he was doing now. Terasawa didn't want to think of himself in those terms. Rather, as a Japanese soldier in the hills of Okinawa, Japanese territory, resisting the American invaders, who had arrived in the water below.

Ten yards above the stream, Terasawa stamped his feet, gave a bloodcurdling scream, "Ai!," and hurtled himself down the hill.

Gladstone whirled around. "What the hell . . . ?" Then he saw the upraised knife and the man with the scar on his cheek. Gladstone nearly jumped out of his boots. Frozen to the spot, he watched with horror as Terasawa stopped next to the cooler, grabbed one of the fish, and gutted it with a single stroke. Gladstone dropped his rod and took off, trudging awkwardly downstream in his high boots.

Terasawa tossed the fish and knife on the ground and raced into the water, chasing him.

In a few seconds Gladstone heard splashing on his heels. Trying to escape was futile. He decided to stop and fight. He wheeled around to confront the man. Before Gladstone could raise his arms, Terasawa grabbed him around the waist and picked him up. He held Gladstone over his head, the way he held barbells that weighed far more than the fisherman. Terasawa spun Gladstone around several times, then tossed him carelessly into the water.

Gladstone's whole body went under. When his head came up, he was choking and spitting ice-cold water. Terasawa grabbed Gladstone's head and held it under. When he finally let him up, Gladstone was gagging, and his eyes were bulging. Terasawa pushed him back under again. Then repeated the process for a third time. As he pulled him up at last, Gladstone's face was blue.

"N-no more," he mumbled in a barely audible voice.

"Then you listen up, you old fool, and you listen carefully."

He nodded.

"You do what you promised the man who called you. Do you understand?"

He nodded again.

Terasawa slapped him hard on the back. Water gurgled out of his mouth. "Say yes," he shouted.

"Yes . . . yes."

"And if you don't, I'll take that knife and gut you, your wife, and your grandson, just as I did that fish."

"It's showtime," Cady said to Bruce Gorman, the head of the FBI's office in Los Angeles. The two of them were having breakfast at an all-night coffee shop on Sunset Boulevard on the strip. The only other patrons at seven on this Sunday morning were three working girls who looked like they'd had a tough night, and their pimp.

Gorman finished a piece of toast and said, "I'm ready. Call."

Cady whipped out his cell phone, then reached into his wallet and extracted the piece of paper with Abdul Azziz's telephone number. The phone rang five times before a woman's sleepy voice answered.

"I want to talk to Abdul Azziz," Cady said.

"Mr. Azziz, he sleeping."

"Then wake him up."

"Maybe you call later."

"Maybe you wake him now." That brought silence at the other end. Cady pressed on. "You can tell him that it's the police and the FBI. Now go wake him."

"I go wake him."

"Fast."

He had to wait awhile until he heard, "This is Abdul Azziz. Who's calling?"

The voice wasn't nervous and trembling. It had a defiant edge.

"My name's C. J. Cady. I'm from the Department of Justice in Washington. Right now I'm in Los Angeles."

"And you can't call during normal hours? You have to wake people up early Sunday morning?"

"I'm being charitable, Mr. Azziz. If you'll look out your front window, you'll see two black cars on Sunset. Each one has four FBI agents. All I have to do is to give the order, and they'll arrest you."

There was a pause while, Cady guessed, Azziz looked out the window. The cars were in place. Cady had been in telephone contact with them.

"You're a very generous man," Azziz said sarcastically. "But I didn't violate any law."

"We could let the judge decide that."

"What do you want from me?"

"I want to talk to you."

"About what?"

"Mill Valley Winery and your purchase of it ten years ago."

"I don't know what you're talking about."

"You're not an American citizen. An alien can't own a wine business, and that's not all that was illegal about your purchase."

"I didn't purchase anything."

"Good. You can tell that to the judge in Houston who sentenced you for the SEC violation. For a second offense you're certain to go to jail. Prisons in Texas are wonderful places. You'll enjoy yourself, and some of the other prisoners will enjoy you, too."

This time Azziz didn't have a sarcastic comeback. Intimidation usually worked sooner or later, Cady had found over the years.

"I want to talk to my lawyer first."

"I'll give you two hours. I'll be there at nine-fifteen. And don't plan on leaving the house. They have it surrounded, and they will arrest you."

Cady hung up and winked at Gorman. Round one had worked according to plan.

Precisely at nine-fifteen, Gorman dropped Cady in front of Azziz's house. He was alone when he climbed the stone stairs and passed the statue of a woman with her privates painted pea green, just as Paul Moore had remembered. He had a beeper in his jacket pocket to call for help if someone tried to strong-arm him.

A frightened young Latino woman in a black maid's uniform opened the door. He guessed she had answered the phone this morning. She didn't say a word. Instead she pointed to the vast living room of the mansion. A dapper, distinguished gray-haired man in a blue polo shirt, navy slacks, and a gold chain around his neck was standing in front of the window. Hearing Cady approach, he wheeled around. "What kind of shit is this?"

"You must be Joe Hughes, Azziz's lawyer. I'm C. J. Cady, assistant U.S. attorney in Washington."

"You ever heard of the Bill of Rights, Cady?"

"Rest it, Hughes; your client's scum. You got him off easy once. You'll never be able to pull it off again."

"You mind telling me what this is all about?"

"He's an alien who bought a winery. That's illegal."

"He never bought a winery."

"Maison Antibes was a dummy corporation to hide his

ownership. If the corporate people in your firm did the legal work, they could be in trouble as well."

The man wasn't going to back off an inch. "You got my attention, Cady, but I also know you're not into alcohol law enforcement. Now, tell me what this is really about."

Cady decided to go on the offensive, hit them hard first. "Your client paid fifty million dollars for a business worth ten million."

"So he made a bad deal for himself. I didn't realize that had become a federal crime."

Bingo, Cady thought. Hughes didn't take issue with the fifty-million-dollar figure. That made him believe the information in the file dropped in his office was right, that Boyd had received fifty million. Now all he had to do was nail it down with credible evidence. Perhaps he wasn't out here on a fool's errand, after all.

Concealing his emotions, Cady regarded Hughes as though he were the lowest of scum. "The man he bought Mill Valley from was running for Congress at the time, and the seller needed the money for his campaign. If you require more than that, I'll draw you a picture."

"What do you want from Abdul?"

"Just to talk to him. That's all right now."

"Informally like this? The three of us?"

"Nope. Under oath and with a court reporter present."

"He doesn't have to talk to you. You don't have a subpoena."

"I can convene a grand jury Monday morning if I have to. You'll have your subpoena by noon today. And instead of doing this in the comfort of Mr. Azziz's living room, with you here, we can do it in the U.S. courthouse downtown without you present and with the reporters having a carnival on Temple Street." Cady shrugged his shoulders. "It's all the same to me. It's like shooting craps. I can make my point the easy way or the hard way."

"You really want to get Senator Boyd, don't you?"

Cady bristled. That wasn't his objective, though he realized that would be the inference people would draw. "I'm trying to do my job."

"And I'm trying to do mine. My client will talk to you if you'll give him immunity. Total immunity from any charges growing out of the Mill Valley transaction ten years ago, including the alien ownership business."

Cady hated making the deal Hughes was asking. It meant that to prosecute Senator Boyd, he had to let Azziz escape all charges. Realistically, though, this was where he had expected to end up when he saw Hughes. With somebody less experienced, they would have haggled for a while, and Cady would have been able to cut a better deal for the government. He could turn Hughes down and try to see if he was bluffing.

Before responding, Cady studied Hughes's face. The hard, cold stare that locked eyes with him told him that Hughes wasn't bluffing. In the end, Cady would have to back down. That wouldn't help him in questioning Azziz. Besides, he disliked negotiating when the result was obvious.

"If I give you the kind of immunity you want," Cady said, "then Azziz answers every question I ask. I don't want any claims of privilege or crap like that. And if he lies, the immunity's off and I go for perjury."

"I think we can live with those terms, but I'll have to talk to my client before I can give you a final answer."

"Understood." Cady felt as if he were on a roll. "And one other thing. I get to bring him to Washington, if I need him live before a grand jury."

Hughes hesitated.

"It's a deal breaker for me," Cady said.

"I'll recommend it to my client."

"If he goes along, you've got a deal for immunity. You have my word on it."

Hughes shook his head. "That's not good enough. I need it in writing from Sarah Van Buren, the assistant attorney general in charge of the Criminal Division in Washington. I don't want to hear later that you didn't have authority."

Cady reached into his jacket pocket and extracted the fax of a two-page letter he had received from the assistant attorney general about three hours ago. With Cady's reputation and the fact that it was Sunday morning, he'd been able to obtain the letter from Washington without having to give an explanation about the investigation. He handed the fax to Hughes, who studied it carefully.

"I'll talk to my client," he finally said.

Cady went over to the front window and waved. A red-headed court reporter dressed in a smart beige suit with a short skirt emerged from the back of one of the unmarked black cars. Her name was Kelly, and she was about twenty-five, Cady guessed. She was carrying Cady's briefcase in one hand and a case with a mini–word processor in the other.

She set up in the living room on a hard-backed chair halfway between where Cady told her he would be and where he planned to put Azziz.

"Sorry to drag you out of bed so early Sunday morning," Cady said, trying to pass the time until Hughes and Azziz appeared.

"Ah, don't worry," Kelly replied. "It was a good excuse to stick my husband with the kids."

They both laughed. His eyes strayed to her legs. She had

great legs, and with her short skirt hiked up, there wasn't much of them that he couldn't see.

Cady heard footsteps and voices. He stood up and looked toward the door. If Cady had two words to describe Abdul Azziz, they would be *fat* and *ugly*. The thick brown mustache didn't do much to enhance his appearance.

"We have a deal," Hughes said. "Under the terms you outlined."

"Good, let's get started, then. Kelly, swear the witness."

Working from notes on a yellow pad, Cady rolled through Azziz's background. Fifteen minutes into his examination he was ready to ask about the Mill Valley transaction. "Mr. Azziz, did there come a time about ten years ago when you purchased Mill Valley Winery in Napa Valley?"

"No, I never purchased that winery," he answered coldly.

"Did a French company by the name of Maison Antibes purchase Mill Valley Winery?"

"I believe so."

"And what was your relationship to Maison Antibes?"

Azziz looked at Hughes, who said, "You may answer the question."

Azziz coughed and cleared his throat. "I owned all of the stock of Maison Antibes."

"And who was the seller of Mill Valley in that transaction?"

"Mr. Charles Boyd."

"Of Rutherford, California?"

"Yes."

"What was Mr. Boyd's business at the time?"

"He owned the winery."

"What else was he doing?"

"I don't understand."

"Was he running for public office?"

"Yes, he was running for a seat in Congress against Chris Broder."

Cady picked up immediately on the venom in Azziz's voice when he mentioned Broder's name.

"Mr. Broder was then the congressman from that district, wasn't he?"

"Uh-huh."

"In connection with this transaction, did you ever have occasion to meet personally with Charles Boyd?"

"Yes, once."

"When was that?"

"When we agreed on the price."

"Who else was present?"

"No one."

"Didn't Mr. Boyd have a real estate agent?"

"Yes."

"Who was he?"

"A Jew. I don't remember his name."

"Was it Harvey Gladstone?"

"That's the one."

"Was he at your meeting with Boyd when you agreed on price?"

"No, I met with him earlier. Not at the important meeting with Boyd."

"Coming back to that meeting, describe how your discussion went with Mr. Boyd on price."

"He told me that he wanted ten million dollars for the winery, the business and the land. Everything."

"What did you say?"

"I told him that I would pay fifty million."

"Isn't that unusual, to offer five times the asking price?"

"I wanted him to have plenty of money for his congressional campaign."

"Why?"

"That son of a bitch Chris Broder was a tool of the Zionists. He was the ranking Republican on an important congressional committee, and he always agreed to give Israel everything they wanted. It was important for Broder to lose. With money, lots of money, Boyd could win."

"Did Boyd know this was why you were paying so much money? So he could defeat Congressman Broder?"

"He knew."

"What makes you so sure?"

"I told him."

"You told him what?"

"He was surprised by what I was prepared to pay. He said he thought maybe he shouldn't ask why that was. And I told him, 'I want you to win the election. I want Broder to lose. He's a slave of the Israelis.' I wanted Boyd to know this."

"Why?"

"Because I wanted Boyd to know that if he took the money, I expected him to be a good boy and vote against the Israelis in Congress."

"And did he do that?"

Azziz wrinkled up his forehead. "Sometimes yes and sometimes no. It could have been worse without my money, and at least he wasn't in a position of power like Broder on that foreign-affairs committee. So I got something from the deal."

"Did Boyd promise you at that meeting that he would vote against Israel?"

"No, but he knew why he was getting the extra forty million dollars. He's a smart man. He understood."

"Did you ever talk to Boyd after that meeting?"

"No."

"After he was elected, did you ever try to influence Boyd in any way?"

"I didn't have to. He knew what our arrangement was."

"Returning to the one meeting you had with Charles Boyd, did he accept your fifty-million-dollar offer?"

"Not at first."

"What do you mean?"

"When I told him why I wanted to pay so much, he said he had to think about it. He said that because of the campaign laws that limit political contributions, he could have a problem with the transaction."

"What did you say?"

"I told him, 'You must decide now. If I walk out of this room, the offer is withdrawn, and you'll never see me again.' "

"You're a good negotiator, Mr. Azziz."

"Your American elections are like a bazaar. You think only the Jews are good in business?"

Cady paused to look over his notes, making sure he hadn't missed anything.

"One other question. Has anybody other than me or Mr. Hughes ever asked you about the matters we have been discussing?"

"No one," Azziz said firmly.

"Never?"

"Never."

"That concludes the testimony."

Cady turned to Hughes. "I'm finished. The court reporter will print out the testimony. I want it read and signed by Mr. Azziz, right now, before I leave."

"Is that necessary?"

"Why, you have a golf date?"

"As a matter of fact, I do."

Cady shook his head in disgust. "Don't worry; I've got a two-thirty plane to Washington. I don't intend to screw around."

"Okay, okay, don't get huffy. I'll push back my tee time."

Not only did she have great legs, Cady thought, but Kelly was one fine court reporter. Less than an hour later, Azziz was picking up a pen to sign and verify his testimony.

As Cady tucked it into his briefcase, Hughes walked him and Kelly to the door. There he handed Cady his card. "You'll send me a copy," Hughes said.

"First thing tomorrow morning."

"You should be happy. You've got a cold-turkey violation by Boyd. Just what you wanted."

Cady wasn't happy. Sure, the Azziz testimony confirmed what was in the package delivered to his office, but Azziz had no credibility. A jury would never believe Azziz against the word of Senator Boyd. Cady also had the computer printout from the Napa County tax office, but Taylor was a good lawyer. She would tear into it because of the missing backup. Even if the purchase price was ridiculously high, she would argue that a French company desperate for a foothold in America was the purchaser. Foreigners frequently overpaid in situations like that.

Cady knew he needed Gladstone, live and in Washington. Without Gladstone, he didn't have a case he could take to a grand jury.

Chapter 12

"Alex Glass wants to have dinner with me this evening," General Ozawa said to Sato. "I came to your office as soon as he called. I didn't want to tell you on the phone."

"That was smart," Sato said. "Did he tell you why?"

"To talk about the tornado preparedness of our self-defense forces, so he can do a story."

"Did you believe him?" Sato asked skeptically.

Ozawa shook his head. "Not for a minute."

"What did you say?"

"My schedule's tight. I said I would check and call him back."

Sato lit a cigarette, leaned back in his plush leather chair, and exhaled with his eyes closed while he thought about what to do. So far Alex Glass and his huge ego had unwittingly been a boon. His articles had helped Sato move from being an obscure fringe political figure to a serious candidate to challenge Prime Minister Nakamura in December. The irony of that didn't escape Sato. From what he knew of Glass's personal views, he was probably appalled by the idea of a rearmed Japan. But that didn't stop the reporter from helping to achieve that result if it served his professional advancement.

The question for Sato was how could he keep using Glass

to his advantage, to lead the young and naive American reporter into writing additional articles that would enhance Sato's chances in December.

An idea popped into his head, and he opened his eyes, leaning forward. "Have dinner with him," Sato said. "The message I want you to get across is how strong and organized the civil defense forces are at the present time. Make the point that if I am elected and the legal restraints on rearmament are removed, as they've been in Germany, in a matter of months we will have a fully operational regular army to assist the United States in responding to any threats to world peace initiated by provocateurs in Beijing or elsewhere. Can you deliver that message?"

"Very forcefully," Ozawa replied.

As the general got up and started to leave the office, Sato began to see a downside to the interview. From his research on Glass, Sato knew that he'd had an affair with Taylor Ferrari, Boyd's campaign manager, when she had been in Kyoto for a global-warming conference a few years ago. That meant Glass might be funneling her information, even if it was not sufficiently substantiated to put in the newspaper. It was a minefield.

"There is one other thing," he said, "old friend."

Ozawa turned and moved back to the desk.

"For all of us, sake sometimes loosens the tongue."

Ozawa knew what Sato was telling him, and he tried to conceal his shame. As much as he hated to admit it, Sato was right, of course. Often at long dinners he tended to drink too much, and he sometimes said things that he later regretted.

"I understand," he said, looking down at the floor. "At this dinner there won't be a problem."

*   *   *

"So you see," General Ozawa said, slurring his words, "once we are permitted to rearm . . ." He stopped in mid-sentence, trying desperately to remember the message that Sato had wanted him to give to Glass, but after three and a half hours, while course after course of the magnificent *kaiseke* meal kept appearing, with the sake flowing like water, his mind and senses were failing him.

Trying to appear sympathetic and helpful, Alex looked across the table at the general. "You'll be able to assist the United States keeping the peace in Asia. Is that what you mean?"

Alex watched Ozawa nod in relief. He too was happy, because at long last he had finished talking about the use of the civil defense forces in dealing with earthquakes and other natural disasters. Alex was anxious to move on to the topic that interested him far more. Plus, his legs were killing him from sitting on the floor. His mind was foggy with alcohol, but compared with Ozawa, he was clear and alert.

Alex had used every trick he could think of to limit his own intake of alcohol. He had tried to give the appearance of drinking, raising the cup to his lips frequently, while taking only small sips. He had spilled out his sake twice into a water glass when Ozawa had gone to the bathroom, and refilled the cup with water. Ozawa showed no restraint at all. When the kimono-clad waitress refilled the cups, Ozawa didn't notice or care that she put much less in Alex's cup. What Ozawa cared about was that his own cup be filled to the top. Still, Alex wasn't used to the potent drink. He was struggling to concentrate, while he realized he was fading fast.

The waitress served pieces of green melon, the final course, and departed unobtrusively.

"I think my articles in the *New York Times* have helped Sato-*san*. Do you agree?"

"Sato shares that view as well."

"Is there anything else I can do to help with his program?"

Ozawa picked up his cup of sake and slurped. "Right now he doesn't need any more help."

"But suppose Senator Boyd is elected in the United States. That could be a problem."

Slouching over, Ozawa laughed. "It will never happen."

Alex looked dubious. "The polls say Boyd is winning."

"He won't even be in the race at the end."

Gulping hard, Alex decided it was time to play his trump card. "You think the American who met with Sato-*san* in Buenos Aires is powerful enough to make that happen?"

Ozawa sat up with a start. He rubbed his cloudy, glazed eyes, trying to achieve some clarity and focus. "How did you know about the meeting in Argentina?"

Alex took a deep breath. *Play it carefully,* he told himself. *We're at the key point. Even soused, Ozawa can't be underestimated.* "Sato-*san* told me in one of our private interviews," Alex said in a negligent voice. "How else could I possibly know?"

Ozawa thought about what Glass had said. The American had a point. If Sato hadn't told him, he couldn't possibly know. Ozawa grunted his acquiescence.

Relieved that Ozawa seemed satisfied, Alex pressed on. "It's amazing that Sato-*san* found the American."

"Never underestimate Sato-*san*," Ozawa said with pride. "His research department is the best in the world."

Not wanting to appear too anxious, Alex paused to eat a piece of the incredibly sweet melon. "You think the American is dependable?"

"Without question. He flew from Washington to Buenos Aires when Sato-*san* asked him to come. Did you know that his father had been an American missionary in China, and he himself was born there in 1942?"

Alex shook his head, letting Ozawa talk.

"Yes, it's true. When Mao's thugs took over, they let all of the missionaries go back to the United States or to Taiwan but six of them. His father and five others were executed in November 1949. So he has a great desire for revenge."

"I didn't know that. Oh, what's his name? Sato-*san* told me, but I can't remember." He shrugged. "Too much sake, I guess."

Glass's words brought the general up short. Sato had refused to tell Ozawa the name of the American he had recruited in Buenos Aires. Could he possibly have shared that name with Glass? That didn't make sense. Nothing was making sense now. He needed time to sleep and to think.

"I don't remember his name," Ozawa said with a sharp edge that Alex had not heard before. "And I think we should go home."

As Alex walked out of the room to pay the restaurant bill, he was elated at how much information he had gotten from Ozawa. As soon as he got home, he'd call the airlines to book a flight to Buenos Aires tomorrow. With the help of somebody in the *Times*'s bureau office there, he'd find a way to get access to the Alvear guest list for August 28. That was how he'd obtain the name of the American whom Sato had recruited to work with him. Then he could write his article— guaranteed to make headlines all across the country.

When Glass returned to the table, he found Ozawa leaning back, propped against the wall, sound asleep in a drunken stupor. The proprietor of the restaurant, a woman clad in a dark blue kimono with white flowers, bowed and told Alex that he should go and not to worry about his guest. "I will take care of the general," she said. So Alex stopped at the door for his shoes and departed.

He headed home on his Kawasaki, roaring through the deserted streets of Tokyo. Suddenly, Alex's elation of a few minutes ago gave way to fear. When Ozawa sobered up, he would realize that Alex had duped him to obtain sensitive information.

Glass cut a sharp right, changing his plans. As a precaution, he would go to his office before going home. There he would write up what he had learned tonight. He would leave it in his desk in an envelope with Taylor's name on the front, just in case anything happened to him. She would know what to do with it. *I'm probably being paranoid,* he thought.

Chapter 13

"I know you don't want to be involved in the Boyd investigation," Cady told Doerr, "but I'm now at the point where you have no choice."

They were closeted in Doerr's office in the U.S. Courthouse.

"Why, what's happened?

"I may be convening a grand jury in a couple of days."

Doerr shrugged. "I told you, I have full confidence in you. Handle it the way you would any other case."

"Wrong," Cady said emphatically. "It's not like any other case. I'm not swinging on this one alone."

Doerr looked insulted. "I would never do that to you."

"Right," Cady said. "No way."

Doerr sighed. "Okay. Give me a summary, but keep it short. I'm due over at the mayor's office to talk about crime statistics."

In staccato sentences, Cady summarized what he had done so far. "My conclusion," he said, "is that I have a case, but I won't convene a grand jury until I get additional evidence. Azziz must have committed other crimes. Somebody could have easily blackmailed him with the threat of disclosure."

"Agreed."

Doerr got up from his desk and reached for his jacket, signifying that the meeting was over.

"There's one more issue," Cady said.

Doerr looked over warily. He knew what was coming next. "Yeah?"

"What do we do about McDermott?"

Very uncomfortable, Doerr said, "What do you mean?"

"He or someone working to reelect the president may have initiated this. Even if he wasn't the one, he may be in it up to his eyeballs. You ever heard of John Mitchell?"

"Don't you think that might have crossed my mind?"

"Well, what do we do?"

Doerr snarled. "Since you managed to drag me into this, that's my call to make. I want to think about it."

Taylor couldn't get past Cady's secretary on the phone. She heard him calling in the background, "Tell her to come down at eleven o'clock. I can't see her until then."

He's not going to be easy to deal with, she decided as she headed along the corridor to Harrison's office.

"Where are you on the new transaction for Fujimura?" she asked him.

"I think you'll be happy."

"Nothing will make me happy today."

"That I can't help, but you should know that my team of associates made it back from Houston last night after working all weekend. We developed a game plan around midnight." He tossed her a spiral-bound document resting on his desk entitled, "Plan of Attack for Project Blue Light."

"Tomorrow at dawn," he said, "we put four units into the air, each one with three lawyers and two paralegals. Each unit will have two plants to investigate in the next two weeks. On week three, they write it all up. Week four you and I get to review it and add our two cents."

"How close will you be to these units during the first two weeks?"

"I'm off for Philly today on another transaction, but you don't have to worry. I'll get a phone call every evening from each unit. They've each got a precise time to call in. Nobody leaves one plant and moves to another until I sign off. You like it?"

She nodded.

"You should." He laughed. "I just saved your ass with Fujimura."

"Let me run your plan of attack by him," Taylor said, "with you on the phone."

Harrison started to fiddle with a plastic cigarette while his secretary tried to reach Fujimura in Los Angeles. "How'd you make out with the good senator at St. Michaels?" he asked.

As she described the bottom line of her conversation along the water on Saturday, she watched Harrison's expression change from interest to bewilderment. At the end he was shaking his head in doubt. "With all due respect," Harrison said, "given what's at stake, you're a little out of your league, dealing with this yourself. And I am too. You should get help from Ken or one of the people in his white-collar-criminal group."

"I suggested that to the senator. He insisted that I handle it myself."

"Not a smart move."

Her sour face showed that she agreed with him. Nevertheless, she said, "I've been involved in several criminal investigations. You've done some yourself over the years. It's not rocket science. For now I'll do it the way the senator wants. If things get dicier I'll talk to Ken. You got a better idea?"

Harrison shook his head. "I suppose you have to respect Boyd's decision. Let's face it, he has the most to lose. When do you see Cady next?"

"Eleven o'clock this morning. My goal is to find out what evidence he has. I'll repeat for him what the senator told me about the Mill Valley transaction. Offer to give him a statement from the senator under oath and try to persuade him to drop the investigation."

"Suppose Cady wants to interview Boyd informally?"

She thought about it for a minute. "Nothing doing. He's not entitled to that."

"Cady could always convene a grand jury and send Boyd a subpoena, figuring he'd have to testify. How could the senator take the Fifth?"

Harrison was right, of course, Taylor realized. Theoretically, anyone given a subpoena to testify before a grand jury could refuse by asserting the Fifth Amendment and claiming that his testimony might tend to incriminate him. But realistically that wasn't an option for a presidential candidate. Everything would become public. A grand jury would be the worst of all worlds. Taylor had to do some rethinking of her strategy.

"Good point. I'll offer up the senator for an informal interview as a last resort."

The intercom buzzed. "I've got Mr. Fujimura."

"Put him through," Harrison said, hitting the speaker button.

Taylor began. "I have my partner Philip Harrison with me, Fujimura-*san*. We want to give you a report."

Taylor pointed to Harrison, who summarized the plan of attack. At the end, she wasn't surprised when Fujimura didn't answer right away. She knew how he operated. He had made notes while they were talking. Now he was reviewing them.

"I completely approve," he said at last.

Pleased, Taylor whispered to Harrison, "Good work."

"If anything serious turns up," Fujimura added, "I want to know immediately and not at the end of the thirty days."

"Absolutely," she said.

"On a totally different matter," Fujimura said, "could I please talk a moment with you in private, Taylor?"

She went back to her own office and had the call transferred there.

"I know you're very involved in Senator Boyd's campaign," Fujimura said in a soft voice, just above a whisper. "From what I hear, it's not good weather for sailing."

Taylor was listening carefully. Over the years, she had learned that Fujimura often spoke obliquely on the telephone where sensitive information was involved. "Is there anything else you can tell me about what you've heard?"

"Sorry, I don't yet know enough to be useful. My schedule calls for me to be here in Los Angeles for the next two weeks. I'll keep listening for more information about the weather. One good friend has an obligation to tell another about dark clouds on the horizon."

Without saying anything else he hung up the phone, leaving Taylor staring at the black handset. Rumors about the senator's problem had somehow reached Fujimura in California. He obviously didn't want to share any more information with her yet. She tried speculating about the source of his information. Several Japanese newspapers with reporters in the United States were following the American election closely, and Fujimura was well connected with the Japanese press. It was possible that one of them had heard the same rumors that had reached Dawson and Cooper at the *L.A. Times*.

Fujimura's warning added urgency to her meeting with Cady. She had better find a way to end his investigation quickly. There was precious little time until the story broke in the press, which would destroy the strategy she and Boyd had decided to follow.

Taylor arrived at Cady's office ten minutes early, but he made her wait a few minutes before he would see her. "I'm sorry, Taylor," he said when she came in at last. "I spent the morning fighting with INS. They're making me jump through hoops to get the Russian mobster in my case deported. Can you believe that?"

"Don't worry about it," she said. She sat in one of the two chairs before his desk. Idly she noticed his nameplate was cockeyed. That set off an idea. She decided to try a little small talk, perhaps loosen him up first. "I always wondered how it got to be C.J.," she said, pointing at the nameplate.

"Oh, that. They named me Conrad Jerome. My mother wanted to call me Jerome, her grandfather's name. My father wanted Conrad. I settled it by opting for the initials."

"Which made them both unhappy."

He smiled. "You're right."

They shared a laugh, one that faded away into uneasy silence. He waited for her to begin. It was her meeting.

"Now that you've had the weekend to do your investigating," she said, "I imagine you've come to the conclusion that there's nothing there, and you're willing to drop the whole thing."

Cady looked at her in earnest. "I'm sorry to disappoint you. Friday I wasn't sure that I had a case. Today I've got no doubt about it."

"What are you talking about? McDermott and the committee to reelect the president are responsible for these trumped-up charges. Don't you see it? It's a campaign dirty trick. You're taking the bait."

He leaned back in his chair and cracked a tiny smile. "I wish you were right, but I've built my own case."

Maybe he wasn't so honest, after all. She'd thought she'd pegged him right, but she didn't know him very well. "There's a crime here, all right," she said heatedly. "You're about to commit it by taking the election out of the hands of the American people, not to mention destroying the life of a good man in the process."

Cady sat up straight. "Whoa. I'm not trying to destroy anyone's life."

"How can you be so dumb? They're using you."

"Okay. Stop." He moved out from behind his desk and sat down on a red leather chair facing her. "I honestly don't think that McDermott's behind this. Both McDermott and Doerr have left me entirely on my own. And I've got no bias or predisposition. You have to believe me. In fact, if you made me choose, my hope would be that Boyd didn't violate the law. Until this came up, I would have voted for him over Webster. And the last thing in the world I want to do is obstruct the presidential election."

"Then why don't you drop your investigation?"

He held his hands out in front of him, as if that would enhance his credibility. "I can't. I believe there's something here, that Senator Boyd violated the law."

"Show me your evidence. Let's talk about it."

Cady got up and started to pace. "You're asking a lot from me."

"If we're not playing games, then let me see what you have."

"No prosecutor would do that at this stage of the case."

"You know this isn't the usual case. I keep telling you a presidential election is at stake."

Cady sighed deeply. Then he walked over to his desk drawer and pulled out the transcript of his interview with Abdul Azziz yesterday in Los Angeles. "I'll let you read it here, but I won't give you a copy."

Now she was getting somewhere. She knew he was a good guy, and this offer of his proved it. As she read, she realized that Cady was watching her face carefully for a reaction. She remained totally deadpan.

When she was finished, she said, "Surely you don't believe this Abdul Azziz. Do you?"

"Of course I believe him."

She looked at him in disbelief. "The whole thing's a fabrication. I've worked closely with the senator for ten years. I know him. This story isn't right. Somebody put Azziz up to it. When I check, I'll bet I find out that Azziz has some other shady dealings in his past."

His hesitation confirmed that her guess was right.

"I'll save you the trouble. He has one SEC criminal violation in connection with a stock issue."

She thought a lot of Cady. She couldn't understand how he could let himself be duped. "And you believe somebody like that over a U.S. senator who has a perfect record for integrity?"

"I don't know what the senator's version is of these events."

"I thought you'd never ask."

She then told the story of the Mill Valley sale exactly as the senator had told it to her at St. Michaels on Saturday.

When she was finished, Cady asked, "Would he be willing to give me his statement orally under oath?"

She was glad she had covered this issue with Harrison. "Let's compromise. You get to interview the senator, but you have to agree that if he sticks to the version of the facts that I just gave you during your interview with him, then you'll drop the entire investigation."

Her offer piqued Cady's interest, and he gave her a counteroffer. "I would be able to cross-examine him about the statement he gives me. Unlimited cross with you present, but without you breaking in to object. Under oath and on the record."

"And if he sticks to his story under those conditions, then you'll drop the investigation?"

"But if I break him, then I can take the case to the grand jury, and he'll testify there."

"If that's what you want."

Cady grew silent while Taylor stared at him, trying to remain calm, hoping he took the deal. She was confident that the senator would stick to his story, even under rigorous questioning by Cady. The investigation would be over. They could go back to the business of winning the election.

"Well?" she asked.

He walked over to the window and looked out. She could guess what was running through his mind. Her offer was tempting. He liked to think that he was a good enough lawyer that he would break Boyd if he were lying, even though the senator was savvy at handling questions. It was a close call. Cady was agonizing over the decision.

Finally he turned around slowly and faced her. "You're very persuasive, but I can't do it. If a secret back-room deal like that ever came out, we'd both look like hell."

She'd been so close. She'd thought she had him. "I'm willing to put my reputation on the line, because it's the right thing to do for the country."

"But that's just the point. It's not the right thing for the country," Cady insisted.

"Then what is?"

"For me to finish my investigation in the normal way."

"Does that mean you're going to convene a grand jury? Wreck a decent man's life and throw the country into turmoil when all you have is the testimony of a convicted felon like Abdul Azziz?"

What she said upset Cady. She was smart, and she was articulating his nagging doubts.

Cady shook his head. "I wouldn't do that, Taylor. But as long as we're being frank, I have to tell you that personally I believe Azziz. Yes, he's a convicted felon, but I sat and looked him in the eye. I believe he's telling the truth."

"Aw, c'mon, C.J., they could easily have found something else he did and threatened to disclose it unless he agreed to lie to you. The senator's the one who's telling the truth."

Cady thought about her words. "One of them has to be lying," he said tentatively.

"So what will you do?"

"Unless I can get another witness, I'll terminate the investigation. There will be no grand jury. No charges will be filed against the senator. I'll do everything humanly possible to keep it out of the press. I give you my word on that."

"If you get something else, would you be willing to discuss it with me before you do anything drastic, like taking the case to a grand jury?"

He looked at her with a gentle, almost apologetic expression. "Sorry, I can't promise you that. I've been more than reasonable letting you read the Azziz deposition. I've got my own job to do."

"Will you at least consider giving me a chance to respond before you decide to go to a grand jury?"

He sighed deeply. "I don't know."

"C'mon, C.J., besides the presidential race, an honest man's life is on the line." She was pleading with him.

"I promise you that I'll think about it. That's all."

Outside the courthouse, Taylor took out her cell phone and called Mark Jackson, the P.I. "Where are you on Gladstone?" she asked anxiously.

"No luck so far. We're still looking."

"Ugh."

"We'll keep trying. Believe me."

She shook her head in frustration. "Do one other thing. There's a man living in L.A. named Abdul Azziz. I know he's had a criminal conviction for violation of securities law. Find out everything you can about him."

"You want to discredit him?"

"You bet. I intend to blast a prosecutor's case to kingdom come."

McDermott raced breathlessly into the Oval Office, bursting in on a photo session with a group of high school science scholars from around the country. He hadn't heard yet, McDermott realized from looking at the president's face.

When McDermott ran a finger across his throat, the president announced, "This will be the last picture." He also instructed his secretary to cancel the meeting with the director of OMB, who was waiting outside the office.

"Senator Boyd is in deep trouble," McDermott said, talking as fast as his brain could process the words. "The U.S. attorney's office in Washington is investigating whether

Boyd accepted an illegal contribution during the campaign for his first election to Congress."

"Run that by me again," an astounded president said.

Sounding nervous, McDermott repeated his words.

"How long have you known about this investigation?"

McDermott's face was twitching. "I just found out this morning."

"But I don't understand. Shouldn't you have been involved?"

"Jim Doerr and C. J. Cady, the prosecutor on the case, decided to keep me out of it, in view of my position in your campaign. I'm grateful to them for that."

The president shoved his hands into his pants pockets and began pacing around the office, trying to digest the mind-numbing news McDermott had given him.

"How did this investigation get started?" Webster asked.

"According to Jim Doerr, an anonymous packet of materials appeared one evening on Cady's desk. Since then he's checked it all out."

The president stopped dead, wheeled around, and stared hard at McDermott. His gaze cut through the A.G. like a knife. "Have you had anything to do with this business?"

The nervous twitching began again. "Absolutely not."

"What about Pug Thompson and his people?"

"I've read him the riot act. I'd have known if it was his idea."

McDermott could tell that the president wasn't convinced. Here was another development McDermott hadn't contemplated.

"Okay. What happens next?" Webster asked.

"We take it one step at a time. I've told Doerr to keep me informed. I'll do the same for you."

McDermott felt trapped, although he had no one to blame

but himself. The situation had deteriorated rapidly. At least matters couldn't get any worse, he wanted to believe, but he knew that was wrong. If truths started to be unearthed, his chance of becoming Chief Justice of the Supreme Court would be blasted to hell.

Chapter 14

General Ozawa woke up with a start. He was still in the restaurant, wearing the clothes from his dinner with Glass. He was stretched out on a futon, but he had no idea how he had gotten there. His entire body was trembling. When he glanced at his watch, he saw it was three-twelve in the morning.

His head felt as if it weighed a ton, but he didn't care about that. Emerging out of his haziness was the gradual realization that he had said some things last night that he shouldn't have. He had done exactly what Sato had warned him against: drinking too much and talking too much. But what exactly had he told Glass?

When he stumbled out onto the street, he found his car and driver still waiting. Without a word, his driver roared off down the empty streets. Once he got home, Ozawa stripped off his clothes. Since his wife had died last year, he lived alone. He fixed an ice-cold bath. He got in it, ducking his head underwater four times to clear his brain, part of his usual regimen when he drank too much, which was more often than he liked to admit. Once he emerged from the bathroom, his teeth were chattering. At least he now had a pretty good idea of what he had said.

Ozawa was mortified. He had really done it this time. He'd never drink too much again.

He considered calling Sato to tell him what had happened, but he couldn't bear the humiliation and Sato's anger. Sato might sever all relations with Ozawa, or even worse. He thought about the vicious murders Terasawa had committed, and he began shaking. Suppose Sato turned Terasawa loose on him?

There had to be another way to solve the problem.

Ozawa racked his alcohol-fogged brain. Slowly an idea took shape. He checked the civil defense force phone directory, then picked up the phone and called a captain who was very dependable, someone he could trust with his life. That was what was involved now.

"Here's what I want you to do," he said to the sleepy man who answered the phone.

They arrived an hour later, in a truck from the local electrical company. The three men in work clothes had toolboxes and all of the paraphernalia that anyone who happened to see them would associate with the repair of an electrical problem.

Two of them took up positions next to the switch box that controlled the flow of electricity into Alex Glass's apartment building. The third one, with an orange hard hat, slipped into the wooden shed adjacent to the building, which Alex had built specially to house his black Kawasaki. The landlord had demanded a month's wages from Alex for permitting the structure, but Alex had the same feelings about that bike that people did about their children. No expense was too great.

The man was a skilled mechanic who had once worked for Kawasaki. In a few seconds, he had the engine exposed and planted a small black square object inside. With the deft fingers of an expert, he hooked up wires between the ignition, the engine, and the black box.

When he was finished and he had closed up the engine, he took a couple of steps back from the motorcycle. It was well tended, and the engine was in perfect shape, better than ones that rolled off the assembly line. It was a shame to destroy something so beautiful.

Alex woke up in a cold sweat. His T-shirt was soaked as well as the sheets, and he knew it wasn't from the sake he had drunk last evening. The alcohol accounted for his humongous headache, but the reason he was sweating from head to toe was because of the magnitude of what he had learned from Ozawa at dinner. Sato's scheme involving a powerful American was frightening enough. The thought of what Ozawa would do when he woke out his drunken stupor was terrifying.

Everything was coming back to Alex. Aware of how explosive the information was, as well as the risks to himself, Alex had swung by his office on the way home, typed out a letter to Taylor, and left it in the center drawer of his desk in a sealed envelope addressed to her. That was smart, he decided. In case anything happened to him, she'd run with his information and find out whom Sato had met in Buenos Aires. If he just left it for that bozo Don Berry, the head of the *Times* office here, Don might think it was too speculative. From the office, Alex had managed to weave his way on his motorcycle to his apartment. His blood-alcohol level must have been off the charts.

In the cold light of morning, two Advil and three cups of coffee eased the headache, but not the terror. Ozawa might have told Sato what he had said. Or Ozawa, a dangerous man himself, might be petrified that Sato would find out. Either way Alex was in deep trouble.

By the time he finished another cup of coffee, he knew there was only one thing he could do: get the hell out of Tokyo ASAP. That wasn't why he had booked the reservation for Buenos Aires in his drunken stupor last night, but he was glad that he had. He stumbled over to his desk, tripping over a pair of shoes, to find the piece of paper on his desk. He was on an ANA plane that left at noon and connected in L.A. for Buenos Aires. He still had plenty of time to leave for the flight, but he decided to hit the road now and wait at the airport. Definitely a lot safer.

Without calling anyone, not even Don, he'd jump on his motorcycle, and head to Narita Airport. Once he was safely in Los Angeles for the connection, he'd call Don with some B.S. story about an illness in the family. That was definitely the way to go.

Moving fast, Alex stuffed some clothes, along with his laptop, into a duffel that fit into the holder on the back of his motorcycle. Out in the hall he waited for the elevator to come. When it didn't, he yelled, "Fuck," and raced down twelve flights of stairs with the duffel in one hand and his helmet in the other.

From the doorway of his apartment building, he looked up and down the street.

Nothing suspicious.

He breathed a sigh of relief. *You guys gotta get up early to catch Alex Glass,* he thought, feeling a surge of renewed self-confidence.

Taking personal risks for a good story was what journalism was all about. He would make it to Buenos Aires. He would find out whom Sato met with on August 28 at the Alvear. His story would earn him a Pulitzer.

Alex hurried toward the shed that held his Kawasaki. His adrenaline was flowing. He'd fly to the airport.

He looked around again as he stuffed the duffel into the holder on the back of the bike and strapped on his helmet. *Buenos Aires, here I come.*

He jumped on the seat and turned the key to start the powerful engine. It began to rev up, but didn't kick over. *Shit,* he thought, *that never happened before.*

He pressed down hard, igniting the engine. This time it didn't die on him, but he heard an unusual click. "What the hell's that?"

Then a huge explosion.

It was the last thing Alex ever heard, because suddenly fragments of his body and the disintegrating motorcycle were being hurled through the flimsy wooden roof of the shed high into the cool morning air.

Chapter 15

"We creamed 'em," an ecstatic Kendrick shouted to Taylor on the phone.

She had arrived at her office at the law firm with a stack of newspapers from different cities that she had picked up at a newsstand in the National Press Building, but she hadn't opened them before the phone rang. "Which polls have you seen?" Taylor asked.

"New York. Washington. Chicago. L.A. And Denver. A clean sweep. Webster is finished."

Taylor was dumbfounded. After watching the debate last night, the most she had expected was a narrow victory. "People really reacted that way?"

"Damn right, and you know what?"

"Tell me."

"Now it's ours to lose. All we have to do is keep the senator out of trouble and we're home free."

Taylor was glad they weren't having this conversation in person, so Kendrick couldn't see the pained expression on her face. She knew that she should tell him about Cady and the investigation, but she couldn't bring herself to do it. It was as if not talking about it would make it go away.

"I'll go out and get a stepladder," Taylor said.

"Why a stepladder?"

"So we can tear down the goalposts." She was trying to fake the enthusiasm Kendrick expected, though C. J. Cady and his investigation had taken over her mind. If something happened on that front today, she'd have to reach Boyd. "Where are you guys now?"

"On the campaign plane, touching down in Miami in about twenty minutes. Morning meetings with big donors and some other stops in the area. Luncheon at the Omni downtown. Then we're off for Tampa and St. Pete. See you."

Putting the phone down, Taylor winced, thinking about Kendrick's words, "It's ours to lose." Unless she found a way to block Cady's investigation, they *would* lose.

Taylor was buried in the newspapers, in which the pundits confirmed Kendrick's analysis, when the intercom rang. "Shawn Emerson from the *New York Times*'s Washington bureau on line one," Kathy said. "Are you in or out?"

Shawn might be calling to talk about the debate. Hopefully he hadn't found out about Cady's investigation. If he had, she couldn't pass up the opportunity to spin the news for damage control. "Morning, Shawn. I hope you enjoyed the debate last night."

"Actually, I did. Your guy did okay, but that's not why I'm calling."

Oh, Christ, she thought. *He's heard about Cady's investigation.* "What's up, then?" She held her breath, while grabbing the bottom of her desk chair.

"There was an accident," he said in a somber tone. "In Tokyo. Your friend Alex Glass was killed in a freak accident with his motorcycle."

"Oh, God, no!" Taylor's voice quavered. "I remember that thing. Alex got me on it once—only once. That was it. I wouldn't do it again. He rode so fast, I've never been as scared in my life. When it was over I pleaded with him to give it up."

"And he laughed at you."

"How'd you know?"

"He laughed at all of us when we told him that. He loved that damn bike. Said it was the only way to get around Tokyo. But here's the strange part. He wasn't in an accident. Somehow it exploded outside his apartment building when he started the engine."

"But that doesn't make sense. He—" She stopped in mid-sentence. Her blood ran cold. Alex had been digging into Sato's life in his coverage of the Japanese candidate for prime minister. Sato had a reputation for surrounding himself with Yakuza thugs. Had Alex pushed too far and offended Sato or one of his people?

"Thanks, Shawn. This is really awful."

As soon as Taylor hung up, she called the *New York Times*'s Tokyo office. The receptionist put her through to Don Berry. "I just heard about Alex," Taylor said.

"We're all in a state of shock." Don's voice was heavy with grief. "Alex wasn't just our star reporter. Everybody in the office loved him. He was a real character."

"What happened?"

"Nobody knows. The Tokyo police are investigating. Apparently Alex started up the bike, and it just exploded."

Taylor wasn't buying it. "That doesn't make sense. Alex spent so much time taking care of that bike. He called it his baby. It was always in perfect shape. It couldn't just explode."

"I know what you mean. That's what I told the police."

She tried to conceal the edge in her voice. "Well, what do they think?"

"At this point they don't have any idea. Or if they do, they're not telling me."

"Listen, Don, if you hear anything, will you let me know?"

"Absolutely. The Kyoto conference was before I got here, but I've heard about you two. I'll keep you posted."

Suddenly Kathy opened Taylor's door. "There's a United States marshal here to see you."

"Oh, shit." Taylor groaned, knowing why he was here. She quickly wrapped up the call with Don.

The marshal was a polite young man, short and squat, built like a tank, with a blond crew cut. There was no point getting angry at him when he handed her the grand jury subpoena. It called for Boyd to testify tomorrow morning at ten.

"I have to ask you," he said, "if you'll accept service for Charles R. Boyd."

"I will."

"Then please sign the return." She scrawled her signature. In addition to the subpoena he handed her a white business envelope with her name on the front. Inside there was a typed note:

> Taylor:
> *I've decided to proceed this way. Regrettably, I had no choice.*
> C. J. Cady

She picked up the phone and pounded her fingers hard onto each button as she dialed Cady's number.

Margaret answered. "I'll get him right away," she said when she heard it was Taylor. "He's expecting your call."

"I'll bet."

In an instant Cady was on the line. "I'm sorry. Really, I am."

"Ah, c'mon. You're not sorry at all. You went to McDermott, and he told you to do it."

"I haven't been near McDermott."

"Then Doerr went to McDermott."

"Truthfully, I don't know what Doerr's done. So far I've been running the case myself. Doerr hasn't given me a single order."

"Next you'll try to sell me the Brooklyn Bridge."

Her response was what Cady had expected. Still, he wanted to convince her that he was behaving decently. "I'm doing everything humanly possible to keep this confidential and out of the press. Nobody has to know about it."

"This could cost you your job and any chance of a career you think you have at DOJ."

"No doubt it will if Senator Boyd gets elected president."

"He is going to be elected."

Taylor called the senator's campaign office at the Omni Hotel in Miami. "Bad news?" Boyd asked as soon as he heard her voice.

"Bad is an understatement. Try horrible. The other shoe fell in the matter we've been discussing."

"You need me back in Washington?"

"Tell Bob to change the schedule and get you back here late tonight. I'll be at your house about seven tomorrow morning. We can take it from there."

"What explanation do I give him and the others?"

"You think you're coming down with the flu. You want a day of rest to get your energy back."

"I'm ready to do battle with this prosecutor."

"It'll be tough."

"Don't worry about me. Nobody's going to force me out over some trumped-up charges."

If Taylor were betting, she'd put her money on Boyd. He hadn't done anything wrong. He was articulate enough to persuade Cady and the grand jury of that fact.

Cady had told her that he would take the case to a grand jury only if he had something more than Azziz. What did he have?

She picked up the phone and called Mark Jackson, the P.I. "Any word on Gladstone?"

"Seems to have disappeared from the face of the earth. One of my people made such a pest of herself that Mrs. Gladstone chased her away with a garden hoe."

"Is it possible that the prosecutor brought him to Washington and has him hidden here? That's why we can't find him?"

"Definitely possible. You want me to check D.C. hotels the Bureau uses for witnesses?"

"Do it and let me know. But don't talk to him if you find him."

"Will do, but I'm not optimistic. As far as Azziz goes, the man's a real slime. A couple of prior convictions. He must have had friends in high places or he'd have done some serious jail time. You'll easily be able to discredit him."

That was comforting news, but Taylor was still worried about Gladstone.

She headed down the hall to Harrison's office. Without saying a word, she handed him the subpoena.

"I'm not surprised," Harrison told her after he looked it over. "I thought it was inevitable. I made my own quiet inquiries around town about C. J. Cady. He's not the type to back off."

"I have to let the senator testify."

"You sure you don't want to run that decision by Ken?"

"C'mon. It's a no-brainer."

Harrison locked eyes with her. "Since you asked my opinion, the way I see it is, if he's innocent he tells his story to the grand jury and you do damage control. If he's guilty or so close to the line that there's a risk he'll lose, he shouldn't waste his time taking the Fifth. He should use the leverage he has as a candidate and have you broker a deal with Cady. He drops out of the presidential race. In return they don't prosecute."

Taylor looked bewildered by these options.

"I'm speaking in plain English," Harrison said gruffly. "What part of that didn't you understand?"

"The senator's consistently told me that he didn't do anything wrong. Now you're talking about a deal."

"Telling you is one thing. Telling a lie to a grand jury under oath is another. That's the worst of all worlds."

"You think I'm wrong to believe the senator. Don't you?"

Harrison shoved a plastic cigarette into his mouth, rolled it around for a few seconds, and pulled it out. "Let me put it this way: I think you're awfully close to your client in this case."

She pounded her fist on his desk. "Don't play games with me. I can't handle that right now. I want to know if you think he's guilty."

Harrison ran his fingers through his unruly hair. "How the hell do I know? I'm not God. I wasn't back in Napa twelve years ago or whenever this stuff happened. I haven't spent enough time with your senator to judge him. I've got strictly a selfish interest in all of this."

"Selfish?"

"Yeah, when the dust clears, I want my partner and friend Taylor Ferrari, whom I have come to value and respect, on her feet and still practicing law."

Chapter 16

Taylor hated grand jury proceedings. Smacking of the old British Star Chamber, they were the most undemocratic institution in the American legal system. The objective in theory made sense: to determine whether enough evidence existed to indict an individual and thereby force him to plead guilty or to defend himself in a public trial. But grand jury proceedings were conducted in secret, and not susceptible to public viewing. Even the transcript of the proceedings was sealed. Present in the grand jury room were the members of the jury, generally around twenty, the prosecutor, and the witness. Lawyers for the witness were barred from the room, though the witness could, at the risk of creating a bad impression, ask for a recess to consult with counsel outside. There was no opportunity for the witness to confront his accusers, and no restraints on what the prosecutor could do. In the end, on the issue of whether or not to indict and thereby force the accused to endure a costly public trial, the grand jury did little more than rubber-stamp the recommendations of the prosecutor.

All of this Taylor explained to a grim and somber Boyd as the two of them huddled behind a closed door Wednesday morning in the den of his Georgetown house.

"Can they force me to testify?" he asked.

"The answer's yes and no."

"Typical lawyer's double-talk response," he said in a sharp tone.

Her own nerves were frayed, her spirits sagging. "Look, Charles, please don't take it out on me. I'm trying to help you."

He groaned. "Sorry. It's just a little frustrating. To get so close and have this come flying in from God knows where. Some fucking bogus charge."

"I know that. I wish I could make it go away, but I can't. So let's come back to your question. The only way you can avoid answering Cady's questions is if you take the Fifth Amendment in response to every question. You have to respond each time, 'On the advice of counsel, I refuse to answer on the grounds that the answer might tend to incriminate me.'"

"And to a nonlawyer, that says I'm guilty as hell."

"Unfortunately, that's right."

"So that's not an option."

She remembered Harrison's advice yesterday. If the senator needed to cut a deal, she would lay that option out for him. She waded in slowly. "But if somebody called to testify before a grand jury knows that he violated the law, then he's better off taking the Fifth and forcing the government to build its case, if it can without his testimony. The worst is to testify and lie. Then a witness ends up with a perjury charge on top of all of his other troubles."

She looked up to find him staring hard at her. "What are you trying to say?"

She paused and took a deep breath. "Is the story you told me Saturday at St. Michaels about your sale of Mill Valley completely true?"

"Absolutely," he said, offended. "Don't you believe me?"

"Of course I believe you. Every good lawyer has to make that one final check before he lets a client testify before a grand jury."

"Is that your guys' version of CYA?" he asked belligerently.

"No, it's called good lawyering."

"Do you have any idea what this prosecutor, what's his name . . . ?"

"C. J. Cady."

"What does he have on me?"

She ran through the Azziz version Cady had shown her Monday.

"Azziz is lying," Boyd said.

"Did you ever meet the man?"

"Never."

"So why'd he say it?"

He shrugged. "They're using him to frame me."

"I thought of that, too. Azziz is a convicted felon for a Securities Act violation."

"That's a hell of a note. In our legal system a criminal can destroy an innocent man."

"I don't know what else, if anything, they've got."

The phone rang. Sally was in Los Angeles with her Italian painter friend, introducing him to some of the gallery owners out there. Taylor and Boyd waited for Donna, Boyd's housekeeper, to answer. Moments later she appeared in the doorway.

"I told you not to disturb us," Boyd said.

She was flustered. "It's a Mr. Cady for Miss Ferrari. He says it's very urgent."

Boyd glanced at Taylor. "Maybe he's decided to fold his hand."

"Don't bet on it."

She picked up the phone. "What's up?"

The sigh that she heard warned her there was more trouble. "Listen, Taylor, there's been a leak. I just wanted to tip you off. I swear I had nothing to do with it."

"A leak!" she said, seething. "You son of a bitch. What kind of leak?"

"I wasn't the source."

"What kind of leak?" she demanded.

"CBS News has gotten word of the grand jury investigation," he said wearily. "They're going public with it on the eight-o'clock news this morning."

"It had to come out of your office. We sure didn't do it."

"It didn't. I swear."

"Then it was McDermott. I'll make sure the Democrats on the Hill fry his ass and yours in the same pan."

"I'm really sorry about this. I'm calling to try to help you out."

Listening to him, she was convinced that he was sorry about what had happened. Still, he was the cause of all of this misery by not backing off on the investigation. "What can you do about it now?" she said bitterly.

"I'll be down at the freight entrance at the rear of the building at ten minutes to ten to help you get him in. That's not much, but it's something."

"Bullshit," she shouted. "The senator goes in the front door with his head held high. I'll be with him. You can be sure that I'll have some choice things to say to the press about abuse of the legal process. We'll bury you before this is over."

"Fine, then, Room two-oh-eight at ten o'clock."

She slammed down the phone and dialed Kendrick at home. "You'd better get over to the senator's house ASAP.

Pick up Governor Crane on the way. Tell him this is more important than anything he's doing."

"What happened?"

"We'll talk when you get here. But do yourself a favor. Don't listen to CBS news on the hour."

"That bad?"

"Worse."

Waiting for Kendrick and Crane, Taylor finished her preparation of Boyd by asking questions that Cady would undoubtedly ask. The phone started ringing furiously. She instructed Donna not to answer it. When Kendrick and Crane arrived, Taylor sent Boyd upstairs to dress while she briefed the others.

As she recounted what had happened, she saw Kendrick getting madder and madder. When she told him about the grand jury proceeding this morning, he looked as if he were ready to explode.

Kendrick roughly pulled her off to one side. "Goddammit," he said in a hiss. His face was red, and the veins in his neck were protruding. "Why didn't you tell me about this fucking investigation as soon as you learned about it?"

"I thought I could make it go away."

"We're supposed to be full partners in this campaign. That was the condition you agreed to when you hired me. You should have told me from the beginning."

He was right. She looked chagrined. "I'm sorry. I was dead wrong. It's been a tough couple of days. I've just been trying to stay afloat. But I would like you to come down to the courthouse with us. Help with damage control with the press."

There was a long pause. She knew what Kendrick was thinking: If this ended in disaster, would he be better off as far away as possible? She wasn't letting him have any choice in the matter. "He'll need you," she stated emphatically.

Crane approached Taylor and Kendrick. "What can I do to help? I mean it. I'll do whatever will help Charles."

He sounded sincere, which impressed Taylor. Even though she had persuaded Boyd to take Crane as his VP in order to get the nomination, she had doubts herself about the silk-stocking, mainline native from Philadelphia. Today Crane was demonstrating that he was a class act. He had the most to gain from a Boyd withdrawal. Yet he wasn't trying to disassociate himself.

"The offer's appreciated," Taylor replied, "but I'm the kind of gambler who likes to hedge her bets whenever possible. The first thing I care about is getting the senator into the White House. The second is getting Webster out."

"Meaning what?"

"You should go home, turn on the television set, and don't answer the phone."

"How can I find out what's happening?"

She turned to Kendrick. "Give him one of our cell phones and write the number down for me on a piece of paper. I'll call you, Governor, when I know something." She paused. "Now, what else are we missing?"

"Sounds to me like you've got a handle on this greased watermelon," Kendrick replied sourly.

"That has to be one of the greatest overstatements of all time. I'll get the senator."

She saw bedlam in every direction around the six-story stone courthouse. Reporters and TV cameramen were two and three deep, swarming like locusts over Constitution Avenue with their equipment.

"A bunch of vultures," Taylor mumbled to Kendrick, who was sitting next to her in the back of the long black bulletproof limousine. Facing them were the senator and Wes Young. As the Secret Service driver navigated through the traffic, another car loaded with more Secret Service followed right behind.

"This is about as close as I can get," the driver said to Young.

"Okay, turn off the engine. We'll take it from here."

At moments like this Young's experience as a fullback at Penn State paid dividends. The agent reached in and pulled Boyd out of the car by the arm. He put his head down and forced a path through the crowd of screaming newspaper and television reporters, with the senator right behind him, followed by another Secret Service agent, then Kendrick and Taylor. *Thank God Sally's out of town,* Taylor thought.

"Senator Boyd," someone shouted, "do you have a statement?"

"Any statement?"

Suddenly Taylor stopped and wheeled around to face the cameras. "I'll make a statement."

They flocked to her, allowing the others to continue unmolested inside.

"I'm Taylor Ferrari, Senator Boyd's lawyer," she began in a calm voice. Just then she spotted Cooper and she nodded to him. "I want to tell you what's happening. We're in the middle of a close election. Suddenly an investigation of the senator is being launched in the name of the attorney general, who just happens to be the president's campaign manager. Now, you can all figure out what's going on." She pointed in the direction of the White House. "They can't beat us fair and square. So they're reaching into their bag of dirty tricks. This time they pulled out the ultimate dirty trick.

All I can say is, you people weren't fooled by the Watergate break-in. So don't be fooled by this latest version of gutter politics."

"Taylor . . . Taylor . . ." reporters screamed.

"Unfortunately, that's all I can say right now."

She pivoted and headed into the building, which was off-limits to the press. Inside, she caught up with the others. In the elevator, a middle-aged African-American woman in a drab blue coat gave the senator the thumbs-up sign. He smiled at her.

For the last stretch to room 208, Taylor proceeded alone with the senator. An armed U.S. marshal was standing in front of the door to preserve the secrecy of the process.

"Remember," she said to Boyd, "I'll be out here in the corridor. Anytime you want to, and I mean anytime, you can come out and talk to me. You've got a constitutional right to do that. Don't let Cady intimidate you."

"Got it."

The marshal knocked twice and the door to room 208 swung open. When Cady came out, he nodded to Taylor and introduced himself to Boyd. The two men disappeared inside.

A battered, dark brown wooden bench with peeling paint on the arms and back lined the corridor wall, but nobody sat down. Young and another agent stood on separate sides of the door to room 208, their eyes darting continually in all directions. Kendrick stood next to the window staring at the courtyard below, which was littered with cigarette butts and pigeon droppings.

Taylor paced restlessly back and forth along the corridor, her head down, dully focused on the marble floor. An awful, eerie recollection kept popping into her mind, of waiting outside a hospital room. At the end, when her mother was dying of cancer, Taylor had maintained a vigil for four straight days and nights. The last words her mother had said to her were, "You're going to make me proud of you. I know that, Maria." No amount of pleading, ordering, or cajoling by her father or brothers could make Taylor leave the hospital. At the end, the doctors tried a last-gasp surgery, while Taylor remained outside the operating room. Afterward a nurse found her in the corridor on the floor, more asleep than awake, and announced the awful news: "Your mother has passed."

"You're driving me crazy with your damn pacing," Kendrick said to Taylor after an hour. "You must have already covered ten miles. I'm going downstairs for some coffee. You want one?"

"A double. Strong and black."

But this wasn't going to end with the senator the way it had with her mother, Taylor told herself. Charles was innocent. He had told her that many times. And she believed him. Now, given the chance to question him, Cady would believe the senator, too. She was certain of that. Charles would walk out of that grand jury room a free man.

At twelve-fifteen, the door to room 208 opened. Senator Boyd's face was flushed with anger and indignation.

Taylor was horrified. "What happened?"

He pulled her into an empty room and closed the door. "The bastards are trying to frame me," he said, pounding his fist on the table.

"What do they have?"

"A phony document from a California tax office that makes it seem like the sale was a fifty-million-dollar transaction instead of ten. False testimony from Harvey Gladstone consistent with the phony document, and a forged canceled check that looks as if I paid Gladstone a commission on ten plus an additional hundred grand that he says was for keeping his mouth shut on the true purchase price. All of it corroborates the bullshit story Azziz told Cady."

Taylor collapsed into a chair. Cady was too smart to be snookered by phony evidence. "How could he let that happen?"

Then Harrison's words came back to her. Had the senator been lying to her all along?

Boyd started moving toward the door. "What are you going to do?"

"Stand out on Constitution Avenue and tell the American people the truth. The short version. Then tomorrow morning we'll have a press conference and turn the tables on Webster and McDermott."

"Let's do it."

With his entourage, he marched down the stairs and out of the building. In front of the microphones, Boyd announced, "Someone is trying to pull off the worst dirty trick in the history of this country. I'm innocent, and I intend to fight back," he vowed. "We'll have a press conference at ten tomorrow morning. I intend to launch my own investigation of the people who played this dirty trick. I promise you that I'll smoke out the people responsible if it's the last thing I do."

The senator refused to take any questions. When they were back in the limo and proceeding along Constitution Avenue, Boyd looked at Taylor and Kendrick. "Listen, you two, I'm going out to St. Michaels. I want to be by myself right now. I have to work on a statement to deliver tomorrow. It's got to be personal in order to succeed. I hope you don't mind if I do it that way."

Taylor did mind. She and Kendrick had a lot to offer. "We could come out and not be in the way."

"Look here, e-mail me your thoughts. You and Bob can be more helpful in Washington getting everything set for the press conference and keeping the wolves at bay. I'll try to e-mail you a draft this evening. In any event, I'll meet both of you at my Georgetown house at eight in the morning. We'll take it from there. I intend to fight this all the way."

She saw no point arguing with him. She had learned long ago that when the senator wanted to do something his own way, that was how he did it. She had to respect his judgment. It was his reputation and political life on the line. Not hers.

She might as well go back to the privacy of her apartment, rough out her thoughts, then e-mail them to the senator in St. Michaels. Together they would come out firing.

Kendrick saw the determination gathering on her face, but he was not impressed. "In this situation, you're guilty until you prove your innocence. And you're going to have a hell of a time doing that."

Chapter 17

In a cold fury, Sato hit the power button on the remote control to turn off the television set in his office. The intensity with which Senator Boyd had delivered his statement was etched on his mind. This wasn't at all how events should be unfolding. Boyd should be on the ropes. He should be withdrawing from the campaign. What Sato saw was a man who was getting ready for a fight.

Sato picked up the phone and called the man he had dubbed R.L. "Not a good day for us, was it?"

"I'm surprised, but it's false bravado on his part. He won't be able to fight the evidence Cady has. It'll take a little longer, but I think we'll get what we want."

Sato's grip on the phone hardened. "That's not good enough for me. There's too much at stake to take a chance."

"It's the only thing we can do."

Sato gave a short, chilling laugh. "You're not as creative, my friend, as I had been led to believe."

The American understood what Sato meant instantly, and he was appalled. "I don't think anything like that is called for."

"That's my decision, not yours," Sato said, his mouth grim. "I'll talk to Terasawa and have him call you. He'll need certain logistical information and assistance from you. That's all. Unlike you, he is very creative."

The American wanted to protest. This wasn't what he had bought into. But he was in too deep for that. His involvement thus far was already a felony. Sato could leak that to the press or a prosecutor. Also, he now understood the consequences if he crossed Sato. The man was very capable of turning Terasawa loose on him.

At Oxford on the eastern shore of the Chesapeake Bay, Terasawa walked into Martha's Marina and followed the script R.L. had given him. "I'm the Chinese tourist who's here to rent the boat."

As Terasawa had been promised, all of the arrangements had been made by R.L. by phone. A thirty-five-foot sailing boat was waiting for him on the dock. That was all he needed to cross the inlet to St. Michaels.

The air was cool and dry. Terasawa was glad he had worn a black leather jacket. A brisk tail wind was blowing, which made the trip even faster than Terasawa had gauged from looking at the charts.

Alone in the sailboat, he pulled out a pair of powerful binoculars at the halfway point. By sailing up and down the inlet like a tourist, he could see Boyd's house from all angles and get a clear fix on security. Outside in the front he spied two Secret Service agents. One was sitting in the black limo behind the wheel. The other was standing next to the car. The two of them were locked in a serious conversation. Terasawa couldn't see anyone in back of the house.

He eased the boat into the dock behind Boyd's house at a ninety-degree angle to minimize the chances that either of the Secret Service agents would see it. He pulled in care-

fully, not wanting to strike the dock and have the sound alert
the agents.

Once Terasawa had the boat tied up, he raced up to the
back door on the toes of his Nike sneakers. He had one hand
on a small burglar's tool in his jacket pocket. Before pulling
it out he turned the doorknob. The door opened.

He tiptoed across the kitchen floor. "Where are you, Senator Boyd?" he whispered.

Upstairs, Boyd ripped off his clothes and tossed them
on the floor of his bathroom. He'd always found that a
good place to think was in the tub. Thinking was what he
had to do: about the kind of statement he should make tomorrow, and about what steps he should take to launch his
investigation into who was responsible for all of this. He
turned on the water and adjusted the temperature in the
Jacuzzi tub.

With his body aching from tension, he looked in the med-
icine closet for Epsom salts to add to the water. The jar was
gone. *That damn Sally,* he cursed to himself. *She takes
things and never returns them.* He turned off the water and,
naked, charged down the hall to her bathroom.

Staying away from the windows with a front exposure,
Terasawa was moving slowly and methodically through the
downstairs, which seemed deserted, when he heard the
water begin running overhead. *Has to be a bathtub,* he decided. *Good, Boyd will be in the tub. That's perfect. I'll give
him a few minutes to get settled in there.*

He walked into the den and saw a television playing on
mute, and a powered-up laptop with a long list of e-mail
messages on the screen. His gaze idly scrolled through the
list on the screen while he waited.

Time to move, he decided finally. He started up the wooden stairs on the toes of his sneakers. A loose board creaked, and Terasawa cursed silently.

Suddenly the water stopped. Terasawa watched the bathroom door open; then Boyd, naked, walked along the corridor in the direction of the stairs. Yanking the .38 caliber revolver from his jacket pocket, Terasawa gripped the gun hard. Terasawa pushed himself against the banister, holding his breath, hoping Boyd wouldn't see him. Terasawa didn't want to kill him when Boyd had so much freedom to move.

As he passed the top of the staircase, Boyd was muttering something that Terasawa couldn't hear. The senator never looked down the stairs. Not then. Not when he returned to his bathroom a few minutes later with a jar in his hand. He shut the door and began running the water again.

Terasawa put the gun back in his jacket pocket. He'd give Boyd five minutes to get comfortable in the tub, he decided, glancing at his watch. Softly he climbed the rest of the stairs with the gun in his hand. He turned into a recessed doorway where he couldn't be seen.

When the time was up, Terasawa extracted a pair of surgical gloves from his jacket pocket and put them on. He removed the revolver and wiped the handle clean with the cloth from his jacket. Then he screwed on the silencer.

Turning the doorknob carefully, he slipped into the room and closed the door behind him. As he crossed the room, the view through the open bathroom door became wider and wider. Senator Boyd was sitting in a huge Jacuzzi with the jets running and his eyes closed. *Perfect,* Terasawa thought. The motor in the tub made so much noise that no one outside would hear a thing. Noiselessly he glided into the bathroom.

Sensing the presence of an intruder, Boyd opened his

eyes with a start. Seeing a strange Japanese man, he recoiled in fear. "Hey . . . what—"

Instinctively Boyd reached for the metal loop along the side of the tub in order to pull himself to his feet, but he never had time. Ramming the gun against Boyd's temple, Terasawa pulled the trigger. Skull fragments and tissue were blasted against the pale blue tile wall. It was precisely the single-shot kill Terasawa had wanted. Boyd was right-handed, so the assassin rubbed the gun against that hand, which was hanging over the edge of the tub, then let it fall to the floor.

Not disturbing anything, Terasawa retraced his steps downstairs. In the den with the gloves still on, he stood in front of the laptop and composed a message.

Please forgive me, Sally, but I can't live with the humiliation of what happened. Love, Charles.

Rather than printing it, Terasawa simply left the message on the screen. Then he departed as silently as he came.

Chapter 18

Don't count us out, Taylor vowed as she fixed a glass of Finlandia on the rocks and took it out on the balcony of her Watergate apartment. She was feeling feisty. *There's plenty of time to expose the perpetrators of this big lie. When we do, the senator will gain sympathy from the public that will enhance his lead.*

She watched boats moving up and down the Potomac as the sun began setting over Washington. The drink tasted good. Maybe she'd have one more before she fixed some pasta for dinner and called the senator to see how his statement was coming. Inside the apartment she checked her watch. Two minutes until the first network news. She turned on the television to hear how the story was being presented to the American people.

The first image she saw was Senator Boyd's house on Chesapeake Bay. She heard the words *St. Michaels* and *Maryland* and then "A Secret Service agent discovered the senator's body when he came into the house about an hour ago."

"What?" she cried out. "What the hell?"

As she turned up the volume, she listened in stunned disbelief. Once she heard the words *apparent suicide,* she couldn't listen any longer. She hit the power button. She took her glass and the bottle of Finlandia out on the balcony. Something was terribly wrong here. Charles would never commit suicide.

In a blank daze, she continued drinking until she finished the bottle of vodka. Finally, trembling from the cold, she decided to go inside. That was easier said than done. Unaccustomed to consuming so much alcohol, she couldn't control her movements. She staggered around the balcony. Objects jumped in and out of focus. She knocked the bottle onto the concrete floor, where it shattered into hundreds of pieces. Too drunk to make her way around the broken glass, she cut her feet in half a dozen places.

Coming inside, she stumbled into the kitchen, then bandaged her feet crudely with paper towels ripped from the roll and collapsed on the living room sofa. She was close to dropping off into a drunken sleep, but she still couldn't forget about what she had heard. Maybe it was all a mistake.

She grabbed the remote control, turning on the television again. She saw a sad reporter, a microphone in his hand. "Maryland officials have confirmed that the cause of Senator Charles Boyd's death was suicide. There is considerable speculation as to whether the senator was in fact guilty of some crime, which is the subject of the grand jury investigation. That may have caused him to take his own life."

"No!" Taylor screamed. "No! He didn't do it!"

She began pounding her fists against the sides of her head. Harder and harder she punched until she thought her head would explode. Somewhere she heard a bell, a doorbell ringing. A man's voice shouted, "Open up, Taylor. Open up right now."

It's Charles, she thought. *He's alive. He's come back to Washington.*

She hurried to the door, staining the Oriental carpet with

bloody footprints on the way. After fumbling with the lock, she managed to open the door. "Oh, Charles," she yelled, and threw herself into his arms.

But it wasn't Charles. It was Coop.

Again the fists. This time she began pounding them against Coop's chest, wanting to punish him because he wasn't Charles.

She began to cry. For the longest time she cried and she cried. Suddenly she pulled away from him. On instinct she ran to the bathroom, where she threw up in the toilet, over and over again in an anguished retching, until there was nothing left but a dry gasp. Then Cooper took her back to the bed, and she passed out.

At one-thirty in the morning she woke up. Except for shadows on one wall from the moon outside, the room was dark. Cooper turned on a night-table lamp. He had been sitting in a chair watching her.

"He's dead, isn't he?" she asked.

Cooper nodded. "Wes Young found him."

She was silent.

"You cared for him a great deal, didn't you?"

She nodded her head. "He was a good man."

"It's over, Taylor," he said flatly.

"What happened?"

"He took a gun with him, went into the bathtub, filled it up with water, and fired a single shot into his head."

"That can't be right," she shouted, bolting into a sitting position. "He didn't kill himself. He never would have done that."

"He left a note for Sally on the computer screen."

The oddness of this fact stopped her for a moment. "Say that again."

"His wife, Sally. He left her a note on the computer

screen asking her to forgive him. Saying 'Love, Charles.' She released it to the media."

Taylor waved her hands, shaking her head. "That proves it. He didn't kill himself. He couldn't stand her. He'd never leave her a note like that."

Cooper gave her a narrow look. "What are you telling me?"

"They killed him. The phony trumped-up charges didn't do the job. *They* realized from his statement that he would never quit. So *they* killed him."

"Who's *they*?" a skeptical Cooper asked.

"The same people who put together this bogus case."

He looked at her sympathetically. "We'd better both get some sleep. I'll go in the other room."

"You don't believe me, do you?"

"Truthfully, no."

"They killed him, Coop, " she mumbled into the pillow, crying herself back to sleep.

In the cold light of morning, nothing made sense.

She found Cooper in the kitchen, sitting at the small butcher-block table with his back to her, eating a bowl of cereal and reading the morning *Washington Post*. When he heard her approach, he stood up and turned around.

"Have you thought about what I said?" she asked him.

"To tell you the truth, you weren't making an awful lot of sense. There's nothing mysterious here. Senator Boyd violated the law. He lied to you, and he took his own life. End of story."

Taylor looked exasperated. "He's innocent. There's some type of conspiracy at work here. Don't you see that?"

She could tell he didn't believe her.

"And just who is this group of conspirators?" he asked.

"I don't know."

"And what's their reason for wanting Boyd out of the race and Webster back in the White House?"

"I don't know that either."

"Oh, great. Then what makes you so sure this conspiracy exists?"

"I know the senator. There's no other explanation."

Cooper frowned.

"They can't get away with this," Taylor continued emphatically. "Dammit, Coop, nobody has the right to destroy a man's life, to manipulate our election process, and then do God only knows what in the next four years."

"You don't even sound rational." Taking her hand in both of his, Cooper said, "To hell with Charles Boyd. I'm concerned about you. I think that you should worry about yourself for a change."

"He was winning," she insisted. "The senator would have made an excellent president. He was a leader in the Senate. Everybody respected him. He could get things done. He had so many good ideas for the country."

Cooper tossed the newspaper across the table. "The top medical people in the state of Maryland and at the FBI dropped everything yesterday and went out to his house in St. Michaels. They all agree that Boyd shot himself. They haven't found any other fingerprints in the house. No evidence at all to support your theory. They're convinced it's a suicide."

"C'mon, Coop. They're just saying that to alleviate public anxiety and because that bastard McDermott made it clear he wants the whole thing wrapped up in a hurry."

"You've got no basis for thinking that."

"I know what Charles told me Saturday at St. Michaels about the Mill Valley transaction. He's innocent."

He looked at her with empathy. "I wish I could agree with you. Really, I do. But I don't see a single shred of evidence to support your belief that he was killed as part of a conspiracy." Cooper was losing the little patience he possessed. "Give me hard information to go on. Not your supposition. Anything."

She thought about his request. In a flash something came to her. "The senator hated the idea of guns in a house. He led the legislative effort on the issue. He repeatedly told me he'd never have one. He criticized me for keeping one in my place in Aspen for protection in the woods. If he killed himself like you're saying, that gun had to be in his house, because the Secret Service limo took him directly to St. Michaels from the courthouse, but it couldn't be. He'd never have had a gun in the house." She rolled her hands into tight fists for emphasis. "Now I know I'm right. And you do, too, because you know what his position was on the issue of gun control."

Cooper shook his head in disbelief. "People often say one thing and do another. Politicians are the worst offenders. I don't have to tell you that."

Frustrated that Cooper didn't believe her, Taylor went for a run in Rock Creek Park. As she tore along the jogging path at a faster speed than normal, she kept replaying in her mind all of the facts Cooper had told her. By the time she got back to her Watergate apartment, soaked with perspiration and breathing hard, she was even more convinced that the senator had been murdered. She wasn't as sure, though, how she would go about proving it.

At home, she had nothing to do. With Charles dead, the campaign was over. She decided to go down to the office at the law firm and catch up on all of her work. It would be better to keep busy, not dwell on the awful death. A memorial service was scheduled for the senator tomorrow. Then maybe she'd be able to start coming to terms with it.

A few minutes after she arrived at her office, Harrison wandered in. "I came to see how you were doing," he said in a kind voice.

"Thanks, Philip. This isn't my best day of all time."

"Well, for what it's worth, I'm very sorry. I know how you feel."

No one ever knows how you feel, she thought. "Thanks for all your help in connection with the investigation and through the long campaign. Particularly your advice in dealing with Cady." She gave a weary sigh. "The surgery was performed professionally, but we lost the patient."

He shrugged. "You can't possibly blame yourself for anything that happened. Boyd never told you the truth about the Napa winery sale. He was guilty on the election-law violation. There's no way you could have pulled a rabbit out of that hat. And as for his suicide—"

Eyes wide open, she stared at him. "It wasn't suicide!"

Harrison pulled back in surprise. "What are you telling me?"

"Somebody shot him and made it look like he did it himself."

Harrison took a plastic cigarette out of his pocket and shoved it into his mouth. "You can't be serious."

"I've never been more serious in my life. There's some type of conspiracy at work."

Harrison shook his head in disbelief. "You've been under tremendous pressure lately. You're imagining things. You have to let it go."

The respect she had for Harrison made her pause for an instant, but that was all. She knew she was right. "Let's think like lawyers," she said, motioning for him to sit down. "Let me lay out the facts in my case."

He moved to the chair she indicated and carefully took a seat. "Okay. Go ahead."

"Fact number one: He hated guns. He would never have had one in his house. He was one of the strongest advocates for gun control both in the House and the—"

"There are plenty of hypocrites on that issue."

She frowned, though she knew he was right. "Fact number two: He went out to St. Michaels to write a speech establishing his innocence. He told me and Kendrick before he left for St. Michaels that he would fight this all the way. His words."

He considered that idea, weighing it for a moment. "Not persuasive. The guilty always say that in the beginning."

"Fact number three: He would never have left a note like that for Sally. He couldn't stand the woman."

Harrison gazed at her keenly. "How do you know so much about their marriage? You weren't having an affair with him, were you?"

Her face reddened. She resented the suggestion, even when it came from Harrison. "No," she said emphatically. "Not ever."

"Good. Then you have to agree with me that nobody knows what goes on in someone else's marriage."

"That may be true, but I knew the senator," she said. "We spent a lot of time together."

He nodded. "That's really what this is all about," he said in a fatherly way. "You admired and respected the man. You don't want to admit that he wasn't what you thought he was."

She stared hard at Harrison. She couldn't believe he was saying that. "That's not what this is about at all. He was innocent. There's some type of conspiracy at work here. I know it."

At the idea of a conspiracy, Harrison smiled sympathetically. "Can I make a small suggestion?"

"What?"

"I think you're tired—"

She slammed her fists on the desktop, ready to pounce on him. "No, I'm not."

"Listen to me, please. I'm your friend. At least let me finish."

She nodded.

"You've had a terrible shock. A man you put a lot of your faith in is dead. My advice is go away for a while. Down to the Caribbean, or maybe the South of Spain or the Greek isles. Someplace far from here. Take about a month off and travel. Forget about Washington totally." He held up a hand to stop her protests. "I'll make sure the management committee understands. I'll cover all of your cases and clients at the firm. I'll get a good litigator to argue the case in the Mississippi supreme court. I'll keep Fujimura happy on the new acquisition."

Taylor appreciated the sacrifices he was willing to make for her. "Thanks, Philip. You're nice to offer that. I really appreciate it. You're a good friend." Her face grew hard again. "But I'm not leaving town. Not until I know what really happened to Charles. I owe him that much."

Harrison frowned. "You're being unfair to yourself. The best thing would be for you to get far away from Washington for a long vacation."

"And besides, I want to help Crane defeat Webster in the election."

Harrison took the cigarette out of his mouth and fiddled

with it, while shaking his head in exasperation. "Now I know you're not thinking clearly."

"What's that supposed to mean?"

"It's not even certain Crane will be at the top of the Democratic ticket. From what I hear, there's total chaos in the party, not only about whom the presidential candidate will be, but the process for picking him. Brill's arguing that since he got the second-highest vote tally at the convention, he should be the candidate. It could take days for them to sort it out."

"Well, when they do, I want to help the candidate."

"That doesn't make any sense. You can be sure that whomever the Democrats pick, you'll be *persona non grata* with the candidate and his campaign staff. They'll want to distance themselves as much as possible from the image of Senator Boyd, and your very presence would bring Boyd front and center. So I would forget about any more political work for a long time if I were you."

Harrison's words rocked her back on her heels. She refused to believe what he was telling her. "But suppose there is some type of conspiracy at work here, and suppose the senator was murdered as part of it?"

"Enough with the conspiracy." His voice was firm. "Let go of this illusion before you wreck your own life."

"I'll never let go of it."

Harvey Gladstone was anxious to get home.

As his weary legs carried him up four flights of stairs and across the parking garage at the San Francisco airport, he was looking forward to the three-hour ride home by himself. It would be a chance to unwind and distance himself from the nightmare that had taken over his life. Climbing into his red Ford Taurus, Gladstone thought about his grandson in a

Los Angeles hospital. For the first time in weeks he felt optimistic. When he had called from Dulles to tell Louise that he would be arriving at San Fran at five this afternoon, she had been ecstatic. The doctor had called from L.A. to say there was a good chance that a heart might be available for Carl. As far as Senator Boyd was concerned, Gladstone felt some sadness, but he had done what he had to do. He had no reason to feel remorse. With the senator dead, he wouldn't have to testify anymore.

Crossing the Golden Gate Bridge as a blanket of fog rolled in over the bay, Gladstone told himself, "Forget about everything that happened with Senator Boyd. It's over."

Half a mile behind Gladstone's red Taurus, Terasawa drove a bulky black Lincoln Navigator. There was no need to follow any closer. After he had confronted Gladstone when he was fishing on Saturday, Terasawa had installed a homing device under the rear bumper of the Taurus. This evening he had picked up Gladstone's trail the instant the car moved toward the exit at the airport. Now that they were crossing the Golden Gate Bridge, Terasawa had another reason to relax. He knew exactly where Gladstone was going. He had already been there once.

An hour later the two cars were traversing the floor of the Napa Valley. Terasawa still kept his distance. There was no need to do anything that would alert Gladstone to his presence. He had a plan. He knew exactly what he wanted to do.

As Gladstone turned west, climbing into the mountains, a light drizzle began to fall. Exhausted and afraid of falling asleep, he opened the window halfway on the driver's side, letting a blast of cold air hit him in the face. The radio was playing country-western music, a ballad about unrequited love. He turned up the volume.

The rain began to make the road slick. Gladstone knew this mountain road like the back of his hand. He also knew how hazardous it could be, even in daylight. The road was full of turns.

Gladstone hunched over the wheel and strained his eyes to see. The fog thickened. He clicked on the lights. *Take it slow and easy,* he told himself.

From nowhere, a large, dark object suddenly appeared along the road in the trees on the right. *What the hell's that?*

A second later the object darted across the road. It was a deer with large antlers. Gladstone slammed on the brakes. His car skidded to the left, crossing the center of the road and crashing against the soft dirt of the hill on the other side.

He didn't think he'd done any serious damage, just dents and some scrapes, so he straightened his car out and continued the upward climb on the winding road. "Goddamn deer," he muttered. "There are too many of them. The state should give the hunters more time."

Gladstone became aware of a car coming up from behind. Nearer and nearer the vehicle approached, until it was sitting on Gladstone's bumper. *The bastard's following too closely,* Gladstone thought. He hated it when another driver tailgated. If the road weren't so narrow and winding, he would have pulled over and signaled the other driver to pass.

He honked the horn and held his hand up above the roof, waving to the rear, hoping the other driver would get the hint. In defiance, the asshole honked back and kept getting closer. *What the hell is this?* Gladstone thought. *Some nut must be trying to play a stupid, dangerous game.*

Nervous, Gladstone kept glancing in the rearview mirror. The car behind turned on its high beams, sending a blinding light into his rearview mirror. *My God, what's he trying to do?*

Gladstone was hugging the edge of the road. A quick glance to the right confirmed what he knew: There was a long, sheer drop into the void below. *What kind of idiot does something like this?*

In terror, Gladstone gripped the steering wheel and pushed everything else from his mind. All that counted right now was that he was alone on this mountain with some lunatic. There were no other cars, no one who could help him. He had a hunting rifle in his house. Once he got home he'd be okay.

It was dangerous on the slippery road, but Gladstone increased his speed, hoping to outrun the jerk. The other vehicle kept gaining. Even worse, it was one of those big monster SUV's.

Then he felt a bump as the SUV struck the rear fender of the Taurus. He was on the verge of panic.

The car's lights shifted to the left, as if the idiot intended to pass.

Let him go, Gladstone decided. It was the only way.

Gladstone edged his car over as close to the precipice as he could.

The driver of the SUV took aim with his car, hit the accelerator, and rammed the Taurus from the side.

The angle was perfect for what Terasawa wanted to do. His Navigator bashed Gladstone's much smaller car off the road and sent it hurling down the hill, flipping over and over as it rolled.

Terasawa braked his own car on the edge of the road and made a 180-degree turn, facing back toward San Francisco. Before he began driving, he kept his eyes riveted on the steep hill and Gladstone's car. There was a stream at the bottom of the ravine and lots of rocks. Gladstone's car hit a large boulder. It burst into flames and exploded. Then the assassin drove away.

"Terasawa successfully completed his assignment," R.L. said to Sato on the phone. "He can fly back to Tokyo from San Francisco."

He had expected to hear relief and appreciation from Sato. Instead Sato said, "What about the girl?"

"Taylor?"

"Yeah. I don't think she'll quit."

"You don't have to worry. I have a plan to get her out of circulation until after the election. At that point nobody will care what happened to Boyd."

"What if your plan doesn't work?"

"It will. I can assure you of that."

There was a long pause. Finally Sato said, "Your assurances about Boyd dropping out of the presidential race were worthless. I have too much at stake not to have a backup plan. Have Terasawa fly to Washington."

"I don't think—"

Sato was getting angry. The man didn't realize who was in control. "I don't care what you think. If your plan doesn't work, I want Terasawa to be in Washington. He'll know what to do about Taylor."

Chapter 19

There was nothing relaxing about Taylor's morning run. She couldn't stop thinking about the senator's death. She knew that it hadn't been suicide. That meant someone had killed him.

That conclusion sent shivers up and down her spine. Her eyes kept darting from side to side, looking for an assailant hiding in the bushes. Twice she thought she spotted someone, and she increased to a sprint, only to realize she was being paranoid. The perspiration that soaked her jogging suit was due in part to physical exertion, in part to nerves. *I'm being stupid,* she told herself. Even if someone killed the senator, there was no reason for them to attack her.

The doorman in front of the Watergate apartment building stopped Taylor as she slowed to a walk, gasping for breath. "A courier just brought a package for you. They have it at the reception desk."

As she looked at the words typed on the upper left corner of the brown envelope—*New York Times, Tokyo Bureau*—her heart skipped a beat. She waited until she was back in her apartment to rip it open. Inside was a typed note from Don Berry clipped to a white business-size envelope. Perspiration was dripping from her face onto the note as she read it:

I found the envelope in Alex's center desk drawer.
We still have not received any further information
from the Tokyo police about Alex's death.

Pulling off the note, she saw that the envelope had her name on the front. The unmistakable scrawl she recognized as Alex's.

She sat down and opened the envelope with care. What she saw was a handwritten note on Alex's stationery. The lines were uneven and words ran into each other. Her guess, as she struggled to comprehend the letter, was that Alex had been drinking when he wrote it, which didn't surprise her. He told her that long dinners with lots of sake were a great way to get information from Japanese men.

She began reading:

Dear Taylor:
I am taking the precaution of writing this note
because I have learned some incredible things this
evening. Now I have a premonition that because of
what I know, I may never make it out of Japan to
complete my investigation.
As I continued to do research about Yahiro Sato
after my recent series, I learned something startling,
which I haven't written in an article because I
needed confirmation and I wanted to understand it
better. What I learned is that Sato has taken an
enormous interest in the American presidential
election. He established, early last summer, a huge
fact-gathering team to assemble information about
all the candidates: Webster, Boyd, Brill, and Crane.
Not merely their statements about Asia and Japan,
but everything about their lives.

I recognize that important foreign leaders follow American elections to a considerable extent, but Sato's attention seemed excessive. So I kept digging. I reached a breakthrough a few days ago when I was studying the tape from a recent television interview of Sato. In it he expressed the opinion, without any doubt, that the man in the White House after January twentieth will support his program to rearm Japan. Knowing where Senator Boyd stands on this issue, I suspected that Sato was somehow involved in manipulating the American election. I have learned that he made a twenty-four-hour trip to Buenos Aires on August 28, after Boyd was nominated. He stayed at the Alvear Palace. My guess is that he went there to meet an American and enlist that person's help in somehow eliminating Senator Boyd from the campaign. That would be consistent with Sato's style.

To confirm all of this, which involved a great deal of speculation on my part, I had dinner this evening with General Toshio Ozawa, who is close with Sato. After far too much to drink, Ozawa confirmed my suspicion that Sato has some scheme for ensuring that Senator Boyd will not be the next president. Ozawa didn't tell me whom Sato met with in Buenos Aires, although he said it was an American man who flew down to Buenos Aires from Washington for the August 28 meeting. He may not know the man's name himself. Nice, isn't it?

She was astounded by what she was reading. What American could be mixed up with Sato in this way? It didn't make sense. She continued reading:

Anyhow, my plan is to fly to Buenos Aires tomorrow, do some digging, and learn the name of the American, hopefully from records at the Alvear Palace.

Now it's very late, and I'm very tired. That's all I can remember of our conversation.

As I write this, I hope to God that you never read it. That I can lay it all out in an article in the Times, *which I intend to write in Argentina as soon as I have the name of the American. I'm close, but not quite there. If you do read this, it means something happened to me. You'll know what to do with this information.*

Beyond Sato and all of this shit, I want you to know I really did love you. For me, it wasn't just a fling. You're the best, Taylor. Take care of yourself and find happiness. Alex.

The letter dropped out of Taylor's hands and onto the floor. Tears welled up in her eyes as she remembered the evening she had been on the back of that motorcycle with him. She had been pleasantly high from the Kirin they had drunk with wonderful sushi at a dive Alex had found in an out-of-the-way neighborhood. She was clutching him around the waist as they roared across nearly deserted Tokyo streets in the wee hours of the morning.

Sato was responsible for his death. She was certain of it.

She put the letter in a drawer of her desk, burying it under some papers. She had to figure out what this all meant. An image of C. J. Cady popped into her head. She should talk to him. Even if he'd been on the wrong side, he'd be willing to help her now.

*   *   *

Taylor fell in step with the crowd, walking into the dimly lit National Cathedral, built on the highest point in the District of Columbia. The massive gothic structure, laid out in the form of a cross, had been designed to match the great cathedrals of the Old World, with its pointed arches and vaulted ceiling shooting up toward the heavens.

Dressed in somber black suits and dresses, Senator Boyd's colleagues from Congress, influential political leaders, campaign workers, staff from his Senate office, family, and Washington friends were in attendance. Scores of people, his oldest friends, had flown in from Napa Valley. Outside, hundreds of D.C. police manned the barricades to keep out the press, photographers, and gawkers.

As Taylor sat down, the organ was playing "Amazing Grace," which Sally had said was her husband's favorite. To Taylor it grated like chalk on a blackboard. The senator had told her several times how much he hated that song.

Taylor wasn't surprised that Sally had decided on a memorial service at the prestigious cathedral, to be followed by a private burial for family at Arlington National Cemetery. As a much-decorated air force pilot in Vietnam, the senator was entitled to that, regardless of the ignominy of his end.

Before the start of the ceremony, Taylor joined other mourners filing by the closed coffin. Most walked with heads bowed in respect. Very few were crying. Boyd had been an ambitious man, and in his drive toward the world's highest office, he had touched their lives, helped advance their careers, and expanded their horizons, but there were few whom he befriended. Like so many of his congressional colleagues passing by that coffin, Taylor thought, for Boyd friendship was a commodity for which there was little time in the long days consumed by the Washington power game and the demands of public office. Friendship existed only outside of the beltway.

Glints of sunlight shone through the ornate stained-glass windows, ricocheting off the rich carvings on the gray stone walls. Looking for Sally, Taylor found her standing in the front row flanked on each side by her sons. The face behind the black veil was expressionless. Both young men were weeping softly. There were no tears on Sally's face. Taylor didn't know what to say to her.

"I'm sorry, Sally. So sorry," she blurted out.

When Sally didn't respond, didn't even acknowledge her presence, Taylor moved on. Against the wall, under a stained-glass window, Taylor saw Governor Crane standing alone, looking exhausted and deep in thought. According to morning news accounts, the Democratic National Committee had struggled through a rancorous twelve-hour marathon session, in which Brill supporters mounted a major effort to seize the nomination. Finally, at about six-thirty in the morning, amid the internecine warfare, the committee had made a decision. The Democratic ticket would be Crane for president and Dale Carlton, the governor of Texas, for vice president. This result generated very little initial public enthusiasm. NBC telephone polls concluded that Crane would win twenty percent of the votes, carrying only the District of Columbia, Massachusetts, and perhaps the candidates' home states of Pennsylvania and Texas.

Wes Young was standing ten feet away, with the ubiquitous earphone of his trade in clear view along with the protruding outline of the revolver in his shoulder holster. He nodded to Taylor.

The bishop began speaking: "Dearly assembled, we have come to pay our last respects to Charles Boyd, who for much of his life was a plowman, laboring literally in the vineyards of the Lord—"

Three rows in front of Taylor, someone's cell phone rang.

The bishop stopped midsentence as myriad irate people looked in that direction. Hurriedly the self-important power broker turned it off.

The eulogy resumed. "While many of us came to know Charles in Washington, it was his work in the lush green fields of Napa Valley that Charles, the plowman, best loved. He . . ."

Taylor didn't need to listen. She had her own memories of "Charles the plowman," the debonair figure who had approached her in a dusty parking lot in Napa, taken her to lunch, and given her a tour of his vineyards that magnificent spring day so long ago. She could recall every detail of that day as if it were yesterday. She was sitting next to him in the front of his red Lamborghini. The top was down. The wind was whipping through her hair.

As she remembered, tears rolled freely down her cheeks. Kendrick reached into his pocket and handed her a handkerchief, which she clutched tightly, closing her eyes while her whole body shook with grief.

"Charles left a comfortable business in order to perform public service," the bishop said. "When we judge a man's life, we must judge all of the days of his life. When we look at Charles Boyd, we see the enormous good he has done for this country and for the world. That's what we must remember.

"All of us are flesh and blood. All created in the image of the Lord. No man, beginning with Adam, has ever been perfect. Perfection belongs only to our Lord."

Implicit in the bishop's words, Taylor realized, was the

implication that the senator had committed a crime, and that was why he had killed himself.

She wanted to stand up and scream, "He was innocent. He didn't do anything wrong." But she kept her seat.

After the ceremony, Taylor went back to the law firm. She had to see Harrison. She had to convince him that she was right that the senator had been murdered as a part of a conspiracy. She'd tell him about Alex's letter. Once she got Harrison on board, he would help her develop a plan for proving it. He was so smart and well connected. He always had ideas for everything. She just had to persuade him to work with her.

She was surprised to find Harrison's suite at the law firm deserted. Not only was his office empty, but Doris wasn't at her desk.

Taylor got the eighth-floor receptionist on the phone. "Where's Philip Harrison?"

"He left this morning on a business trip. I'm sure Doris knows where he went, but he didn't tell us. About all I know is that he was going out of the country. I imagine he's on an airplane right now."

"Doris isn't here either."

"Oh, yeah, I forgot. She took the rest of the day off."

Feeling alone, uncertain what to do, Taylor stumbled in a fog back to her own office. The whole world came sharply into focus with a start when she saw two policemen in dark gray uniforms standing next to the desk of her secretary, who had a contentious look on her face.

"What's going on, Kathy?" Taylor asked.

"These two state troopers from Mississippi said they had to talk to you right away, but I wouldn't bother you at home. You're entitled to a day of mourning. I told them I didn't know when you'd be in. They could just come back tomorrow. If they didn't like that, they could go pound sand."

"Thanks, Kathy. But I think I can deal with them. It can't be any worse than everything else that's happened today."

Taylor turned to the two state troopers, who were holding their bubble-top hats in their hands, fiddling nervously with them. "You two looking for me?"

"Yes, ma'am," a heavyset man in his mid-twenties with a cherubic face and carrot-red hair answered in a Southern accent. "If you're Taylor Ferrari."

She nodded.

His tall, thin partner, intense-looking with bushy brown eyebrows, produced a Mississippi State Police ID with his picture. The heavyset trooper followed suit.

"We'd better go into my office to talk," said Taylor. Kicking the door shut, she directed them to chairs in front of her desk. "What can I help you gentlemen with?"

The heavyset one was the spokesman. "Well, we're sure sorry to bother you right now, but we've got a serious matter that couldn't wait."

His tone sounded ominous, putting Taylor on her guard. "You've got my attention, Sergeant Billings."

"Were you in the town of Hattiesburg, Mississippi, on May twelfth of this year?"

"I was in Hattiesburg at about that time." Taylor was trying to remember the exact dates of the trial in the power case. She was tired. Her mind refused to give her more than early May for the trip to Mississippi, and the fact that it had been very hot. She picked up the calendar on her desk and flipped back to May. "I was there from the fifth to the fourteenth of May."

"Miss Ferrari," Sergeant Billings said politely, "I've got a warrant here for your arrest."

Taylor leaned forward in her chair. "You've got what?"

"I'm sorry, Miss Ferrari—really, I am—but the sheriff of Forrest County has sworn out a warrant for your arrest. Gus here 'n' me were sent on up to serve it on you and to bring you back."

"And what in God's name does the sheriff of Forrest County think I did?"

"Hit and run." Billings looked down at the document he was holding. In a somber voice he began reading: "'At about ten o'clock P.M. on the night of May twelfth, Taylor Ferrari was driving a blue Toyota Camry that struck and killed a ten-year-old girl named Sue Ellen Westin.'"

Taylor's mouth opened in dismay. "Is this somebody's idea of a stupid prank?"

"No, ma'am. I'm awfully sorry."

Her eyes moved from one of the troopers to the other. They were squirming in their chairs.

"Give me that warrant. I want to see your IDs again." Taylor examined the documents carefully. They all seemed genuine. The warrant cited a blue Toyota Camry, which was what she had rented for the trial. But she had never driven at night. She was positive of that fact. She had worked every single night in her bed-and-breakfast. Besides, she was reluctant to drive at night in a part of the country that was foreign to her, particularly because emotions in the community were running high on the issue of expanding the power plant.

There had to be some mistake. Her blue Toyota had been confused with another car of that type. She studied the Mississippi license plate number shown on the warrant—ZKA 372. That had to be the answer. Someone had mistaken another blue Toyota with the license plate ZKA 372 with the car she had rented. She knew how she could easily establish her innocence.

She buzzed Kathy. "Please bring all of my expense reports from the Mississippi trip in May, and the backup, particularly the car rental agreement with Hertz."

"These things sometimes happen," Sergeant Billings said. "The country roads are dark at night. Kids walk on the edge of the highway. People don't realize when they've hit something."

"I never drove at night when I was in Mississippi," she replied emphatically. "I have no idea what you're talking about."

He didn't respond. A heavy silence settled over the room until Kathy entered minutes later with Taylor's expense reports. A copy of the Hertz agreement was flagged with a yellow sticker.

As she fumbled through the file to reach the car-rental agreement, Taylor's palms were damp with perspiration. Sure enough, the dates coincided. She had rented the car on May fifth and returned it on the fourteenth. Her eyes jumped to the license plate number on the upper left of the document: ZKA 372.

A bad joke had turned into a horror story. With her eyes still riveted on the document, her mind searched for possible explanations. Someone could have stolen the car at night from the parking lot of the bed-and-breakfast where she had been staying. Yet each morning the car had been in the same place where she had left it the night before.

She ran her hand through her hair, thinking, trying to come up with an explanation for what was happening. Then it struck her: There was no mistake. Whoever was responsible for the senator's death had decided to take her out of circulation. Somehow they had gotten to the sheriff in

Hattiesburg. If she went with these two troopers, the sheriff would toss her into a rural Mississippi jail until the election was over—and maybe for a lot longer. They must think the senator had given her information that would permit her to figure out who they were.

Her attention shifted to the arrest warrant. It had been issued by a Mississippi state court, which meant it had no legal effect outside of Mississippi. They were counting on her cooperating and coming down to Hattiesburg with the state troopers to try to clear her name.

She glanced up at Sergeant Billings. "Sorry, guys," she said. "This is all a big frame. I didn't hit anybody. As I said, I never even drove at night. So I'm not going with you."

"I have to warn you that by refusing to come with us you could face serious consequences."

"Such as?"

"The local D.A. in Hattiesburg will file extradition papers with the court in Washington in a matter of days. Once they get the warrant up here, the D.C. police will arrest you and bring you down to Hattiesburg. If it goes that way, I'm afraid the judge will never let you out on bail."

Her eyes hardened. "And if I come with you now, are you prepared to guarantee me that I will get out on bail?"

He shuffled his feet nervously. "Gee, I sure don't know about that. I mean, I'm not a lawyer. I was just trying to be helpful."

"I appreciate that, but I think I'll do my own lawyering."

"Yes, ma'am. Whatever you want."

When they left, a sobering thought ran through her mind. She couldn't remain in Washington. Whoever was responsible for the senator's death was now focused on her. They were dangerous people. If she was going to find out who killed the senator, or even stay alive herself, she'd better get the hell out of town fast.

That was easy to say, but where could she go? She thought about driving out to the senator's home in St. Michaels. There might be clues she would recognize, but that was too dangerous. Also, the police might still have the house sealed.

She thought of trying to reach Harrison, but his business trips abroad frequently lasted several days. Often he was unavailable even by phone if he was in the middle of negotiations. She couldn't sit here waiting to talk to him.

Think, she told herself. *Think.*

Kendrick? He'd never put his own life on the line for her, or to find out what happened to the senator.

Cady? Somebody had been feeding him information. He was the logical place for her to start. He was decent and honorable. Once she made him understand that he had been used, he'd join her in finding out the truth.

She tried his office. "Sorry, he's out of town on vacation," Margaret, Cady's secretary, said. She offered to pass on Taylor's message when he called in, but she was unwilling to give out his number. With a little more cajoling, Taylor got Margaret to confirm that Cady was at his mountain cabin outside Mendocino.

Once the secretary clicked off, Taylor picked up the phone to get information for northern California. After punching in only two numbers, though, she slammed it down. *Get smart,* she told herself. Whoever worked up to this elaborate Mississippi arrest scenario could have tapped her office phone. Maybe even Cady's phone in California, because he had been an unwitting participant in this scheme. She had to show up there cold.

"I've got a couple of errands to run," she told Kathy.

Once in the hallway, she slipped into the inside fire staircase, which permitted her to exit the firm's office building through a side entrance. She had to move fast, not even stopping at home for clothes. She strode quickly to an ATM on Pennsylvania Avenue in order to use cash for her plane ticket.

A cab was cruising down from the Capitol, and she shot her hand in the air to stop it.

"Dulles Airport," she told the driver.

Chapter 20

He had a wooden country cabin. An A-frame house on a small hilltop, with a view of the Pacific off in the distance, it was located at the end of a dirt road, at least a mile from any other house. It was a far cry from the palatial country homes that Philip Harrison and some of Taylor's other partners owned in the mountains or on the eastern shore of Maryland. The kind of place that was perfect for someone who wanted total privacy.

With only the address she had gotten from telephone information, Taylor had a great deal of trouble finding Cady's house. After several inquiries in the center of town, Jed Doyle, an elderly man with a thick, bushy beard who operated a convenience store, drew her a crude map. Even with that, finding the way was difficult. Heavy clouds filled the night sky and blackened the moon. Hunched over the steering wheel, peering through the windshield of the rental car, Taylor was straining her eyes as she followed a winding road.

Finally she spotted an old, rusty mailbox with the name *C. J. Cady* carved in the metal. She turned left and drove slowly up the narrow road as Doyle had told her.

In the light of the high beams of the car, she caught Cady, alone on the front porch, sitting in a wooden rocker with a book in his hand. A lamp with a single bulb stood next to the rocker. Two tennis rackets were leaning against the side of the porch.

Startled to see a visitor, he leaped to his feet. He was wearing old, faded jeans and a bright checked shirt. He had the stubble of a beard from a couple of days' growth.

The moment she saw Cady, all of the exhaustion from the long plane ride and drive drained away. He was her last chance, her only chance. It wouldn't be easy, but she'd have to persuade him to help her. She brought the car to a halt in front of the house and jumped out.

"Taylor, for God's sake," he said, putting his book down on a table. "What in the world are you doing here?"

She climbed the steps wearily to the porch. "Please help m-me," she stammered, to her surprise. Despite her resolve to remain strong, she began to cry.

He looked at her with a mixture of bewilderment and sympathy. "C'mon inside."

Trying to regain her composure, she followed him into the cluttered living room. Books, clothes, dirty dishes, and empty wine bottles were strewn everywhere. Old newspapers were piled haphazardly in a corner. Cady struck a match and lit the kindling in the stone fireplace. He tossed on a couple of logs and then turned to her.

"Sorry for the mess," he said, embarrassed. "I get totally out of my lifestyle up here."

He saw that she was trembling. Her teeth were chattering. "Sit down near the fire," he said. "I'll get you a glass of wine. Then we'll talk."

When Cady returned from the kitchen a few minutes later, carrying two glasses of Matanzas Creek chardonnay, he found her leaning forward in a wooden chair, close to the fire, warming her hands and pulling herself together.

"Before you say anything," he said as he handed her a glass, "I want you to know that I'm sorry about the senator. Real sorry. I almost called to tell you that."

"It's not your fault. You were doing your job. I would have handled the case the same way if I were on your side."

"In the heat of the battle I sometimes get carried away. I never wanted him to kill himself. I just wanted to make him pay for what he had done. Not that way. I hope you'll believe me."

She summoned up a smile for him. "I do. Thanks for saying it."

There was an awkward silence. Finally Taylor said softly, "Please listen to what I have to say. You'll find out why I came all the way out here."

Cady took a sip of wine and sat down. "Okay, I'm ready to listen."

In a monotone, she repeated to him the facts she had presented to Cooper and Harrison that persuaded her that the senator had been murdered. Then she told him about her confrontation with the two Mississippi state troopers. As she spoke, Cady occasionally asked a clarifying question, but gave no reaction to what she was telling him.

"So now I'm a fugitive from justice," she concluded. "Whoever killed the senator tried to have me arrested."

He pulled back and raised his hand. "Easy, Taylor. That's a powerful charge you've just leveled, that we're dealing with a murder, not a suicide."

His response rocked her back on her heels. "After listening to me, you still believe that's what happened to the senator? That he killed himself?"

He eyed her closely to see if she'd come unhinged. "That's what the FBI and the Maryland medical examiner have concluded. You're telling me that they're part of this conspiracy you're imagining?"

"I don't know about the police. I just know that *they* killed the senator and made it look like suicide."

"How do you know that?" he replied without making any effort to conceal his disbelief. "And who are *they*?"

Take a deep breath, she told herself. *Don't blow your cool.* She counted to ten before continuing.

"C'mon, Taylor, I need facts. We're both lawyers. We act on facts. Give me facts. Then I'll believe you."

"Let me ask you something," she said, trying to be patient. "As you went through your investigation, didn't some things seem strange to you? I had the impression that your case came together too quickly and too easily. Like someone was feeding you stuff. You know what I mean?"

Cady walked over to the fireplace. He nudged the burning logs with a poker and tossed on a couple of fresh ones. The scent of pine filled the room. He was troubled by what Taylor had said, not only because he liked and respected her, but because her last point was a good one. He had felt uncomfortable about the envelope being dumped on his desk mysteriously. The backup records that had been missing in Napa. Gladstone had been unavailable, then suddenly called and came. Azziz was a convicted felon.

"Let me ask you," Cady said, "who you think is behind this conspiracy you're talking about."

She took a deep breath. "At first I was convinced it was McDermott and Pug Thompson."

"The logical choices."

"But now I've changed my mind."

She told him about Alex Glass and then recapped Alex's letter.

That was too much for Cady. He shook his head in disbelief. "Let me get this straight. You think that a Japanese political figure is responsible for all of this?"

"That's exactly what I think."

"Isn't that a bit over the top?"

"If you give me half a chance, I'm going to prove it to you."

"How?"

"Through Harvey Gladstone. You interviewed him. I never got a chance because you did such a good job of hiding him."

Cady nodded.

"Gladstone was the key to your case. Right?"

"He was one of the pieces," Cady said stubbornly.

"Mill Valley was really sold for ten million, like the senator said. Somebody got to Gladstone and persuaded him to make up a false story, which you bought in your zeal to make a case and become famous."

He ignored the jab. "What about the tax records?"

"They must have been cooked."

"And Azziz?"

"C'mon, C.J., don't make me laugh. Anybody could have gotten to that guy. They were using you. They were feeding you phony evidence as if you were a hungry pig at a trough."

"That's hardly a flattering analogy." He finished his glass of wine, then looked at her sympathetically. "I know that's how it seems to you, because you were close with the senator, but truly I think my case against Senator Boyd was sound. I wanted a just result."

"Bullshit!" she shouted, totally exhausted and frustrated. "If you really want a just result, then tomorrow morning you'll get in a car with me and go see Gladstone. Subject him to a rigorous cross-examination."

Cady was annoyed at her shouting, and he still didn't believe her story. Her feelings for the senator were driving her to irrational conclusions.

"Well, will you stop being defensive and go with me to see Gladstone?" she demanded.

Cady locked eyes with her. "In a word, no. The Boyd case is over. Finished. Concluded. Wrapped up." He took a deep breath. "As I said before, I'm sorry the senator is dead. Really I am. But I can't bring him back. And neither can you."

She glared at him.

"And you want to know what else I think?" Cady said.

Furious at him, she responded, "I really don't give a damn what you think."

"I think somebody in Mississippi made a mistake in bringing those charges against you. There was some type of clerical or computer error. I think you should go down there and straighten it out. After that, you should head off to the Caribbean for a good long vacation."

His last comment was too much for Taylor. Her face turned bright red with anger as she shot to her feet. "You're the third fucking man," she screamed, "who's told me in a condescending way that I'm being irrational. Well, I may be a woman, but I'm not some emotional cripple. If you're too goddamned stupid to see a picture that's absolutely clear, then that's your fault and not mine."

"Listen, I didn't say that because you are a woman—"

"And right now I don't give a damn what you meant. I don't intend to bother you any more or stay in this house one more minute."

She stormed toward the front door.

"Hey, it's late. You can stay here tonight."

"I don't want a thing from you. I saw the Mendocino Inn in the middle of the town. I'd rather stay there."

"Listen, I'm sorry. Really. It's just that I don't think—"

"That's your trouble. You don't think. Period."

Before he could respond, she was through the front door, slamming it so hard that the entire wall vibrated.

Chapter 21

At seven o'clock in the morning, Cady climbed out of bed, ending a miserable night of tossing and turning. He liked Taylor. He had even thought about asking her out last spring when they had finished the Warden case, which was why he had suggested that they go rafting in West Virginia. Then he got busy with the Russian mobster case and never followed up. That was the way it went for hardworking, single professionals.

All of that made him feel terrible for handling the discussion with her so poorly last evening, letting it degenerate into a shouting match. But damn, she had frustrated him. She was leaping to conclusions without having the facts to back them up.

Walking down the dirt path to the mailbox for the morning newspaper, he couldn't get her out of his mind. If she hadn't rushed out of the house last night, they could have talked things through. He could understand that she was upset about Senator Boyd's death. But that didn't justify her leap into an irrational void with her crazy theory about conspiracy and murder. She was hopeless, he thought, shaking his head. Still, he had to admire her spunk, coming all the way out here to enlist his help.

Back in the house he spread out the *San Francisco*

Chronicle on the kitchen table and fixed a bowl of Cheerios with berries and skim milk. On the front page there was nothing new about Senator Boyd's death. Just a rehash of the old stories.

Another front-page story related that Governor Crane was trying to jump-start his campaign with interviews on all three television networks in the next twenty-four hours. The Crane campaign was making a massive effort to hit the ground running and get into the race. Eighteen-hour days were being crammed together as the candidate planned to crisscross the country, stopping in each of the forty-eight contiguous states at least once. In the meantime his campaign headquarters in Harrisburg was cranking out a daily flow of position papers and blasts against the ineptitude of the Webster administration. According to the analyst, it was a high-risk, go-for-broke campaign that Crane was running, a far cry from Boyd's carefully planned, cautious effort that had put Boyd gradually in the lead. But conditions were different now. Crane didn't have the time that Boyd did. He had no choice, if he wanted a chance to win.

The apolitical Cady admired what Crane was doing. He always liked the gutsy underdog who refused to give up. He doubted that there was enough time for Crane to pull ahead, but swings in American public opinion were often hard to predict.

Eating cereal, Cady flipped the pages of the newspaper, rapidly scanning headlines. The Forty-niners were playing at home on Sunday against the Rams. On the first page of the business section was a long article about fluctuations in the value of the Japanese yen. According to a Stanford economist, Japanese exports would be more expensive and their position would erode further in world markets. The economist was predicting even harder times ahead for Japan, with the Japanese standard of living certain to fall some more. Cady thought about Glass's letter. It seemed preposterous that Sato or any foreign leaders could manipulate the American presidential election.

Cady kept turning pages. The *Chronicle* that Cady received in Mendocino had a supplement with a news roundup for areas north of the city. On the second page of that supplement a picture caught his eye. *Whoa, wait a minute.* He did a double-take. *My God, that's Harvey Gladstone's picture.* Next to it, the caption read, *Realtor Killed in Automobile Crash.*

With a lump in his throat, Cady began reading:

Late on Thursday evening, Harvey Gladstone, a retired realtor, died when his car crashed off the road in the mountains west of Napa Valley and burst into flames. It is unclear what caused Gladstone to veer off the road. Conditions were wet and hazardous. The police are still investigating.

Gladstone is survived by his wife of forty-one years, Louise, a son, Jonathan, and a grandson, Carl, in Los Angeles. For many years he operated Gladstone Realty, one of the major realty firms in Napa Valley, from its founding in 1960 until his retirement in 1988. Gladstone was also a past president of the Kiwanis and the Elks.

"Oh, shit, it can't be!" Cady blurted out.

He thought about what Taylor had told him last night. Maybe she was right. Maybe somebody had used him. They had made the investigation easy enough, guiding him to all the right places.

You dummy! Gladstone's dead because of you.

He tried to review in his mind the points Taylor had made last evening, which he hadn't taken seriously. If what she was saying was true, then her own life was now on the line. Whoever had killed Boyd and Gladstone was after her next.

Oh, God, I let her leave here on her own last night. Cady cursed himself. She could've been followed. He tore the article about Gladstone from the newspaper and shoved it into his pocket. Then he ran outside the house and climbed into his dark blue Jeep Cherokee. Dirt and pebbles sputtered as he tore down the driveway.

Chuck Harley, the owner of the Mendocino Inn, was a tennis partner of Cady's.

"Hey, I'm looking for—"

Harley interrupted him. "She's in the dining room having breakfast."

"How'd you know who I wanted?"

"Well, last night when I checked her in, I asked, 'What brings you to Mendocino?' She said, 'That asshole C. J. Cady.' That gave me a clue."

"Is she okay?"

"Unless she ate a double portion of the cook's corned-beef hash." Harley laughed at his joke.

In the dining room Taylor was the only guest. Confused and uncertain about what to do next, she had decided to take a long walk after breakfast on the beach. That was always good for thinking. She'd find a way out of this mess. In the meantime she sipped coffee and picked at a blueberry muffin while glancing at the *San Francisco Chronicle*. She had the cup in her hand when she saw Gladstone's picture and article. "Oh, no," she cried, and the cup fell out of her hand onto the table, then rolled to the wooden floor, spilling the coffee along the way. "It can't be."

From the entrance to the dining room, Cady watched the cup fall, saw the expression of terror on her face, and knew that she'd seen the Gladstone article. He rapidly approached.

"Oh, Taylor. I'm so sorry," he said grimly. "I was used. I should have been smart enough to know what was going on."

Cady glanced around. Harley had left them alone in the dining room, but they couldn't stay here. He needed to get her out of sight. "Let's go back to my place."

"C'mon, we'll go over your story again," Cady told her as they walked through the front door of his house.

Feeling buoyed by his support and concern, Taylor swallowed hard, took a deep breath, and went through all the different steps.

When she was finished, Cady said, "I have to try to get to Dorfman at the FBI."

She shook her head solemnly. "You can't do that."

"Why not?"

"We don't know who we can trust. If we accept what Alex said in the letter, then Sato has an influential American working for him. Perhaps more than one. Dorfman could be part of it. As the FBI director, he has to be spending time with McDermott and Webster. They might both be involved."

"You really think—"

"I don't know what to think. Two people have died. I don't want us to become numbers three and four. If you know Dorfman well enough to tell me it's a reasonable chance to take, I'll trust your instinct. But I don't think you do."

"Yeah, you've got a point," he said thoughtfully. "If you

follow that reasoning, then we'll have to operate on our own for now."

She thought back over what she had told him. "When the senator came out of the grand jury room, he said that you had a phony document from a Napa, California, tax office that made his Mill Valley sale seem like a fifty-million-dollar transaction instead of ten."

Cady was aware of the weakness in the computer print-out he had gotten from Karen without the backup being available. "Yeah," he said sheepishly.

"What exactly did you have?"

As Cady told her about his meeting with Karen and what she had given him, Taylor looked at him incredulously. "C'mon, C.J., that woman was conning you. They wouldn't have destroyed the backup on a ten-year-old transaction."

"What makes you so sure?"

"I worked for the California government. That's how I met Boyd. Unlike industry, they didn't have efficient document-disposal policies. At least when I was there."

Cady was defensive. "That was a long time ago, and you never worked in that office."

"Agreed. Who can we call to find out?"

Cady paced around the room, thinking. "When I spent a year with my old law firm in San Francisco, I was friends with a corporate partner, Al White. A good guy. He'd give me the info without asking any questions."

Taylor watched Cady's face as he made the call and asked White about document disposal. The chagrined expression on his face told her the answer before he hung up.

"I screwed up," he said simply.

She put a hand on his shoulder. "I wouldn't put it that way. I'd say you were tricked by some people who will stop at nothing to get what they want. It's time for us to pay a visit to Karen. She's in this up to her eyeballs."

"Exactly what I was thinking. We have to make a couple of stops first."

"What do you have in mind?"

"Now that I've bought into your story, I don't want us to be victims three and four."

Cady opened the top drawer of a bureau in the living room. He reached under a navy blue cardigan and took out a .38 revolver and a box of bullets.

"Do you know how to use that thing?" Taylor asked.

"Chuck Harley taught me to shoot a couple of years ago to scare off animals. I've never killed anything in my life."

Cady parked the Jeep in front of a large office building on California Street, deep in the heart of the gloomy canyons of San Francisco's financial district.

"Now do you want to tell me what we're doing here?" Taylor asked impatiently as he cut the engine.

"Remaking you."

"Remaking me?" Unconsciously she raised her hand to pat her hair.

"Yeah, I don't want any of Sato's henchmen nailing you before we get our case together, and I don't want you rotting away in a Mississippi jail. So right now you can say good-bye to Taylor Ferrari for a while."

"I don't understand."

He liked that he'd taken her by surprise. "Didn't you like to play dress-up when you were a little girl?"

"I never had a chance. All I had were brothers. They needed me for football or baseball. Now, would you mind telling me what you're planning to do with me?"

"There's an office in that building," he said, pointing,

"with the name Epsilon Industries on the door. That's where the Justice Department operates its West Coast witness-protection program. They provide new identities to people who testify in Mafia cases and the like. Before we left Mendocino I called Tom Miller, a friend of mine who's the head of the FBI office in Sacramento. He promised to make all the arrangements. They should be waiting for you."

She flashed him a flirtatious smile. "Will I get a choice about what to be? I always wanted to be one of those tall, slim, blond, leggy models, the type you see in *Vogue* magazine."

"Personally, I prefer your current Sophia Loren natural look."

She stroked his arm as she prepared to open her door. "Cady, you're really not such an uptight SOB."

Taylor got part of her wish. Five minutes after they entered the offices of Epsilon Industries, Ken Linderman, head of the DOJ's West Coast witness-protection program, fitted her with a blond wig. Linderman and Cady were both standing behind her, staring at her in the mirror, when Cady said, "Well, you always wanted to be a blonde. You should be happy."

She screwed up her face and shook it from side to side. "Ugh, I meant a classy blonde. This wig makes me look like a bimbo. Talk about cheesecake."

"Don't pay any attention to her, Ken," said Cady. "She's never happy. She had a miserable childhood that she hasn't gotten over."

Linderman was ignoring both of them. He fitted her with tortoiseshell glasses.

"They're plain glass," he said. "They won't affect your vision."

Then he had a photographer take a series of pictures of her.

"Smile, Taylor," Cady said. "We're not doing a root canal. Blondes are supposed to have more fun."

Thirty minutes later Linderman handed her a California driver's license, a passport, and three credit cards, all in the name of Caroline Corbin. She stared for a moment at the license and the Santa Monica address.

"You live on Wilshire Boulevard, close to the beach," said Linderman.

"I used to live in that area once. It's a perfect address for a bimbo."

Humorless, Linderman stared at her dourly.

"What about the credit cards?" she asked. "Are these valid? I've got to buy some clothes. I left Washington in a hurry."

Linderman looked at Cady. "Tom Miller told me to set these up for the max. There's a twenty-thousand-dollar limit on each card."

Cady scratched his head uneasily. To Taylor he said, "I authorized all of this without approval from any of the top people in DOJ. Since you're a rich partner in a prestigious Washington law firm, I'll trust you to repay Uncle Sam for any charges on the credit cards when this is over. Otherwise, it comes out of my meager government salary."

"Or your trust fund," Taylor said lightly, having read Cady's bio.

"Does that mean you'll be responsible for the charges?" Linderman asked her, wanting to get this point cleared up.

"More likely I'll put twenty thousand dollars on each of the cards and drop you both a postcard from Rio."

Cady couldn't help laughing. "I'll sign for it," he said. "She's hopeless."

When Cady had signed all of the forms and they were getting ready to leave, Linderman said, "I hope you two have a good time, whatever you're planning to do."

Taylor had no sooner gotten back in the Jeep than she took off the wig and glasses and stuffed them into her purse.

"Hey, wait a minute," said Cady. "I didn't go to all this trouble for nothing."

"The wig's hot, and it itches." Taylor untied her black hair, let it hang down, and ran a comb through it. "Also, one of the things in life I was always grateful for was that I had good eyes and didn't need glasses."

His lighthearted mood of before was gone. "I guess you don't like staying alive."

"I'll put them back on if it looks like there's any danger."

"That's real smart. You know that sooner or later they're going to try to kill you. I doubt if they'll give you much warning."

He started the engine and pulled away from the curb.

"Where are we going now, boss?" Taylor asked, trying to restore the camaraderie they'd had upstairs.

"Napa."

"Can we stop at Neiman Marcus on the way? I'm getting a little tired of wearing this one suit."

He checked his watch. "You've got an hour. We have to get there before Karen closes up for the day. So don't turn into one of those women shoppers on me."

He smiled, and she punched him playfully in the ribs. "That was a disgusting sexist comment. Men can shop as well as women. Or did your mother just call Brooks Brothers and have the family chauffeur pick up your clothes?"

"Methinks you have a tongue as sharp as a—"

"Serpent's tooth? You got that right."

*　　*　　*

"Where's Karen?" Cady said to the woman with flaming red hair behind the counter at the Napa tax office. The name tag on her black cotton blouse read, *Samantha*.

She shrugged. "That seems to be the sixty-four-thousand-dollar question."

Cady was nonplussed. "What do you mean?"

"It's the damnedest thing. Apparently they hired her last week. Then a couple of days ago she didn't show up for work. Now nobody can reach her."

Cady and Taylor exchanged looks. They were thinking the same thing. Either Karen had gotten scared when the senator died and took off for the hills, or whoever put Karen into this office wanted her out before Cady or anyone else came to dig further about Mill Valley.

"So who are you?" Cady asked.

"I should ask you the same question."

Cady showed her his DOJ identification. That was good enough for Samantha, and she said, "Actually, I work at the motor vehicles office. Somebody from government services called and told me to come over here to cover the office as a temp until they get a replacement for Karen."

Taylor broke in. "Who was here before Karen?"

Samantha shrugged. "I have no idea."

"Do you know where the backup documents are for the records in the computer?"

"I haven't a clue. Like I said, they just asked me to come over and cover the office."

Cady sighed. "Thanks for nothing."

She shrugged. "Hey, it's not my fault."

As they walked outside, he muttered, almost to himself, "We'll never find Karen now."

Taylor pointed to Ed's Diner across the street. "Let's head over there."

Cady shook his head. "I'm not hungry," he said, dejected. "If you want something, though, I'll go with you."

"Oh, I want something, but it's not food. Come on. It's my turn for a surprise."

They took a seat at the counter. Cady ordered a diet Coke, and she was served a cup of coffee brewed hours ago that looked and tasted like mud. There were only two other patrons in a booth in the corner. Ed, tall and thin, in his late sixties, Taylor guessed, was behind the counter in his stained white apron surreptitiously studying them.

"Have this place a long time?" Taylor asked.

"About thirty years. I guess that's a long time. You two from back east?"

"Washington."

He shook his head. "Too bad what happened to Senator Boyd. Out here we still love him no matter what he did."

Taylor bristled. The implication was that the senator had been caught with his hand in the cookie jar. But that wasn't surprising. People thought most politicians were crooks. "Actually, I worked with the senator a bit," Taylor said. "He was one of my favorite people."

Ed nodded. He liked that. "What are you guys doing out here?"

Cady was watching her, wondering how she was going to handle this. She went on smoothly, "We're working on a lawsuit. Wanted to get some info from the tax office, but there's nobody over there now who can help us."

He raised his eyebrows. "Really? Trish is usually pretty helpful."

"Well, she's not here anymore."

"Hmph, I didn't know that. She ran that office for nearly fifteen years. Must have just happened." He thought about what they had said. "Actually, I was thinking that it's been a while since I've seen her. Lots of days she brings her own lunch, but she usually gets over here once a week. Always has BLT on whole-wheat toast. 'Hold the mayo,' she says, as if I wouldn't remember. I like her even though I feel sorry for her. She's one of those decent women who married a real bastard. We all cheered when she filed for divorce a couple of years ago."

Ed was rattling on. It was obvious that he liked to talk to his customers. That must go with the territory.

"Being a single mother with a teenage boy isn't easy these days," he added. "If you know what I mean." They both laughed. "But it beats having that piece of shit around the house. He was her second husband, too. Why's it always happen to the nice ones?"

"Does she live in Napa?" Taylor asked.

"Up in Rutherford. Behind the Chevron."

"You wouldn't happen to have a phone number, would you? Maybe she can help us."

Taylor held her breath while Ed pulled back and studied his visitors. They seemed honest and decent, and she had worked with the senator. "I don't have a number," he said, "but her name's Patricia Bailey. She's in the book."

"I should make the call," Taylor said when they were back in Cady's Jeep.

"Why, because you're a woman?"

"That and the fact that I worked for the senator. Ed told us people here loved Boyd."

"Be my guest." He handed her his cell phone. "Also, you should use my phone in case anyone is getting access to calls being made on your cell."

"Good point."

Taylor got the phone number from information and dialed. A teenage boy answered.

"Can I speak to Trish?" Taylor asked.

"This is Kevin," he said. "My mom's not here." He sounded polite, not surly, like lots of children who answered calls for their parents.

"Do you know when she'll be home?"

"Actually, she's off on an overnight," he said, and laughed, which gave Taylor the idea that Trish had gone with a man. The teenager apparently found this role reversal amusing. "She'll be back in the morning."

Then the boy caught himself. This woman sounded nice, but he was giving away a lot of information to a stranger. "Can I ask who's calling?"

"I'm a friend of Senator Boyd's," Taylor replied.

"My mom went to high school with him," Kevin said.

Taylor had lived in Washington so long she had forgotten what small towns were like. Everybody knew everybody.

"Any chance I can reach her by phone now?"

"No way," Kevin said. "I don't know where she is." He giggled. "She said, 'Don't call me on my cell unless it's an emergency.' "

Taylor didn't push. Tomorrow morning would be soon enough. They were making progress.

Cady started up the engine. "I'm impressed how you handled Ed and Trish's kid. You're good with—"

She completed his sentence. "Ordinary people. Real people, you mean?"

"Yeah. Like that."

She smiled. "I didn't have the advantage of a prep-school education."

He frowned. "Hey."

"That was a joke. There's nothing at all pompous and arrogant about you, C.J. You're a decent human being. You've definitely risen above your upbringing."

"Does that mean I have to turn off the road at the cheapest motor lodge I can find to prove a point?"

"Actually, I was thinking of Meadowwood."

He laughed. "Who's the snob now?"

"So have we made any progress?" Taylor asked Cady once the waitress poured some Kistler chardonnay and departed.

They were sitting in a booth in the corner of the Meadowwood dining room. It was almost nine o'clock, and they had both unwound. Taylor had run for an hour on trails that cut through the woods around the property, while Cady had hit with the tennis pro on one of the lit courts. She was wearing a white Gucci pants suit with a black tank top she had bought that afternoon. A fire was crackling in a fireplace not far from their table, which warmed the high-ceilinged, wood-paneled room.

"What do you mean?" Cady said.

"Well, if Karen was the person they installed in the Napa tax office to mislead you, then I don't see how Trish is going to help us."

Without hesitating, he said, "I don't want to talk about it tonight."

"What do you want to talk about?"

"Let's order, then I'll tell you."

After their first course, a cold crab salad, arrived, he said to her, "I feel really sorry for everything that happened in my investigation of Senator Boyd. I like to think that I'm a savvy prosecutor, but those guys had me for lunch. If it weren't for me, Boyd would still be alive and you'd be running his campaign. I hope you'll forgive me."

"Of course I'll forgive you. This was so brilliantly orchestrated that no one could have seen through it. Still, you don't have to beat yourself up, because I'm not sure it mattered."

He was puzzled. "What do you mean?"

"Even if you didn't take the bait, they would have found another way to get the senator out of the campaign."

He sipped some wine. "You liked the senator a lot, didn't you?"

She gave him a cool look. Why did everybody think they were sleeping together?

He could sense her reaction. Awkwardly he clarified: "I didn't mean it that way. I meant as a person and a leader."

That was better. "Yeah, I did. He would have been good for the country. He was an honorable man. I can't believe he's dead. It's like a bad dream. I expect to wake up and find him walking through the door, saying 'Taylor, what's on for tomorrow?' "

Cady looked at her sympathetically.

"Enough," she said. "Let's talk about something else. How about you? Tell me how you became a white knight."

He held off until the waitress deposited their main course of grilled quail and a pinot noir of Au Bon Climat. "Well, actually, it all started with my divorce. Janet, my ex, was a paralegal at Hunt and Brenner when I was a senior associate. We didn't get to know each other until a firm weekend outing at the Greenbrier, where we ended up as a doubles team, quite by chance, in the tennis tournament. I wasn't into all of this 'firm togetherness' stuff. Still, I decided to participate." He shook his head sadly, remembering what had happened. "Anyhow, we won the tournament in a walk. To celebrate, we got roaring drunk at the firm party that night and ended up in bed together."

"You sound like quite the social animal."

He smiled. The quail was getting cold, but he didn't care. "Hardly. I was shipped off to a boy's boarding school when I was ten because my dad, a superb Wall Street lawyer, and my mother, a superb social climber, couldn't be bothered having their only child around." He gave a shrug, meaning he was long past caring about it. "At Stanford, I was a nerd whose only activity was varsity tennis. I socialized, but had no relationships. For the first seven years at the firm, until I met Janet, I dated, but I was too busy to have a life. I wanted to make partner on my own, not on my family's connections. Though she was ten years younger, Janet was a lot more experienced at these things. She knew exactly what she wanted." Bitterness crept into his voice. "If you get him in bed, the wedding ring will follow. After I made partner, we had a great life ahead of us, or so I thought."

"What happened?"

His eyes hardened. "A few years into the marriage she told me I was a cold, unfeeling WASP with ice water in my veins. How's that?"

"Oh, dear."

"Then one day I came home early from New York because an oral argument was canceled. I found her sitting on top of the club tennis pro in our bed, pushing herself up and down and shouting for joy."

She reached over and put her hand on his. "I'm sorry."

"It forced me to reexamine my life. Tennis certainly was her game. I felt like a chump."

"What did you do?"

"Filed for divorce. For a cash payment of a hundred thousand, she was willing to grant it without a contest. No alimony. Then I got the firm to transfer me for a year to our San Fran office. I went up to Mendocino most weekends to the cabin, walked in the woods and looked at the ocean. From all of that, I lost my taste for corporate law. I decided to try to do some good for the country. With my skills, I figured the U.S. attorney's office was a good place. I've gotten rid of real scum, like that Russian mobster, Kuznov. Despite the problems that come from working for an ambitious ass kisser like Doerr, I've been happy there. That's it. End of story. Now let's eat."

For several minutes, they attacked the quail in silence. All the while Taylor was thinking about what he had told her.

"You know," she said, chewing, "we're not so different. My mother died when I was twelve. After that I had no real family. My father worked hard in a steel mill. When he came home he had a wall around himself. My brothers had no use for a girl. I knew I had to get out of that town." Her face brightened at the next part. "Fortunately I got a steel company scholarship to Carnegie Mellon, which included a summer job to study mining in Colorado. Once I saw the Rocky Mountains, I was never the same. I was planning to go to grad school in environmental engineering, but then a funny thing happened."

"What's that?"

"As I began reading about global warming in a senior seminar in college, it became clear to me that scientists should be the advocates in our society on environmental issues, but they aren't. The lawyers are. If I wanted to make a difference, I'd have to become a lawyer and join their club." She saw him nodding in agreement. "One of my professors knew somebody at USC law school who helped me get admitted late in the process. After law school, I took a job in the governor's office doing energy work. That's how I met Boyd—at a hearing. We hooked up again after I came east to Washington to do good on the Hill. When the excitement of that work turned to boredom, Philip Harrison convinced me I could do something worthwhile with a law firm as my base. Contrary to the public perception, all lawyers in private practice aren't villains. So here we are."

He studied her. "You're right. We're not so different." He hesitated. "Can I ask . . . have you ever been married?"

"Nope," she said. "The right man never came along, and I was hell-bent on my career." She thought about Alex. "I've had a number of relationships over the years, though. I don't have any regrets." Suddenly she was overtaken by a huge yawn. "I don't know why I'm so tired. In about five minutes I'm going to embarrass you by falling asleep on the table."

They walked slowly back to their rooms, which were next to each other in one of the small cottages that dotted the property. A thousand stars filled the moonlit sky. From the chill in the air, she had goose bumps on her arms. At her door they stopped.

"One thing I want to tell you," she said.

"What's that?"

"I appreciate everything you did for me today. The wig and the false ID. Everything. You're not a cold, unfeeling WASP with ice water in your veins."

He touched her shoulder, and his hand lingered there. "Thanks."

"I had a really nice evening. And the wines you picked were incredible."

"As long as you're giving compliments, I'll give you one: I think you look great in that pants suit. Smashing."

"Thanks, C.J."

He pulled his hand away reluctantly. "Breakfast at seven-thirty?"

"Sounds good."

He leaned forward and kissed her on the cheek.

She held her breath, wondering if he'd ask to come into her room. She didn't want to tell him he was being too aggressive.

When he took a step backward, she said, smiling, "See you in the morning."

Terasawa entered Taylor's apartment building—the Watergate—through the garage.

He had been lurking behind an oak tree near a large metal door that was locked shut. Tenants, a couple in a black Cadillac, came home late at night and activated the remote control that raised the door. Terasawa waited until their car had passed through, and slipped inside before the door closed.

Squatting behind the nearest car, he watched the couple climb out of the Cadillac and walk toward the garage elevator. The man was dressed in a tuxedo. The woman had on a mink coat and was carrying a jeweled evening bag.

Once the elevator door opened, Terasawa moved forward rapidly and followed them inside. He looked like a tenant, dressed in a suit and tie with a topcoat, carrying a black leather briefcase. The couple paid him no attention. Exhausted and tipsy, they had just come back from a party. The woman said, "I never thought we'd get out of there."

As the elevator started its ascent, Terasawa tensed, prepared to go for the Berretta in his shoulder holster.

Yet the couple exited on the fourth floor. The man nodded to Terasawa and mumbled, "Good night." The woman's eyes were half-closed.

The elevator continued its ascent to the eighth floor, Taylor's floor. Terasawa walked softly down the thick beige carpet of the deserted corridor. He didn't know whether Taylor was in her apartment or not. He had called repeatedly that evening, and there had been no answer. That didn't prove a thing. She might be screening her calls.

In front of her door, he stopped and glanced around. There was nobody in sight.

With a small loop of wire and a thin metal bar, twelve seconds was all it took for him to pick the lock.

Once inside, Terasawa closed the door and looked around the dark apartment. She could be sleeping. With the gun in his hand he moved on tiptoe through the living room to peek into the two bedrooms. Nobody was there.

Terasawa was disappointed. It would have been so easy to dispose of her once and for all and go back home. Now he couldn't do that. He had to stay until he finished the job. Even worse, he had no idea where she was or when she'd come back home.

"Search it first," Sato had told him. "Then do your other work."

Terasawa didn't want to turn on any lights for fear of arousing suspicion. Instead he used a pocket flashlight with a powerful beam. He thoroughly searched the apartment, particularly the drawers, for any papers Taylor might have that could support the idea that the senator had been murdered.

Terasawa didn't find anything until he got to the center desk drawer in Taylor's study. Buried under some papers was an envelope with the address of the *New York Times*'s Tokyo bureau. Terasawa sat down in her leather desk chair and began reading Alex Glass's letter. Terasawa was dumbfounded. Glass had pieced together everything Sato had planned. That damned Ozawa had betrayed Sato.

He thought about it some more. No, Glass didn't know

everything. He didn't know the name of the American whom Sato had met in Buenos Aires. The man Sato called R.L.

And Ozawa . . . What a fool the general had been. Terasawa's mind was churning. He now had something powerful to hold over Ozawa and use as he wanted.

In the meantime he slipped Glass's letter into his pocket. Since she had read it, one thing was clear: Taylor had to die.

He opened his briefcase and shined the flashlight inside. All the components were encased in bubble wrap.

First he removed the plastic bomb with great care. It was packaged to resemble a mass-market paperback book. The cover had been torn from *The Eye of the Needle*. He placed it on a wooden coffee table in the living room.

Then he unwrapped the detonator, which was flat and a foot long. He placed it under the edge of the Oriental carpet just inside the apartment door. When Taylor came home, she'd have to step on it.

Finally he removed a clear plastic wire and connected one end to the book. He ran it under the carpet. The other end he connected to the bomb.

Terasawa walked around the detonator with great care as he left the apartment.

It didn't matter any longer what Taylor had found out from Alex Glass or anyone else, Terasawa decided. Sooner or later she'd come home. Then the bomb would finish her off.

Chapter 22

Trish looked apprehensively across her living room at Taylor and Cady. She was chewing gum furiously. "The available men out there," she said, pointing to the picture window, "are the dregs. The absolute bottom of the barrel."

It's obvious her overnight didn't go well, Taylor thought. She felt bad for the tall, willowy woman with curly blond hair who was wearing gold rings on four of her fingers and large gold hoop earrings.

"I'm sorry," Taylor said.

"Ah, don't worry about it. I'll survive. Besides, Kevin's a great kid. He's an honor student."

They had already been here ten minutes, and Trish hadn't asked why they wanted to see her, which Taylor thought was odd. Glancing at Cady, she decided to jump in. "I was a good friend of Senator Boyd's."

Trish turned instantly wary and apprehensive. "Kevin told me."

"He said you knew the senator from school."

"Uh-huh. He was Chuck then. We were in the same class. I liked him. Everybody did. None of us could stand her."

"Sally?"

"Yeah. She was a year behind us. She never even started college. At least I went two years to junior college. Her father owned a little grocery store down in Oakville, but once she married him and went to France, she took on airs. She opened a ritzy antique shop, and after that she didn't want to have anything to do with any of us, which suited me fine." Trish began chewing harder, thinking about her dislike for Sally. "Some people are like that."

"So why'd he marry her?"

"Oldest reason in the book: He knocked her up. Now he's dead, and the bitch has all his money." Trish shrugged. "That's life."

Cady thought he saw an opening. "Was there much money?"

Trish looked at them anxiously. "Who are you people? What do you want?"

Taylor responded before Cady could. "As I said, my name's Taylor Ferrari. I was the senator's campaign manager. You may have seen my name in the newspaper in articles about the campaign."

Trish looked her up and down. "Yeah. I thought I remembered the name."

"I was the senator's friend, too." Taylor gave the woman a measuring look. Leveling with her was a gamble, but her instincts told her Trish could help if they got her on their side. "I don't think he killed himself. I'm trying to find out what really happened."

To her relief, Trish agreed with her. "I couldn't see him doing that myself. Chuck loved life too much." After her immediate response, her expression turned puzzled. "So why'd you come to see me?"

Trish was smart, Taylor decided. She knew why they were here, but she was trying to avoid it. "You worked down in the Napa tax office. With the records. Didn't you?"

Trish jumped to her feet. "I don't want to talk about it."

She stormed out of the house into the backyard. Taylor followed her, signaling with her hand for Cady to remain behind. There was no question something had happened, and she thought she could pry it out better by herself.

Trish had settled on an old swing. She was rocking back and forth. Terror was written on her face.

"What happened down there?" Taylor asked.

Trish didn't respond. She kept swinging and chewing her gum. The silence became long and heavy.

Finally Taylor said, "Cady in there is a government prosecutor. He could get a subpoena and make you tell us, but I don't want to do that."

"I wouldn't talk anyways."

From the fear in her eyes, Taylor knew Trish meant it. She decided to take a different tack. "On the other hand, Cady can also call on people from the FBI. He can protect you and Kevin, if you're worried that somebody might try to harm you."

Trish hesitated. "Yeah, I'm worried. You would be, too."

"I'll go in and talk to Cady. I'll let him tell you what he can do."

Once he learned what Taylor wanted, Cady quickly made a call to Tom Miller.

"Two men from the FBI will be here within the hour," he said, after he had hung up. "One to guard you, the other for Kevin, until this is over. We won't leave until they come. So you can talk to us now."

"Correction," Trish said. "I don't talk until they come."

Miller had decided to send three agents. He thought Cady might need another one, depending on what Trish said.

An hour later two of them had taken up position outside

Trish's house. The third was in the stands at the field where Kevin was playing football.

That was good enough for Trish.

"I'm not real good with dates," she began in a halting voice, "but about two weeks ago or so—more like ten or twelve days—a guy came in to see me. He said he was from Washington, and he wanted all of the backup documents for Chuck's sale of Mill Valley. He also said that he wanted access to the office computer to check what the computer said about that sale. He didn't fool me for a minute."

"How do you mean?" Taylor asked.

"I knew this guy would change what the computer said. Once I gave him the backup, nobody could ever prove he'd changed it."

Cady, who was taking notes, winced. They had totally pulled the wool over his eyes.

"What'd you tell him?" Taylor asked.

"I said NFW."

"NFW?"

"No fucking way. I said that Mr. Knowles was my boss. He's the only one whose orders I follow."

"What did the guy say?"

"He got all huffy. Said he had the power of Hugh Mc-Dermott, the U.S. attorney general, behind him."

At the mention of McDermott, Cady dropped his pencil. This was what he had been afraid of from the beginning.

"He didn't intimidate me," she said proudly. "This bozo. I took enough crap from my second husband over the years to hang in with anybody. So I repeated that I only do what Mr. Knowles tells me. I don't take orders from him or his attorney general."

"And then?"

"When he saw he couldn't get his way, he put his briefcase up on the counter and opened it. He had piles and piles of hundred-dollar bills. Like in a movie. And he said, 'How much do you want?' "

"What'd you say?"

"I laughed at him. Told him that back in Washington everybody might be for sale, but out here there are honest people. That really pissed him off. So he said I'd be hearing from Mr. Knowles, and he stormed out."

"Can you describe the man?" Cady asked.

"Sure. Tough-looking. Broken nose."

"Pug Thompson," Taylor blurted out.

"Did he give you a name or show you an ID?" Cady asked.

Trish shook her head. "Nope, but I'd recognize him."

"We need a picture," Cady told Taylor.

She turned to Trish. "Do you have a computer in the house."

"Sure, everybody does. I have one. Kevin has two."

"Internet access?"

"Natch. We may be in the country, but we're not in the Stone Age."

Five minutes later the printer was spitting out a picture of Pug Thompson, whom Trish immediately identified as the man who paid her the visit.

"Did you ever hear from Mr. Knowles?" Taylor asked.

"A couple of hours later. He called to say I was fired for unsatisfactory work, which was total bullshit. All my reviews had been good."

"What'd you do?"

"I was madder 'n hell. I was thinking of hiring a lawyer to sue, but then I got a call from the man with the broken nose. I'll never forget what he said: 'If you ever mention this to anyone, first I'll kill Kevin and then I'll kill you.' I was sure this Pug, or whatever his name is, meant it. He scared the shit of out of me. So I never mentioned a word to anyone until now."

Cady blew out his breath in a whoosh. "Jesus, what a story. What happened to the records of Mill Valley?"

She shrugged. "I got no idea where they are now. After this guy left and before Mr. Knowles called, I checked the storeroom; they were there then. I doubt very much if they're still there."

"When you computerized, you didn't destroy any records?" Cady asked.

She looked at him as if he were daft. "We don't throw out anything."

"Did you happen to see the purchase price for Mill Valley when you looked at the records after Pug left?"

She shrugged. "Didn't have to. I was working in that office ten years ago when Chuck made the sale. The sales price was considered confidential, which you could do in those days. I saw it, of course. Ten million bucks." She whistled. "A hell of a lot of money. I was happy for Chuck, though sorry the bitch would get to spend some of it."

Her words put the final nail into the coffin of Cady's case against Senator Boyd. Taylor had been right all along: Someone had framed the senator.

"Where can we find your boss, Mr. Knowles?" Cady asked.

Trish walked over to a table and picked up a telephone book. While Cady wrote, she said, "William R. Knowles, 240 Stone Canyon Road, Yountville.

"That's not far from Domain Chandon winery," she added. "I hope you nail the bastard. I want my old job back."

*   *   *

In the Oval Office, Webster and McDermott were watching video clips on CNN of Governor Crane's speech in New York earlier in the day.

Crane literally had taken over Times Square. A huge platform had been erected, and a gigantic throng, thousands and thousands of people—New Yorkers, tourists, men and women of all ages—gathered around on a sunny and breezy Sunday afternoon to listen as Crane presented his blueprint for revitalizing the American economy. At first most listened in silence. He was even heckled. But slowly, with his booming, resonant voice, he gained their attention.

"I have a message for you," he said. "A bold new plan to unify all Americans in a gigantic program to jump-start the economy and increase the wealth of all Americans."

The television broadcast showed the crowd at the end of Crane's speech, cheering wildly as he closed with a single powerful point: "Hold your decision until the debate. Then you decide who should be the president of the United States."

Chants of "Crane for president . . . Crane for president . . . Crane for president," echoed off the walls of the huge skyscrapers.

Crane stood on the platform waving to the crowd.

President Webster snapped at McDermott, "Turn that damn thing off. Get the Redskins game and put it on mute."

The A.G. hit the remote-control switch.

"Nobody has worked a crowd like that since JFK in the 1960 campaign," said Webster in a tone that mixed admiration with envy. "We're just lucky the Democrats started with Boyd and not Crane. We've only got a twenty-five-point lead. Do you think Crane has time to close the gap?"

McDermott didn't hear the question. His mind was miles away. Last evening at a charity benefit he had run into Jim

Doerr, who had said Cady was out in California. What was he doing there? McDermott wondered. Doerr had said Cady was tenacious. Christ, he hoped that Pug didn't leave any loose ends out in Napa.

McDermott felt a tug on his arm. It was the president. "Hey, are you okay? You seem spaced out."

"Yeah, I'm fine," McDermott said glumly. "Just a little tired. I thought I'd get some rest when Boyd died. It looks like Crane intends to make a run out of it."

"Unfortunately, that seems to be the case. Crane may have started late, but the public always loves a new face."

"And he's got a pretty one to boot."

"We have to maximize our prep time for the debate. We didn't take the last one with Boyd seriously enough."

"I'll talk to Boudreau. We'll get started ASAP."

Webster sipped the drink in his hand. "Did you ever find out who sent that anonymous package about Senator Boyd to C. J. Cady?"

This time McDermott was ready for him. He had reluctantly come to the conclusion that Webster wouldn't forget about the question. So he had studied Cady's file from the investigation. To his great relief, he could provide an answer to Webster that was plausible and safe.

"I just found out," said McDermott. "I wasn't going to bother you with it today."

The president looked up anxiously. "What's the answer?"

"A man by the name of Abdul Azziz bought the Mill Valley property from Boyd. He didn't like Boyd's sympathetic views toward Israel. He thought your administration would tilt toward the Arabs. Since he was a party to Boyd's sale of Mill Valley, he had all of the facts. It was an easy matter for him to hire someone to deliver the package to Cady."

"How certain are you of this information?"

"I personally read the entire file of the investigation, even the transcript of the deposition of Azziz."

"Should I read that transcript myself?" Webster asked.

"I don't see the need for it. It's very clear."

McDermott held his breath. *If he wants to see the file, I'm in deep trouble.*

The president moved on. "Who else is aware that Azziz started this whole thing?"

"Only the two of us, and C. J. Cady, of course. Doerr, if he bothered to read the file or talk to Cady, which I doubt."

"Do we have an obligation to disclose these facts to the public?"

McDermott coughed and said, "I don't see why. No one in your campaign organization was responsible. Or even involved."

Webster rubbed his chin, weighing McDermott's words. "You're sure that Pug Thompson and his people didn't put Azziz up to this?"

"I doubt if they even know who Azziz is. I didn't until I dug into the file this morning."

"And you're certain that you're not making this up to protect me from something?"

"Absolutely."

Webster was satisfied. "Good work. Let's consider it a dead issue. Turn on the volume for the game."

"Willy just left for the country club to play golf," Knowles's wife, Monica, told Cady when he called.

Well, isn't that nice, Cady thought.

"He plays up at Silverado. I don't know where you are, but you might be able to catch him before he tees off."

Cady and Taylor had the third FBI agent, Curt Donner, follow them in his own car. Upon their show of federal authority, the manager of the club fully cooperated. He checked around before telling them, "Willy hasn't gotten here yet. His tee time's not for another half hour."

"I think we'll wait for him in the parking lot," Cady said. "Do you happen to know what he's driving?"

"Brand-new maroon Lexus sedan. He just bought it last week. I know because he was showing me this unbelievable computer guidance system the car has."

Bingo, Cady thought. He looked at Taylor, who was smiling too. He knew exactly how to handle Willy Knowles.

Cady was standing at the rear entrance to the country club, flanked by Taylor and Donner, watching the parking lot, when a shiny new maroon Lexus with temporary plates pulled in.

Knowles was alone in the car. When he opened the door to get out, Cady was right there, holding out his ID from DOJ. "Are you Mr. William Knowles?"

The quavering response was: "Yes, I am."

"I'm C. J. Cady. This is FBI agent Curt Donner," he said, pointing. "We're here to investigate a conspiracy that involves the Mill Valley records."

Donner removed a pair of handcuffs from his pocket as Cady had instructed him.

"I didn't do anything wrong."

"Then answer a few questions we have," Cady said. "If we're mistaken, we won't bother you anymore."

Knowles briefly considered calling a lawyer, but decided that might only make matters worse. Cady had said this was about the Mill Valley records. He could handle these guys. They'd never be able to prove he had done anything wrong.

The manager of the club made an empty conference room available. Cady and Taylor took up places across the table from Knowles, while Donner waited outside.

Cady said, smiling, "Nice new car." Knowles squirmed, and Cady's smile hardened. "How much did Pug Thompson pay you in cash?"

The direct frontal assault without any warning threw Knowles off guard, which was, of course, why Cady did it.

"I don't know what you're talking about."

Cady noticed beads of perspiration breaking out on Knowles's forehead. "I saw on the plates that you bought the car from Napa Lexus. I think I'll call them and see whether you paid by cash or check. If they say check, we can subpoena your bank account. We'll find out how much the cash deposit was that way."

Knowles's lime-green golf shirt was growing wet under the arms. Cady decided to turn up the heat. "Conspiracy to commit murder is a tough crime to be involved in, because everybody who played a role can go to the electric chair. Even the bit players. Did you know that?"

Knowles's teeth were chattering. His knees were knocking. "Did you say mur-murder?" he stammered. "I have no idea about any murder. Who was murdered?"

Cady didn't want to answer that question. "You tell me what you know, and I'll decide how deeply you're involved."

"Can I take a leak?" Knowles said with an urgency that made Cady think he might wet himself. It was tempting to let that happen, but Cady decided not to. "Agent Donner will go with you. To make sure you return okay."

When he was back, Knowles said, "If I tell you everything I know, will you agree not to prosecute me?"

"I won't make any promises. You play ball and we might not bother you. That's the way it works."

A long silence followed, which Cady let stretch out as long as it would. Finally Knowles sighed. He was going to confess. "A man from Washington came to see me about ten days ago. He said he worked for Attorney General McDermott."

Taylor pulled out the picture they had gotten from Trish's printer. "Is he the one?"

"Yeah."

"What did he want?"

"He wanted me to fire Patricia Bailey, who works in the Napa tax office."

"Did he say why?"

Knowles shook his head. "Not a word. I swear it."

"And you didn't ask?"

"That's right."

"You didn't want to know?"

Knowles looked down at the table as if he could find a clue there for some way out of this mess.

"I'm right, aren't I?" Cady asked.

Knowles nodded.

"And he told you who to put in that job. Didn't he?"

"Yeah. He said she'd just be there for a couple of weeks. He assured me that she wouldn't screw anything up."

"So you did it?"

Knowles nodded again.

"How much did he pay you?"

Knowles hesitated.

"Well?" Cady pressed.

"A hundred thousand," Knowles whispered. "In cash."

"Enough to buy the Lexus and remodel the den?"

"Actually, we're redoing a bathroom," he said sheepishly.

"After you heard about Senator Boyd's death and the nature of the grand jury investigation, you knew why they wanted Trish out of that office and their own person in. Didn't you?"

Knowles said weakly, "Yeah, I kind of figured it out."

Taylor looked at Knowles with disgust. "I don't know whether Cady will prosecute you or not, but I do know one thing."

He was staring at her with eyes the size of saucers, waiting for her to continue.

"From this day forth, you have to live with the fact that you helped kill a good man so you could have a new Lexus and a bathroom."

Back in the Jeep, Taylor was steaming. "That scumbag. Some people have no shame."

Cady glanced at his watch. "I checked the flight schedule this morning. If we hustle, we can make the last afternoon plane out of San Fran back to Washington."

She muttered, "I can't believe it. The senator's dead because of that asshole."

"We're going for it," Cady said. "I hate red-eyes." He floored the accelerator, and they tore down the Silverado Trail.

"So let's take stock of where we are," she said. She patted her briefcase. "We've got a written affidavit from Knowles. That's powerful evidence to use against Thompson and McDermott."

"Precisely. We also know that our thinking about Sato was wrong. It was McDermott and Pug Thompson, which is what you thought at first, and which is logical."

"So how do we go after an attorney general?" she asked.

Cady sped into the left lane to pass a slow-moving truck. "We keep eating the little fish," he said. "Then when we're ready to go after the shark, we call in a big fish of our own to help us out."

Chapter 23

It was midnight when they arrived at Dulles Airport. "I've got a car here," Cady said. "I'll take you home."

They climbed into his XK8 Jaguar convertible, in British racing green, and roared down the airport access road toward Washington. She heard him saying something about their plans for tomorrow, but she couldn't stay awake. The motion of the car after the long flight and the grueling last several days was putting her to sleep. "You're right, C.J.," she mumbled.

"Right about what?"

"I don't know," she replied, and she was out.

Twenty-five minutes later he pulled up in front of the Watergate apartment building and nudged her. "Wake up, Sleeping Beauty. You're home."

Taylor yawned. "A very fast ride."

As she reached for the door handle, Cady put a hand on her shoulder. "I'll be back here at eight tomorrow morning to get you."

She squeezed his hand. "Thanks, C.J."

He decided to wait until she was inside the building to pull away.

Cady wasn't the only one watching Taylor. Across Virginia Avenue in a hotel room that had a clear view of the entrance of the Watergate apartment, Terasawa stood at the window with high-powered binoculars pressed against his eyes. He had never seen Taylor before, but he had been given a picture. He recognized her immediately with that long black hair. He was glad she was finally home. He felt uncomfortable in this high-rent part of Washington, where he might stand out. Much safer was the seedy Capitol City Motel on New York Avenue, where he had been staying before. He had kept his room at that hot pillow joint. People went in and out all the time. No one noticed anyone else.

Terasawa jotted down the license plate number of the car that had dropped Taylor off, just in case. In another five minutes or so she would walk into her apartment, and bam. He smacked his right fist into the palm of his left hand. That would be the end of her.

Once Cady saw Taylor enter the apartment building, he eased his XK8 away from the curb. *Dammit.* He remembered that she wasn't wearing the wig and the rest of the Caroline Corbin disguise. With everything that had happened in Napa, he had forgotten about it. Tomorrow morning he'd insist that she begin wearing it. In the Russian mobster case he had just finished, Kuznov had killed two witnesses with a powerful bomb in their apartment. Taylor had to understand that dangerous people did horrible things when they were cornered.

Though he knew that, he had still been surprised that Kuznov had someone plant the bomb. He never thought—

"Oh, my God," Cady cried out. "Oh, my God."

He did a 180-degree turn and roared back to the Watergate. These people were as dangerous as Kuznov and his gang.

He slammed to a stop in front of the building. Waving his DOJ identification in his hand, he ran up to the door. "Please," he said to the doorman. "We've got to stop Taylor

Ferrari before she gets to her apartment. There could be a bomb. Please, it's life and death."

His desperation was so genuine that the doorman, who liked Taylor, waved Cady through and pointed to the elevators. "Eight-oh-four is her apartment."

Riding up in the elevator, Cady felt a twinge of foolishness. What if there was no bomb? He'd seem like an idiot. Still, he couldn't take the chance.

Nervously he glanced at his watch. *Shit.* It had already been several minutes. She was probably opening the door right now while this elevator crawled along. *I should have taken the stairs. I'd be there already.*

The instant the door opened, Cady looked down the hall. Taylor was walking with a duffel bag in one hand and the mail she had stopped for in the lobby in the other. He began running and shouting, "Taylor. Taylor."

At first she didn't hear him. She stopped in front of her apartment, the key in her hand.

"Don't go in there!" he screamed.

His momentum carried him into Taylor, and the two of them tumbled to the floor, scattering her mail. "Thank God I caught you in time," he cried out."

She was flabbergasted. "You want to tell me what this is all about, C.J.?"

He explained it to her as he helped her gather up envelopes.

"Do you really think that—" she started to ask.

Cady cut her off. "I didn't think so in my Russian case, and I ended up with two dead witnesses. I've gotten to like you more than either of them. I don't want to lose you."

She flashed him a grateful smile. Out in California, she'd gotten to like him too. "That's very sweet, C.J. What do you want to do now? Suppose I open the door carefully and look around. See if anything's been disturbed."

He wouldn't hear of it. "We need a professional. You and I will never be able to tell. If we find something, we won't know what to do." He whipped out his cell phone. "I'm calling the FBI bomb squad. You don't set foot in there until they say it's okay."

An hour and a half passed before the bomb squad, with great care, disconnected the powerful bomb that had been planted in Taylor's apartment.

Shell-shocked, Taylor was sitting down, leaning against the hallway wall.

"Pack a bag," Cady said. "You can stay with me until this is over."

He carried the duffel with her things to the car. As they pulled away in the XK8, he said to her, "Dammit, Taylor. Put on that blond wig and the rest of the Caroline Corbin disguise. I don't care how much it itches."

She didn't respond. Tears were running down her cheeks.

He leaned over and gently fastened her seat belt. "We're going to my house," he said. "You'll be safe there."

Across the street, Terasawa cursed when the Jaguar pulled away with Taylor inside. He knew what would happen once he saw the driver come back, then the van with the words *Bomb Squad* painted in red letters.

He couldn't believe they had thwarted his plan. Well, it wasn't over yet. He had the license plate of the Jaguar. She was probably going to stay with the driver. In the morning Terasawa would find a way of getting his name and address from the D.C. motor vehicle office.

Terasawa was a patient man. Taylor wasn't going anywhere.

Chapter 24

Taylor woke with a start and sat up in bed when she heard a door slam downstairs. The bedroom was strange. It took her a few seconds to remember what had happened last night and that she was in Cady's house.

She heard footsteps on the stairs, coming her way. That had to be Cady, she thought, but what if it wasn't? She wrapped the sheet tight around her upper body and held her breath.

The footsteps were getting closer. Suddenly a face appeared in the doorway. It was Cady, carrying two mugs of coffee and the morning newspaper. Taylor let out a sigh of relief.

"Did you sleep all right?"

As he sat on the bed, she clutched him tightly, remembering the bomb that had been planted in her apartment. If Cady hadn't come back when he did, she would have been killed. Her body quivered against his, and she began to cry.

"You don't have to worry. It's over now."

"Those people will try again. You know that, C.J."

"They'll never be able to find you. They have no idea you're with me."

When Taylor finally pulled away from him, he stood up.

He tossed her a blue terry-cloth bathrobe and said cheerfully, "Breakfast is on the kitchen table."

Fifteen minutes later Taylor was in the kitchen munching a piece of toast when the sound of sirens shattered the morning calm. A wave of panic engulfed her as she heard a commotion outside on the street in front of the house. She watched Cady cross quickly to the living room window. On his way, he grabbed the gun lying on the shelf above the fireplace. She was two steps behind him.

Out on the street they saw two blue-and-white D.C. police cruisers and an unmarked black Chevy Caprice. Cady, gripping the gun hard, carefully watched the figures who stepped out of the car.

"Clint Perry," he said to her. "A member of the local D.A.'s office. I know him fairly well."

"Why are they here?"

"My guess is that he's legit, but I'm not going to take any chances. I'll stall him for a few minutes. You go upstairs and put on the blond wig. Then return to the kitchen. Get ready to play the bimbo. Look like you're hungover. Just keep your purse and your Caroline Corbin ID nearby."

He stuck the gun in the drawer of an end table.

"Should I get dressed?" she asked.

"What do you have on under the robe?"

"Nothing."

"Leave it that way. If the going gets tough, let the robe open a bit and show them a little tit. It distracts cops every time. And if it really gets tough—"

"You're a sexist pig."

He held up his hands in innocence. "You want to end up in a Mississippi jail? Or even worse, if these guys figure out who you are?"

"Not if I can help it."

"Then do what I said."

She was hastily adjusting her wig in his powder room mirror as the doorbell rang.

Cody waited until she emerged and sat back down at the kitchen table. "All right, all right, I'm coming," he shouted.

"Sorry to bother you," Perry said when he opened the door, "but we're looking for a woman by the name of Taylor Ferrari. We've got a Mississippi extradition order for her. We're supposed to fly her down to Jackson. I'll show you a picture."

Listening in the kitchen, Taylor held her breath.

"I don't need a picture, Clint," Cady replied casually. "I know Taylor Ferrari from the Boyd case. I haven't seen her since the grand jury last week. Why would you possibly think she was here?"

"We got a tip this morning."

"A tip from whom?"

Perry shrugged. "I don't know. It was phoned in. Guy knew all the details."

Cody seemed genuinely puzzled as he said, "Well, your tip was wrong. She's not here."

"You mind if we look around? I'll have to file a report. Even though I know you and it's your house, I'd better do this according to the book."

"Be my guest."

Through the open kitchen door, Taylor saw one uniformed policeman go upstairs to look around. Another one went down to the basement.

Cady took Perry aside, close to the kitchen door. "Listen, Clint, last night I picked up this broad in Georgetown. A real looker, with a shape like you wouldn't believe."

"You must have had a hell of a night then."

"Actually, we did. Anyway, she's in the kitchen now. I don't want you guys scaring her away."

Perry smiled at Cady and gave him a thumbs-up.

"I'll owe you for this," Cady added.

Perry went into the kitchen himself and scrutinized Taylor carefully. "D.C. police," he said. "Can I ask your name?"

"Caroline Corbin," she said, sounding intimidated by the police.

"Can I see some ID?"

She got up from the table to get her purse, which was on the counter next to the sink. From the corner of her eye she was watching Cady, and his advice—show them a little tit—popped into her mind. She'd be damned if she would do that. She pulled the belt, and the blue robe tightened in the front. She handed Perry her driver's license and one of her credit cards.

"Looks okay to me," he said quickly.

At the front door, as they were leaving, Perry asked Cady, "Got any idea where we can find Taylor Ferrari?"

"Beats me. If I hear from her, I'll let you know."

Perry winked at Cady. "Have a nice morning, C.J."

Terasawa was in a gray Mercedes parked across the street from Cady's house and two doors down, when, without any warning, the door of the garage alongside the house went up and the green Jaguar shot out. Terasawa started his engine, but as the Jaguar passed, Cady was alone in the car. That meant Taylor must still be in the house. Without Cady being there, Terasawa would have an easy time with her.

Terasawa glanced at the clock in the car. He'd wait a few minutes before going in, just in case he came back.

When the time was up, Terasawa sneaked around to the back of Cady's house. Without any difficulty he picked the lock on the back door and went inside.

With a gun in his hand, on his tiptoes, he searched the house. It was empty. Terasawa was furious, realizing they had tricked him. Taylor must have been in the trunk of the car. He cursed in Japanese.

Terasawa had no idea where they went. With a deep scowl he decided to go back to the Capitol City Motel and keep out of sight. This evening he'd return to Cady's house. If they weren't home, he'd let himself in and wait inside for them.

Pug Thompson was sitting at a table in the back of the Corner Bakery restaurant in Chevy Chase when Taylor and Cady walked in and looked around.

Pug had initially objected to meeting in a public place when Cady called to say, "Willy Knowles thought we might want to talk." Pug had suggested Rock Creek Park, but Cady was afraid to take a chance. He and Taylor needed the protection that a public place offered. Chevy Chase was far enough away from town that they would not be recognized.

Pug sipped his cappuccino as they sat down. At the nearest table, a woman was giving a bottle to one child and rocking another one in a stroller while she talked to a friend who had a child on her lap. Coffee break in the 'burbs.

"Glad you could meet us," Cady said, "but I guess you didn't have any choice."

"Shh, keep your voice down," Pug responded. "And tell me what the hell this is all about."

"I think you know."

"Humor me."

Cady told him about their conversation with Knowles, deciding to omit any mention of their meeting with Trish to minimize the danger to her. He snapped open his briefcase and showed Pug the Knowles affidavit.

"So you see," Cady said at the end, "we've got you dead to rights. We can—"

Pug cut him off in midsentence. "Let's not waste our time farting around. I have a law degree. Don't forget that."

"Actually, I didn't know it," Cady said. He looked at Taylor, who shrugged her shoulders. "What do you have in mind?"

"You give me complete immunity, and I give you McDermott. It's that simple."

That was precisely what Cady had been hoping for. "How good's your evidence?" he asked.

"Don't worry about that. It's enough to give you a solid case against McDermott. Are you ready to deal?"

Cady gave him a hard stare. "If I don't think your evidence is good enough, the deal's off."

"That doesn't seem right. I open my kimono and you—"

Cady narrowed his eyes. "Don't play games with me. There's no other way I'll do it."

Pug sighed. "Word around town is that you're an honest guy, but I'd still be taking a hell of a chance."

"You're not doing me a favor," Cady said. "You're about to drown. If you want to go down alone, be my guest." Cady snapped shut his briefcase and stood up. "C'mon, Taylor. We're outta here."

Pug grabbed his arm. "All right. We'll do it your way. Give it to me in writing."

"I can't do the deal myself," Cady said. "I need the approval of Sarah Van Buren, the assistant A.G."

"Go call her then. I'll wait here."

It took a while for Cady to get what he needed from Sarah, then put the agreement in writing. When he laid it on the table, Pug reached into the briefcase at his feet. He pulled out a scientist's lab notebook with a black-and-white cover bound on the side.

"I made contemporaneous notes of every discussion I had with McDermott about this business from the time it began."

"Why did you do that?" Taylor asked.

Pug gave her an ugly smile. "In case we ever got to this point. To save my own ass. The way I'm doing right now."

"Let me see the notebook," Cady said.

As he read through the notes, he was amazed. McDermott had directed the whole Napa records fabrication each step of the way. He had supplied the woman, Karen, who Pug said had been a paralegal at McDermott's Chicago law firm, which would be powerful corroborating evidence. According to the notebook, Pug had delivered the Mill Valley backup documents to McDermott. He had no idea where they were now.

When Cady finished reading, he handed the notebook to Taylor for her assessment. "It's all good stuff," he told Pug, "but McDermott may deny he had any role. He may say you did it on your own. You have to give me something besides this to nail McDermott."

Pug reached back into his briefcase and pulled out a single piece of paper. "I needed McDermott's authorization to get the hundred K that I used to pay off Knowles. I couldn't do that myself."

With the glint of victory in his eye, Pug handed Cady

the page. It was a photocopy of the authorization for a
check request. The stated purpose of the hundred thousand
was "miscellaneous expenditures."

The date fit the Napa time frame perfectly. Pug had carried out his end of the bargain: He had given them McDermott.

Chapter 25

Cady parked the XK8 on Capitol Hill, raised his head out of the car, and looked around. He didn't think they had been followed, but he didn't want to take any chances. He gripped the gun in his jacket pocket.

Once he was convinced the coast was clear, he leaned back in the car and said to Taylor, "Okay, let's go." He hid the gun under the front seat.

They entered the Supreme Court building from the side door on Maryland Avenue. A group of high school students were milling around the white marble corridor as a tour guide gave a lecture about the first chief justice, John Marshall. Cady led Taylor through the crowd and up to the guard's desk.

"Hey, C.J.," the guard said in a friendly voice. "How's it goin'?"

"Couldn't be any better," Cady said. "We're here to see the Chief."

Taylor pulled out her Caroline Corbin ID, and after a quick glance at it he waved them through. "I'll call the chambers of Chief Justice Hall and let them know you're on the way up."

Cady also received a warm greeting from Helen, the Chief's secretary. Taylor raised her eyebrows, impressed that Cady was so well known and liked in the building. In the court's hallowed halls, with its multitude of armed guards, she felt safe and secure. After everything that had happened, that was a very good feeling.

"He's on the bench now," said Helen. "He'll be back here in about half an hour."

"That's what he told me when I called this morning. You mind if we wait in his office?"

"No, not at all. Make yourselves comfortable."

The Chief's office was gigantic, Taylor discovered as she followed Cady to the far end, to a red leather sofa, where they sat down. She peeled off the wig, which was itching like crazy, and stuffed it into her briefcase. The glasses went next. They passed the time reviewing everything that had happened to them in order to present a precise, persuasive case to Hall.

When the Chief shuffled into his office, Cady and Taylor rose to their feet.

Watching the Chief take off his black judicial robe after Cady introduced her, Taylor found a single thought running through her mind: *This man is sick, very sick.* He could hardly lift his arms. She wanted to go over and help, but she was afraid that would offend his dignity, which Cady confirmed by a subtle shake of his head. Finally Hall succeeded in taking off his robe and draped it over a chair. His face was pale, almost ashen, thin and drawn. His gait was slow and halting as he joined them.

"Helen told me you're up here on a great emergency," Hall said. "I assume it has to do with your Boyd investigation."

Cady gave his former boss a smile. "It's possible that the entire American government is hanging in the balance."

Hall was amused. "If you wanted to capture my attention, you certainly did that."

"I'm afraid it is serious, sir."

"Okay, you two. Talk."

For the next forty minutes Cady and Taylor had what amounted to an oral argument before Hall. They alternated in telling their story about the events concerning the Boyd investigation and his death while the Chief interrupted to ask clarifying questions, just as he did on the bench. Physically he seemed weak, but his mind was lucid and sharp. He asked to see a copy of the Knowles affidavit and the notebook, as well as the check authorization they had gotten from Pug. He picked up his reading glasses and studied them, tapping his fingers on the desk.

When he was finished, Hall leaned back in his chair. "Unfortunately, you weren't exaggerating," he said. "This is serious business. But why did you come to me? What do you think I can do?"

For Cady, the Chief's question was a lob up to the net. "Quite frankly, sir, I was hoping that you might help us confront McDermott. On our own, I'm afraid he'll dismiss our charges and arrange to have someone kill us the way he arranged the murders of Boyd and Gladstone."

"That's a powerful charge."

"I wish it weren't true."

"Why not go to the president or the FBI?" Hall asked.

"They might be involved as well. Also I don't think you'll have the same ability to persuade them as you will McDermott."

Hall wasn't so sure of that. "What makes you think McDermott will talk to me? He's hardly one of my admirers. In fact, we've never liked each other."

Again Cady cracked a smile. "Well, I remember from my

days up here that you can be very persuasive with top lawyers in the government."

Hall chuckled. With great effort he pulled himself to his feet and walked over to the large window facing the Capitol across the street.

Taylor was watching him carefully. Would the chief justice decide to pursue the case, or would he hand it back to them? The few minutes that he spent in front of that window seemed like an eternity.

Hall turned around slowly, returned to his desk, and pressed the intercom. "Helen," he said, "get Attorney General McDermott on the phone. Tell him I want to see him up here in an hour. If he asks what the subject of the meeting is, tell him that you have no idea, and I'm not available until then."

Hall turned back to Taylor and Cady.

"You think he'll come?" Taylor asked anxiously.

"Oh, he'll be here. He'll assume that I want to talk to him about my resignation and his appointment to replace me. He'll cancel anything to talk about that."

"We really appreciate your help, sir."

"Thanks, but I haven't done a thing yet. McDermott will be a tough nut to crack. We'll see what happens." A dark shadow crossed his face. "Unfortunately, though, going after McDermott may not be the hard part," Hall said solemnly. "What scares me is the possibility that the president could be mixed up in this as well."

Taylor had never seen anyone as surprised as McDermott when he walked into Chief Justice Hall's office and saw her and Cady. Hall was seated behind his large red leather-topped desk, looking stern and judicial. Taylor and Cady were sitting off to one side. An isolated chair in front of the Chief's desk was intended for the stunned McDermott.

"Take a good look around," Hall said in a raspy voice when McDermott was seated. "This will probably be the last time you'll be in these chambers."

McDermott was not one to back down from a challenge. "With all due respect, I don't think that's for you to decide. As I recall my constitutional law, the president is the one who will appoint the next chief justice, and the Senate confirms."

"But his name won't be McDermott. You can bet on that. You'll be publicly disgraced and almost certainly serving time in jail after what I've just learned from my two young friends here today about your role in the Boyd affair."

"Now, wait a minute," McDermott said in an indignant voice, "what kind of lies have these two been telling you?"

"Spare us the dramatics. They have a notebook Pug Thompson made, a copy of a check authorization of yours, and an affidavit from a California official who supervised the Napa land office. I've personally looked at all the evidence in the hope of finding it didn't prove what they told me, but it does. At a minimum, it proves you created false evidence against Senator Boyd." Hall's voice was cracking with emotion. "And that's at a minimum."

The A.G. wasn't cowed. "Let me see the so-called evidence."

Hall pointed to Cady, who handed it to McDermott.

As the attorney general examined it, all of the color drained from his face. Though he tried to maintain a righteous demeanor, to Hall, Cady, and Taylor he looked like a kid whose mother had caught him looking at pictures in a porn magazine.

At last the Chief said, "I want to know why you did this.

I want to know the rest of your involvement in the Boyd affair." His tone was harsh and accusatory.

McDermott refused to be intimidated. "You can't address me like that. You've got no right to conduct an inquisition. Even for a chief justice, you're way out of line. I can get up and walk out right now. You can't stop me."

McDermott rose and started toward the door.

"Be my guest," Hall replied calmly. "You're free to go. But if you do, you should know that I'm planning to pick up the phone and tell the president everything." Those words alone were enough to stop McDermott on the spot. Sensing that McDermott was now in trouble, Hall continued: "I'll go to key figures across the street on the Hill. Taylor here is prepared to go to the press. You'll be publicly disgraced, and Cady will charge you with the murder of two people."

McDermott's head snapped around. "What two people? What are you talking about? I didn't have anything to do with anyone's murder."

Cady jumped in. "The case against you for conspiracy in the murders of Senator Boyd and Harvey Gladstone is solid. That'll get you murder one times two."

A look of bewilderment enveloped McDermott. Perspiration was running down his forehead. His lower lip was quivering. "I never had anything to do with anyone's murder," he said weakly, while raising his right hand. "Jesus, I didn't even know Harvey Gladstone was dead. I'll swear to that on a stack of Bibles."

"Which is worth about as much as Al Capone authenticating his own tax return," Cady said.

Oddly enough, as she listened, Taylor found herself believing that McDermott wasn't mixed up in the two murders. The thought of Alex Glass and his letter came to her. With him, there were actually three murders. Then she had a powerful realization: They had made an error thinking it had to be Sato or McDermott. Why not Sato *and* McDermott?

She moved toward McDermott and leaned her head forward as she did when she bored into a hostile witness. "Don't give us your lies," she said. "You met with Yahiro Sato in Buenos Aires on August twenty-eighth. We know that. You've been working with him. The two of you wanted the senator out of the election for your own separate reasons. You're the U.S. end of this conspiracy. You engineered the Boyd and Gladstone murders, using Pug Thompson or someone else."

McDermott pulled away from Taylor and sat down. He was trying to absorb everything he had heard. He pulled a small calendar out of his jacket pocket and checked it, rubbing his eyes to make sure they weren't deceiving him. A ray of hope began to appear, a way out of this nightmare. "You've got the wrong man," he said boldly.

"Yeah, right, and I'm Michael Jordan," Cady snapped back.

Realizing that he would never get anywhere with Cady, McDermott turned toward Hall. "I never met with Yahiro Sato in my life, and I wasn't in Buenos Aires on August twenty-eighth. On that date I was in Las Vegas, speaking before a conference of state law-enforcement officials. Five hundred people heard me in the morning, two hundred and fifty at dinner that evening." He pointed to the phone. "Call any state attorney general. "They'll all back my story."

Cady reached for the phone and called Peter Dorsey, the Maryland state attorney general in Annapolis. Sure enough, he had seen McDermott. "Yes, thanks for the info," he told Dorsey.

As Cady put the phone down, he thought he knew exactly

what had happened. "Okay, let's go back to square one," he told McDermott. "What you can't refute is the evidence of your involvement with Pug in connection with the Napa documents relating to the sale of Mill Valley."

McDermott looked down at the backs of his hands without responding.

"Since you didn't go to Buenos Aires," Cady continued, "you must be taking orders from the person who met with Sato in Buenos Aires on August twenty-eighth. Now tell us who that was."

McDermott realized that he now had leverage. "And if I give you what you want, you'll agree that I won't face any charges or suffer any adverse consequences for my minor involvement in all of this."

"Are you crazy?" Cady said. "You—"

The Chief cut him off. "Here's what I'm prepared to do. On your side, you tell us fully and honestly everything you know about this Senator Boyd business, and you agree never to accept a Supreme Court appointment. In return, we won't mention a word of your involvement to anybody. So you won't be charged criminally. You'll resign immediately as A.G. If the president gets reelected, you will respectfully decline any position in his new administration for personal reasons, as people always say. You'll be able to go back to private life with your honor and license to practice law intact." He saw McDermott's jaw working, as he waited for his turn. "That's the deal. It's more than generous. The only reason I'm offering it is because we have to know for the good of the country what happened. And we have to know before the election."

"It's a goddamned shakedown."

"It's a lot better than you deserve."

McDermott sat brooding for several minutes, staring at the carpet and pondering Hall's offer.

"Suppose I were to agree not to be chief justice. Could I at least be an associate justice on the court if Webster appoints me?"

The Chief scowled. "Forget it. We don't need people like you up here."

"But my whole life I've dreamed—"

"You have nobody to blame but yourself."

Hesitating, McDermott glanced over at Taylor and Cady, then back to a grim-looking Gerhard Hall. "I'll take it," he finally said.

"Good. Now, tell us everything you know about this mess. And if you lie, the deal is off."

McDermott took a deep breath and began talking. "One evening a couple of weeks ago—I can't remember exactly when—I got a call at home from Philip Harrison. He—"

Taylor thought she had heard him wrong. "Who did you say?"

McDermott sneered at her. "Philip Harrison, sweetie. Your distinguished partner."

Taylor shot to her feet. With a wild look in her eyes, she pointed a finger at McDermott. "Philip had nothing to do with any of this. Don't you try to tarnish a good man's name to save your own vile skin."

McDermott chuckled. "Sorry, sweetie, Harrison—"

"And don't you call me that again."

Cady broke in. "Just tell us what happened."

"Well, anyhow, Harrison called and asked if I would meet him at a parking lot in Great Falls. He said it was urgent. So I went."

Taylor was still on her feet glaring at McDermott.

"At the meeting," McDermott continued, "Harrison told

me that he knew certain embarrassing facts about my personal life. He even showed me some photographs to prove his point."

"What facts?" Taylor asked.

McDermott looked at the Chief. "That's irrelevant to the issue. Nobody needs to know."

Hall smiled. "Oh, c'mon. The fact that you have a second family in Florida is one of the most widely known secrets in this town."

McDermott seemed startled, but continued. "Harrison said he would tell my wife and the president, who don't know about this relationship. He threatened to leak it to the press unless I helped him." McDermott paused, cringing even now at the thought.

"What did he want you to do?" Cady asked.

"He told me that there would be an investigation of Senator Boyd relating to his sale of Mill Valley. He explained that it would begin with an anonymous package being dumped on a prosecutor's desk. Because he knew so much about it, my guess is that he or someone working for him actually placed that package on your desk."

Taylor balled her hands into fists, seething.

"What did he want you to do?" Cady repeated.

"He wanted me to have the records changed in the Napa tax office and to deliver the backup documents to him. He said that as attorney general I could find a way to roll over state officials and get that done."

"And you agreed to do it?"

"What choice did I have? So when I left the meeting, I called Pug. I told him to take care of it, and we talked about how. Also, I want you to know, Harrison's threat to expose my other family wasn't my only motive."

"Yeah. What else was there?"

"At this first meeting, I saw a sinister-looking figure lurking behind a tree. Harrison never said it, but I felt that man would harm me if I didn't do what Harrison wanted."

"Why did Harrison want Boyd out of the presidential race?"

McDermott said, "Hmph," and glowered at Taylor. "Why don't you ask your partner that, sweetie?"

She had hesitated to interrupt, but now that McDermott had directed his comment to her, she was ready for him. "You're lying through your teeth."

She was taking this too personally, Cady thought. She couldn't bear to think this Harrison had betrayed her. But Cady wanted to move on. "A minute ago you said this was your first meeting with Harrison. How many others were there?"

"Just one more. The night before you convened the grand jury, Harrison called me to come to the same place. He also asked me to bring the Napa backup records, which I did."

"Where are they now?"

"I gave them to Harrison. I have no idea what he did with them."

"What else happened at the second meeting?"

"He told me that your evidence was so strong that Boyd should be agreeable to a deal: He would offer to withdraw from the race in return for immunity from prosecution. He said that you would probably oppose it, but I should force you to accept it."

"Did you agree to do that?"

"Yeah, but Harrison's prediction proved to be wrong: Boyd never agreed to withdraw."

"Was the man lurking in the area again?" Cady asked.

"Yeah, but this time I had a very good, tough P.I., a former Chicago cop I've used before, follow me to the meeting. My guy was hiding in case anything happened. I told him about the man lurking behind a tree, and he was there again. Afterward my guy tailed this guy to the Capitol City Motel up on New York Avenue, room two-sixteen.

"Why'd you do that?"

"I wanted to get an edge on Harrison, a sort of insurance policy, that I could use if this business turned south, like it is now."

"Did you check the motel registration to get the man's name?"

"The P.I. did."

"And?"

"He's Japanese. His name is Terasawa. The P.I. said he has a large scar on his left cheek. That's—"

Cady interrupted him in midsentence. "Are you sure of that?" He remembered seeing a man parked in a Mercedes across the street from his house this morning—a Japanese man with a scar on his cheek. Jesus, he must have been the one who had planted the bomb in Taylor's apartment. He had found them.

"Uh-huh." McDermott gave a deep sigh. "That's all I know. You now have the full extent of my involvement in this."

"Haven't you forgotten something?" Taylor said.

"What's that?"

"How you arranged the Mississippi warrant for my arrest."

He looked puzzled. "I have no idea what you're talking about."

"You're lying again," Taylor said.

"Why would I lie after everything I've already told you?"

"Then who arranged for my Mississippi arrest?"

"You'd better ask Harrison. He must have done that too, sweetie."

She was outraged. "You don't expect us to believe the bullshit story you just told us."

"Look, you can believe what you want, but Harrison betrayed you. I'll bet you were feeding him all your campaign info. He made a fool out of you."

Taylor's face was crimson with anger, and Cady rallied to her aid.

"Leave the personal attacks out of this," he said, sounding irritated. "Do you have any proof of what you've told us?"

A haughty smile filled McDermott's face. "I thought you'd never ask. I've got proof of everything."

Six eyes were staring at McDermott. "What kind of proof?" Hall asked.

"I recorded both of my conversations with Harrison without him knowing it."

"You're kidding," Cady said. "Why?"

"I'm an old gutter fighter from Illinois politics. I know how to protect myself. I wasn't going to take the rap and let Harrison skate."

"Where's the tape?" Hall asked.

"In a safe-deposit box in a bank out of town."

"I want it."

McDermott held up his hand. "If I give it to you, I want to be able to finish out my job as A.G. until the end of the president's current term. It's only a couple of months. Otherwise people will suspect something. My reputation will be tarnished."

Cady was about to say no when Hall raised his hand, cutting him off. "Okay, you can have that provided you agree to sign any extradition orders Cady wants for Sato or any-one else."

McDermott nodded.

Hall said, "How soon can you get us the tape?"

"I'll have it here tomorrow morning at ten."

Taylor waited until McDermott had gone before she ex-ploded. "I can't believe that you two bought that lie." Her breath was coming in loud, short spurts. "All he's doing is trying to save his own skin, the scumbag," she shouted.

"Take it easy," Cady said.

"Don't tell me that. I hate it when anyone tells me that."

Hall looked at her with kindly eyes. "At this point, we're not accepting anything he said. Let's see what kind of tape he has."

"Ah, c'mon, tapes can be phony. You both know that. He controls the FBI. As long as they have a recording of Mc-Dermott's voice and one of Philip's from any speech he's given—and he's given plenty that have been recorded—the FBI lab can make a tape. They can make it sound authentic following any written script McDermott gives the techni-cians."

Hall looked at Cady. "Is she right?"

"I think so, but—"

"But nothing," Taylor protested. "That's the whole point."

"Tell you what," Cady said to Taylor. "It's a long time until tomorrow morning. Suppose you and I keep digging. See if there's anything else that'll tell us whether McDer-mott or Harrison is Sato's man in Washington."

"Good idea," she said. "I'll bet I can prove that McDer-mott was in this from the beginning, and that Philip wasn't in Buenos Aires on August twenty-eighth."

Cady looked at her sympathetically. "I hope with all my heart you can do that." Then he whipped out his cell phone.

"Who are you calling?" she asked.

"John Frazier, an FBI agent I used on my Russia case. I want him to go up to the Capitol City Motel, find this Terasawa, and arrest him. If he's not there, Frazier can stake out the place and begin searching for him around town. We've got a description and a name. We're going to find this guy and get him to tell us the name of his American contact."

When they hit the ground floor, Cady told Taylor, "You wait here inside the door. I'll get the car and pick you up."

Cady didn't want to alarm her any further by telling her that he had seen the man with the scar on his face parked across from his house that morning.

Terasawa had planned to take a short nap back in his motel room to harness his energy for what might be a long evening ahead. Yet he was too restless to sleep. He climbed out of bed and turned on the radio to see if there was any news about the discovery of the bomb in Taylor's apartment or anything else about the Boyd case.

As he listened to the radio, he walked over to the window and peeked through a crack between the brown vinyl curtains. The seedy motel had two floors, and access to all of the rooms was from the outside rather than from the lobby. A balcony ran the perimeter of the building on the second floor.

Terasawa spotted two cars in the parking lot below that hadn't been there before, one on the right of 216 at the far end of the parking lot, the other on the left. They were dark, late-model American cars without any markings. There was one man behind the wheel in each car.

The telephone rang. On the third ring Terasawa picked it up. Without waiting for him to speak, the caller hung up.

That was too much of a coincidence for Terasawa with the cars out front. Each of the drivers must have partners who were in the motel office, Terasawa decided. One of them had called to determine if he was in the room. That was all Terasawa needed to round out the picture.

He strapped on his shoulder holster with the Berretta and put on his jacket. Three different passports, car keys, and money were in his pockets. He looked around quickly to make sure there was nothing else he needed, and nothing left that would give away his identity.

If he moved fast, he would have the element of surprise on his side. Approaching the door of the motel room, he pulled the car keys out of his pocket. He envisioned the scene outside in his mind. Metal staircase ten yards to the right along the balcony. His gray Mercedes twenty yards across the parking lot, facing forward toward the room.

As he opened the door, he hit the panic button on his key ring to flush out and distract the cops. The car alarm in the Mercedes began blasting its shrill warning, and both drivers jumped out of their cars and ran with guns in hand. One ran toward the Mercedes, the other toward him.

Terasawa made it to the second step of the metal staircase before the cop reached the bottom. He raised his gun to confront Terasawa. "FBI. Stop right there. Drop the gun. Hands in the air," the man shouted, his gun pointed up at the assassin.

Terasawa had no intention of complying. He fired his own gun, winging the agent in the shoulder. The man's gun fell to the ground and skidded across the oil-stained asphalt.

By then the other one had run behind the Mercedes. He dropped to one knee and took aim. Terasawa raced down the rest of the stairs and ducked behind a car, which deflected two shots. He knew that he didn't have much time before the other two agents came racing back from the motel lobby. He hit the button on the keypad that started the Mercedes engine by remote control. Then he began running toward the car, weaving in the parking lot, dodging shots and firing as he ran. His first shot narrowly missed the agent's head. His second one hit the man in his exposed knee. He screamed in pain and crumpled to the ground.

The Mercedes was idling when Terasawa grabbed the door handle. Before he jumped in, he fired one shot each at the two FBI cars, flattening the tires.

As he slammed the car door, the other two agents came running around the corner of the motel building with their guns in their hands. The time it took them to survey the scene was all that Terasawa needed to roar out of the parking lot and into the flow of traffic.

Running after him, they tried to take aim at the Mercedes. But New York Avenue was a main artery with lots of traffic and pedestrians—too many people to risk a shot as Terasawa moved in and out of lanes.

Behind the wheel, he considered his options. They must have recorded the number on his license plate. The car was hot. He had to get rid of it. Two blocks from a Metro station, he ditched the Mercedes, then took the Metro north and east to New Carrollton, next to the Amtrak train station. It was a short walk to the parking lot used by train passengers. Hoping that the owner of the car he picked wouldn't be back to report his car missing until Terasawa was through with it, he easily opened the door of a beige Toyota Camry and hot-wired it. The driver had obligingly left a parking ticket on the front seat.

Terasawa breathed a sigh of relief. He had to make a

change in his plans, but only a slight change. No longer could he wait at Cady's house. That was too risky. But there was nothing wrong with sitting on the street in the car, a few doors away. And, of course, that wasn't the only way he could get Taylor. He still had one other possibility, but that depended on her and where she went today.

"I'm sorry, we blew it," a distraught John Frazier said to Cady on the phone.

"What happened?" Cady asked anxiously.

Frazier gave him a complete report. "I'm kicking myself for being in the motel office along with George. If only I had been in the parking lot at the time. Now I've got two agents in the hospital."

"How serious?"

"After surgery they should be okay, but I'm angry with myself."

Cady tried to conceal his disappointment. "You'll get him soon."

"We've got an all-points bulletin out for the man."

"Is there any chance you can put a man in front of my house?"

"You think he'll go there?"

"He was there this morning."

Eavesdropping, Taylor pulled back in fear.

"I'll get a man in front ASAP," Frazier said. "How about your office?"

"I've got the security of the U.S. Courthouse. We'll be okay here."

"And when you leave?"

"I'm in the garage. I'll make sure I'm not followed."

"I don't know, C.J. If I were you—"

"Your resources are limited. Use them finding this Tera-sawa. I've got a gun myself. We'll be okay."

He hung up the phone and turned back to Taylor. "Since we can't interrogate Terasawa, we're back to the issue of how we uncover additional facts on the issue of whether it's McDermott or Harrison."

"It's not Harrison," she insisted.

When Cady didn't respond, she said, "I'll go see Philip and talk to him. It's time to refute McDermott's nonsense once and for all."

"Don't you think we should both go?" Cady asked.

She raised her hand. "Please, C.J., this has to be me alone."

He didn't agree, but he backed down.

"Let me call and make sure he's in," she said, pulling out her cell phone.

"Don't forget about the police order for your arrest on the Mississippi warrant. You might want to meet him outside of the office."

When there was no answer on Harrison's line at the office, the call rolled over to the receptionist.

Taylor tried to disguise her voice in case all firm personnel had been given orders to notify the police if they heard from her. "Is Mr. Harrison in today?"

"Out of town on business," was the polite answer.

"And his secretary?"

"On sick leave. Who is this, please?"

She hung up and dialed Harrison's home. "It's Taylor," she told Celia, his wife.

"Oh, how are you?" Celia replied in a relaxed, friendly voice. She and Taylor had always gotten along well together.

Taylor breathed a large sigh of relief. At least the Mississippi business hadn't reached Celia, but then again, not much from the law firm ever did.

"Is Philip in?" asked Taylor, holding her breath.

"He's in Japan on business."

Taylor was blown away. "Japan?"

"He's been over there a few days on this trip."

Taylor was even more confused. To her knowledge, the only Japanese project Harrison was working on now was the one for Fujimura. In fact, all of his work for Japanese clients came through her and Fujimura.

"When's he coming back?" Taylor asked.

Celia laughed. "I don't even bother to ask that question anymore when he leaves on a business trip. The answer is always, 'When the negotiations are over.' You want me to give him a message if he calls?"

Taylor suddenly had an idea. "No message, but do you have your calendar around for last August?"

"Sure. I'll get it."

After a couple of minutes, Celia returned to the phone.

"Take a look at August twenty-eighth," Taylor said. She heard papers crinkling. "Do you know whether Philip was in town?"

"Definitely away. I wrote 'Philip out of town. Dinner with Mary Ann at Cosmos Club.' "

"Do you happen to know where he was on August twenty-eighth?" As soon as the words were out of her mouth, Taylor knew the answer.

Celia laughed again. "I can't possibly keep track of him. He's always going so many places. He tells me, but I never bother to write it down."

"Did he happen to mention Argentina?"

"I honestly don't remember."

*   *   *

Cady went to the men's room.

Sitting alone in his office, Taylor was reeling from everything she had heard today. It couldn't be. Philip couldn't have done this to her.

When Cady returned, he looked at her with great tenderness. He felt sorry for the enormous pain she was feeling. Still, he had to bring her back to reality. "What Celia said is consistent with what McDermott told us."

"There has to be another explanation," she said without any of the vehemence she had displayed in Hall's office.

"How well do you know Philip Harrison?"

She felt as if she had been smashed in the stomach with a sledgehammer. "Until now, I thought very well."

He shook his head grimly. "A picture that was grainy is now becoming very sharp."

"It can't be right."

"What's he doing in Japan?" Cady had meant it as a rhetorical question. Taylor still wasn't willing to believe Harrison was involved.

"If it weren't for all of this, I would have assumed that one of his American clients is negotiating an agreement with a Japanese company or obtaining financing from a Japanese bank. Now I can't even guess."

Cady pulled up a chair close to Taylor and sat down. "I really do think that Harrison's working with Sato. He's the American Alex Glass was trying to discover when they killed him."

Taylor refused to believe it. "Harrison's not working for anybody in this mess."

Cady didn't want to be too hard on her. Over and over again he had seen situations in which people didn't want to face what friends or loved ones had done. Yet he had to help her see it. "I'll bet Harrison spent enough time with you in the last couple of weeks to know what moves Senator Boyd was making in his campaign before he made them. That would have let Harrison plan this thing perfectly."

She shot a scathing look at Cady. "I can't believe that." As soon as the words came out of her mouth, Taylor felt like a fool. Cady had to be right. She had kept Harrison informed. He had been interested. She had wanted his advice. It had seemed natural.

God, she was stubborn, he thought. And loyal to a fault. He decided to take another approach. "If Harrison was involved with Sato, then he might have some documents in his office in the law firm that confirm it."

"And how do you propose to get access to his office? You couldn't possibly get a judge to issue a search warrant with what we now have."

"You're right. But you could easily get into his office. You're a partner in the firm."

Taylor stared at him, wide-eyed. "You want me to break in and search Philip's office?"

"That puts it bluntly, but that's the idea. If he's involved, I bet he has got some incriminating documents stashed away. With attorney-client privilege and work-product rules, we lawyers never imagine anyone will get access to our own files. Besides, Harrison may have wanted to keep some papers to protect himself if Sato ever decided to let him take the fall alone."

"I don't want to search Philip's office," she said emphatically.

"Why not? If you don't find anything, that should give you a powerful argument that he's innocent."

"The answer's no. *No.*"

"Afraid of what you'll find?"

Cady had hit the nail on the head. She couldn't accept the conclusion that Harrison had betrayed her.

"All right, I'll do it," she said reluctantly. "But we'll have to wait until about ten this evening, when the place is pretty much deserted. I don't want anyone seeing me there."

Chapter 26

With the gun on the flat panel next to the gear shift, Cady roared out of the underground parking garage in the U.S. Courthouse. He cut a sharp right, looking in the rearview mirror. He headed down one avenue and up another in random directions for five minutes until he was convinced he wasn't being followed. Then he proceeded to the law firm, parking on the street in front of the building in case he and Taylor had to make a quick getaway.

In the lobby of the building, Bruce, the regular evening guard, sat at a desk close to the elevators.

"Evening, Bruce," Taylor said, taking the security key from her purse that operated the elevators after normal business hours.

Bruce stood up at his desk and looked awkwardly at her. "Sorry, Miss Ferrari. I can't allow you to go up in the elevator."

Taylor was flabbergasted. "What did you say?"

"I-I'm sorry," he stammered, "but you can't go up."

"I'm a partner in this law firm. Have you forgotten that?"

"No, Miss Ferrari, but I have orders not to let you go up."

"Orders?" she shouted. "Who told you that?"

"Mr. Harrison himself called me about an hour ago. He gave very strict instructions. He said that you were a fugitive from a Mississippi warrant. That I shouldn't let you up in the elevator. That if I saw you, I should call the D.C. police. He gave me a special number at police headquarters."

Taylor was too stunned to respond, but not Cady. He whipped his wallet out of his pocket and flashed his Department of Justice ID in front of Bruce so fast that Bruce never had a chance to see his name. Then he took the .38 from his jacket pocket and pointed it at Bruce.

"Now, listen up," Cady barked. "I'm with the FBI, here on an official government investigation. I've asked Miss Ferrari to go up to her office and get me some papers. If you don't let her go up in that elevator right now, I intend to haul your sorry ass to jail for obstruction of justice. Do you know what that is?"

Bruce shook his head weakly from side to side.

"It means that you go to jail for not letting the FBI do its job. Mr. Harrison doesn't go to jail. You do. You got that?"

Cady gripped the gun in one hand and reached for the phone with the other. "Now, do I call headquarters at the FBI to have you arrested, or do you let her go up?"

Bruce pointed to the elevator.

As Taylor disappeared from Cady's sight, he said to Bruce, "Don't make any effort to reach for the phone." Cady moved to a position halfway between Bruce's desk and the glass front doors of the building. He wanted to keep an eye on both his car and Bruce.

Having worked closely with Harrison for so many years, Taylor knew a great deal about his personal habits. He never kept the door to his office locked. His most confidential papers were in two locked drawers at the bottom of one of the built-in bookcases that lined a side wall. Most important, the key to those drawers was inside a silver cup resting on the bookcase, which had been his prize for being on the winning team of a Newport-to-Bermuda sailing race three years ago. Once when she was alone in his office waiting for Harrison to return from a meeting, she had watched his secretary take that key, unlock the drawer, and retrieve a file that Harrison needed.

Not wanting to draw the attention of anyone who might be working late, she walked softly down the dimly lit corridor lined with Oriental carpets. At the entrance to Harrison's office, she turned on the lights, took a deep breath, then went inside. Her chest was pounding as she crossed the carpet toward the silver cup.

Quickly she opened the top of the two drawers. Inside were half a dozen red file folders, all neatly tied and arranged in a row. One by one she took them out and leafed through the papers inside. They all contained documents relating to the law firm's business. She put them back carefully and opened the bottom drawer, where she found two more red file jackets.

The first one contained documents related to a top-secret hostile corporate takeover being planned by a large French conglomerate, one of Harrison's major clients, for a Fortune Fifty American corporate manufacturer. She tied up that file and returned it to the drawer.

From the tension of what she was doing, her hands were moist with perspiration. The last folder had an S on the front. She carried it over to Harrison's desk, opened it, and began leafing through the papers inside. Japanese writing caught her eye. She felt more bewilderment. It was inconceivable that Harrison could be doing work for a Japanese client without involving her, unless . . .

She was fighting hard against what was now the likely conclusion. She went back to the beginning of the file and examined the documents one by one.

On top, Taylor saw a draft speech in Japanese dated October 2 of this year, and a typed English translation below it. It was a speech for Yahiro Sato to deliver at the Japan Defense Agency the day after the American presidential inauguration in January.

Taylor began reading the draft:

> The banner that led Japan into the modern era was "Rich Country, Strong Army," [fukoku kyóhei], and these two have always been linked together throughout history. A strong military is absolutely essential for Japan's survival in the modern world. This thinking was expressed by Fukuzawa Yukichi at the end of the nineteenth century, when he wrote, "There is no single example of a nation maintaining its independence by relying on treaties and international law."
>
> Today, our nation's economic development has stagnated because of our limited landmass. We have a population that is approximately half of the United States', but the total land of all of our islands is equal in size only to California, and very little of that is arable. To expand our economy we must reach out to our neighbors in Asia. This is critical if we are to expand our markets and obtain less expensive raw materials. In addition, if our neighbors compete unfairly with us in world markets, they must be persuaded to change their behavior. Finally, we must be sensitive to the threat that we are facing as the Chinese economy expands, and they continue to develop more sophisticated weapons.
>
> All of these factors taken together have led me to suggest a major program for development of an

expanded military, which is necessary for Japan's defense and to assure its proper role in the world.

The draft then outlined the first steps of the program for militarization, which would begin early next year:

> *(1) January 30, Sato, as defense minister as well as prime minister, publicly announces that all U.S. troops must leave Japan within 30 days.*
>
> *(2) February 15, repeal Article IX of the Japanese constitution, which General Douglas MacArthur forced on Japan, contrary to the sovereign rights of every other nation of the world. It provides, "aspiring sincerely to an international peace based on justice and order, the Japanese people forever renounce war as a sovereign right of the nation. . . . Land, sea, and air forces, as well as other war potential, will never be maintained. The right of belligerency of the state will not be recognized."*
>
> *(3) March 1, develop plans for increases in manpower and equipment in the army, navy, and air force, and begin development of a nuclear arms program.*
>
> *(4) June 1, begin negotiations with Taiwan for a mutual defense treaty.*

In the margin of the speech were a number of handwritten revisions in a script that Taylor recognized to be Harrison's.

The next document in the file was the final version of the speech, in Japanese, dated October 20. With her knowledge of the language, Taylor compared the final with the draft. All of the changes Harrison had suggested had been made.

With a sick feeling in the pit of her stomach, Taylor turned the speech over and looked at what else was in the folder. There was a copy of a fax addressed to Yahiro Sato, which read, *No need to worry. Everything is proceeding on schedule.* It was signed, *R.L.* That must be the code name for Sato's American contact. Under the fax was a report from a French investigator that linked Abdul Azziz and Maison Antibes and made the bribery case against Boyd.

She pulled out the calendar that Harrison kept in the center drawer of his desk. With trembling hands, she flipped back to August.

There it was staring her in the face. A line through August 27 and 28 with a note that read, *Y.S. The Alvear Palace, Buenos Aires.* Precisely the date that Alex Glass had said Sato had recruited his American supporter in Argentina.

There was no doubt it was Harrison.

Taylor felt light-headed and weak in the knees. She collapsed into Harrison's desk chair, and sat there for several minutes as the full measure of the conspiracy sank into her mind.

Sato's motivation was easy for Taylor to understand—his distorted view of what was good for Japan. But what about Harrison? What possibly could be motivating him? That had Taylor stumped. It couldn't be money. He had all he could ever want. Power? He had turned down important positions in the American government. Then what?

Whatever it was, it had to be significant enough to involve him in the murders of Boyd and Gladstone.

She would have bet anything that Harrison wasn't capable of arranging those, but now she realized that she would have been wrong. *Goddammit.* Cady was right. Harrison had been able to plan precisely every move because he always knew from her where the senator was and how he was reacting to Cady's investigation. She had been the perfect stooge.

Suddenly Taylor realized what else Harrison had done to her. He must have sneaked into her office and examined her Mississippi travel records in order to frame her for the hit-and-run that would have put her in a Mississippi jail.

Waves of anger and betrayal flooded her mind. She knew that she had to move, but she felt frozen. She couldn't get up from that chair.

Cady saw someone approaching his car, and he raced toward the front doors of the building, the gun in his hand. Once he saw it was just a young couple who stopped to admire the XK8, he breathed a sigh of relief.

While Cady was looking out front, Bruce reached down and pushed the button on the two-way pager hooked to the belt on his waist.

Terasawa was parked in the Toyota Camry a couple blocks away from Cady's house in order to avoid detection by the FBI agent parked in front. When Taylor and Cady came home, he planned to make a frontal assault, even if it meant killing all three.

Once he heard the beeper, he knew what it meant: Taylor was at the law firm. He started the engine and headed toward the building.

Taylor rose with a start and collected all of the documents she had been examining, as well as Harrison's calendar. With swift, purposeful strides, she walked down the hall to the copying machine and made two copies of each. Then she went to her own office, stuffed one set into a brown mailing envelope, addressed it to Chief Justice Hall at the Supreme Court, and applied more than enough postage to get it there.

The second set she placed in a red folder. After that, she returned the original documents to Harrison's office.

On her way to the elevator, she stopped in the firm's mail room and tossed the brown envelope into one of the bulging gray sacks of outgoing mail that would be taken to the post office first thing in the morning. The red folder she clutched tightly in her hand.

They walked quickly from the lobby to Cady's car. "Let's go back to my house," he said. "Then we can take a careful look at what you have in that folder. While I drive keep your eyes open, and I will too. Let's make sure we're not being followed."

Cady drove west on Pennsylvania Avenue and then cut over to Rock Creek Parkway and Beach Drive, which sliced through the large park in the center of the city. From the passenger seat in the front, Taylor kept glancing back, watching the flow of cars behind them. When they passed the P Street exit, she said to him, alarmed, "I think we're being followed."

"Keep watching," Cady said tersely.

Minutes later they went through a brightly lit tunnel. At this time of the night very few cars were on the road. Taylor kept her eyes riveted to the side mirror next to her window.

"It's still there," she said. "Looks like a beige Toyota Camry."

"Buckle up and hold on. I'm going to lose him."

For the next few minutes, Cady raced around the winding narrow roads that snaked through the park, with the Toyota hot on his tail. He was frantically trying to lose his pursuer, but the Toyota gradually gained ground. Cady slowed down slightly to cross a narrow stone bridge.

Through the rearview mirror, he watched the Toyota close most of the gap.

Taylor turned around in her seat. Terrified, she saw that the driver was a Japanese man clutching a pistol. "He's got a gun," Taylor screamed. "It must be Terasawa."

Cady floored the accelerator and shot around a bend. They heard a gun firing. The bullet sailed over the top of the green Jaguar. A second one shattered the rear right taillight. Cady stomped on the accelerator.

Just ahead a narrow road cut off to the right. At the last instant, without any warning, Cady swerved sharply and took the turn. The driver of the Toyota couldn't react in time, and he missed it. With a couple of seconds' lead time, Cady roared along the road. He turned left into a parking lot for a picnic grove and slammed on the brakes.

"What are you doing?" Taylor asked frantically.

"Out of the car. Fast," he snapped. "Follow me."

He turned off the engine, jumped out, slamming the door behind him, and ran into the grassy, leaf-filled area just ahead. Taylor followed him with the red file folder in her hand.

When he dove behind a bush, she was right with him.

It was quiet on the road.

"Maybe he won't find us here," she whispered.

"Let's hope so," he said anxiously.

Then they saw a set of headlights coming toward them. It was the beige Toyota. The car stopped on the road, adjacent to the parking lot. As they watched, Terasawa rolled down the window on the driver's side. In his hand he was holding a bottle. He raised it and flung it in the direction of the green Jaguar. It smashed the front windshield and burst into flames, exploding and triggering an explosion in the car's engine.

"Holy shit," Cady hissed, glued to the spot. "He thought we were in there."

The flames were shooting into the air with a savage heat that threatened to engulf Taylor and Cady. She grabbed him by the arm and pulled him away. "We've got to get the hell out of here," she said. She began running with the folder clutched tightly in her hand. Cady was two steps behind.

Back on the road, Terasawa saw a flicker of movement in the darkness. Cursing, he grabbed his gun and ran after them.

Taylor and Cady sprinted through the park, which was thick with trees and covered with leaves on the ground. Glancing over her shoulder, Taylor saw Terasawa coming after them. Shots flew over their heads. She was on the verge of panic. Then she cautioned herself, *Don't be stupid.* She knew her way around Rock Creek because she often ran in the park. They had an advantage here. She had to decide how to use it.

She jumped over a small stream. Cady followed her.

"I hope you know where we're going," he blurted out between short breaths.

"Just follow me," she called over her shoulder.

Another round of shots rang out. One narrowly missed Cady, blasting the bark of a tree.

Taylor looked back to make sure Cady was okay. That was a mistake. She stumbled over a log, crashing down into some branches and scratching her knees, arms, and face. She was stuck in a mess of branches on the ground. Another shot flew over her head.

Cady grabbed her by the arm and pulled her to her feet. The delay permitted Terasawa to close the gap.

In a renewed burst of energy, with Cady right behind,

Taylor practically flew over a tiny stream and hurdled a tree trunk on the opposite side.

She heard Cady gasping for breath. "Not far to go," she called, encouraging him. "Fifty more yards or so. You can do it."

That energized Cady. "I'll make it," he said, "but hurry."

A shot ricocheted off a boulder, but neither of them broke stride.

Ten yards ahead, across the road, Taylor saw a gray stone building. It was the Beach Drive Station of the U.S. government's park police. Half a dozen patrol cars were parked in front. Emerging from the woods, Taylor dashed across the road. She burst into the open door of the park police station, with Cady right behind.

"We're being chased by a killer," she cried out.

Alerted, two officers pulled out their guns and ran to the door.

Before they could see Terasawa, he took off back into the trees. Cautiously the two officers crossed the road, their pistols drawn. With no one in view, they returned to the station.

"You want to tell us what happened?" one of the other policemen asked Cady. Producing his DOJ identification, he explained that they were being chased by the man who had been involved in the shoot-out at the Capitol City Motel. "It involves one of my cases," he said, not telling them any more about it.

As he spoke, Cady was considering his options. Going back to his own house was out of the question. Terasawa would attack there. But if the assassin couldn't find them, they would be safe. They had to get out of the area before Terasawa could get to his car and return to follow them.

"Will you drive us to the Willard Hotel?"

*   *   *

When Harrison arrived at Yahiro Sato's country house in the mountains west of Tokyo, Sato was waiting for him near a small pond with carp in the back. "Let's walk," Sato said.

Despite his age, the Japanese leader was in excellent physical shape. With long, purposeful strides he walked swiftly. Harrison, a full foot taller than Sato, struggled to keep up the pace. For several minutes they went on in silence, with Harrison waiting patiently for Sato to begin talking.

They stopped in a clearing, where Sato motioned for Harrison to sit down on a tree stump. The American took a cigarette, a real one, from a pack in his pocket and tried to light it, but the wind made it impossible. He cursed under his breath, crumpled the tobacco into his hand, then tossed it on the ground.

Grim-faced, Harrison said, "It's all turning to shit on us."

Sato stared at the American in dismay. "That's ridiculous. Boyd's no longer a candidate. Everyone believes he took his own life. Regardless of who wins the election in the United States, I'll get what I want: support in the White House for my program."

Harrison frowned. "When I agreed to help you, I didn't think anyone would be killed. You didn't tell me that."

Sato tossed the blame back to Harrison. "And you told me that Boyd would drop out of the race once he saw the evidence."

Harrison's face tensed. "I was wrong, but that didn't justify two murders."

Sato picked up a twig on the ground and snapped it in two. He had to be patient with this naive American fool. He couldn't afford to have Harrison turning on him. "Sometimes unforeseen things occur. We do what we have to do in order to prevail."

Distraught, Harrison threw his arms in the air. "You don't understand. Now we have two murders that could be investigated. It can get back to both of us. You should never have sent Terasawa to the United States in the first place."

Harrison's words infuriated Sato. The American had assisted Terasawa with everything he had done. Now Harrison was trying to disassociate himself. Struggling not to lose his temper, which would be counterproductive, Sato gestured for calm. "We can ride this out if we don't panic. Unless Terasawa is arrested and talks to the American authorities, which will never happen, no one will be able to prove a thing against either of us."

Harrison disagreed. "You underestimate Taylor. I know her well. When she grabs onto something, she's like a dog with a bone. She'll find the truth with or without Terasawa. She's even tied Alex Glass's death into this whole business."

Sato looked worried. There was no longer any doubt in his mind that Ozawa had spilled his guts to Glass at dinner. The walls were closing in. "I'll do whatever it takes to avoid having this destroy us."

His words were spoken with such vehemence that Harrison's despair lifted. He thought about the cryptic conversation he'd had a couple of hours ago with Bruce, the guard on the desk at the law firm. Initially Harrison had developed the elaborate plan with the judge in Mississippi to have Taylor arrested and taken out of circulation—in jail, where she wouldn't be harmed until the election was over. It was only when she foiled that effort that he had reluctantly concluded that he had to give Terasawa the support he needed to kill her. The assassin should have done that tonight. Yet he had never received the telephone verification that she was dead. "The steps I've taken to eliminate Taylor," Harrison added glumly, "haven't succeeded."

"So what? If the police don't capture Terasawa, Taylor has nothing."

Harrison thought about Sato's words. He had to assume the worst. That meant Taylor had searched his office. But everything that was incriminating he had carefully locked up. And even if she did find it, at most it was circumstantial. There wasn't enough for her to build a case against him. Besides, she had nowhere to go with it. If she tried to get to President Webster, McDermott would block her. If Harrison were back in Washington, she would confront him and kick up a fuss. Until he received some confirmation from Terasawa that she was dead, he had to remain in Japan.

"Terasawa will take care of Taylor," Sato said.

Harrison nodded in abject resignation. God, he hated what he was doing. What this had come down to. In Buenos Aires everything had seemed simple enough. All he had to do was get Cady launched on the investigation. Aided by his relationship with Taylor and his ability to control McDermott because of the woman in Sarasota, Harrison was confident he would be able to force Boyd into withdrawing from the presidential race. And certainly nobody would be hurt or killed. Webster would be reelected, or possibly Crane. It didn't matter. Sato would become the Japanese prime minister. With support from the White House, a remilitarized Japan would offset China's military might. At long last he would be avenging the death of his father. It would have all played out that way if it weren't for that fool Boyd refusing to drop out in return for immunity from prosecution, even though the evidence against him was overwhelming.

Now Harrison was cornered. He kicked at the muddy ground in anger and frustration.

Reading his mind, Sato said, "This battle's not over." His

eyes were blazing with fury and determination. "You don't have to worry. We'll find a way to destroy Taylor before she destroys us."

"We're safe now," Taylor said as Cady threw the dead bolt and put the chain on the door of their room at the Willard Hotel. "We're finally safe from that awful man."

While she went into the bathroom to clean her cuts and bruises, Cady got on the phone to call John Frazier and tell him what had happened.

"I'm sending two men to the Willard," Frazier said. "One to stand out in front of your room and the other at the entrance to the hotel. They'll stick with you tomorrow. This guy's not going to quit."

As Taylor came out of the bathroom, the full enormity of what had happened to them tonight struck her. Her body began convulsing wildly, and Cady put his arms around her. "He'll never be able to find us here," he said as he held her tight. He led her over to the bed and hugged her. "We're going to get even with Harrison. Before this is all over, he'll pay for what he did to both of us."

Hearing Harrison's name, and remembering his betrayal, Taylor leaned forward, threw her arms around Cady, and began to cry. For several minutes she trembled against him. Rivulets of tears flowed down her cheeks.

Cady held her close. "It's going to be all right. We're going to get even with him. We'll find a way."

All we have to do, he thought grimly, *is stay alive that long.*

Chapter 27

Two FBI agents escorted Taylor and Cady out of the Willard, looking in every direction as they walked down the front steps. Terasawa was nowhere in sight. "We must have lost him," Taylor said, hoping she was right.

Another agent was in the car, behind the steering wheel. As they began moving, Cady muttered, "I loved that XK8. I'll kill the bastard if I ever find him."

Once they arrived in Chief Justice Hall's office, Taylor opened up the red folder from the law firm and spread out the Harrison documents on Hall's desk. The Chief took his time examining each piece of paper carefully. He tapped his fingers on the desk as he looked at the documents. Taylor didn't like the frown that was growing on his face.

Finally he lifted his head. "I'd say that these documents build a good case against Philip, but it's all circumstantial. It's not as strong as I'd like to prove a conspiracy that's responsible for two murders."

"But his work on the speech itself is enough," Taylor responded. "The handwriting in the margin is Philip's. All of the changes he proposed were picked up in the final."

"He's a Washington lawyer. They provide advice to foreign leaders all the time." The Chief's tone was thoughtful.

"Even on actions contrary to the interests of the United States. That's not a crime. You know that, Taylor."

"How do you dismiss the fax? It's obviously a coded message."

"I agree, but it will be hard to prove that Philip sent it."

Frustrated, Taylor said, "Then look at the diary entries. He had a meeting with Yahiro Sato on August twenty-eighth in Buenos Aires."

"Assuming that Y.S. is Yahiro Sato."

"But isn't that reasonable, given the dates on the two speeches, and everything else?"

The chief justice waggled his hand back and forth. "It's all reasonable. Personally, I'm convinced that Harrison and Sato planned this whole thing together to knock Senator Boyd out of the race. If all we had was this, I'd want to go forward and confront Harrison. Still, I'd like a little more evidence linking Harrison and Sato. I don't have to remind you, Taylor, that Philip's a skillful lawyer. You don't want him arguing that there's a reasonable doubt."

The intercom rang. "Mr. McDermott is here," Helen said.

"Send him in," the Chief replied.

McDermott had no sooner entered than he reached into his pocket, extracted a microcassette, and placed it on Hall's desk. "I made a copy. You can keep this one."

Sitting by the recorder, they listened to the tape, which confirmed everything McDermott had said yesterday. At the end, Taylor blurted out, "We've got Harrison nailed to the wall."

McDermott looked bewildered by her change of position. Yesterday she had been his most ardent defender.

"What role did the president play in all of this?" Hall asked McDermott gently.

"None. He had no knowledge of any of it."

Cady broke in. "You're covering for President Webster. Trying to take the rap."

"Absolutely not. He had no idea that I met with Harrison. I knew damn well that Webster would not have gone along with it, even if it enhanced his chances for reelection. He's not Nixon. He would have let me take my lumps rather than become a part of something like this."

Cady thought that was highly unlikely. "Why should we believe you?"

"You've got too much on me. I can't afford to lie to you. The truth is that the president's not involved. They didn't need him. They had me to do their dirty work."

"Who killed Senator Boyd?" Cady pressed.

McDermott drew back. "Beats me. Why don't you ask Harrison?"

"Harvey Gladstone?"

"Same answer. Until you told me yesterday, I didn't even know he was dead."

With his flat denials, the interrogation came to a halt. Silence fell over the room. Finally Hall said, "Seems to me we're about finished with you. The only other thing I want is a promise that you'll never mention a word of this conversation to anybody, including the president."

"You don't have to worry," said McDermott, perspiring freely. "Boyd and Gladstone are dead. Talking about this meeting would be like signing my own death warrant."

When McDermott was gone, Hall turned to Taylor and Cady. "Despite what McDermott said, do you think President Webster is involved?"

"I can't decide," Cady replied. "McDermott's such a slimeball that I'm not willing to trust him. He could still be covering for Webster. Certainly I'm not convinced enough to risk telling the president or Dorfman at the FBI what we now know. Not with this killer on the loose."

Hall weighed the sensitive issue in his mind. "I have to agree with your last statement," he said reluctantly.

Taylor was standing in front of the window, facing the Capitol, with her fists tightly clenched.

"Our next move's easy," Cady said, glancing at her. "With McDermott's tape, we've got an ironclad case against Harrison. Let's extradite him from Japan."

Taylor turned toward them and shook her head sharply. "We can't go after Harrison alone. We have to get Terasawa and Sato as well."

"Do you really think the Japanese government would ever extradite Sato?"

The desire for revenge was burning inside her. "We've got to find a way to make Sato pay for what he's done. And Terasawa, too."

Cady could tell she was leading up to something. "I'm open to suggestions."

"There's a Japanese lawyer I know by the name of Fujimura," Taylor replied.

"Kenzo Fujimura," Hall said.

"You know him?" Taylor asked, surprised.

"We've met several times over the years at international legal conferences. He's a superb lawyer. I have a great deal of respect for him."

"Fujimura's in California now, working on a corporate transaction," Taylor said. "I want to fly out today, tell him about our Harrison-Sato case, and seek his advice. Perhaps enlist his support."

The Chief took off his glasses, leaned back in his chair, and closed his eyes, mulling over Taylor's proposal. "It's not a bad idea," he replied at length. "Fujimura's well connected with the Japanese government. He could approach Prime Minister Nakamura for us and try to gain Nakamura's acquiescence before we make the request for Sato's extradition." Hall saw Cady cringing in his chair, and stopped. "Why don't you like the idea, C.J.?"

"I'm not sure we can trust Fujimura. If he's worked with Taylor, he probably knows Harrison. How do we know he isn't mixed up in this as well?"

"I say we give it a try," Taylor replied.

"And there's something else," Cady said.

"When the chips are down, the Japanese stick together. If it's Sato against us, they'll all close ranks behind Sato."

The Chief was taken aback. "C'mon, C.J., you're not serious."

"Unfortunately, I am. Look, I'm not as much of an expert on Japan as she is," he said, pointing to Taylor. "But even I know how intense nationalism in Japan is."

Taylor couldn't believe what Cady had said. "That's ridiculous. The Japanese are like any other people, some good and some bad."

"Listen, you two," Cady said defensively, "I'm not a racist. All I'm saying is that until we know for sure that Fujimura and Nakamura aren't involved, we're running a big risk to trust them."

Cady and Taylor turned to Hall, wanting to see what side he would come down on.

"I have to agree with Taylor," Hall said. "I'm prepared to trust Fujimura."

Cady stared at the Chief before he realized any further effort was futile. Glumly, he said, "I'll do it your way. I just hope you two are right."

"Clearly it's a risk," said the Chief. "But our only hope now, with Harrison in Tokyo, is to get some help from the

Japanese side. Fujimura's our best bet. I would only change one thing."

"What's that?" Taylor asked.

"You two can't take a chance on going out to California yourselves. This is too big for the three of us, and too dangerous. Last night proves that. Let's face it, we're two lawyers and one old sick judge. On our own we wouldn't have a chance."

Cady disagreed. "But we managed last night. . . ."

"You got lucky last night, C.J. Before you go to California or anywhere else, the two of you need logistical support. You need somebody to protect you."

"I'd love that," said Cady, "but how do we get it without involving the president?"

"Let me try Paul Clayton," the Chief said. "He's been a close friend of mine for many years."

Taylor interjected, "General Clayton, the chairman of the Joint Chiefs?"

"You know him, Taylor?"

"Senator Boyd was an air force buddy of Clayton's in Vietnam. They flew F-4s together, and they kept up a friendship over the years. Even though the senator wasn't on the Armed Services Committee, General Clayton usually stopped by the senator's office when he was testifying on the Hill. I met him a number of times when I was with the senator."

"But General Clayton works for the president," protested Cady.

Hall replied, "I think I can persuade Paul to give you the help you need without the knowledge of the president. He's not a big fan of Webster, and he's got a large petty-cash fund."

*   *   *

Forty-five minutes later, crossing the Fourteenth Street Bridge in the back of a dark blue unmarked Ford Crown Victoria with Cady and the Chief, Taylor thought about what she knew of General Clayton. He was an example of what a military hero should be. Besides having an outstanding war record in Vietnam, he was well regarded by the men and women serving under him. He was viewed as honest and forthright. He wasn't afraid to be outspoken if he thought the issue justified it. Guiding the air force through a difficult time of sharp cuts in the defense budget was no easy task, but somehow General Clayton managed it. He also enjoyed a remarkable degree of good feeling with congressional leaders.

They entered the vast and gloomy Pentagon parking lot at the north gate. The marine driver made his way around rows of parked cars and into an underground garage. Inside, he led them into a private elevator that went straight to the office of the chairman of the Joint Chiefs.

General Clayton, a tall, imposing figure with a full head of black hair, was waiting in the doorway to his office. His shoulders were broad and his chest large, thrusting forward the four gold stars on his blue uniform and his numerous decorations.

"I'm sorry about Charles," he said to Taylor. "I was at the memorial service at the National Cathedral. I wanted to talk to you after it was over. Somehow I missed you in the crowd."

"It wasn't a very good day for me, I'm afraid."

"Or the country, for that matter. I liked Charles. I thought he would have made a good president." He held a hand out to the chief justice. "Should we all go into my office, Gary?"

"It would be best if I briefed you alone first," Hall said.

The two of them disappeared into Clayton's office, leaving Taylor and Cady to wait outside.

For the next thirty minutes, Cady and Taylor impatiently flipped through old magazines to pass the time. They both looked up when the door to Clayton's office opened. Standing in the doorway, the general had a tense expression on his face.

The Chief took Taylor and Cady aside. "I've told him everything. He'll give you all the help you need. Not only because he liked Senator Boyd, but he knows that it's in the best interest of the country. He agrees that until we know for certain that Webster isn't involved, the president can't be told anything about this."

"What do we do now?" asked Cady.

Hall coughed, a long, hacking cough that gave Cady a chill inside.

"You two go in and talk to General Clayton," he said. "I'm going back to the court."

About a dozen model airplanes were scattered on tables, bookcases, and credenzas in General Clayton's huge office.

"I have to tell you two," General Clayton said, "if I hadn't heard it from Gary, I would never have believed it. It's a classic case of American intelligence making the wrong judgment."

"I'm sorry," Taylor replied. "I don't understand."

"We have a score of people at the Pentagon in military intelligence who do nothing but watch Asia and try to predict what's going to happen there. But all of them have discounted any immediate threat being posed by Sato. They've been worrying about the risk posed to Taiwan by China's increased militarization and North Korea's nuclear development program. They missed the real issue. It's like Saddam Hussein all over again."

General Clayton stopped and tapped his fingers lightly on the desk. "I take it back," he said, "there is one of my people in intelligence, Major Jonathan Green, who has been writing memos warning us to focus on Sato because he has a good chance of being the next prime minister, and he's strongly committed to Japanese militarization. The difficulty is that nobody, myself included, paid much attention to Major Green."

"Then you view your role in this as more than protecting us," said Taylor.

"Exactly. This is the Pentagon. Everybody has their own agenda, myself included. As I see it, you two are a little gift from heaven that dropped into my lap. If I can use you two and this conspiracy to disgrace Sato and prevent him from achieving a position of power in Tokyo, then the world will be a safer place."

"Did the chief justice tell you about Taylor's plan to meet with Fujimura in Los Angeles tomorrow?" Cady asked, appealing to a new arbitrator.

"I think it's a fine idea. It gives us a possible solution. Most important, it may give the Japanese government a face-saving way out as well. If—and it's a big if—Sato is operating without Japanese governmental approval, and if disclosure is made in the right way to his government, we may be able to induce Nakamura to extradite Sato along with Harrison to the United States." He turned to Taylor. "The trouble is that I don't know Fujimura personally. If you and Gary are prepared to trust him, that's good enough for me. Where's he staying in Los Angeles?"

"He has a suite at the Hotel Bel Air," replied Taylor.

Cady hung his head, knowing he was defeated.

"Call him, Taylor," Clayton said. "Try to set up a meeting there this evening at six. Just the two of you—you and Fujimura. I'll fly you out in a military plane. You'll have bodyguards and a military escort, but I want them and Cady in the background. My suggestion is that you act as if you're still on your own."

"That's risky for her, isn't it?" asked Cady.

"My people won't be too far away. Even if Fujimura's working with Sato, I doubt that he'll try to harm Taylor in his own hotel suite. You comfortable with that, Taylor?"

"Very much so. Let's do it."

She was starting to feel better about this plan. They would be protected by the military, and she'd be meeting a man she'd known for years. Together they would find a way to unmask the conspirators and make them pay.

Chapter 28

The L.A. basin was shrouded in fog when General Clayton's plane began its descent at Edwards Air Force Base. In her seat next to Clayton, Taylor closed her eyes and tried to make a final decision about how to play her meeting with Fujimura. The difficulty was that all of Cady's arguments, which he had continued to press through the long plane ride, had managed to plant a substantial doubt in her mind. Suppose Cady was right and Fujimura was a part of the Sato-Harrison conspiracy? Even if he was not involved, would he instinctively support his countryman? If so, would she be laying a new trap for herself?

A black Dodge Caravan was parked on the runway. From the outside it looked like any other minivan, except that the glass was treated to prevent people from looking in. But the inside of the van was anything but ordinary. Because it was the van that was used to accompany the president when he made trips to California, it was loaded with sophisticated telecommunication and recording gear. There were also enough arms, including machine guns, inside this traveling fortress to outfit a small army. The side glass paneling of the van was bulletproof and doubly reinforced. Two marines were sitting up front, and four more were in the back as Clayton, Taylor, and Cady climbed in.

Not knowing how Fujimura would react, and wanting to avoid a leak that would eliminate the element of surprise, Clayton had decided not to alert the Hotel Bel Air, the LAPD, or the private security force that patrolled the Bel Air community about their visit. His plan was to drop Taylor off at the hotel and then park nearby, where he would monitor her conversation with Fujimura, broadcast from a microphone he planned to fasten to the clasp of her purse.

As the van crawled along the San Diego Freeway in the heavy traffic, Clayton asked one of the marines to hook up the microphone. Taylor balked.

"I changed my mind," she said emphatically. "I don't want to do it that way, secretly recording my conversation with Fujimura."

"Why not?" Clayton asked, puzzled. "That's the way we agreed to do it."

"It may be silly, but it's a matter of honor. He's been a good friend, and I want him to help me. We have no reason to believe he's with Sato on this."

"He'll never know that the conversation is recorded."

"That's not the point, General Clayton."

Cady was upset, thinking about the risk to her. "C'mon, Taylor," he said. "General Clayton's proposal is the way to go."

"I won't do that," she said stubbornly.

"So how do you want to do it?" Clayton asked her.

"Drop me off at the hotel. Come back in an hour. If I'm not in front then, return an hour later. When you pick me up I'll give you a complete report."

"You're putting yourself at great risk," Cady said.

"What's he going to do? Drown me in the hotel pool?"

"At least let me go with you," Cady said. "We can meet with him together."

"It has to be me alone."

"But—"

Clayton cut him off. "We'll do it your way," he said to Taylor. "But if you're not out in front the second time we return for you, then we're coming in for you fully armed."

On one other occasion Taylor had been at the glamorous Hotel Bel Air. When she was working for the California governor, she had attended a power breakfast there with half a dozen top executives in the electric power industry. At the time she had been staggered by the sheer luxury of the place, which was surrounded by ten-million-dollar private homes. Unlike other hotels, the Bel Air wasn't a building, but a series of cottages scattered throughout carefully tended grounds. Swans gracefully adorned the pond created in front. Here, the aura of Hollywood's fabled years lived on in unparalleled splendor.

As Taylor exited the van, an attendant came up, dressed casually, California style, in khaki slacks and a white sport shirt. "Can I help you, miss?"

"I'm here to meet with one of your guests."

The front desk called Fujimura's suite to verify that she was expected, and a bellman led her along a tree-lined path to a large cottage at the back of the property. Incredibly, everything looked the same as she remembered. It was chilly in the early evening air, and, whether from the cold or apprehension, Taylor found herself trembling as she walked.

Dressed in a suit and tie, standing in front of his cottage, Fujimura bowed, then led her inside. Flames were leaping in the stone fireplace. Coffee, tea, and a tray of small sandwiches were spread out on a table in the living room. Two waiters clad in white jackets stood by the table to serve.

Taylor nibbled a chocolate-chip cookie and sipped coffee as Fujimura told her how sorry he was about Senator Boyd. Then he made small talk in English about the beauty of the hotel. She knew that he wouldn't talk business, even in Japanese, until they had finished eating and he could politely dismiss the two waiters.

When they were gone, he lit a cigarette and continued talking in English. "You told me on the phone that you had a serious matter to discuss with me. I assume it's about the gas company acquisition you and Harrison are working on."

"Unfortunately not. It's a political matter of the greatest urgency."

He was taken aback by this announcement. Then, as he remembered her conection to the senator, he recovered himself. "Please tell me."

She gulped hard, then began her saga with her conviction that Senator Boyd had been murdered. She talked about Cady's role, then the investigation in Napa, and how they had almost been killed by Terasawa in Rock Creek Park. She omitted only the involvement of the chief justice and General Clayton, making it appear as if she had come to Los Angeles by herself, because that was what General Clayton had told her to do. Like any good lawyer, she decided instinctively to hold back one piece of evidence, so she didn't tell him about the recording McDermott had made of his conversation with Harrison. In all, she talked for almost an hour. Fujimura listened intently, smoking one cigarette and then another, but showing no emotion or visible reaction. When she was finished, she handed him copies of the materials she had taken from Harrison's office. He put his cigarette down and studied the documents.

"You've made some very serious accusations," he said

solemnly. "With tremendous implications for the relationship of our two nations."

"Only with the greatest reluctance. I firmly believe that they're true."

His eyes, magnified by his thick glasses, looked up at her. "Could someone be intentionally misleading you?"

She paused for a few seconds before answering. "I honestly don't think so. It all fits together too well."

He still wasn't satisfied. "Is it possible that Harrison alone is responsible, and he's arranged matters to appear as if Sato is his partner?"

She shrugged her shoulders. "All of the evidence seems to suggest otherwise."

He stroked his chin with his thumb and forefinger, weighing her words. "Why did you come to me?"

"For your advice, if you feel comfortable providing it. Cady is waiting for me in downtown Los Angeles. He has official orders issued by the Justice Department for the extradition of Harrison and Sato. He's prepared to deliver them to your embassy in Washington tomorrow."

"Which would precipitate an enormous crisis between our two countries."

"Precisely. That's what I hope to avoid. I'm aware of your personal relationship with Prime Minister Nakamura. I believe that these matters warrant his attention. Perhaps he can suggest a less formal way to resolve this matter. If he cannot, at least we will be providing him with the courtesy of advance notice, to which he is entitled as the leader of a close ally."

Fujimura lit another cigarette, rose, and paced slowly around the room, deep in thought. She closed her eyes, letting a wave of weariness pass over her body, and waited.

"I'm prepared to fly back to Tokyo this evening," he said

softly. "There's a late plane. But I don't know whether Prime Minister Nakamura would be willing to discuss these matters with me."

Taylor decided to press her case, even at the risk of alienating him. "May I respectfully suggest that when you talk to the honorable prime minister, you give prominence to the recent death of Alex Glass, which occurred in Japan. Were that fact to be made public along with everything else, it would be unfortunate."

Irritated, Fujimura responded in a cool voice, "I'm well aware of that."

Realizing she had gone too far, Taylor quickly backed off. "Would you like to take the Harrison documents with you? I could make copies here at the hotel."

"For now, you keep them safe. My suggestion is that you stay at the Bel Air tonight in my suite. From Japan, I'll call you here tomorrow and give you a report."

Taylor glanced at her watch. In fifteen minutes the second hour would be up. Clayton with his marines would descend on the Bel Air. She stood up abruptly.

"I have to go back to my hotel to get my things," she said. "Later, when you're gone, I'll return."

He didn't notice her distress. Instead he handed her a room key. "It will all be arranged with the reception desk."

As she started toward the door, she turned around and looked at the worried Fujimura. The furrows had deepened on his forehead. He looked much older than when she had arrived.

"Would you say that he was surprised by what you told him?" Clayton asked when she returned to the van.

"He's not a man who shows his emotions, yet I dropped a bombshell on him. He had to be surprised."

"Unless, of course," interjected Cady, "he's been a part of this from the beginning, in which case he wasn't surprised at all."

Cady's observation troubled her. "Do you really think—"

"At this point I don't know what to think. He could have been their California contact. His being out here is a hell of a coincidence. He knows both Sato and Harrison. How many other people fit that description?"

After the way Harrison deceived her, she wasn't sure she could trust anyone. She turned to Clayton. "What do you think, General? Am I letting my friendship with Fujimura cloud my judgment?"

He shrugged. "At this point I can't tell. After Fujimura leaves I'll make an arrangement with the hotel so any phone calls or messages you receive are sent out to the air force base where we'll be. We'll wait there and see what he does in Tokyo."

"Wouldn't it be better if I stayed in his suite at the Bel Air," she asked, "as he suggested?"

"You can't expose yourself that way," Cady pleaded.

"You're missing the point, C.J. That's how we can find out if Fujimura is a part of this with Harrison and Sato. Nobody else will know I'm in his suite at the Bel Air. If someone does come, I'll have to agree he's involved. If they don't, then you have to admit that we can trust him." He was still worried, and she added, "There's no risk. We have six marines who could ensure my safety. Right, General Clayton?"

The general was weighing her idea. "If you're willing to take the risk," he said, "I'm game. It would be good to know for certain where Fujimura stands. I'm sure I can get the hotel to cooperate with us without telling them what it's all about. I'll have the van take you back to the Bel Air once

Fujimura leaves. Cady and I will go out to the base for the night."

"I want to do it," she replied. "I've got to show you two that Fujimura's not mixed up with Sato and Harrison in this."

"Well, if Taylor's going to stay at the Bel Air tonight, I'll be there, too," Cady said to General Clayton. "I'm not taking a chance of leaving her alone."

Taylor and Cady watched a rerun of the evening's presidential debate on the television set in the living room of Fujimura's suite while they ate dinner from room service—power food: sirloin steaks and baked potatoes followed by hot-fudge sundaes.

Unlike the Webster-Boyd debates, which had been civil and dignified, this was a no-holds-barred slugfest. As she watched, Taylor had no doubt who was coming out on top. Crane sounded fresh and sharp, with a vision for the country. The president looked tired. Whether Crane could pull off the impossible, to turn next Tuesday's election into a real contest, remained to be seen.

Once the debate ended and the spin doctors took over, Taylor turned off the set.

"Who won?" she asked Cady.

"Tweedledee and Tweedledum."

"Gee, I thought Crane came across so much better. It's clear that he wants to make sweeping changes to improve things. Webster just wants to stay in office."

"Get real. The way I see it, they're both posturing for the public. Who knows what they'll do if they're elected?"

"You're such a cynic."

There was a rustling in the trees outside in the back of the suite. Cady jumped to his feet and grabbed the revolver from his jacket pocket.

"Get under the bed," he shouted to her.

She hit the floor. On her elbows and knees, she crawled toward the bed.

"I'm going to look around outside," he said.

She heard the door slam. Minutes later he reentered the suite and called to her, still under the bed, "False alarm. Nothing."

She scrambled to her feet.

Cady said, "It finally struck me when I was walking around outside that I was being stupid. You're right, of course. Nobody will attack us here tonight."

"Then you agree with me that we can trust Fujimura?"

Cady shook his head. "That's not it at all. I finally figured out how this thing's playing out. It's like a vortex, a sort of giant vacuum cleaner, sucking us in slowly. They're not going to make any effort to harm us here in California. They don't have to. With Fujimura's help, Harrison and Sato will lure us to Japan and kill us there."

"You really believe that?"

"Absolutely. You'll probably get a call from Fujimura tomorrow asking us both to go to Japan. That'll be part of the setup."

He waited as she mulled over Cady's words, but not for long. "So what are you going to do if Fujimura asks us to go to Japan?"

"It'll never happen."

"Meaning that you don't know what you'll do."

When she didn't respond, he said, "Ah, to hell with all that."

He walked over and put his arms around her, pulling her close. For an instant he hesitated, waiting to see if she would resist. When she didn't, he leaned down and kissed her. She returned the kiss with an urgency that answered any doubts he had. He slid a hand around to her front and stroked the side of her breast.

When she finally pulled away, her face was flushed. "There's a large Jacuzzi in the bathroom."

He smiled. "But I didn't bring a bathing suit."

"Neither did I. Let's crack some champagne." With her next thought, a devilish twinkle appeared in her eye. "Also, why don't you get the leftover fudge from the sundaes?"

"Why do you want that?"

Turning him by the shoulder, she pushed him in the direction of the bar. "Do you always have to be in charge?"

When he entered the bathroom a few minutes later, she was wearing only her white lace panties. As he watched, she slipped out of them and leaned over the tub, adding bubble bath and adjusting the temperature. It was the most erotic sight that Cady had ever seen.

He placed everything on a small table and reached for her. She was too fast for him, slipping into the tub and disappearing under the suds, except for her head. She turned on the jets as he yanked off his clothes. "Hey, hurry up."

Inside the tub, he sat down facing her and poured two glasses of champagne. As he raised his glass, he said, "Getting to know you has been the only good to come out of this mess."

She tapped her glass against his. "Ditto. I'll drink to that."

They relaxed in the tub, intensely aware of each other's naked bodies, while they finished their champagne. Then Cady leaned forward and kissed her again. He ran his fingers slowly around her breasts, first one and then the other. They were soft and warm from the water. When her tongue darted into his mouth, he dropped his hand lower, rubbing and stroking while he continued to kiss her. He spread her legs apart and inserted two fingers inside as he continued caressing her with the heel of his hand, rubbing it in a clockwise motion, faster and faster until her whole body convulsed.

Once she recovered from her flight to ecstasy, she moved her toes over his penis and testicles. She kissed him deeply, touching his chest lightly with the tips of her fingers, playing with his nipples, exciting him even more.

"Bed," he mumbled, standing up and holding out his hand to help her up. "Let's go to bed."

But she refused to budge. Instead she ran her fingers over his rigid member, touching and probing, sending twinges throughout his entire body.

"Bed," he mumbled again. "I want you now."

With her knees on the floor of the tub, she reached for the silver pitcher with the thick, cold fudge. She poured it over his erect penis, then spread it around with one hand. When he was coated, she ran her tongue over the tip of his penis and then along the shaft, licking as she went. "Um, I like fudge," she said.

He closed his eyes and gave himself over to her. She took the whole thing into her mouth and sucked. He was powerless to do anything at all. She had achieved total control over him. With her wet mouth around him, he felt the excitement rising to a climax. But then she squeezed the bottom of his penis firmly just above the balls, and that pulled him back from the brink.

At last she rose and led him to the bed. With their bodies still dripping wet, she pushed him down flat on his back, and she mounted him. They moved together in a slow, undulating rhythm. When his body began to shudder, at long last finding relief, she drove herself to climax as well. Their bodies trembled together. She remained on top of him, pressing down, resting her head on the curly hairs of his chest long after he slipped out of her.

She leaned up and kissed him gently once more. Then she rolled off. That was the last thing either of them felt before they disappeared into a deep sleep.

A powerful storm worked its way through the Pacific and lashed the island of Honshu. Torrents of water poured from the sky, flooding narrow Tokyo streets. A large black limousine pulled up in front of the office of Prime Minister Nakamura. Yahiro Sato emerged from the back of the car. Under an umbrella held by a staffer, he walked smartly into the building. Despite the hard rain, Sato had a broad smile on his face, projecting the image of a man close to attaining his cherished objective: becoming the prime minister of a remilitarized Japan. Inside, though, his stomach was churning. He wasn't able to dismiss Harrison's warning, despite his verbal bravado to the American. As long as that woman, Taylor, was in pursuit, everything he had worked for was at risk.

An hour later, when Sato left the building, an expression of grim determination marked his face. As the limousine pulled away, Sato turned to Ozawa in the back of the car and gave him a series of instructions.

"There is no room for error," he said at the end.

Ozawa was dropped at the headquarters of the Self-defense Forces. With the rain pounding down, he stood and bowed politely to his leader until the car pulled away. Then he walked swiftly inside.

The car continued driving west toward Sato's country house. When they arrived, it had stopped raining. Sato stood in front and stared up at the Japanese flag, the red sun on a white background, swinging gently in the breeze from a pole above the house. If he did not act fast, his entire plan could be ruined.

Waiting for Sato to return, Harrison soaked in the natural hot spring half a mile from Sato's house. Usually the water, so hot that steam rose into the air, relaxed him, but not now. He closed his eyes and thought about that day in Shanghai so long ago. Every detail of that morning—November 21, 1949—was indelibly etched in his memory.

An hour before sunrise, they had come, pounding on the door of the house in which seven-year-old Philip and his mother had been held in house arrest since his father's imprisonment. Petrified, his mother opened it to see half a dozen armed soldiers waiting out front. "You come with us," the officer in charge said.

"Is it my husband? Will they release him?" she said. "Have they decided it was all a mistake?"

Her words were met with a stony silence. The two of them were tossed in the back of an army truck with a red star painted on the hood. In the bitter cold of the morning, the boy huddled close to his mother.

At the gate to the prison, armed guards pushed them forward. As they were hustled up three flights of cracked and decaying concrete stairs, the terrified boy clutched his mother's hand. On the top floor, the guards pushed them out onto a balcony which overlooked the muddy yard in the center of the prison compound. At the far end stood a single wooden post.

The boy's mouth opened to cry no as he realized what was happening, but he couldn't speak.

"This is what happens to spies and traitors," an officer

said. He gave an order, and another soldier restrained the boy and his mother to stop them from jumping.

When they led his father from the jail to the post, he walked with resolute dignity—a man of God who had come to China to do the Lord's work as a missionary. A man who had no regrets about how he had spent his life on earth. A man who had no fear of the world to which he was passing.

They tied him with his back to the post, his face pointed toward the boy and his mother.

A soldier offered to put a black cover over his head, but he waved the man away. He wanted to face the six soldiers who constituted his firing squad.

As the order was given—"Ready, aim . . ."—the boy saw the words forming on his father's lips, "The Lord is my shepherd. . . ." Bullets from six automatic weapons tore into his father's body.

His mother uttered the most searing, heart-wrenching screams, which the boy often heard in his sleep at night even decades later. But the boy did not cry out. His mouth opened, but not a sound came out.

Philip and his mother came back to New York to live with her sister and brother-in-law on the Upper East Side. The firing squad might as well have killed her, for she never recovered. She died of a stroke two years later.

Two young women approached Harrison, holding towels in their hands. "Sato-*san* has returned and would like you to meet him," one of them said.

Harrison climbed out of the pool of water and grabbed a towel. Anxious to hear what Sato had learned, he dressed quickly and returned to the house.

As Sato told him that Fujimura had been present with the prime minister and reported on the meeting, Harrison became more and more disturbed. He was in deep trouble. The decision to extradite Sato was complex and troublesome for Nakamura, but not the decision to extradite Harrison. Nakamura would grant that in a heartbeat.

Harrison's only chance now was with Sato. He looked at his Japanese ally hopefully, waiting to see how he had responded.

"I suggested to Nakamura that he invite Taylor to come here along with Cady," Sato said.

Harrison was incredulous. "To Japan?"

"I told him that we should have a chance to confront them and answer these baseless charges. Once he hears both sides, I explained to Nakamura, he will have no choice but to reject the demand for our extradition."

"But I don't understand. They'll ruin both of us."

"A trap is being laid," Sato said firmly. "We will prevail one way or the other."

"But how will you stop them from destroying us?"

Sato said coldly, "In the United States you were in charge. It hasn't gotten us what we want. Here I make the decisions. We do things my way. This time we won't fail."

Chapter 29

At six-thirty Taylor was awakened by a thump outside their bungalow as one of the hotel's employees tossed the *L.A. Times* on their doorstep. Remembering how wonderful last night had been, she kissed the still-sleeping Cady on the cheek. She headed to the front door and snatched up the newspaper. On the bottom of the first page was a box with the results of four postdebate polls.

"Oh, damn," she moaned as she studied the numbers. In all four polls Crane had made significant inroads, but he was still trailing by five percentage points on the average.

The phone rang. It was General Clayton. "You two all right?"

"Yeah, fine."

"There's no point having you stay at the Bel Air any longer. You accomplished whatever you set out to do. Lieutenant Farnsworth will bring you back to the base."

"What about Fujimura's call?"

"I'll have the Bel Air board patch it through. He'll never know where you are."

The call from Fujimura didn't come until noon. By then General Clayton had his electronic gear in place. As Taylor talked on the phone, her conversation would be broadcast into another office down the hall, where General Clayton and Cady could listen. The general even had an interpreter standing by, a Japanese-American air force first lieutenant.

"Is that you, Taylor?" Fujimura asked in Japanese.

Relieved to hear his voice, she let out a deep breath. "Yes, Fujimura-*san*," she answered in English.

"I think it would be better if we spoke in Japanese. Would it be convenient for you to fly to Tokyo with C. J. Cady?"

Taylor rocked back onto her heels. This was precisely what Cady had predicted: that Sato and Harrison would use Fujimura to lure them to Japan to kill them.

Cady came racing into the room, shaking his head furiously. "Tell him we won't come," he whispered. "I'll deliver the extradition papers to their embassy in Washington." Then he ran back to the other office.

Taylor hesitated, unsure how to respond.

"Are you still on the phone, Taylor?" asked Fujimura.

Confused, Taylor answered, "I'm surprised by your sudden invitation."

"Reservations have been made for the two of you in first class on JAL flight one-twenty-four leaving Los Angeles at four o'clock this afternoon. They're holding your tickets at the airline counter."

"What can you tell me about your discussions in Japan?" she asked.

"It would be best if we spoke about these matters when you arrive in Tokyo. The issues are quite complex."

"It would be useful if I had some idea of what happened."

"That's not possible, I'm afraid."

"Are you certain that it's necessary for me to come?"

Fujimura sighed. He realized that he had to tell her something. "Unless you and Cady come and provide the prime minister with an opportunity to evaluate the facts, he will agree to extradite Harrison, but not Sato. Now, is it convenient for you to come?"

Cady came back into the room. "Tell him no," he said in a hiss.

She looked at Cady and hesitated.

"It's convenient for me," she finally replied.

"And Cady?"

"I'll have to talk to him. Do you want me to bring anything?"

"All of the documents that you showed me at the hotel. Prepare Japanese translations to the extent possible."

"And where should I go when I arrive?"

"I'll be there personally to meet your plane."

As Taylor put the phone down, she thought Cady would explode in anger. General Clayton was standing in the doorway looking at her with a combination of admiration and concern.

"I'm sorry, C.J.," Taylor said, "but getting Harrison isn't enough. Sato started all of this. He has to pay for what he did. The only way that can happen is if we go."

He was livid. "Goddammit, Taylor, we're a team. You shouldn't have said yes like that. At least, you should have told him that you'd talk to me and call him back."

All trace of last night's romance was gone. "We don't have a choice. We can't talk to the president because we don't know where he stands. Going to the press is out of the question because it would wreck American-Japanese relations."

"I know all of that. I still think I should have been consulted before you put my life on the line."

"What do you mean, your life?" she asked tensely. "I only answered for myself."

Cady snapped, "Yeah, right. Do you really think I'd let

you make that trip on your own?" He turned to General Clayton. "Can you fly us over to Tokyo in an air force jet?"

Clayton nodded. "Sure."

"I don't understand," Taylor said. "Fujimura told me they're holding seats for us on JAL one-twenty-four. We can get there in time."

"This time I'm the one who's making a unilateral decision for both of us," Cady said emphatically. "We're not flying on JAL one-twenty-four."

"What's wrong with JAL one-twenty-four?"

"I don't want to take any chances."

"You really don't trust Fujimura at all."

"It's Sato and Terasawa I'm worried about. They're capable of anything."

"You really think that—"

"Look, Taylor, we may not make it back from Japan, but I'd sure like to be certain we get there."

She sighed deeply. "Okay, I'll call Fujimura and tell him about the change in our flight plan."

Terasawa was dejected. He sat in his car across from Cady's house and continued his vigil. Deep down he knew it was hopeless. The FBI agent had left yesterday. Terasawa knew that Taylor and Cady would not return.

He also knew that he had totally failed Sato because of his inability to kill Taylor and Cady. The humiliation was almost too much to bear. He hung his head in shame, uncertain of what to do or where to go.

His cell phone rang, jarring him back to reality. It was Sato.

"You're worthless and incompetent," Sato shouted angrily in the phone. "No more use than a piece of dog shit."

Terasawa didn't argue. He didn't want to admit that he

had no idea where Taylor and Cady were. "Should I come back to Tokyo?" he asked.

"I don't care what you do. You'll have to live with the disgrace. I never want to have anything to do with you again."

As he hung up the phone, Terasawa vowed to return to Japan and find a way to redeem himself with Sato.

Chapter 30

After the air force jet landed, it taxied past the headquarters building at the large American base outside of Tokyo. One of the facilities, Taylor thought, from which the Americans would be expelled if Sato became prime minister. With Cady behind her, she descended the stairs into the dreary light of an overcast afternoon, clutching a briefcase in her hand.

Accompanied by their six-member marine escort, in military dress, Taylor and Cady walked along a series of interminable walkways until they reached the base headquarters building. Fujimura was waiting for them in the lobby with a somber expression.

"This is C. J. Cady," she said to Fujimura, who bowed politely.

Fujimura looked at the six-member marine contingency and then back at Taylor. "I'm sorry, but you must come with me alone," he said. "Those are the rules decided upon by Prime Minister Nakamura."

"But—" Cady interjected.

"We'll come alone," she said, cutting him off.

"And no weapons please," Fujimura added.

She stared at Cady. He didn't move.

"Please, C.J.," she said.

He took the .38 out of his pocket and tossed it to Lieutenant Farnsworth.

Satisfied that the ground rules had been accepted, Fujimura turned and led the way out of the headquarters building. A jeep drove them to the front gate, where a black sedan was waiting just outside the base. The driver, sitting behind the right-side steering wheel, scrambled out as they approached. Wearing white gloves, he opened the back door.

The black sedan pulled slowly away from the base. They were now on their own in Japan.

"Where are we going?" Cady asked.

"Tonight we're staying at a *ryokan,* what you would call an inn. It's south of here in Shuzenji on the Izu peninsula, about three hours' driving time."

Trying to relieve the tension with small talk, Taylor said, "I remember reading about Shuzenji in history, but I can't recall what happened there."

"It's famous from the Kamakura shogunate. The second Kamakura shogun was assassinated there in 1204."

"That doesn't give me a good feeling," Cady muttered.

His comment made Taylor squirm in her seat. "What happens tomorrow?" she asked Fujimura.

"A meeting has been arranged. You'll have a chance to tell your story."

"To whom?"

"Prime Minister Nakamura will be there, Suzuki-*san,* the minister of justice, Sato, and Harrison. Just the seven of us, and an interpreter."

Cady broke in. "But didn't you already report to the prime minister what Taylor told you in Los Angeles?"

"Of course. As soon as I returned to Tokyo I reported everything to him. Now he wants to hear it directly from you." Fujimura paused while the car entered an expressway and began driving south. "The prime minister also wants Sato and Harrison to have an opportunity to hear you as well."

"It sounds to me like a trial."

"You might say that, Cady-*san*."

The cell phone in Fujimura's pocket rang, and he quickly pulled it out. After listening for a few seconds, he said, frowning, "Yes . . . I understand . . . yes."

"Is there a problem?" Taylor asked when he hung up.

"Both a problem and a solution," he said in his typically enigmatic way.

Cady returned to the topic of their previous discussion. "Who's on trial: the two of us, or Sato and Harrison?"

"You're not on trial," Fujimura responded.

"But the question is whether the prime minister will believe us or Sato."

"You could put it that way. Or you could say, in the language of your American lawyers, that Sato and Harrison are being given an opportunity to confront their accusers."

"And if the prime minister doesn't believe us?"

"We'll deal with that at the time, Cady-*san*."

That wasn't enough for Cady. "What is the role of Suzuki, the minister of justice?"

"To conduct the proceedings and to advise the prime minister. I believe Taylor is familiar with him."

"I met him a number of times in your office," Taylor replied. "That was before he was justice minister. When he was still a law professor and a judge."

"Precisely."

Taylor felt better knowing that Suzuki would be there. He had an international reputation as a scholar. Like Chief Justice Hall, he was known for his integrity, and as someone outside of the political process.

A sign on the road read, *Toll, 1 km.* As they approached, the driver slowed down and reached into his pocket for some bills. Four tollbooths were open for southbound traffic.

The driver was trying to decide which booth to select when Fujimura said, "Pull all the way to the right and stop the car."

As the driver complied, Taylor and Cady became alarmed. "What's wrong?" Cady asked.

Fujimura ignored the question. He put one hand on the door handle. The car stopped next to a police car with its back doors open under the large canopy that covered the tollbooths.

The instant the black sedan was stopped, Fujimura opened the back door on the right side. "Come with me," he said abruptly to Taylor and Cady.

"Where are we going?" Cady asked.

"Please, Cady-*san*," Fujimura replied in an authoritative tone. "It's essential. Now! I don't have time to explain."

Fujimura was already out of the black sedan and standing along the right side. Taylor grabbed Cady by the arm and pulled him out.

With his two visitors in tow, Fujimura ran toward the police car, which had one uniformed policeman behind the wheel and another up front on the left side. Fujimura pointed to the back of the car. The three of them climbed in.

The driver started the engine, but the police car didn't move until the black sedan had left the tollbooth and was out of sight.

"What was all that about?" Cady demanded from Fujimura.

"I was instructed to change cars at this tollbooth."

"Why? What's going on?"

"Security reported that a man with a scar on his face had been loitering near the black sedan in a suspicious manner when it was parked outside of the American base."

Taylor gripped the car seat tightly. "Terasawa," she said, her voice quavering.

"I don't know," Fujimura replied.

"Where are we going now?"

"Our destination remains the same. The *ryokan* on the Izu peninsula."

Outside, it was twilight. Taylor strained her eyes to look through the windshield to see where the sedan had gone. Suddenly she heard a loud blast, a percussive boom. There was a bright light as a fireball shot skyward.

Fujimura's cell phone rang again. He answered immediately. When he hung up he looked grim. "Someone planted a bomb in the black sedan. The car was in a field, empty, when it exploded."

Taylor gasped, too stunned to speak. "Terasawa," she finally said.

Cady agreed. "No question about it."

She turned to Fujimura. "We thank you for saving our lives."

"Switching cars was not my idea," he said modestly. "I was only following instructions."

"Given to you by whom?" Cady demanded.

If Fujimura was offended, he didn't show it. "The instructions came from Prime Minister Nakamura directly to me."

"How many people know that we're staying tonight at this inn in Shuzenji?" Cady asked.

"Only the prime minister, myself, and the policemen in this car."

"I know what you're thinking, C.J.," Taylor said.

"There's no point in changing the *ryokan* tonight. If Prime Minister Nakamura wanted us dead, he would not have instructed Fujimura to have us change cars at the tollbooth."

She had a point, and Cady acquiesced. Still, the idea that they had been riding in a car that had blown up left them both nervous and tense.

They exited the expressway and turned onto a narrow rural road. Fujimura said it was nearly two more hours until they reached the *ryokan*. The car climbed into the Amagi Mountains, amid hot springs. Exhausted from the long plane ride and aided by the motion of the car, Taylor couldn't keep herself from dozing. When her eyes opened from time to time, she glanced at Cady. He was watching the driver and Fujimura intently.

They reached the *ryokan* without any further incident.

The proprietors spared no effort to make their guests from the United States comfortable. Dinner was a never-ending series of traditional Japanese cuisine, but after the bomb scare, Taylor and Cady didn't have much of an appetite.

During dinner, Taylor found Fujimura surprisingly pensive. When he spoke, he limited himself to small talk. He asked Cady about his prosecutor's job in Washington. He explained to them about the hot springs in the area that made this a center for resorts, and also a center for country homes maintained by some of the wealthy and powerful in Japan. After dinner Taylor and Cady walked back to their adjoining rooms, each furnished in traditional Japanese style with tatami mats and futons.

Taylor whispered, "Now that you've spent some time with Fujimura, are you willing to trust him?"

"I still haven't seen anything that sways my mind that way."

"His life was on the line with ours today. If we didn't change cars, he would have been killed with us."

"But we did change cars."

"Meaning what?"

"Meaning that the whole thing could have been an elaborate scheme to lead us to the very conclusion that you're coming to now, namely that we can trust Fujimura."

"You're a stubborn man, C.J."

"Just a cautious one. But listen, I'm not an idiot. You know your way around here. Don't worry. I'll follow your lead."

After a hot bath, the jet lag hit Cady. He lay down on the futon and immediately fell sound asleep.

Inexplicably, Taylor was no longer tired. Dressing in a navy blue–and–white kimono that had been left out for her, she wandered around the *ryokan*. She found Fujimura sitting alone in a small lobby area, smoking a cigarette and sipping Armagnac.

He pointed at the glass. "Would you like to join me?"

"Yes, thank you."

He motioned, and a young woman immediately appeared with another snifter.

"Cady-*san* doesn't trust me. Does he?" Fujimura said.

"He doesn't know you the way I do. Also, trust doesn't come easily to C.J." She thought of his ex-wife, and wondered if his distrust extended to all women.

"He's your friend. So I must speak carefully."

"With me you never have to speak carefully."

"Cady-*san* doesn't trust me because I'm Japanese. I know that—"

"That's not right. He's just—"

"No, I often see it in the eyes of some of your countrymen. Unfortunately, the same emotion in reverse exists on this side of the Pacific—contempt among some Japanese for Americans. Sixty years isn't that long a time in the history of a nation as old as ours." He paused to puff deeply on his cigarette. "I don't blame your friend for being disturbed and worried. Yahiro Sato is a powerful man. He has strong allies."

"How powerful is he?"

"I don't have a precise answer to that question. I do know, however, that people have been underestimating him. Many of the army—sorry, the Civil Defense Force—might very well support him in an open conflict with Prime Minister Nakamura."

Taylor sipped some Armagnac, troubled by this possibility. "Does that mean that we're on the verge of a military takeover of the democratic government in Japan?"

He shrugged. "Perhaps not now. If Sato continues to gain power, then it could be difficult to say."

Taylor paused to ponder what Fujimura had just told her. "What will happen tomorrow?" she asked.

"You must persuade Prime Minister Nakamura what you told me in California is true."

"And if we succeed in persuading him?"

"Then I'm hopeful that he will agree to extradite both Harrison and Sato. Prime Minister Nakamura is an honorable man." He stared at her through the thick lenses of his glasses, looking for understanding.

"He's also a politician. They're no different here than in Washington. I learned that long ago."

"That's true."

"Suppose we don't persuade the prime minister tomorrow?"

Fujimura pursed his lips and shook his head. "I don't like to consider that possibility."

An involuntary yawn forced its way out of Taylor's mouth.

"Perhaps you should go to sleep," Fujimura said. "You'll need your strength tomorrow. It will be an important day for you."

She left him and walked down the hall, stopping in Cady's room first. He was thrashing on the futon, moaning in his sleep. She bent down next to him. He was sweating profusely. His arms were swinging wildly.

Careful to avoid being struck, she leaned in and touched him, waking him up. "Are you okay, C.J.? Are you sick? What's wrong?"

He shot up to a sitting position. "Oh, God, I was dreaming. It was terrible."

"What about?"

"We were in a Japanese POW camp. Fujimura and Sato and some other men were torturing you. I was forced to watch. God, it was so awful. They were—"

She stopped him in midsentence by putting one hand over his mouth. With the other she opened her kimono. She pulled his naked body, damp with perspiration, close to her, burying his head against her breasts. When he was calm she pulled him down with her to the futon, still keeping his head against her.

He soon fell asleep again, but she remained awake long after. She kept returning to the idea that Sato had allies in the military. If tomorrow did not go his way, he would be desperate. Did he already have alternate plans in place?

Chapter 31

As the police car pulled away from the *ryokan,* two more police cars joined them, one in back, the other in front.

"Where's this hearing going to take place?" Cady asked Fujimura, who was sitting in the front seat.

"Prime Minister Nakamura's country house in Hakone. Near the base of Mount Fuji. A complex like your Camp David."

"Whose decision was that?" Cady asked suspiciously.

"Prime Minister Nakamura selected the venue."

After that answer they rode in silence. Taylor looked out the window at the breathtaking scenery. The sides of the road were thick with bamboo and evergreens. At regular intervals they had to slow down to cross small wooden bridges that went over fast-moving mountain streams. In the distance she could see snow-covered mountain peaks. Yet even among such beauty Taylor wondered where Terasawa was. Out there, somewhere in that wilderness, plotting his next move.

Taylor tried to imagine what it was like centuries ago during the shogunate, when warring tribes fought never-ending battles. Was that what she and Cady had gotten swept up in now? A modern-day version of one of those battles with Yahiro Sato, samurai, making a military grab to wrest control of the government from Nakamura?

The police car turned into a narrow paved driveway.

"The prime minister's country house," Fujimura announced unemotionally.

As the car passed two large catering trucks and pulled up to the stone gatehouse at the entrance, Taylor looked around. In the center was the main house, a large wooden building. On five sides of the main house, like spokes on a wheel, were a series of cottages that served as guesthouses. The entire complex was surrounded by a thick forest filled with bamboo and tall evergreen trees. A small stream ran along one side of the property.

The main house was surrounded by soldiers, about twenty in all. Taylor saw each armed with a submachine gun. On the roof two sharpshooters were scanning the area.

The sentry in the gatehouse motioned to their driver to turn off the engine. Four soldiers descended on the car, each one opening a door. When they all climbed out, the soldiers frisked them for weapons and checked Taylor's briefcase.

"Why so many soldiers?" Taylor asked Fujimura.

"Those are members of the Japan Self-defense Force. The charges you have brought are serious. Prime Minister Nakamura thought the presence of the soldiers was appropriate."

"But will the troops follow the orders of Nakamura or Sato?" Cady asked.

"All of our troops are loyal to the democratic government of Japan," Fujimura said sharply.

The large main house, like the cottages, was constructed and furnished in Western style because the prime minister frequently entertained Western leaders at this complex. As they walked through the front door, Taylor whispered to

C.J., "Cool down. Here we can't use the kind of confrontational approach that we employ at home. They're the judge and jury. If we're going to win, we have to do it their way."

"I'll behave," Cady replied, sounding chagrined. "I promise. You take the lead."

Inside the door stood another half dozen armed soldiers. As Taylor took off her shoes, she heard a rustle of activity. A man whom Taylor recognized from his pictures as Prime Minister Nakamura came forward. Fujimura introduced Taylor and Cady to him in Japanese.

"It's a great honor," Taylor said, bowing graciously. She nodded to Cady, directing him with her eyes. He followed suit.

"My thanks to you," the prime minister said in Japanese, "for making such a long trip to help us."

"We just hope that we can be of assistance," she answered in his language.

Involuntarily he raised his eyebrows, showing how surprised he was by her perfect Japanese pronunciation. "You learned your Japanese well."

She blushed in response to the compliment. "Fujimura-*san* is an excellent teacher," she replied.

At that point Suzuki, the Japanese minster of justice, appeared, dressed in a suit and tie. He looked a lot older than Taylor remembered, but it had been about ten years since she had last seen him. He was in his mid-seventies now, Taylor guessed. Like Fujimura, he wore very thick glasses.

Again, Fujimura introduced Taylor and Cady. More bowing. Then Fujimura and the prime minister left the room.

"Let me tell you a little about our proceedings today," Suzuki said to Taylor and Cady in English. "The honorable prime minister and I want to listen to what you have to say, and also to Sato and Harrison. This isn't a trial. It's more like an informal hearing. Everyone can make any statements they want. There won't be any cross-examination. And no record will be made of this discussion. At the conclusion, the prime minister, after consulting with me and Fujimura-*san,* will make a decision on your extradition requests."

"I assume that the discussion will be in English," Taylor said.

"I'm afraid that's not possible. For Prime Minister Naka-mura, it is preferable to use Japanese. Earphones and simultaneous translation will be provided so that Cady and Harrison may understand and speak in English. You have the choice of language."

"I will use Japanese," Taylor replied. "I prefer my own words to those of an interpreter."

He was pleased with her request. "As you wish."

"Where's Philip Harrison?" she asked.

"He's in the large room in back with Yahiro Sato. He asked if you would be willing to speak with him privately before we begin."

Cady caught her eye and vigorously shook his head, but she ignored him. "If it's acceptable to you, Suzuki-*san,* I will talk to Harrison."

He nodded. "I see nothing inappropriate in that."

When the justice minister left the room, Cady said to her, "Are you crazy? Harrison's going to try to turn you around. That's why he wants to meet with you."

"You really think he has a chance after everything that's happened to me?"

"He has a reputation for being persuasive."

Suddenly she realized that, in his bristling way, Cady was trying to protect her. "He's done a lot for me. I owe him this much."

"Because he tried to have you killed?"

"No, for everything before that."

"Well, at least behave like a good trial lawyer. Talk to him in generalities. Don't lay out our case for him. He doesn't know what papers of his you have. If you tell him, he'll be able to concoct some explanation."

He was being overbearing, and she had to restrain herself. "What could he possibly say?"

"Please, Taylor, this one time, listen to me."

Moments later a soldier led her to a small room that was empty. Patiently she waited for Harrison to appear. When he did, he strode in exuding self-confidence.

"For God's sake, Taylor," he said in a tone of surprise and righteous indignation, "what in the world have you done to me?"

He intends to intimidate me, Taylor thought. *He thinks he can prevail if he forces us into our normal roles of senior and junior partner.*

"Me? What have I done?" she said, tossing it back to him.

He ran his hand through his ruffled hair. "You don't think I was responsible for any of the things that happened to Senator Boyd, do you? Yahiro Sato built a trap for me because I was your friend. You're playing into his hands, forcing me into that trap."

Taylor wanted to scream, but she kept herself under control. "I don't believe I'm hearing this," she said in a firm, calm voice.

"How long have we worked together?" he said. "Do you really think I could do anything like that?"

"It turns out that I didn't know you at all."

Her coldness didn't faze him a bit. "What evidence do you have to back up any of these charges you made against me?"

She thought about Cady's warning. Harrison was on a fishing expedition. "All of the facts establish that you directed this conspiracy with Sato."

"You're dead wrong," he said, sounding annoyed. "Sato's a vicious man and a manipulator. He tried to draw me into his scheme. I was going to be his alibi if anything went wrong. You're playing into his hands."

Taylor laughed. "You'll have to do better than that."

"You don't get it. Do you?"

She couldn't believe he could lie so well to her face. "You can't think I'm stupid enough to believe you—"

He interrupted her. "I guess you don't get it. Sato's devious and smart. He's tricked you. Don't you see that?"

She had an acrid taste in her mouth. The words *You bastard, how could you?* were on the tip of her tongue, but she held them back.

"I was hoping that you'd be honest with me, Philip. I was obviously wrong."

Terasawa drove the four-wheel-drive vehicle recklessly on the dirt mountain trails, avoiding the paved roads. All of the usual approaches to Hakone were swarming with police and soldiers. He couldn't risk being stopped. He had to assume that they knew he was responsible for the bomb in the black sedan yesterday, that they had his picture.

Thinking about the bomb infuriated him. How had the police found out in time to have Taylor and Cady switch cars? He hadn't told anyone what he was planning. Terasawa concluded that he must have been sloppy in the execution. He was so unstrung by everything that had gone wrong lately, he wasn't careful enough. Seething at the thought, he smashed his hand against the dashboard.

Terasawa increased his speed, then missed the next bend

in the road and landed in a ditch. Five minutes later, when he maneuvered his way out, skidding and kicking mud high in the air, he made up his mind to slow down.

Besides, there was no reason to hurry. He knew from Ozawa where Taylor and Cady were. He had the perfect line of communication. Sato kept Ozawa informed of all developments by a state-of-the-art cell phone that worked even in the deepest mountains. And Ozawa, terrified that Terasawa would tell Sato about Glass's murder, passed along Sato's information to him the same way.

Terasawa patted his jacket pocket containing the gun and stiletto. He would find a place to hide in the hills above Nakamura's house. Then he would wait for the right time to make his move.

He would make it up to Sato. With Terasawa's help, Sato would emerge victorious.

Suzuki had cleared the large formal dining room of its normal furniture to set up a hearing format. There was a small table in front, which he sat behind as a judge. Facing that table and on both sides were longer tables. At one, Sato and Harrison were seated. At the other were Taylor and Cady.

All the way in the back, at the center facing Suzuki, sat the prime minister and Fujimura as an audience or gallery of two. Off in one corner, in a glass-enclosed booth, was the translator, a thin, intense-looking young woman.

As Taylor glanced around the room, she thought about what Cady had said yesterday in the car. A shiver passed through her. Were Sato and Harrison on trial? Or she and Cady? It didn't matter. Taylor couldn't afford to lose. Both of their lives were on the line. If they returned to America without Sato, he would direct Terasawa to follow them.

Suzuki began by introducing Taylor and Cady to Yahiro Sato, who rose and stood to his full height of five-foot-four. He resembled precisely the pictures she had seen with Alex's articles. His hair was still black and thick despite his age. Today he had a bitter scowl on his face.

When they were all seated, Suzuki turned to Taylor and Cady. "You should please begin. You two may divide the presentation in any manner you would like."

Taylor stood up. On the long flight to Tokyo they had decided that she would handle the proceedings. If she missed any facts, he would jump in.

Standing in a position from which she could alternate her gaze between Suzuki and Nakamura, she began talking slowly and precisely, straining to find the right words in Japanese. She described her relationship to Senator Boyd and her role in his campaign. She told them that all of these events began with a meeting that Sato and Harrison had had in Buenos Aires, followed by a mysterious package being dropped on Cady's desk. She talked about the murders of Senator Boyd and Harvey Gladstone. She recounted Alex Glass's letter. She explained how McDermott finally confirmed beyond question Harrison's involvement in this conspiracy. "I reviewed documents in Harrison's office," she said, "that establish the involvement of Yahiro Sato and the objective of this conspiracy, which was to eliminate Senator Boyd from becoming the next American president because he would block Sato's program for the renewed militarization of Japan."

In all she spoke for nearly an hour, presenting their case. She never said that she had copies of documents taken from Harrison's office, only that she had reviewed them.

As she spoke, she tried to focus equally upon Suzuki, Nakamura, and Fujimura, not knowing whether the prime minister would form his own opinion or rely heavily upon his justice minister and Fujimura. All three were listening carefully without any visible reaction. From time to time the prime minister leaned his head back and closed his eyes for a few moments, but she knew that he was still listening intently.

During her long monologue, she also watched Harrison. With earphones that gave him an English translation, he looked more and more outraged. In contrast, Sato remained cold and aloof, making no effort to conceal his contempt for her and the proceeding.

"And so I called Fujimura-*san*," Taylor said in conclusion. "Whom I have known for many years. I flew to California to meet him. I explained to him the entire story. A day later he asked me and Cady to come to Japan."

Suzuki turned to Harrison and Sato. "Would either of you care to speak?"

Harrison rose to his feet, looking at Taylor with a sympathetic eye. "Miss Ferrari has unfortunately taken some facts and jumped to very strange and unjustified conclusions. I feel sorry for her because of what happened to her close friend, Senator Boyd. It is regrettable that he violated the law relating to campaign contributions the first time he ran for Congress. When it was clear that the facts would become known, he killed himself rather than face the consequences. He committed the crime ten years ago that caused his disgrace. It's understandable that he would take his own life rather than live with the humiliation that he alone caused."

Harrison continued in the smooth voice that made him such an effective lawyer. "The real estate man, Gladstone, was killed when his car crashed off an icy mountain road. Driving conditions were hazardous. He was old and tired, and should not have been driving that night. Those are the facts. The rest of her story is fabrication. A creative story worthy of a novelist. Not the truth.

"As for her claims of a conspiracy being directed by me and Yahiro Sato, there's absolutely no evidence, just the conjecture of a troubled woman who, as she told us, is wanted for arrest by American legal officials. In other words, she herself is a criminal and a fugitive. Is that whom you would believe? Someone like that with no evidence, with no proof?"

With a look of righteous indignation, Harrison finished his speech and sat down. He was good; Taylor had to admit that. If she didn't know better, she might have believed him. When she glanced at Cady, she saw he was impressed too. Yet he was already reaching into her briefcase for more ammunition.

Suzuki turned back to Taylor. "Harrison-*san* has asked about evidence and proof. Do you have anything to corroborate your story?"

She took the material Cady handed her. Harrison was acting as if nothing she brought forth could possibly harm him. She handed the documents she had copied in Harrison's office over to Suzuki, who studied them for a moment. "Would you explain these?" he asked.

"They all came from Mr. Harrison's office. Please look at the two speeches first, Suzuki-*san*. What you have is a draft and the final version of a speech to be delivered by Sato immediately after his election. The speech calls for the United States to remove all of its forces from Japan and for radically increased Japanese militarization. The draft has handwritten changes in the margin in Philip Harrison's handwriting. All of the changes proposed in the margin were made in the final."

Suzuki spent several minutes looking at the speeches to

satisfy himself that Taylor was correct about the changes. Then he silently handed the speeches to Harrison.

Harrison didn't deny what she had said. "Of course I suggested those changes in Sato's speech. I'm a Washington lawyer. Sato asked for my advice on a speech that impacted the United States. I regularly offer suggestions to the French finance minister on his speeches as well. There's nothing inappropriate in that."

"But the program of militarization he proposes," Taylor said to Suzuki, "it's—"

Harrison interrupted her in midsentence. "It's an internal Japanese matter. It wasn't my business, and it shouldn't be yours. But since you're so concerned about what's proper, why don't you explain to Mr. Suzuki that you broke into my office and stole these speeches from a locked drawer?"

"Don't let him bait you," Cady said quietly to her.

"I won't." Instead she directed Suzuki to the next document. "It's a fax of a message that Harrison sent to Yahiro Sato confirming that they were involved in this conspiracy together."

Suzuki looked at the fax and passed it to Harrison. He studied it carefully. "I have no idea what this is," he said flatly, "or where she got it."

"It came from your office. You obviously used a code."

"And you obviously mixed some forged papers in with the ones you stole from my office."

She glanced at the back of the room. The prime minister's face told her that he was annoyed. She felt a sick wrenching in the pit of her stomach. This hearing was all a great show to discredit her and Cady.

"Next?" Suzuki asked her in a crisp, impatient tone.

"There is an entry from Philip Harrison's diary showing

that he met in Buenos Aires on August twenty-eighth with Yahiro Sato."

Again Suzuki examined the documents. "It only has the initials Y.S. It doesn't have the name Yahiro Sato."

He held out the document to Harrison, who waved it away with his hand. "I'm happy to concede that I met with Yahiro Sato on that occasion. He asked me to advise him in preparing the speech we spoke about earlier."

She had now exhausted the pile of documents she had given to Suzuki. She looked flustered and defeated. Harrison was staring at her with contempt.

"Do you have any thing else, Miss Ferrari?" Suzuki asked scornfully. It was as if his time and that of Prime Minister Nakamura had been wasted with false accusations.

"There is one other thing," Cady said. He reached into her briefcase again and extracted a microcassette and a recorder. He smiled at her, filling her with renewed confidence. Harrison, she saw, was leaning forward, straining to see what it was.

"This tape," she announced, "contains a recording of two conversations between Harrison and McDermott, the attorney general of the United States. May I play a portion of it?"

Harrison shot to his feet. "Those recordings were made without my knowledge. They would not be admissible in an American court of law."

Suzuki was irritated at Harrison's outburst. "You may sit down, Harrison-*san*. I don't know if they are admissible in an American court, but that's not where we are now. Besides, I doubt if an American court would be sympathetic to someone who helped manipulate their presidential election." He looked at Taylor. "You may play the tape."

She had the tape set at the most dramatic part of the second Harrison-McDermott meeting.

"I don't like the idea of accepting that deal if Boyd offers it," McDermott's voice said. "I'd rather make him go to trial."

"Either you accept the deal, or I'll tell the president and the newspapers about your girlfriend and child in Sarasota," Harrison's voice replied.

"The first time we met, you said that all I would have to do was help you with the California records relating to Mill Valley. Now you want me to blindly follow your orders and tell Cady and Doerr how to run the case against Boyd. You're asking for too much. This could be a conspiracy to harm the United States. President Webster is my friend. I'll risk the embarrassment of your disclosure before I'll agree to what you want. You have to tell me what this is about."

"Just do what I say."

"You tell me, or you can go fuck yourself."

There was the sound of a car door slamming.

"Okay, I'll tell you," came Harrison's voice.

"Well?"

"This is all being engineered by Yahiro Sato."

"The Japanese politician?"

"Yes."

"Why?"

"If Sato is elected prime minister, and Boyd is in the White House, he'll never be able to proceed with expelling American troops and remilitarizing Japan."

"But Webster will let him do those things. He would like an Asian counterpoint to China's growing military might."

"Precisely."

"So you're an agent of Sato's. Why? For money?"

"I never received a cent."

"Then why?"

"That's none of your business."

Taylor turned off the machine and stared at Harrison. He was as white as a sheet. How in the world had he been such a fool as to let McDermott tape their conversation, and how in the world had she been able to get that tape? For the first time in all the years she had known him, he was speechless.

"Very nice," Cady told her softly.

She turned around, facing Nakamura. "So I respectfully request that you grant our request to extradite Sato and Harrison to the United States, where they can stand trial for these events."

Suzuki looked at Sato. "Do you have a statement?" he asked.

Sato remained seated. "I have no denials and no apologies to make," he said. "Some time ago I became convinced that Japan was being treated unfairly by the United States and that we were facing great danger from China. We have succeeded economically with our exports of technologically superior products, but we refused to assert our own national pride. Well, that time is over. Japan is a great nation, and a great nation needs a powerful military. We have as much moral right to be the policemen of Asia as the Americans, who don't understand our part of the world. Even Germany, with all of their crimes against the Jews and others in the war, was permitted to return to normalcy. We alone continue to be punished. The reason for that unfair treatment is American racism aimed at us."

"You want us to be an aggressor again in Asia?"

"You're an intelligent man, Suzuki-*san*. Don't you understand what's happening? The Chinese are already heavily arming with modern technology. Soon they'll be able to fire missiles at us across the sea. Can we afford to be ill prepared for the next war with China?"

Suzuki broke in. "But even if you believe all of this, why did you interfere in the American election for president?"

"Because it's imperative to ensure that the White House is occupied for the next four years by someone who will not block Japan's rightful attempt to regain its fair military place in the world. It is in the best interests of our nation. We're victims of American imperialism. They don't keep their troops here to protect us. They keep them here to dominate us and to make certain that our military doesn't pose a threat to them."

"How did you become involved with Harrison-*san*?"

"After research to find an American who could help me, I discovered that Harrison was perfect. He shared my hatred for the Chinese. So I invited him to meet me in Buenos Aires. There I persuaded him to help me achieve my goal. When I enlisted his help, I told him to operate legally. To force Boyd out by lawful means. He got carried away and violated the law. That's not my responsibility."

"In the last month, two innocent people have died in the United States," Suzuki said. "Senator Boyd and Harvey Gladstone, because of what you and Harrison did."

"Correction," Sato said forcefully. "I had nothing to do with those deaths." He raised his hand and pointed a finger at Harrison. "All actions in the United States were being directed by him."

Harrison was appalled that he had ended up in this situation. When Sato had sent him the note with the date of his father's death and an invitation to meet in Buenos Aires, he had been sufficiently intrigued to go. When he had heard about what Sato wanted to do, he had eagerly agreed to help. It was the perfect way of avenging what the Chinese did to his father by helping to rearm their mortal enemy. There wasn't any thought that violence or murders would be involved. He figured that all he had to do was get carefully prepared evidence about Mill Valley into the hands of a strong-willed prosecutor and help Sato with some speeches. He had thought he was so smart, yet somehow he had lost control over events. And Sato was too clever for him. His desire for revenge had blinded him to the grim realities of what was happening. That desire for revenge had destroyed him—had taken the entire life he had built for so many years and reduced it to rubble.

"And what about the death of Alex Glass?" Suzuki asked Sato. "How do you explain that?"

This was the question Sato had been dreading, the one loose end that couldn't be laid at Harrison's door. He was boiling with anger toward that fool Ozawa and toward himself for letting Ozawa go to dinner with Glass. "An unfortunate accident," he said in a cold voice. "The Tokyo police have not found a single shred of evidence to the contrary."

Suzuki looked dubious. "An odd coincidence coming at that moment, wouldn't you say?"

"Life is full of coincidences."

"Do you have anything else to add?"

"Only that if you put my actions to a vote in Japan, many others, surely a majority, would agree with me."

"I very much doubt that," replied Suzuki. "Most of our people would recall with horror that similar thinking by militarists in the thirties brought a great disaster on our country and its people. Now I think we should take a recess."

Nakamura, Suzuki, and Fujimura went into another room to confer. As Harrison headed toward the bathroom, Sato slipped outside and took his cell phone out of his pocket.

He turned on the power and pressed a single button. "Ozawa here," came the response.

"Where are you?" Sato asked.

"About seven miles away. I have two truckloads of soldiers with me, fully armed and ready to move if you give the order."

"What about here in Nakamura's compound?"

"Of the thirty soldiers, at least ten will support us, perhaps more if a battle starts."

Sato nodded with satisfaction. He planned to speak with Nakamura later and help him reach a peaceful resolution of this matter, one that preserved the integrity of the Japanese nation. If Nakamura didn't accept that, then what followed would be his responsibility. Sato didn't feel any remorse about his plans. For thousands of years patriotic warriors had undertaken actions precisely like the one he was planning. Technology might be more sophisticated now, but people were still the same. Power belonged in the hands of bold men like him, not bureaucratic cowards who were serfs of a Western nation, like Nakamura.

When Harrison came out of the bathroom, his face wet from the cold water he had splashed on it, Taylor was waiting for him. Alone, out of earshot of the others, she grabbed his arm and pulled him aside.

"How could you do it?" she demanded. "Sato I can understand. I don't think he's right, but I can understand his motives. But you? Why did you do all of those horrible things?"

He took a deep breath and stared at her, debating whether to tell her the story he had never told anyone else—about his father and about China.

"You wouldn't understand," he finally said.

His words enraged Taylor. "Ah, c'mon, Philip, two people were killed. Decent human beings. Boyd, an honorable senator who was trying to improve the country. Gladstone, a kindly man with a wife and a sick grandson who was dying." Her voice was cracking with emotion. "How could you have done it?"

It was too much for Harrison. He had to say something. "That was Terasawa on his own. I couldn't control him. I warned Sato he was a loose cannon."

As Taylor thought about what had happened, she became even angrier. "And the trumped-up charge in Mississippi? Don't tell me that was Terasawa. You arranged that."

"Just to get you out of circulation until after the election. No one would have harmed you."

She shot him a look of loathing. "You're disgusting."

"As I said, you would never understand."

"Once you're extradited, you'll be the one spending time in jail. If you're lucky and Cady doesn't charge you with murder one."

He looked at her with contempt. Then he turned and walked away.

She stood alone for several minutes, balanced on the verge of tears and uncontrollable anger. Blurry-eyed, she saw Prime Minister Nakamura approaching her. Speaking in Japanese, he asked if she would walk with him outside.

It was chilly, but she didn't mind the cold. He was walking two steps ahead of her with his hands behind his back, a deeply troubled man. She moved quickly and fell into step with him.

"I want to emphasize," he said grimly in Japanese, "that Yahiro Sato was operating on his own. This was not a project authorized by our government. Do you understand that?"

She had no doubt on that issue. "I do. You were very cooperative. More than that, you saved my life and Cady's yesterday by moving us from that car that exploded. If you honor Cady's extradition request and send Sato and Harrison back to the United States with us, I will emphasize your government's lack of complicity when Cady and I report to the president in Washington."

"And what action do you think the American government will take?"

"My guess is that they will prosecute both men under American criminal law for murder, among other crimes."

"And will there be a public trial?"

"Unless the defendants agree to a plea bargain. Even in that case, the arrangement will be made public."

He was weighing her words carefully. "Sometimes it's better if certain matters are not publicly disclosed."

"Unfortunately I don't think we have a choice in this situation. Public exposure is necessary to ensure that Harrison and Sato are punished for what they have done."

When Nakamura didn't respond, she studied his face carefully. She hadn't convinced him; she realized that.

In a slow, halting voice he said, "I'm afraid if there's a public trial of Sato and Harrison in the United States, these events will be misunderstood. Others in your country don't have your knowledge of Japan. They will view this as something more than the aberrant behavior of a Japanese extremist. They will seek to erode what has been a cooperative relationship between our two great nations for the last fifty years."

"That thought concerns me as well, but I don't see an alternative."

There was a heavy silence as they continued walking. At last Nakamura broke it. "You said a moment ago that I saved your life."

"That's right," she replied warily.

"Then I would like a favor from you in return."

"What's that?"

"Remain here at my country house for twenty-four hours while I ponder my decision on extradition. During this time, don't talk to anyone in the United States by telephone. Don't disclose to anyone else what Harrison and Sato did."

She hesitated.

"I want you to wait only twenty-four hours," he repeated. "Then I will give you my decision." He could see that she was uncomfortable with his request, and he added, "You must appreciate the enormous political implications for me on the issue of Sato's extradition. He is a viable candidate against me for prime minister. I need a little time to weigh this momentous decision."

She thought about his request. Actually, she liked it for her own reasons. If they waited twenty-four hours and then flew home, the American presidential election would be over. That would be better. It would be a disaster if this story broke before then.

"We'll do what you asked," she replied, knowing that Cady would be upset because she hadn't consulted with him. Yet she was the one who understood the sensitivities of the Japanese, so she had to decide. "We will wait the twenty-four hours. You should know, however, that Gerhard Hall, the chief justice of our Supreme Court, has copies of all of the documents. Should anything happen to me and Cady, extradition for prosecution of Harrison and Sato will still occur."

"I rather expected something like that," the prime minister said. "I'm asking everyone else to remain here for this twenty-four-hour period as well."

"Sato and Harrison too?"

He nodded.

Nakamura had taken charge. His words meant virtual house arrest for all of them.

In their walk they had made a wide circle. They were now coming back to the house. "Before we separate," Nakamura said, "I want to say thank-you for what you've done by coming to me privately. I intend to try to find a reasonable solution to this matter."

She bowed politely, then held up, letting him walk into the house first with her two steps behind.

What in the world did he mean by "a reasonable solution"? she wondered.

Chapter 32

"We're prisoners." Cady said to Taylor angrily.

"Why do you say that, C.J.? We're just staying for twenty-four hours until Nakamura decides on the extradition petition."

He began pacing the floor of the cottage they had been given for the night. "This afternoon when you were out walking with Nakamura, I wanted to call someone at the American base to get patched through to General Clayton. My cell phone didn't work here so I tried to use one of the house phones. I was told that it's not possible to make calls."

She sighed, knowing how unhappy Cady was with her decision. "We're all being treated that way. Harrison's in another guest cottage alone. Sato's in a third one. Nakamura, Suzuki, and Fujimura are staying in the main house tonight while they discuss the issue and try to find a reasonable solution."

Cady picked up on her words. "The reasonable solution is to turn Harrison and Sato over to us for extradition."

She put a hand on his arm. "That's where I think we'll end up. We have to give Nakamura the time to get there by himself."

He was not soothed. "Will they even feed us?"

"Room service."

"You know what I think?"

"I doubt if I'll like it."

"I think that Nakamura will make a deal with Sato. In return for rejecting the extradition request, Sato drops out of the election. Nakamura will look the other way when some of the soldiers kill us, and nobody will ever hear from us again."

Taylor looked outside at carp swimming in a pond encircled by bamboo trees. "There's something wrong with your scenario," she replied.

"Yeah, what?"

"Both General Clayton and Chief Justice Hall know everything that happened. Hall has a set of the documents."

Cady gave a short, nervous laugh. "I guess you're right. I just don't like waiting around while the leader of a possible coup is parked next door to us." Cady made a sour face. "Anyway, there's nothing we can do about it. If we tried to leave, they'd restrain us physically. All we can do is wait and hope that I'm wrong."

His words troubled her. "Maybe you will be wrong about how this is going to play out."

"In the movies," Cady continued, "we would end up together happily ever after, and Sato and Harrison would be destroyed."

"But in real life?"

"Soldiers rush up to us with machine guns firing."

Nakamura and Sato dined together—just the two of them—in the main house. Kimono-clad women left food and sake, then retreated quickly behind a closed door. Armed soldiers paced in the corridor.

"You have placed me in a difficult situation," Nakamura

said. "I want to find a reasonable solution, but so far it eludes me."

Sato gripped a piece of octopus sashimi in his chopsticks. "Surely you can't be considering my extradition to the United States."

Nakamura frowned. "From all of the facts presented, I have no choice."

Sato struggled to control his anger. "You'll be hated throughout the country. People will say that your motive is political. That you realized you would lose the election to me. That was how you stole it."

Nakamura bristled at Sato's harsh words. "I'm aware of that, but we're a democratic government. I have to do what is right."

Sato snarled. "What is right for whom? For you. Surely not for the Japanese people."

"The United States is an ally."

"Allies should treat each other with dignity, as equals. When the Chinese use their military might to erode our economy, this ally of ours will stand by and watch our nation be wrecked."

Nakamura frowned, troubled by Sato's words. "Three people have died."

Sato was ready for that comment. "How many died in the American bombing of our homeland night after night? My mother and sister were two out of hundreds of thousands. Try to imagine your mother burning to death before your own eyes. First her hair. Then her clothes and her flesh. How many died in China? My father survived, but he was destroyed fighting there. And I know that your brother and uncle were two others."

"But that was years ago."

"People haven't changed. People never change."

Nakamura blew out his breath and sipped a tiny bit of sake. Sato was clever, his arguments powerful. "What would you have me do?" he asked.

"Refuse the request to extradite me."

"And Harrison?"

"He should have an unfortunate accident. Dead men can't be extradited."

"Cady and Taylor will pursue you publicly. Through legal channels."

"Without Harrison to testify to my involvement, there is no case against me. You will be able to turn away their request."

"Let me ask you hypothetically—if I agree to do that, will you drop out of the election for prime minister?"

Sato locked eyes with Nakamura. "Never."

After waiting for Nakamura to grasp the firmness of his conviction, Sato rose. "I'm going back to my cottage. You consider your decision carefully tonight. If you decide on my extradition, you will be responsible for the consequences."

Nakamura's face flushed with anger. "Are you threatening me?"

"I am simply pointing out that I have loyal supporters. They may not accept your decision."

Sato had tossed the threat of civil war on the table. The usually stoic Nakamura raised his hand to point a finger at Sato. But before he could do that, Sato turned and marched out of the room.

Ozawa had called to tell Terasawa that they would be in the compound all night. He had also repeated to him Sato's detailed report of who would be staying in each of the buildings, the strength of the defenses, and their location.

At ten o'clock, with high-powered infrared binoculars, from his position on a wooded hill above the complex Terasawa looked through a window of the main house and watched Nakamura, Suzuki, and Fujimura convening around a table. They must be trying to decide what to do.

Slowly and stealthily, Terasawa crept down the hill. With the heavy cloud cover it was pitch-black. With his dark leather jacket he melted into the shadows. The night-vision glasses he was wearing showed him there was no fence. No dogs. Just twenty men in place around the main building with significant distance between them. Others were guarding the cottages. Ozawa had told him to go in through a side entrance to the main house, where Kenji, the soldier on duty at that door, would let Terasawa pass.

At the bottom of the hill Terasawa took a narrow path behind a wooden shed, close to the side entrance. Crouching, he watched and waited. So far, so good. No one knew he was here.

After a minute Terasawa picked up some pebbles and tossed them to the left of Kenji, the signal Ozawa had told him to use. As the pebbles hit the ground Kenji turned toward the noise. While he did, Terasawa made his move.

Inside, the house seemed deserted. Terasawa crept surreptitiously toward the room in which Nakamura was meeting with Suzuki and Fujimura. Once he heard their voices, he paused in the next room out of their sight and listened. He heard Nakamura say, "I don't like the idea of extraditing Yahiro Sato. Harrison is different. With Sato, people will say my motive was political."

"You have no choice," Suzuki responded.

"He's right," Fujimura added. "The evidence against Sato is strong."

"It's a dangerous decision. He has powerful supporters," Nakamura said in a voice cracking with nervousness.

"And you are the elected prime minister of the country," Suzuki replied.

There was a long silence. Finally Nakamura said, "You're both right. I'll honor the American extradition request. I'll announce it in the morning."

Terasawa had heard enough. He crept out of the house through the side entrance. When Kenji heard his footsteps, the soldier turned the other way. In seconds Terasawa raced back into the woods that encircled the property.

Ozawa had told Terasawa that only a single soldier was guarding each of the three cottages that were being occupied. The guard in front of Sato's cottage was loyal to Sato and Ozawa. He would let Terasawa pass.

Terasawa emerged from the woods behind Sato's cottage, caught the soldier's attention with his eyes, and whispered the words, "General Ozawa said I can pass." As the guard looked away, Terasawa slipped by.

Sato was pacing back and forth across the living room of the cottage. What would Nakamura decide? he kept asking himself. He had no intention of honoring an extradition request. Soldiers loyal to his cause were waiting outside. Others were in the two trucks waiting with Ozawa. Nakamura was a smart man. He had to understand the serious consequences of a decision directing Sato's extradition.

Sato heard a rustling at the rear door of the cottage. Hairs stood up on the back of his neck. Had Nakamura decided that the reasonable solution was to kill him? He hurried into the kitchen and grabbed a knife. He raised it high over his head and moved noiselessly by the doorway.

Astonished, he watched Terasawa enter. Their eyes met;

then the assassin bowed. Sato wanted to kill the man. If Terasawa had disposed of Taylor and Cady in Washington, there would never have been this proceeding. Sato wouldn't even be here.

Terasawa understood how Sato felt. "If you wish to use the knife on me," he said, his head still bowed in front of Sato, "I willingly submit. At least I beg you to listen first to what I have to tell you."

"Stand up," Sato said. "It is tempting, but now's not the time. What information do you have?"

"I was in the main house, Sato-*san*," Terasawa said. "A few minutes ago."

"And?" he asked, tightening the grip on the knife.

"Prime Minister Nakamura intends to extradite you. The decision will be announced in the morning."

Initially Sato was surprised. As Terasawa's words sank in, though, surprise gave way to fury. "Are you certain of that?"

"I heard it myself."

"It's civil war he wants then," Sato said, thinking aloud.

"I'll do whatever you want," Terasawa said. "You can count on me to fight to the death."

Seeing the determination on Terasawa's face, Sato loosened his hold on the knife. If he prevailed tonight, there would be plenty of time to deal with Terasawa's incompetence in Washington. "Are you armed?" Sato asked.

"Pistol and stiletto."

Sato's mind began racing. It would be best to make his move now, at night. "Go get the two Americans and bring them here."

"Immediately." Terasawa started toward the door.

"Alive. And I mean that." Sato's eyes bored into Terasawa like lasers. "As hostages they're of value to me. Dead, they're useless. Do you understand?"

Terasawa nodded. "And Harrison?"

"He's of no use to me," Sato said coldly. "Quite the contrary. He is the key witness against both of us."

"Understood."

"Go now. Be back here with the two of them in precisely twenty minutes. Before you leave Taylor's cottage, set it on fire. In exactly twenty minutes."

Terasawa bowed deeply. "It will be done."

As the assassin exited the cottage, Sato pulled out his cell phone and called Ozawa. "It's time to act. How soon can you be here with the two truckloads of soldiers?"

"I left the soldiers in the trucks a few miles away. I'm on the road at the end of the driveway to the compound. I can be in your cottage myself in one minute. I'll make a call to the soldiers. They can be here in twenty minutes."

"Good. Do it then. Also, give the order by phone to the soldiers in the compound loyal to us that in twenty minutes one of the cottages will be set on fire. That's their signal to kill the other soldiers and occupy the main house. In the confusion, hold Nakamura, Suzuki, and Fujimura prisoners. Tell your people that two truckloads of soldiers are coming for support."

"I'll give the orders immediately."

Terasawa took up position behind a tree near Harrison's cottage. The single guard was circling the cottage on foot. Terasawa waited until the guard was in the back to bound across the open stretch and slip in the front door. He found Harrison lying in the Western-style bed on his back, snoring loudly.

As he stood in the doorway, watching Harrison, waves of

anger and rage engulfed Terasawa. The idea that he had been taking orders in the United States from this pathetic, weak American tore at his insides. If Harrison weren't so gutless, everything could have been done neatly and quickly. Because of his insistence on the Mississippi extradition, Terasawa had lost his chance to kill Taylor before she ever got to Cady and plunged them into this quagmire.

With the stiletto in hand, he advanced silently and jumped on the bed, straddling Harrison's body. Terasawa didn't want to kill Harrison in his sleep. The American should know what was happening. With his free hand Terasawa grabbed Harrison's throat, cutting off his windpipe so he couldn't scream.

Harrison woke with a start. When he tried to sit up, Terasawa forced him down, flat against the bed. He tried to twist away, turning his arms, kicking his legs. His struggles were hopeless. Terasawa was too powerful.

A thin ray of light from outside reflected off the stiletto. Harrison, his eyes bulging with terror, looked into Terasawa's face. He could sense the man's hatred—a wild animal beyond reason.

Terasawa went to work, using the knife to slice off his genitals, then jab his abdomen. Blood began spurting from Harrison's body. Backing away, Terasawa tied one of Harrison's legs to the bedpost so he couldn't move. Then Terasawa wiped the blood from the stiletto on a sheet and left him to die a painful death.

Terasawa checked his watch and grimaced. Too much time with Harrison. He had better move fast to get Taylor and Cady.

He covered the distance quickly. Outside their cottage a single soldier was standing in front of what looked like the only door. Terasawa circled around in the woods to ambush the guard from the rear.

Hiding behind the corner of the building, Terasawa waited until the soldier was looking the other way. Then he made his move. He looped his left arm around the guard's neck, squeezing it. Yet the soldier reacted instantly, shoving an elbow hard into Terasawa's ribs and knocking the wind out of him. Terasawa fought back, pressing his forearm against the soldier's neck while he dragged the man backward into the woods, where their struggle wouldn't be seen. The soldier swung his machine gun wildly, aiming for Terasawa's head, but the assassin deflected it with his other arm holding the stiletto. Forming a fist, Terasawa punched the soldier in the side of his head, knocking him out. Then Terasawa slipped the stiletto into his heart for a clean kill.

Inside the cottage, Taylor and Cady were fully dressed, lying on different sides of the Western bed, too tense to sleep. "Are you awake?" Cady asked.

"I'll never sleep tonight."

"I heard some noises outside."

"Didn't we do this at the Bel Air?"

"This time I'm sure. I'm going to look."

"Probably an animal. Or the guard in front."

Cady put his shoes on and walked toward the door of the cottage. As he was about to open it, Terasawa burst into the room with an automatic pistol with a Sionics suppressor. Before Cady had a chance to shout, Terasawa clamped his hand over Cady's mouth and shoved the gun against the side of his head. In that position, Terasawa forced Cady toward the bedroom.

Taylor heard the sound of approaching feet and turned on

the light. "Oh, my God," she blurted out when she saw Cady and Terasawa.

"If you make a sound, I'll kill both of you," Terasawa said.

They knew he meant it and kept still. Unarmed, they were no match for the assassin.

"Now, it's going to be like this," Terasawa said. "The gun's going back into my pocket. The three of us will walk over to Sato's cottage. If anyone asks, Sato-*san* wants to talk to you, and I'm the translator. If either one of you makes a false move, you're both dead. You understand?"

They nodded.

As they were leaving the cottage, Terasawa struck a match and lit the sheets on the bed. It would take a few minutes before the entire cottage caught on fire.

No one questioned them as they covered the fifty yards to Sato's cottage. The guard in front, loyal to Sato, let them pass. Inside, Ozawa and Sato were sitting in front of a roaring fireplace, poring over a crude map of the compound Ozawa had drawn to show Sato where his men were. A duffel bag filled with guns and ammunition lay at Ozawa's feet.

Once Terasawa herded them inside and closed the door, Sato said, "Well, well, my persistent American friends. We meet again."

"What do you want with us?" Cady demanded.

Sato sneered. "Nothing. It's you who want me."

"You're making your legal situation worse," Cady said. "You won't get away with this."

Sato laughed. "You may find this hard to believe, Mr. Cady, but we're not operating under American rules of law. You two are my insurance policy."

Taylor understood exactly what was happening: They had become hostages in a coup being launched by Sato.

"Tie them up," Sato barked to Terasawa. "Then leave them on the floor. They won't be going anywhere."

Ozawa kept a gun aimed at Taylor and Cady while Terasawa roughly pushed them to the floor. Then he tied their hands behind each of them. He tied their ankles separately, then together, facing each other like a couple of Siamese twins.

The coarse rope cut into Taylor's skin. She grimaced, biting down on her lower lip. She was kicking herself for not seeing that this was coming. Cady had tried to keep his hands apart when Terasawa tied them so he'd be able to wiggle free, but the assassin was too strong. He had forced Cady's hands together in a viselike grip behind Cady's back.

"Where are your troops?" Sato asked Ozawa.

Anxiously the general pulled out his cell phone. "Give me your location," he barked to the officer in charge.

"We're on foot, passing the catering trucks. We'll be at the gatehouse in less than a minute."

Ozawa turned to Sato. "They're almost at the gatehouse."

Sato nodded. "Good. Give the order I told you."

Ozawa swallowed hard, overcame his doubts, and spoke quickly: "Move into the compound now. Once you're inside the gate, send twenty men to the main house. Kill everyone inside. Then burn it to the ground. Have the other twenty disperse around the perimeter and open fire on any of Nakamura's troops still standing."

Prime Minister Nakamura was looking out of the window of the main house, watching flames shoot out of Taylor and Cady's cottage high into the air. At that instant he had no doubt what Sato intended.

He grabbed his cell phone and called Captain Tanaka, the head of Nakamura's personal security detail, who was on guard outside of the main house. He knew that he could count on Tanaka's support. "It's war," the prime minister said. "They're going to try to kill me. I need you in here to take charge."

"Yes, sir," came the terse reply.

Tanaka called to two men he could trust, and the three of them hustled into the building through a side entrance.

Taking charge, Tanaka told Nakamura, Suzuki, and Fujimura, "I want the three of you behind that chest." He pointed to a heavy wooden piece of furniture. "It may deflect bullets. At least it's some protection."

"I won't act like a coward," Nakamura protested.

"With all due respect, Mr. Prime Minister, it may save your life, and the life of our country."

Nakamura looked at Fujimura and Suzuki, who were nodding. "Okay, let's go," he said.

Tanaka yanked the cell phone out of his pocket and called Akashi, the commander of the thirty soldiers he had handpicked because he could count on their loyalty to Nakamura. They were sitting in the two catering trucks close to the gatehouse. Each of them was gripping an Uzi submachine gun. On their upper arms they each wore a white band with a red circle, the symbol of Japan, to distinguish themselves from Sato's supporters.

"The attack has started," Tanaka said. "Move now. Fast. Into the compound."

"We're on the way," Akashi said as he silently pulled back the tarp hiding the troops in the back of the truck.

Tanaka's next call was routed to a small town three miles away, where two Boeing Apache helicopters sat on a grassy field, pilot and copilot at the ready. "Come immediately," he said.

The engines were started, whining as they spooled up.

Once the rotors were at maximum speed, the choppers lifted off into the heavy darkness. Clouds blocked out light from the half moon.

Inside the glass-enclosed gatehouse, three bewildered sentries watched the Sato forces, heavily armed, approach. The leading edge of the unit was now twenty yards away.

"Do you know what's going on?" one of the sentries turned to a second and asked. Before he had a chance to respond, there was a blast, a burst of fire, and a crash as the glass walls shattered. A hail of bullets ripped through two of the sentries before they could grab their guns from the holsters. As those two fell to the ground, the third one, miraculously unharmed, threw himself on his comrades and covered his head with his hands, protecting himself from flying glass and pretending he was dead.

Behind the advancing Sato soldiers, Akashi led his troops stealthily out of the catering trucks. He knew that they had the advantage of position and surprise. He was determined to use it to his advantage.

At a distance of thirty yards, he whispered into his mouthpiece, "Fire now!" The sound of over a score of firing Uzis drowned out every noise of the night.

Never expecting an attack from the rear, and intent on advancing into the compound, the Sato forces were slow to react. In the first seconds ten members of their unit were hit and down, most dead, some seriously wounded. The others recovered quickly. "Take cover in the trees!" the commander of the Sato forces shouted. His troops spread out and ducked behind trees to return the fire. They were part of a fierce fighting unit Ozawa had picked for this assignment.

The two groups fired at each other from only twenty yards away.

Akashi was behind a tree when a shot slammed into the trunk and ripped off the bark. He blasted away, returning the fire with a staccato burst that caught the soldier in the neck. The man let out an animal-like cry and fell to the ground.

Cady tried to twist his hands free, but it was hopeless. He looked around, seeking a way out. All the while he was cursing himself for not arguing more forcefully to talk Taylor out of taking this damned trip.

He tried to catch her eye, but she was straining to watch Sato and the others, waiting for them to give her and Cady an opening. What happened to Fujimura? she wondered. If he was still alive, he'd find a way to get them out.

Nakamura refused to remain behind the wooden chest. Over Tanaka's objections, the prime minister stood at the window, straining his eyes in the darkness to follow the action. Cold fury surged through his body. He couldn't believe this was happening. Japan was an honorable democratic nation, but Sato wanted to turn back the clock over sixty years to her militaristic past—a past that had caused so much pain and death. Until his dying breath, Nakamura was determined that Sato wouldn't get away with it.

Suddenly a fierce firefight erupted in the compound as the ten remaining Sato supporters began firing at the other troops. A deafening noise filled the air. The Sato forces mowed down six in the initial burst of fire.

Now it was the Nakamura loyalists who raced for cover and began firing back. Gunfire was blazing everywhere. Bursts of automatic weapons pierced the night, the flames from firing guns sending a continual series of flashes into the darkness.

Tanaka threw the switch that turned on the floodlights for the compound. He shouted to his two colleagues inside the house, "Guard the prime minister. I'm going outside to try to secure this building."

Tanaka slipped out through the side door and quickly took stock of the situation. He looked up at the roof of the main house just as one of the two soldiers stationed there, a Sato follower, took down the other one in a hail of fire. Tanaka dropped to one knee, aimed his submachine gun, and got off a burst of fire that hit the other one in the stomach. The man screamed and tumbled off the roof to the ground below.

Tanaka moved along the side of the building to the front. To his horror he saw Kenji, who had been guarding the front entrance and who he thought would be loyal, running into the main house through the front entrance, gun in hand. He must be going for Nakamura. Tanaka raced through a side door and cut him off.

"Stop right there," Tanaka shouted.

Kenji whirled around and opened fire. Tanaka took a bullet in the left shoulder, but got off two shots of his own, the second one of which blew Kenji's face away.

At the sound of fire, one of Tanaka's men raced over. When he saw what had happened, he grabbed a bedsheet and tightened it around Tanaka's shoulder. Then each of the three security men inside the main house took up positions at one of the entrances to secure it and protect the prime minister.

*   *   *

From the window of his cottage, Sato watched flashes of gunfire erupting all around the compound. There was more firing in the distance.

"What the hell's going on?" Sato shouted at Ozawa. "We knew it would be tough inside the compound, where they had us outnumbered, but your troops from outside should be here by now. Where are they?"

"Any second," Ozawa said. "Any second. They'll be here. Then it'll be over."

A shot crashed into the wall of the cottage.

Sato grabbed a gun and stood next to Ozawa and Terasawa, who were firing Uzis. A soldier in front of Sato's cottage was behind a tree, blasting away with his automatic weapon at the cottage. The window shattered. Sato, Ozawa, and Terasawa ducked. As a Nakamura loyalist leaned out for a better aim, Terasawa, wearing his night-vision glasses, drilled a bullet through his head. The man collapsed onto his gun.

On the floor, Taylor and Cady tried to figure out what was happening. When they heard the sound of glass shattering, they pressed their bodies together to protect their faces. Shards of glass landed on Taylor's bare legs. She felt blood oozing down her calf.

Cady saw the blood and was horrified. "Are you okay?" he asked. Pieces of glass were embedded in her skin, and it hurt like hell.

"Yeah, it's nothing," Taylor said through clenched teeth. "Just a little souvenir I can point to when we make it out of here."

"I sure hope you're right," Cady said.

She heard not so much fear in his voice as resignation.

At the gatehouse, the troops were firing furiously at each other from behind trees when the two Apaches appeared overhead. With their night-vision glasses, the gunners in the choppers looked for the white bands of the Nakamura loyalists. Once they had their positions noted, they opened fire on the others. Flashes of light suddenly lit up the night sky. The commander of the Sato forces cursed. He had never figured that Nakamura would bring in helicopters. The choppers were hovering just above the treetops, close to the ground. One of them let loose with a Hellfire missile. It wiped out five enemy soldiers and set some trees on fire.

The pilot of that helicopter saw one of Sato's troops pull something out of a case and hold it up. It was a missile launcher he had planned to use inside the compound. He aimed for the Apache.

"Oh, no!" the pilot cried out. He tried to pull up. It was too late. The missile tore into one of the two engines. The chopper veered wildly for several seconds with the pilot losing control. It crashed into the woods, setting off a huge fireball.

The other Apache moved into position and took out the missile launcher with a Hellfire. Then he supported the Nakamura troops by firing more Hellfire missiles. The co-pilot lobbed a grenade into the forest at Sato's troops.

From his vantage point inside the cottage, Sato saw the choppers. Now he knew he was in trouble.

"Your soldiers!" Sato screamed at Ozawa, who pulled the cell phone out of his pocket again. "We need them now!"

Ozawa was frantically punching in numbers.

From the floor across the room, Taylor saw Ozawa's face fall as he listened to the other end.

"Well?" Sato demanded.

Ozawa solemnly put the cell phone away. "We are ruined. Nakamura outsmarted us. He had troops of his own hidden in catering trucks at the entrance to the property. They ambushed my people. The battle's raging now."

"You idiot!" Sato shouted at Ozawa. "You destroyed me! First you tell our secrets to Glass. And now this. You should have anticipated a counterattack."

Sato raised his gun and slammed the hard steel against Ozawa's face, breaking his jaw and nose and knocking him unconscious. As Ozawa fell to the ground, his gun dropped out of his hand and skidded across the floor.

Two of Sato's supporters saw that the battle was going poorly. Armed with Uzis, they made a mad dash for the front of the main house, intent on killing the prime minister. At least they would have that much to show Sato.

Finally, having yielded to Tanaka's frantic pleas, Nakamura was now back behind the heavy wooden chest with Fujimura and Suzuki. One of Tanaka's colleagues, guarding the front door, saw the attackers coming and yelled for help.

He killed one before taking a bullet in the ribs. Tanaka, a gun in his right hand, a bandage on his left arm, opened fire and took the other one down.

At the gatehouse the shooting was dying down. The rest of Sato's troops were no match for the Apache. All of them were on the ground, dead or wounded. Akashi rallied the remainder of the Nakamura supporters, the twelve survivors. "Let's go," he said. "Let's finish this up." They ran inside the compound with their guns in their hands.

On the floor of Sato's cottage, Taylor had an idea. She twisted around. "Slide with me," she whispered to Cady. Awkwardly and with great difficulty, she moved the two of them so her hands tied behind her back were close to the fire. Terasawa and Sato were facing the other way, firing their weapons out the window.

She bit down hard on her lower lip as she forced her hands against a burning stick that had fallen forward out of the fire. The heat seared her skin and flesh. The pain was intense, but she felt the rope loosen as the fire burned through it. Her hands were free.

Cady was watching her closely. She put an index finger to her pursed lips, then placed her hands behind her back, hiding the fact that she was free until she decided on her next move.

A booming voice on a loudspeaker from the main house overrode all other noises and stilled the guns for an instant. "Yahiro Sato, you are surrounded," Tanaka announced. "You have no chance. You must come out with your hands in the air."

An Apache helicopter hovered overhead, the gunner ready to let loose with a Hellfire missile on Sato's cottage. From her position on the floor, Taylor saw the helicopter. If it fired she and Cady were as good as dead.

Terasawa looked at Sato, prepared to follow his decision. "I will never surrender," Sato cried out.

That was all Terasawa needed to hear. He grabbed one of the Uzis Ozawa had brought with him and began firing it furiously. A hail of shots blasted back into the cottage and flew over Taylor and Cady. Sato began creeping toward the kitchen and the rear of the house.

He must be planning to escape through the back door, Cady thought. He was leaving Terasawa to die defending the cottage while he escaped. They had to get out. Taylor had to make her move now. She reached into the fireplace with a pair of tongs to grab a small log that had caught fire only at one end. She used it to burn through the other ropes binding them.

The first thing Cady did when his hands were free was remove the fragments of glass from her leg. It stung so badly that tears rolled down her cheeks. Her leg bled more freely. He hated causing her pain, but at least the glass was out. Then he pointed to the back door and whispered to Taylor, "Let's get the hell out of here."

The Apache was hovering closer. Its searchlights bathed the cottage in an incandescent white glow.

Taylor and Cady were crawling on the floor away from the fireplace when Terasawa ran out of bullets. He cursed loudly, dropped his gun, and turned around to grab another one from the floor. From the corner of his eye he saw that Taylor and Cady were free.

Locking eyes with Terasawa, Cady knew that the instant the assassin got his hands on another gun, he would kill them.

Cady propelled himself through the air from his crouching position and smashed into Terasawa. They went down to the floor with Cady on top. Terasawa clawed at Cady's face and eyes, refusing to be pinned down. Cady was strong, but he was no match for Terasawa. With a grunt, the assassin pushed his body up and rolled, forcing Cady to roll with him. In an another instant Terasawa was on top, with his hands around Cady's throat.

Taylor was ready to attack when she spotted Ozawa's gun on the floor. She grabbed it and aimed as Terasawa was cutting off Cady's breath. With the two men struggling, there was little margin for error. Taylor's hand was slick with perspiration. She aimed for Terasawa's head and pulled the trigger.

Despite the sound of the hovering helicopter, in the small cottage, the roar of the gun was deafening. At the last instant

Terasawa jerked, but the shot still grazed the side of his head. He gave a bloodcurdling scream. The assassin staggered to his feet, reaching for Taylor, but his body suddenly sagged. He collapsed on the floor.

"For all the evil you've done," Taylor shouted, and fired three more shots at Terasawa's heart to finish the job.

Now that the shooting from inside the cottage had stopped, those outside held their fire as well. Again the demand to surrender was made on the loudspeaker.

Cady picked up one of the guns, and the two of them walked slowly and cautiously toward the back of the cottage. At the door to the kitchen, Taylor stood and gaped in horror. In the manner of a samurai warrior, Sato stood naked except for a cloth around his loins. His feet were planted firmly on the floor. In both hands he held in front of his body a sharp knife used for deboning fish.

Taylor wanted to scream, "No!" She wanted to fire her gun. To run over and grab him. To do anything to stop him from committing *seppuku,* but she was paralyzed and immobile. Sato was in a trance. He had no idea she was even there. In the way of the bushido, he was preparing to join other Japanese warriors in the land of honorable soldiers.

In a single swift motion he inserted the knife into his abdomen. With all the force in his body he brought the knife upward, twisting it as it went in to complete his disembowelment. At the end, at the moment of death, a smile of peace and harmony appeared on his face. He collapsed in a pool of his blood and intestines.

Taylor turned to Cady, who looked as stunned as she felt. Slowly the two of them backed away. She was reaching for him, needing his support, when two soldiers burst in the front door.

Chapter 33

At the American air base outside of Tokyo, the pilot was ready to take off for the United States, but Taylor insisted on using the secure military phone first. When she had General Clayton on the line, she told him everything that had happened. He promised to report it all to Chief Justice Hall.

"One other thing, General Clayton," she added. "I see no need to disclose these events to anyone other than Hall. Do you agree?"

"Absolutely, and I'm certain Gary will as well."

"It's finished, then."

"It's all finished. By the way, you want to know about the presidential election?"

"Oh, my God. I forgot about that."

"Webster won," Clayton said. "All three networks are predicting a clear victory for him."

As she hung up the phone, Taylor felt none of the disappointment she thought she would have only days ago. She now believed that other things in her life were more important.

"The election is over," she said softly. "The election is finally over."

Cady shrugged, reflecting the indifference he felt. Then

he threw his arms around her and kissed her for a long moment.

She called to Lieutenant Farnsworth, "Can you drop us somewhere close to Mendocino, California?"

"Anywhere you want," he replied.

Cady put an arm around Taylor's back. Together they walked toward the waiting airplane.

Acknowledgments

I want to thank my wife, Barbara, who continues to read each draft of my novels, offering constructive suggestions before they leave the house. Her insights were invaluable. She particularly helped me develop the characters of Taylor and C. J. Cady. Pumping life into Taylor was a challenge, and I could never have done it without Barbara's help.

Our daughter, Rebecca, an Asian studies major who lived in Japan, served as a wonderful resource for this book.

Once again, Henry Morrison, my skillful and talented agent, has been incredibly invaluable. The genesis of this novel, like that of *Spy Dance* and *Dark Ambition*, occurred at lunch one day in New York when I pitched the idea to Henry. "What if . . . and what if . . . and what if . . ." After he reshaped the concept, he said, "Prepare an outline." We were in business. Henry carefully read each draft and proposed revisions that made the book much stronger. Henry truly was a partner throughout the process.

I cannot offer enough thanks to Doug Grad, my dedicated editor at NAL. Doug has a unique ability to enhance creatively each manuscript. He did it for me with *Spy Dance* and *Dark Ambition*, and he has done it again here. Doug knows what has to be expanded, what has to be cut, and what has to be reshaped in order to keep a tight flow in the novel. Doug's entire team at NAL—John Paine, Adrian Wood, Ron Martirano, Tina Anderson, and the art director, Richard Hasselberger—are phenomenal and a pleasure to work with. They forced me to justify each sentence. In reviewing the edits, I felt like a witness undergoing cross-examination—always an uncomfortable position for a lawyer who is accustomed to asking the questions.

⊘ SIGNET   (0451)

Next Victim

By *New York Times* Bestselling Author

Michael Prescott

He calls himself Mobius—and he's a serial killer
who has eluded the FBI for years. Catching him
is an obsession for Agent Tess McCallum.

Her name is Amanda Pierce. She's on the run from
the feds—wanted for the theft of a military chemical
weapon. In an exclusive Los Angeles hotel, she
meets with Mobius. It's the last date of her life.

But for Mobius, it's the beginning of a new
life-and-death game. His opponent is
Tess McCallum. And the stakes are not one victim,
not two victims…but thousands.

0-451-20753-X

Coming February 2004
IN DARK PLACES
0-451-41127-7

**Available wherever books are sold, or
to order call: 1-800-788-6262**

S808